To Kim, Allison, Mike, and Tommy

ACKNOWLEDGMENTS

There are many people whom I would like to thank for making this book a reality. I would have to start with my mother, Margaret O'Neil Burns, who provided me with a belief that I (an engineer!) could actually write a work of fiction. Although our conversations occurred decades ago and she has been gone for many years now – here it is! Mom, I hope you enjoy the finished product somewhere up in Heaven's library. My colleagues at Cincinnati State are also owed a debt of gratitude. For many years they have immersed me in an environment of continuous learning, challenged me to step outside the box, and encouraged me to succeed. My three decades of teaching have undoubtedly made an impact on me. I would like to also thank my editor, Mike Waitz of Sticks and Stones Freelance Editing, who provided an enormous amount of guidance and support in helping me produce the final manuscript. Being new to the world of fiction, it was extremely helpful to have someone who took an interest in making this project the best that it could be. Finally, and most importantly, I would like to thank my wife, children, family and friends for a lifetime of support in ways that I cannot even begin to mention. It is easy to take the constants in one's life for granted but, believe me, I am very grateful for everything I have been given.

Equilibrium:

A state in which opposing forces are balanced.

FOREWORD

The world we live, work and play in is composed primarily of man-made materials constructed by people into the electrical grids, water systems, roads, buildings, and bridges that we rely on for almost every human activity. Our dependence on these technological creations is so interwoven into our very existence that they have become, in a way, as necessary as air, water and sunlight. We have come to accept that our environment – the space in which we live – is an environment significantly shaped by the power of human creation and creativity.

Our acceptance of man's need to build using concrete, steel and other materials is an interesting phenomenon. The ubiquity of the existing systems and structures has lulled us into a comfortable acceptance of their reliability, because let's face it, we expect these things to work. The lead story of the evening news will <u>not</u> be "All Planes Land Safely Again Today," "Clean Drinking Water Available," or "Motorists Stage Thank-You Rally for Getting Home in One Piece." The normalcy of modern infrastructure working without incident belies the real complexity involved in that infrastructure's design and construction.

For the most part, structural engineers work in the shadows of the public's consciousness. Unlike with other professions (e.g. doctors, lawyers, etc.), the public's awareness of what structural engineers do is rather murky at best. But this is okay with those engineers – most are happy in their anonymity and eager to finish their current project and move on to the next. Continue to produce a design that is economical, practical and safe. Continue to produce a design which is turned into a building, bridge or other structure that functions as it is supposed to – day after day, week after week, for a lifetime. In equilibrium.

PART I

Equilibrium Lost

1

Friday June 20, 1986
4:55 PM
Cincinnati, Ohio

Misty Kunkel was damp with perspiration as she stepped out of the taxi in front of the Grand Plaza Hotel. The summertime heat and humidity are always oppressive in Cincinnati but this year was the worst Misty could remember. As she approached the hotel's chrome and concrete portico, she felt her baby girl twist and roll inside her. Misty instinctively stopped walking and cradled her belly. After catching her breath, a soft smile crept across her face. *Only another five weeks, baby girl. I can't wait to meet you.*

Misty hesitated slightly in front of the hotel. Revolving door or regular door? The extra 35 pounds the pregnancy added to her waifish frame slowed her reflexes and made her more cautious about many 'take it for granted' activities.

Getting off the couch, stepping into the shower, and going through a revolving door. I certainly don't want to get stuck in there.

Her husband, Dan, had insisted on keeping their monthly date night even though Misty would rather spend this Friday night in the air-conditioned comfort of their suburban home. Misty knew Dan enjoyed these date nights, but after struggling to get pregnant, she wanted to be as careful as possible. Still, Dan was excited, and the Plaza's TGIF Dance was the talk of the town, which made it hard for her to say no. Besides it could be their last date night for a while.

Misty chose the regular door on the right to enter the Plaza. Having to be rescued from inside a revolving door by the fire department did not seem like the best way to start the evening. Besides Dan would be upset if they missed the first slow dance. *I think slow dances are all that we are up for tonight, baby girl.*

Stepping into the hotel, she welcomed the cool air which made her notice the small tendrils of perspiration rolling down her chest. She pulled on her pink cotton top and readjusted it to break the suction between her skin and the fabric. The lobby was at least twenty degrees cooler than the city sidewalk she had occupied only moments ago. Already feeling more refreshed, she looked for someone who could point her in the right direction.

Brad Kessler stood with his left foot propped up on a chrome-plated luggage carrier peering into the hotel lobby. His black bellman's jacket was too loose for his lanky frame, and his black, wavy hair speckled the satin trim around his collar with dandruff. Like many nineteen-year-olds, Brad was socially anxious and struggled with people, so this job was an opportunity to gain a little more than just a paycheck. It forced him to interact with people and, lucky for Brad, those interactions followed a standard script.

Hello, Mr. Smith. Is this your first time staying with us? We have several great restaurants here at the hotel. What are you in town for? We have a lot of things to see in town. Where would you like your luggage? Is there anything else I can do for you?

Brad could stick to the script and, for the most part, it kept him from making eye contact. He hated to make eye contact with people. Instead, Brad would find himself looking at people's shoes when going through his script. He found that shoes were much easier to look at and, besides, shoes don't look back.

Misty spotted the tall bellman leaning on the luggage carrier. As she approached, Brad was engrossed in the task of watching two nubile teenage girls painting their fingernails on an overstuffed leather couch in the corner of the lobby. Besides tip money, surreptitiously observing the female guests was the other major perk of Brad's job. Much like interacting with hotel guests, Brad believed this surveillance was a prime opportunity to maybe one day introduce himself to someone of the opposite sex. Thoughts rolled through his teenage brain in no particular order but focused on a singular topic. *God, they are hot. I wonder if they are here for the cheerleading competition. Her hair is braided just like Bo Derek's. Two of them, one of me. Both are 10s. Is she wearing a bra? What would happen if they invited me to the competition? Where are their parents?*

Like many teenage boys, Brad was more thought than action. He stood there, oblivious to the world, pondering the possibility of walking over and striking up a conversation. *This time I'll do it. I just need the right opening.*

"Excuse me, could you tell me where the dance is tonight?"

Startled out of his daydreaming by a fatigued voice over his left shoulder, Brad turned around awkwardly, momentarily feeling off-balance as if the person behind him was reading his thoughts. With adrenaline coursing through his body, he tried to compose himself and erase any thoughts of possible escapades with the young ladies before speaking.

"I, um…I'm sorry. I didn't hear you?" Brad said as he backed up slightly. His reply certainly wasn't part of the standard script, and he was not about to make eye contact. Gazing at the floor, he searched for her shoes and immediately was drawn to Misty's rounded belly. Brad's anxiousness increased to new heights as he faced the reality of this stranger. A pregnant stranger who was asking him for something. *Oh God, she didn't say she was having a baby now, did she?*

Misty sensed the young man's discomfort. She taught a Greek literature course at a local community college and was familiar with the startled look on Brad's face. It was not the first time this had happened during her pregnancy. The ancient Greeks used the word "tokos" for pregnancy. It amused Misty how many young men, who spent a vast amount of time preoccupied with sex, were stricken with fear that someone could have an actual baby in front of them. Just another case of tokophobia.

She softened her voice and said, "I was looking for the ballroom – where tonight's dance will be."

She gestured as she spoke, and a silver charm bracelet dangled from her wrist. The shiny object gave Brad something to focus on as he tried to keep his nerves under control. He was not very knowledgeable on women's fashions or accessories, but he did appreciate the beauty of the bracelet with a charm that looked like the letter 'K'.

"Oh, right – the dance. Right this way. I will show you where it is."

The Grand Plaza Hotel had opened the previous year as part of the revitalization of Cincinnati's downtown business core. The hotel consisted of three main sections – a high-rise section containing the hotel rooms, another section of meeting rooms and an atrium that connected the two. The city had been able to entice the developers of the Grand Plaza by passing a prevailing wage waiver. This waiver allowed construction projects built within city limits, like the Grand Plaza project, to pay lower wages to construction workers, thereby reducing the cost of the project considerably. A boon for the developers, these waivers were not popular with local labor unions, who had retaliated using an assortment of picketing, blockages, and petty harassment during construction of the Grand Plaza. But this was all in the past and was way over Brad's head. All he knew is that he liked his job.

The lobby where Misty spoke to Brad was ornate but not opulent, characteristics which fit Cincinnati perfectly. After all, this was a city where people would walk six blocks in ninety-nine-degree heat to a Reds game rather than pay five dollars to park at the stadium. Brad walked in front of Misty slowly across the blue-gray Carrera marble that was stitched together in a herringbone pattern and punctuated with in-laid fleur-de-lis mosaics. They walked away from the cherry and gold-trimmed front desk counter and towards a portal that was becoming crowded with other patrons.

"So how long have you worked here?"

"Oh, since the hotel opened. A little more than a year I think," said Brad looking straight ahead. Misty was a step behind.

"Must be an interesting job. Seeing so many people."

"Yes, it is. I do like watching people."

An instant bolt of teenage anxiety shot through Brad like he had just confessed to a crime. *Watching...ugh. I should have said seeing.*

Misty laughed effortlessly placing her hand across her chest. Her laughter soothed his fear, and he quickly glanced back at her and made eye contact.

"Watching people – me too. That is all I will be doing tonight in my condition – just watching."

"This will be a good place for that tonight. People tell me these dances are a lot of fun, and it looks like there is a good crowd."

Approaching the atrium they brushed by a line of people waiting to purchase drink tickets.

"I don't think I need any drink tickets."

Misty glanced down at her silver-rimmed Timex watch with the black leather band. Water weight gain of her pregnancy had even spread to her wrist as the clasp was now on the last notch of the leather band. *It might be time for a new band if this little girl doesn't come on time.* Her watch read a few minutes after six.

"I'm meeting my husband, so we only need a table for two."

"Oh, okay. Let's look for a place over there," replied Brad, pointing to the far end of the atrium across from the stage.

Reaching the entry way of the atrium Brad led her down the three steps to the floor. She slowly navigated the steps holding onto the cold metal railing. She was always careful around steps these days. Everybody would move more slowly if they couldn't see their feet.

The band was setting up on a small raised stage at the far end of the atrium. The stage was a collapsible steel structure ideal for a quick set-up and tear-down. The translucent whiteness of the tile floor amplified the sunlight streaming into the atrium from the massive windows along the west wall, giving an operating room-type glow to the space.

"Still have a few tables open. There and over there."

Brad pointed to the possible targets. He was getting more comfortable in being off script with this pregnant lady whose water was still intact. That comfort did not mean that he wished to linger. He had a feeling that the longer she stood, the more likely that something unexpected might happen.

Misty's eyes took a couple of seconds adjusting to the brightness. She pointed towards several round tables that Brad had spotted located across from the stage and under a walkway which crisscrossed the atrium. The tables were out of the main flow of foot traffic and the shadow of the walkway provided some refuge from the room's glare.

"I think a table over there will work just fine."

Misty glanced up at the beautiful olive green stucco planters on the walkways. The planters were stacked full of tropical bromeliads which were brimming with red and orange flowers. The blooms were larger than anything she had ever seen, even in the conservatories which she frequented. The cascade of colors over the railing of the walkway accentuated the festive atmosphere of the evening perfectly and, although ready to get off of her feet, Misty appreciated their beauty for a moment longer. Brad reached the table and turned around to see Misty looking up at the walkways. Smiling at her, he became embarrassed when she returned his smile. She then continued over to meet him in front of the table.

"Those flowers certainly are beautiful," she said.

"They sure are," the young bellman responded. "The staff here spends a lot of time taking care of them."

Misty's steps grew shorter as fatigue was catching up to her.

"I appreciate your help…..Brad," she said as she read his name off his badge for the first time.

Hearing her say his name, Brad relaxed even more with the stranger whom he had known for about sixty seconds. He looked at her dark, shoulder length hair that framed her girl-next-door Midwestern features. She was pretty, pregnant, pleasant and just one of those people that made you feel at home.

"Thank you, ma'am. I hope you have a nice night."

Misty extended her right hand to the young college student. Brad grasped her hand gently, and looked first at her silver charm bracelet again and then at her almond-shaped blue eyes.

"Oh, I will. Watching people," she said smiling. "Thanks again for your help, Brad."

Feeling good about himself, Brad smiled back to her before turning around to snake his way past the burgeoning crowd that was streaming into the atrium.

2

Friday June 20, 1986
5:45 PM
Lexington, Kentucky

Nick Kremer balanced the Kentucky Building Code on the highest shelf in the small library of the J. B. Jones Engineering office. Code books – one of many arcane resources for engineers, like Nick, engaged in the practice of structural design and construction. *Damn things are getting bigger all the time.* Its plastic cover made a soft scratching sound as he pushed it back into its designated position on the wooden bookshelf.

He paused at the bookshelf a moment feeling satisfied but tired. He had just completed the structural plans for a twenty million-dollar wastewater treatment plant for the Fayette County Sewer District. Nick was well aware that the sewer district was both a new and important client. The city of Lexington, home to the University of Kentucky, was located in Fayette County and was projected to experience a robust population growth over the next decade. Population growth is good for the engineering business as it leads to development which needs infrastructure – roads, bridges, sewers, and water. Impressing the sewer district could result in a strong pipeline of engineering work for years to come. Working late for the last several weeks, Nick and his team needed to meet today's deadline, and they delivered. Feeling the relief of another project completed, Nick was ready for another work week to come to a close.

"Another day, another dollar, Nicky," shouted Joe Jones across the rows of light green vinyl covered drafting tables.

"Amen to that," replied Nick as he turned around. He smiled at the old man who shared his last name with the company. "Not enough time in the day."

Joe Jones was a short, barrel-chested man with salt and peppered hair that he wore in a close-cropped military-type style. Joe believed in order as it had always been part of his life. Many years ago Joe had replaced the order of military life with the order of the engineering profession. Order meant everything had a place and a process that could be used to find the right place. The place for his black, thick-rimmed glasses was high on the bridge of his nose. The front pocket of his solid blue cotton dress shirt was the place for a plastic pocket protector holding two mechanical pencils, a six-inch plastic ruler, and a gold Parker fountain pen. Every day. Everything. With no room for variance.

From Nick's perspective, Joe was old school. His boss was an engineer from an era without the tools used today. Nick found it humorous that Joe still didn't even own an electronic calculator, much less use one. Maybe his stubby fingers didn't have the required dexterity for it or maybe learning wasn't worth it at his age.

"Time and money, Nicky. Time and money. Time is the same for everybody, my friend. A lot of folks will say time is money, but you have to remember it's about people too. Don't get me wrong. I need you all to make money for me. But you have to remember we have a responsibility to a lot of folks around us."

The old man was right about that. Engineering, at its core, is a people business. Clients. Contractors. Developers. Designers. People. Nick loved the challenge of designing on paper the structures that one day would be standing in the real world. He liked driving down the road and looking at a bridge or building and thinking 'I designed that'. But he was just one cog in a process that took projects from concept to reality. That process was full of other people who wanted to be a part of something that would stand the test of time. Nick appreciated his clients because they were the ones willing to take the risk hoping to turn a paper-based design concept into a physical reality. Nick also liked the interaction with others on the design team -- architects, other engineers, fabricators, and vendors. Project design was a lot like sports. A well-run project had the team working as one towards the common goal while not-so-good projects saw the team fragmented and interested only in themselves. Sometimes people can be real pricks.

"I know. A lot of folks. Why don't you tell me again about all the folks you worked with on the Great Pyramids? I heard the pharaohs could be real assholes, right?"

Joe was special to Nick – a mixture of boss, colleague, and father-figure. The latter was important to Nick as his father had been non-existent since the death of Nick's mother. From almost as early as he could remember, Nick had lived with the thought that he wanted to be different than his father. He wanted to be different in the manner that he approached his family, his work, and his life. He especially wanted to be different in his relationship with his wife and children.

Nick thought that his mom was an angel. She played the role of both father and mother to Nick, her motherly tenderness interspersed with stern warnings to stay on the right path and use his God-given gifts. She had died of breast cancer late last year and Nick still felt the pain. His father had used her illness to physically desert the family that he had emotionally deserted years earlier, leaving Nick and his sisters with choices in their mother's last weeks that young people are ill-equipped to make. Her passing had relieved some of the emotional grind of being a caregiver and his work filled that void left by his mother's absence.

Joe Jones was the rudder in the life of this young engineer. Joe's small town, down-home advice always made Nick feel both listened to and protected. The old man with the gap-toothed grin standing in the front of the office provided the young engineer equal measures of comfort and motivation.

"Yeah, the pharaohs could be real assholes. But like I say, you do your job well, and your clients will keep coming back. Did you know I used those damn pharaohs for a reference when I applied for a job with George Washington as well?"

Nick laughed. He and Joe were the two licensed structural engineers at the company. Working at a small firm, Nick was given freedom and responsibility more quickly than most other 27-year-olds. In theory, young engineers are considered to be "in-training" and required to work under the auspices of a veteran engineer for four years before they can take the state exam. Nick's four years with Joe had been a whirlwind moving from one complex project to another. His performance had not gone unnoticed. Joe Jones had asked him months ago to be a partner in the firm and Nick had signed the papers last month. His professional life was off to a fast start and headed in an upward trajectory. Nick smiled a tired smile as he walked back to his desk. Life is certainly moving fast.

The partnership was especially gratifying to Nick because many of his college friends had not found work right away. Nick had chosen engineering because it was a relatively stable profession. That apparent stability is deceiving because the engineering business depends on the state of the general economy. And the economy in 1986 was much better than it had been when he'd graduated four years earlier. Interest rates were falling, and that lowered the cost of borrowing money. A reduction of uncertainty among developers accelerated the pace of putting new projects "in the pipeline" throughout the country.

"Well, Joe, I don't know if George Washington is going to put in a good word for us or not, but I will certainly try to keep folks coming back – until I am your age at least. How old are you anyway? A hundred?"

Nick enjoyed ribbing Joe about his age. It was part of the camaraderie that the two shared and the old man took it all in stride. He knew that the mirror was not lying as he looked every bit of being sixty years old.

"Shit, boy. Even at my age I still work harder than a two-dollar whore on nickel night," Joe chortled.

His use of 'shit' sounded more like 'sheet', betraying his ancestral roots that connected him to the hills of eastern Kentucky. Joe took great pride in his humble beginnings and pegged success to the values his father had preached – respect, hard work, and honesty. Coal country had reinforced these values in a smart kid who spent his youth thinking there was more to the world. At sixteen, he was lucky enough to be presented an opportunity to see the world, if fighting Hitler can be considered lucky. Assigned to an Army engineering battalion, Joe had worked building temporary bridges to move Allied troops across rivers in Europe. That experience had sown in him the desire to engineer new designs and build a life in Lexington.

Nick laughed. Two dollar-whore. Where does he come up with these?

"Well I don't know anything about nickel night," Nick replied. "All I know is that Jenny is probably holding dinner for me and my honey-do list is getting longer by the minute. If you keep me here any longer, I am going to be busier than a cat trying to bury its crap on a concrete floor."

The old man bellowed in laughter and slapped his hand on his stomach.

"You've got that right, Nicky. Believe me, you are right about that."

Nick smiled and shoved the last few papers into his brown leather briefcase. He was happy that he used the saying correctly and made his boss, a connoisseur of redneck wisdom, laugh. The clock on the wall read ten minutes till six o'clock. Nick hoped rush hour was winding down and traffic would be light. He also hoped that he wasn't too late and that Jenny was in a good mood.

"See you tomorrow boss," yelled Nick with a short-armed wave towards the front of the office.

"See you, Nicky. Give Jenny my best."

3

Friday June 20, 1986
5:50 PM
Cincinnati, Ohio

The atrium of the Grand Plaza Hotel pulsed with music and motion as people began to unwind at the end of another work week. A crowd of professionals gathered from various downtown and suburban businesses. Men milled around in open-collared short-sleeve shirts, while women in a variety of semi-formal dresses and suits conversed casually. Co-workers, friends, and spouses engaged in a litany of introductions, followed by small talk about families, the weather, and vacation plans. Men lined up, three-deep, at the bars on either side of the atrium where the queue conversation centered mainly on the major league baseball strike that had been going on for more than a week. The Reds were in the midst of a good season and an angst hung in the city about what the strike would mean on the hometown team's postseason chances.

Sunlight streamed into the faces of the eight-piece band occupying the raised stage on the east side of the atrium. They played instrumental staples from the 1950s – *Moonlight Serenade, Around the World*, and the syrupy sounds of Glenn Miller's *In the Mood*, which currently wafted through the air.

The atrium floor in front of the stage formed a semi-circular dance floor that was currently being used mostly as a conversation space. Couples, herded into groups of varying sizes, stirred like tumbleweeds on a desert plain. Groups of people, cocktails in their hands, stayed stationary for a few minutes until their drinks ran dry, at which time they were uprooted and blown away to a new location.

Several slightly older couples were dancing close to the band. They moved in geometric patterns – circles, boxes, and arcs. Hand-in-hand they seemed content to stay close to the stage as if it were some fertile farming valley, careful not to venture into the cocktail-infused desert region.

Beyond the desert region of the dance floor, concentric rings of tables cordoned off the seating area on the atrium floor. The round tables, shrouded in white cotton tablecloths, spread out from the dance floor like spokes on a wheel of a bike. Twenty tables formed the primary boundary line and six more rings of tables filled this area of the room. The sunlight reflecting off the dance floor tile still bathed the atrium in an ethereal luminescence complementing the lazy notes of the band music perfectly.

Three steel and concrete walkways crisscrossed the air space above the atrium floor, allowing guests to efficiently traverse the distance between the hotel portion of the Grand Plaza and its four-story function block. The second- and fourth-floor walkways occupied the same vertical ribbon of space, stacked on each other like miniature versions of a highway overpass. With the workday complete, the walkways were no longer conduits shuttling conventioneers to and from their meeting rooms. Tonight the walkways formed a convenient perch for those interested in people-watching and wanting to stay removed from the bustle down below.

Misty Kunkel enjoyed people-watching from her small table as well. Over eight months pregnant, she was happy to be tucked back away from the crowds. She sat with her right shoulder to the west side of the room, a location where there was not a lot of foot traffic. The exterior wall consisted of large rectangular panels of glass intersected at right angles by a checkerboard grid of dark aluminum mullions. The panels occurred at regular intervals and Misty's seating position allowed her to people-watch in the atrium as well as out on the street while waiting for her husband to arrive. She was good at identifying the ever-present personas always found in a crowd.

There's the forty-something loud and obnoxious conversation monopolizer.

She's the young 'I'm bored and am only here to climb the corporate ladder' blonde.

She's giving him the 'he's going to pay for this' stare for being fixated on the much younger female co-worker.

Outside at the bus stop, there was a sixteen-year-old, frizzy haired teenage girl with her equally greasy-haired teenage boyfriend with one arm wrapped around her and his hand resting just below her halter top. A typical two-month teenage love story.

Misty passed the time easily in this spot with so many people to watch. The table was also a short walk to the restroom, which Misty frequently needed nowadays. With her kidneys cleaning the blood for two people, it seemed like the urge to go happened every fifteen minutes. *Geez, I would hate to see how often I would need to pee if I were having twins.* As she had found out carrying her first child, also a girl, a nearby restroom at the eight-month mark is a good thing.

Finally, Misty spotted Dan standing at the atrium entrance near the steps that she had walked down a little while ago. She saw him surveying the crowd looking for her. Dan was methodical in his approach to everything in his life. Daily activities had a way of being done in a specific order to accomplish these in the most efficient manner possible. Mowing the grass, painting a room, laying out his work clothes – all activities he approached in a standardized fashion.

Now Misty saw him looking for her in the manner she knew so well.

Where could she be? Left side of the stage. Row 1, row 2, row 3 don't see her. Row 4, 5, 6, 7 don't see her. Next line over from the left side of the stage.

Misty was not a systematic part of Dan's life. Spontaneous, romantic, and carefree. One minute she would be going out to get mail and the next minute she would be lying on her back in the grass watching clouds in the sky. She absorbed life, appreciating its sights, sounds and smells. They were good for each other, and both were happy in their young marriage. Dan proved to be the kite string that tethered Misty to the world of tasks that needed attention. Misty was the camera lens that allowed Dan to appreciate life's big picture.

Misty waved her arms for a while before realizing that her five-foot-five height was not conducive to being seen in the growing crowd. She was all too aware of her husband's systematic approach to things.

He might be standing there for another hour if I don't get him.

She did not want to leave the table unattended. Staking her claim to the table, Misty tilted both chairs diagonally onto the table and made her way over to retrieve her husband.

Dan continued his scan of the room.

Middle right of the stage. Row 1, row 2, row 3 don't see her.

He stopped this process when he heard the familiar husky voice belonging to the love of his life.

"Hey, sweetie. Over here!" Misty yelled again waving her arm in his direction.

Dan smiled when he saw his wife. He knew it was cliché, but she was even more beautiful pregnant if that were possible. With an agility reminiscent of his younger days, he quickly bounced down the three steps and eagerly made his way over to her.

"Hi, babe. You look beautiful," he said as he lightly put his hands around her and bent down to kiss her firmly on the lips. He loved the way she smelled, a mixture of lavender and lilacs.

"You smell so good."

Misty giggled like someone thinking about the punchline of a joke before they say it out loud. He told her she smelled good no matter what – the chlorine smell after swimming, the garlic smell after cooking, and the salty sweat smell after working in the yard.

"Thanks, sweetie. I wore it just for you tonight."

"Really, what is it?" Dan asked curiously.

"Baby powder, just for you. I went all out," she laughed. "I thought with the heat wave out there that I might need a little help staying comfortable tonight."

"Baby powder works for me."

Maybe love does that to a man because to Dan she did smell good tonight.

"I have a table over here. Let's get this date started."

She grabbed his hand and put it on her waist. The happy couple, arms around each other, walked back to their table almost oblivious to the music, conversations and socializing around them.

4

Friday June 20, 1986
7:00 PM
Lexington, Kentucky
Nick Kremer pulled his Chevrolet Monte Carlo into the Whispering Hills subdivision, a four hundred acre development situated in the flat farmland off I-64 northeast of the city. Right onto Bold Ruler Avenue, another right onto Cannonade Drive, past Sir Barton Court and finally left onto Proud Clarion Lane. Nick paid little attention to the streets named after past Kentucky Derby winners. He'd grown up in nearby Paris, Kentucky and the business of thoroughbred horses – breeding, selling and racing – was a natural part of central Kentucky life, as natural as the change of seasons.

Whispering Hills was street after street of two-story, brick houses with two-car garages situated on seventy-foot by two-hundred-foot lots. The typical two thousand square foot floor plans had first-floor laundry rooms, spacious kitchens with avocado-colored appliances, adjacent eating areas, and wood paneled family rooms with thick shag carpeting. The subdivision was a place for families looking to step up to a better slice of suburbia. It was the perfect place for mom, dad, two children and a family pet.

Nick drove slowly down Proud Clarion Lane amidst the waving of lawn sprinklers trying to postpone the onset of brown grass in what had been an unusually dry year. The front yards he passed were full of bikes, big wheels, and baseball bats. True to his engineering background, Nick scanned both sides of the street cautiously looking out for a stray ball that might be followed by an oblivious child. He had lived here for only six months and, although a few years younger than most of his neighbors, he liked the place.

The white "22" on the black aluminum mailbox signaled his house, and as the Monte Carlo eased over the curb, he pulled up the driveway's slight incline. The humidity draped him like a wet towel as he sat there in the car's black interior girding himself for the awaiting reception. *How pissed will she be? I told her that I would be a little late. Is two hours late a little late?* With a long slow exhale he stepped out of the car. Walking through the open garage, climbing over boxes and other items in his way, he opened the door and entered his home.

They had met in college. Nick, a not-so-typical engineering student, who spent a lot of time studying the fluid mechanics of beer, and Jenny, an equally hard-partying education major, and a queen bee in the sorority circuit. She had come with some of her sorority sisters to a local hangout in celebration of her twenty-first birthday, and Nick was there to kill a few brain cells with his roommates. He'd noticed her immediately as she walked in the door. Perfect hair, tight blue jeans, bejeweled and beautiful. Sorority girls always carried an air of superiority wherever they went.

In Jenny's case, superiority had its familial roots. Born into a wealthy family, she was the youngest child of a stockbroker father and socialite mother. Growing up people had considered her the 'it' girl. Smart, popular, good-looking, and athletic, Jenny had floated through life without working hard for anything. Nick, fueled by several drinks, had put on a charismatic smile and interrupted the 'girls' night out' to buy her a drink. The special that first night was a 'buttery nipple' – a blend of butterscotch schnapps and Irish cream. She had laughed when she heard the name and Nick loved how she laughed. The buttery nipple was a great icebreaker drink. I mean, how can you not get into a conversation with a girl after asking if she would like a buttery nipple? The conversation had led to another drink, and several others before finally ending in a wobbly walk back to the sorority house.

That night was six years ago. Six years is an eternity as a young man moves from the excesses of college life – time, booze and sex – to the responsibilities of fatherhood and marriage. In six years a lot can happen, and a lot had happened to Nick. An unplanned pregnancy, two college graduations, one successful job search, one job search put on hold, marriage, a baby girl, and a baby boy.

"Jenny, I'm home," Nicked called out as he slipped off his shoes and kicked them into the corner. As he turned around the corner of the entryway, a whirlwind of bouncing brown curls and a pair of outstretched arms ran towards him.

"Daddy, daddy you're home!"

"There's my big girl," Nick yelled to his three-foot tall little lady. He thrust out his arms as his daughter, Mary, launched herself at her dad. He swept her up in his arms and she screeched with joy as he twirled her around. "How's my girl? Did you have a good day today? Tell me what you did today."

"Lemme see," chirped the five-year-old placing a sticky index finger on the side of her plump cheek. "I played with my Barbies, painted some pictures, and colored. And lemme see, I helped take care of baby Robby too."

"Wow… that sounds like fun. You are such a big helper, do you know?" He said squeezing her tightly before gliding her back to the block patterned vinyl kitchen floor. "Where are Mommy and Robby now?"

"Mommy is upstairs sleeping. She doesn't feel good today."

"Really? Why don't you stay down here and watch some TV? Daddy will check on mommy. I will be back down in a minute."

Nick took a deep breath as he walked through the kitchen – countertops full of plates, spilled milk, a still-open peanut butter jar, slices of white bread and cereal bowls. The sink was full of dishes from the past several days, and the garbage can reeked of decomposing scraps. Jenny was not the best housekeeper, but Nick didn't care that much to make an issue out of it. Hell, this place is still cleaner than my college apartment. What did bother Nick was that Jenny seemed different late- ly as if every day was a chore to get through. She hadn't been herself for quite some time. Since after Robby was born. Hell, maybe longer than that. Jenny, who had once floated through life in a carefree bubble was now a tired, stay-at-home, young mother struggling to keep her head above water in this new reality.

Nick opened the door to the baby's bedroom. Shades were drawn, the playpen sat in the corner with a sleeping toddler snuggling into a blanket and pressed up against the meshed netting. Robby was a good baby, a better temperament than Mary as a baby, but now his easygoing disposi- tion was starting to change. He wanted to see and touch everything and therefore needed to be under constant surveillance. He wanted to climb, pull, shake and eat everything. Nick was sad to see him asleep as he looked forward to playing with his little guy after work. Asleep at seven o'clock would mean play time would be after midnight. Nick was not looking forward to that.

Jenny was lying in bed, sleeping on her back, her summer cotton night- gown raised up revealing her white bikini underwear. There was a time not too long ago when Nick would have calculated how much time they would need to have sex compared to how much time it would take Mary to become bored with the TV. He knew, however, tonight wasn't one of those times.

As he crept over the carpeted floor to the bed, a loose piece of sub- flooring let out a low groan and stirred Jenny from her sleep. Her eyes fluttered and, in a half-conscious state, she rolled over towards the door.

"Nick?"

"Yeah, dear. It's me. How are you feeling?" he said sitting on the edge of the bed. He reached out and stroked Jenny's leg.

"I'm just tired," she said rolling over in the direction of his voice. "Another long day here taking care of the kids. I thought you were coming home hours ago."

"I know. I know. I was hung up at work. We needed to get a project out the door. Now that I'm a partner it's something I just needed to get taken care of."

There was an awkward pause. Jenny tucked her elbows into her sides and lifted her back up off the bed to directly see her husband. Her face was puffy as she opened her eyes completely.

"Jesus, Nick. You don't know what my day is like. There are things you need to do *here*," Jenny declared in a sharp, clipped tone as if she were a balloon beginning to expel its air. "I'm tired of hearing about how important your job is – the kids and I are important too. Getting some help around here would be nice. I am with the kids all day long – feeding, cleaning, and changing them. I don't get to go out to meetings or lunches with people. The only adults that talk to me are on the damn TV."

Nick had been on the receiving end of Jenny's rants before and realized that the late nights at work over the past months had irritated what seemed to be an open sore in their marriage. With all the other things going on in his life, he struggled to find a balance that made everyone happy. He had thought about how to fix things because engineers are, by their nature, problem solvers. Every problem is composed of variables that can be manipulated to find possible solutions. Sure, the variables change in every problem, but finding them and adjusting them is just part of finding something that works. The tools of the trade reflect the methodical nature of this process – the rows of dusty codes on the bookshelves, the mechanical pencils stuck inside a pocket protector, and the lines of calculations written on the pads of three-hole punched quadrille paper. His marriage, however, was teaching him that some problems are not solved by simply adjusting the variables. Some problems were not looking for solutions, while others were only looking for an audience. In this case an audience of one.

"Okay, I hear you. How about we look at getting you some help around here. Maybe someone to do some cleaning or help with the laundry."

"And where are we going to get the money for that?"

This was a good question. The young couple's lifestyle in Whispering Hills was one that produced substantial financial strain. Purchasing a starter home like other young couples would have been smart, but Jenny had fallen in love with the subdivision when they first drove through it. A personal loan from Jenny's parents had provided most of the down payment for their mortgage, the size of which had made Nick uncomfortable. Although engineers made a decent salary, it was nowhere near enough. Jenny's expectations of her husband, especially one who fathered their first child out of wedlock, were steep. Nick always felt like he had to make that up to Jenny's parents and the best way to do that was to give their daughter what she wanted. The problem with providing for Jenny was that her wants were burying him. She wanted this house because anything less just wouldn't do. She wanted a nouveau riche décor that people would envy. She wanted Robby because she didn't want Mary to be alone. A lifestyle built on credit, coupled with the necessities of two small children, left Nick desperately trying to stay afloat.

"I know, I know. I hope that our profit sharing will help out."

Nick stuttered realizing that the long-term financial impact of partnership at J. B. Jones was not a short-term solution for the credit card balance that they had built up to furnish much of their house.

"I hope so too," Jenny sighed. "You know I gave up a lot staying at home to raise the kids. It hasn't been easy. You need to think about what this family needs. You need to help me out more. You need to be a better father than your father."

Nick had spent his adult life trying to be different than his father in almost every way. Those words from his wife cut deep into his soul. He pushed himself off the edge of the bed and walked towards the door.

"Yeah. I will do that."

He winced as if he was in pain walking out of the bedroom. The mere mention of his father flooded him with bad memories. At least now he could spend some time with Mary before it was bedtime.

5

Friday June 20, 1986
7:04 PM
Cincinnati, Ohio

Density is a physical property possessed by all materials. In the engineering world, this property helps define many other properties such as specific gravity, strength, and weight. An easy explanation of density involves visualizing a box measuring one foot long by one foot wide by one foot tall. Such a box contains a volume of space measuring one cubic foot. Density is what the box would weigh after filling it with a certain material. The two most common building materials used for building construction are steel and concrete. A one cubic foot box of steel would weigh four hundred and ninety pounds; a one cubic foot box of concrete would weigh one hundred and fifty pounds.

Dan Kunkel was stroking Misty's right hand across the small table. He enjoyed being here with his wife and the shadows cast by the second-floor walkway above their table provided a romantic ambiance. She was the most important person in the world to Dan, and he was happy that she had agreed to come out for this date. He smiled at her softly thinking how they fit together so well and how excited he was about the impending arrival of their second child.

"What?" she asked playing with the bracelet on her right wrist.

"I was just thinking about you and me. Our family. About how lucky I am. Any chance of getting you out on the dance floor tonight? Might be the last dance we get for a while."

Misty rolled her eyes playfully and decided to play the 'hard to get' card.

"Boy, oh boy, you ask a lot from a girl. First, you drag me out here, and now you expect a dance out of me. What else are you going to be expecting tonight?"

The band started their third set, and the couples on the now-crowded dance floor swayed to Duke Ellington's *Satin Doll*.

"I don't know. If I play my cards right, who knows?"

"Slow down there, big boy," Misty cackled. She loved that Dan still found her sexy in her eighth month even though her libido didn't feel turned on too much anymore. The additional thirty pounds on her small frame made everything, including sex, uncomfortable. Dan knew how she felt now and would never push the issue. One more reason she loved this man.

"You have a better chance getting me back out on the dance floor than getting into my pants tonight," she replied. "But you never know what the future holds or which way the wind...you know, will blow," she said blowing her husband a kiss.

"You mean I have a chance...tonight?"

"There's always a chance, sweetheart."

Misty considered herself fairly adept at satisfying her husband, and given that it had been three weeks since they'd last had sex, she knew tonight might be the last chance for them to be together for a while. Squeezing Dan's hand she giggled while slipping her bare foot across the table and rubbing it on Dan's leg.

Dan's eyes widened and, although no waiter had waited on them yet he raised his right arm to signal excitedly.

"Check please!"

Misty laughed loudly at that.

Misty's laughter coincided with a metallic popping sound overhead. The sound, by itself, was not alarming given the amount of activity in the atrium. Lost in the enchantment of the evening, the young couple did not react to the hundred thousand pounds of steel and concrete falling on top of them.

The human body bears a striking functional resemblance to the structure of a building. The human body has a frame made from bone and tendon which supports and protects the systems that allow the body to perform the activities of daily life. This frame allows the nervous system to control respiration, communication, and reasoning. Similar to the human form, the frame of a building supports the building itself. Failure of a single part can place the systems of each under extreme distress. Failure of multiple parts can jeopardize either's very existence.

The human skull protects the command center of the body – the brain. Damage to the brain disrupts the commands sent to and from the brain to the rest of the body. Interrupting these commands can affect motor functions, analytical reasoning, spatial recognition, and even the ability to get an erection. Contrary to popular belief, the skull is somewhat deformable and can bend under a blow and rebound to its original shape. It bends as long as the force of the impact is not too large. While a mild knock to the head does not leave a lasting reminder of the impact, impacts that are large enough result in skull fractures. Doctors have identified a variety of possible skull fractures, but the most serious of those are the ones where shards of the skull punch their way into the intracranial space. If this happens, grave damage can result with the bone lacerating arteries and shredding pieces of the brain itself.

The steel beam that struck Misty Kunkel weighed three hundred pounds and fell from a height of 10 feet. The intractable scientific laws governing the interaction between Misty and the second-floor walkway beam were unwavering in their application. Physics tells us that an object falling from this height struck Misty in approximately three-quarters of a second. The same laws also dictated that the velocity at the time of impact would be twenty-five feet per second. Principles of energy conservation dictate that Misty's parietal bone buckled under three thousand foot-pounds of energy at this time. This level of energy is sixty times greater than the energy required to produce a simple skull fracture.

The collapse pushed a quarter-sized piece of Misty's skull through the dura mater and blood vessels covering the brain, stopping at a depth of one inch into her brain. The falling steel beam severed her left leg below the knee, and a reinforcing steel bar from the walkway slab punctured her rib cage. Pinned under the wreckage, she could only see blackness in front of her. The damage from the skull fracture prevented her from speaking, and her heartbeat began to quicken. She wheezed with each breath due to a partially collapsed lung. Under the pile of rubble, in the darkness of the small void, she heard only silence until the wailing of the victims started. Her charm bracelet dangled from her wrist as she reached out her right hand searching for Dan.

6

Friday June 20, 1986
7:05 PM
National Engineering Laboratory
Washington, D.C.

Nassir Yassim unfolded the letter slowly. The luminosity of fluorescent lights bore down upon his cubicle, making his eyes ache today like they did at the end of every day. The National Engineering Laboratory, a branch of the Department of Commerce, provided technical services to other agencies involved in solving problems to enhance national competitiveness; though if you asked people in government circles, the NEL was just another agency existing anonymously in the overlapping web of redundancy.

Educated as an engineer in Egypt, Nassir was happy in his position as a research associate in the NEL. His degree in material engineering was useful as job prospects in that field were rising in the West, although prospects in Egypt were poor. Leaving Egypt to come to America had seemed like a good choice, maybe really his only choice. Being a research associate was just a chance to get some work experience and, at the same time, stay in America a little longer. Although his job mainly involved collecting data from federal agencies and preparing technical reports, he knew it was better than trying to find a job back home.

Nassir's jaw clenched every time he thought of the word 'home.' For a Palestinian living in Egypt *home* was not synonymous with warm and comfortable feelings. His family had fled to Egypt during the 1967 war, relocating in Rafah, a city in the northeast section of the Sinai Peninsula. Captured during this campaign, Rafah and much of the Sinai fell under Israeli control. Growing up under Jewish governance was not a bad thing as far as he was concerned. Although refugees, his family was accepted and he was allowed to pursue an education as if they were native-born citizens. However, that had changed when an Egyptian writer was assassinated by a group of extremists and almost overnight, public sentiment turned against the Palestinians. Recrimination had followed and when Israel turned the Sinai back to Egypt in 1982, Nassir knew that education overseas was an opportunity to get out. That opportunity had come by way of Virginia Tech.

As he read his mother's letter his hands trembled. His soul filled with a mixture of sorrow, helplessness, and guilt over his life in Washington versus his family's life back in Rafah.

> *Nassir,*
>
> *We are getting along as well as can be expected. Things have not improved since I last wrote. Your father and brothers cannot find work, other than odd jobs and the hauling of trash from the market. We have sold most of our belongings to allow for our necessities. Your father is considering moving back to Gaza thinking that he would stand a better chance of finding work. Still, we have it better than your cousins in Lebanon as there is so much unrest there. I am afraid it will boil over one day. We hope that you are safe and doing well. Please stay in good health and ...*

Nassir's eyes ached some more, but this time it was not from the light. Pangs of guilt slowly ate away at him. He was here enjoying a good education, a good job, and freedom to do what he wanted but he knew that life for his family was bleak. The thought of this hopelessness combined with his guilt began to manifest itself into something else. In disgust, he crumpled up the letter and threw it on the floor.

7

Friday June 20, 1986
7:15 PM
Cincinnati, Ohio

Scientists know that gravity is the force that attracts a mass toward the center of the Earth. Newtonian physics states that the gravitational pull is in direct proportion to the mass of the object. This concept necessitates that any object on Earth is attracted to every other object. But since the mass of our planet is millions of times larger than anything else its gravitational pull dominates. Structures must resist different types of loads including the natural tendency of the Earth to pull a structure down to its core. The balancing of the loads applied to a structure by the resistance of the structure is called equilibrium.

The collapse started a few minutes past seven o'clock in the fourth-floor walkway, which measured one hundred and seventy-seven feet in length. The walkway consisted of four sections supported at one end by the hotel and at the other end by the function block of meeting rooms. Three steel box-shaped beams supported by a vertical steel rod on either side provided the support of the walkway in between its ends. The two rods and the beam formed a support that was similar to a circus trapeze with the walkway resting on the seat of the trapeze. The steel rods hung from the roof of the hotel and connected to the beam using a bolt and washer on the bottom side.

As one connection between a vertical rod and steel beam failed, the other fourth-floor trapeze-type supports failed in a quick progression.

Snap. Snap. Snap. Snap. Snap. Snap.

As the six connections unzipped one at a time, the pieces of the fourth-floor walkway came crashing down. The second-floor walkway was thirty feet below and directly underneath its fourth-floor counterpart. Identical in form and material composition, the second-floor walkway mirrored the walkway above it with one exception. The vertical steel rods of the second-floor walkway were connected directly to the fourth-floor walkway instead of being connected to the atrium roof. Because of this configuration, the failure of the connections on the fourth floor immediately left the second-floor walkway unsupported. Similar to a trapeze artist holding onto the trapeze if the ropes supporting the trapeze were cut, with nothing to resist the pull of gravity, the walkway crashed down to the atrium floor followed by the fourth floor a split second later. Within the blink of an eye, gravity pulled the two walkways down to the floor of the atrium, where two hundred people were enjoying a Friday night in Middle America.

Brad Kessler was standing in the hotel lobby when the collapse occurred. The sounds of shattered glass and a hollow thud announced the impact of the walkways and shook the floor beneath Brad's feet. The vibration disoriented Brad for a moment. Guests and staff in the lobby all turned in the direction of the atrium and stared. A deafening quiet seemed to shroud the atrium where only moments ago the hum of conversation, music, and laughter had streamed forth into the lobby. Frozen, like figures in a wax museum, the hotel staff in the lobby waited for someone to make the first move. Suddenly a middle-aged man in a short sleeve oxford shirt ran out of the atrium towards the front desk.

"Call 9-1-1. Call 9-1-1. The walkways fell. Fell on people. They are trapped underneath!"

The reservation associates behind the check-in desk lifted their phones simultaneously. Brad noticed a grayish translucent cloud, a mixture of debris, billowing out of the entrance to the atrium. New sounds quickly followed – screaming, yelling, and the stampede of feet.

Brad, along with several others, ran towards the atrium entrance. The cloud of dust thickened as he approached the atrium. He was met head-on by dozens of patrons helping the injured out to the lobby. They were people, mostly middle-aged, business-types who had come to the Grand Plaza for an evening out with friends. The first wave of people were all in decent shape from Brad's perspective. Those with injuries were walking on their own or with minimal assistance from others. Besides the coughing and the crying, this group did not appear to have any severe injuries. Brad had a sense of relief as he squeezed his way towards the right handrail.

Cuts, bumps, bruises, limping…not so bad.

Even those requiring assistance in the first wave had no serious injuries as far as Brad could tell.

Brad turned pale as he cleared the bottleneck of people at the atrium steps and stepped down onto the floor. His eyes widened at the sight of the two walkways resting on the west side of the atrium floor. The scene seemed so out of place that Brad paused, studying it for a moment and trying to let his brain make sense of what his eyes were seeing. The walkways sat in a contorted pile of rubble on the floor, the southernmost section of the fourth-floor walkway still hanging at an odd angle from the function block wall. The walkways did not collapse in perfect synchronicity but were stacked haphazardly as if someone had just dumped a giant puzzle of steel and concrete on the atrium floor.

"We need help! We need help over here right now!" yelled a dust-covered man who was standing on top of the rubble. The dust had cleared where he was standing as a stream of water made a splashing sound on the rubble less than twenty feet away. The water came from a sprinkler pipe up near the void where the fourth-floor walkway had sat only moments ago. "Get some help!"

Brad's heart raced as he ran towards the man. Chairs and tables were tipped over around the periphery of the impact site, and he slipped on some broken glass crunching under his feet. As he reached the rubble his stomach tightened as he saw arms and legs jutting out from beneath the crumpled pile of steel and concrete. Rivulets of red mixed with the water cascading off the rubble to form larger puddles next to the wreckage. Several planters of bromeliads lay in pieces on the atrium floor, mounds of dirt with the vestiges of red and orange flowers scattered haphazardly. Several people were being helped up off the floor, conscious but unable to walk. Others huddled around people on the floor trying to lend first aid.

Jumping over the debris and puddles, Brad froze in his tracks. A floral dress with some legs jutted out from under the concrete walkway and atrium floor without a person attached. Brad's mind attempted to associate what he saw with another memory that was not as brutally real. Where have I seen this? His mind tried to connect this sight with something familiar, and it finally did. *The Wizard of Oz. The house that fell from the sky. The Wicked Witch of the East.*

Even though that part of the movie had shocked him as a small child, he always knew it was only a movie. The groaning and crying of the injured snapped him back to reality.

"He's not breathing."

"Help me. Help me. My foot is stuck!"

"Get this fucking thing off me. Please. I can't feel my legs!"

"Where's Linda? Linda!! She was right here a second ago!"

A strong, calm voice broke through the muddle of noise, pleadings, and questions.

"You. Come here. I need help here."

Scrambling up to the rubble Brad jumped onto the remains of the fourth-floor walkway. The man who had called him was now on the other side kneeling on the atrium floor. Turning his head, he pressed his right ear on the ground and peered under the pile with a small flashlight. Brad approached and knelt down beside him. He felt a coldness on his legs as his pants became wet from the water which pooled where they were kneeling.

"There is someone in there. I saw them a second ago," said the man.

The area he was shining his flashlight into was a small opening where the concrete walkway had arched itself into a small peak. The fourth-floor walkway was lying on top of the lower walkway but offset to the east by about two feet. Brad figured that the weight of the steel beam from the fourth-floor walkway had somehow caused its concrete to buckle upwards creating a space that could fit a couple of suitcases at best.

"I can see someone. I can see an arm. An elbow. Hey, hey, can you hear me?"

A slight gurgling sound was barely audible over the activity that was occurring on the atrium side of the wreckage.

"Move for me if you can hear me."

His flashlight glowed on a torn piece of fabric and a gray, dust-covered arm which moved towards them about an inch.

The man looked at Brad with a mixture of excitement and apprehension.

"I see movement. Someone's alive in there."

The hopefulness of those words contrasted with the image of thousands of pounds of steel and concrete lying on the floor of a hotel atrium. Brad nervously eyed the man.

"How are we going to get to them?"

"I don't know. We have to move this up and off."

Brad's mind raced with options.

Could we get a bunch of people and lift it? Could we get a jack of some type? A hoist? A crane?

"A forklift?" Brad blurted out. "The hotel has a forklift out on the loading dock."

The dust-covered man looked at Brad and with no hesitation nodded his head.

"Get it. Get it right now."

Brad raced over the rubble out to the atrium floor. Pockets of people clustered in various areas along the wreckage. Arriving fire department personnel roamed the room assessing the situation. Running past the portable stage, Brad noticed a musician sitting with his feet tapping the floor. Shell-shocked, the man stared blankly at the scene unfolding in front of him.

Exiting the atrium through a double service door on the far southeast corner, Brad ran down a corridor of crème-colored concrete block bathed in fluorescent light. His footsteps emptily echoed behind him, although he was unaware. Turning a sharp corner into the kitchen prep room he banged his knee directly into a hook holding kitchen utensils. The metal ripped through his pants and gouged his leg although the adrenaline coursing through him masked the pain. Sprinting into an adjacent hallway, he made it finally to the hotel garage.

The garage area had a large metal overhead door that led out to the loading dock. To the right side of the garage door sat a beaten-up yellow forklift. Brad ran over to it and was relieved to see the key seated in the ignition. He had some experience with forklifts from a job a few summers ago when he worked in a lumber yard. Although he had no formal training, running a forklift never struck him as being too much different than driving a car. Release the brake. Click the gear shift to the drive position. Push on the gas.

Brad turned the key, and the forklift rumbled to life. He checked the position of the forks making sure they were slightly off the ground. Shoving the gear shift into reverse, Brad steered the vehicle back a few feet. Placing it into forward and pressing on the gas Brad retraced his path back to the atrium. The forklift was small enough to fit most anywhere in the hotel given the proper amount of expertise. Brad was finding out that he wasn't quite the expert as the forklift banged hard into the block walls as he turned into the prep area. Brad tried turning it again with the same result. Exasperated, he backed up and correctly positioned the forklift to enter the prep room and continue on his way to the atrium. Once in the atrium, he made a beeline for the west wall.

"Coming through. Coming through. Watch out," yelled Brad to anyone and everyone within the sound of his voice.

Driving up to the rubble of the walkways about twenty feet from the point where he had scrambled over it five minutes earlier, he stopped as a new panic crept over him. I can't drive over these piles with a forklift. There's no way to get to the other side. Now what?

Brad's head throbbed as his mind raced searching for possible solutions. Suddenly he felt a hand grab his shoulder.

"What are you doing?"

Brad turned and saw a fireman standing next to him. His tan suit was streaked with dirt and the stenciling above his shirt pocket read 'LT. DAVIS'.

"We found someone trapped alive over on the other side. We have to lift the concrete up. But they are over on the other side," Brad said in a staccato-like manner.

"Okay. Okay. Take a breath," Lt. Davis said forcefully.

The grizzled twenty-five-year veteran wanted to calm Brad down but also wanted to let him know that the Cincinnati Fire Department was in charge now. Although the actual extent of the situation was still unknown, the lieutenant knew they were dealing with a mass casualty event. "We have a lot of people trapped from end to end," he said pointing to the north and south ends of the atrium, which had supported both walkways just a short time ago. "You can't just go trying to move the slabs in one place without thinking about what will happen somewhere else."

A blanket of despair fell over Brad as he realized there were others entombed beneath the wreckage. The blood felt warm dripping down his gashed leg, which was now throbbing with each heartbeat. He was focused on helping the one person in the one place that a dust-covered stranger had discovered. With two walkways on top of each other, he was beginning to grasp the enormity of the situation.

"But this forklift might work. We have a heavy crane on the way, but that will take a while to get here. Let's see what it can do," Lt. Davis said. "Where was the person you were trying to get at?"

"Right over there," Brad said pointing over a mass of people – some in need of rescue, others the rescuers.

"Get out and show me."

Brad jumped out of the forklift and ran to the pile. As he scrambled up the debris, his foot slipped, and his knee smacked down violently on a serrated edge of some broken concrete. Stunned by the pain, he was grabbed by Lt. Davis and pulled up. They made it to the other side and quickly located the dust-covered man a dozen feet to their south. He was still kneeling on the floor and talking through the opening.

"I'm back. I got the forklift on the other side," Brad said. "The fire department is here to take a look."

Lt. Davis crouched down and peered into the small opening. "What do we have?"

The dust-covered man in a raspy voice replied, "A person...I think a lady, in there. She's alive. She moved her arm a couple of times."

The fireman removed a large flashlight from his belt and pointed it into the void. He crawled up to the opening and said, "I'm with the fire department. We are going to try to get you out. Hang with us, okay?"

Davis could see the elbow move. He stood up and surveyed the pile of rubble to the left and the right. He pulled his radio off his belt and climbed up the pile to be visible from all parts of the atrium. He barked into the radio, "Johnson, this is Davis. My location is on the west wall – forty feet off the south wall. Can you see me?"

There was a long pause. The seconds crept by slowly. The radio crackled to life, "Davis, come again."

"Location is west wall – forty feet off the south wall. Can you see me?"

There was a shorter pause. "Yes, I see you."

"We have a person trapped, but responsive. Need to know the location of closest entrapment from my location."

The radio was silent again for what seemed like an eternity to Lt. Davis.

"Lieutenant, about twenty feet north of your location. Closer to the atrium side."

Davis climbed back down and took a position behind Brad and the dust-covered man, who were kneeling down. He surveyed the wreckage focusing on the arched slab that had created the opening. Twenty feet was good news. Moving the slab would not be a clean process, not like picking a book up off a table top. The slab, although broken, was still connected by sinewy pieces of reinforcing steel bars embedded into the concrete and running the length of the walkway. The lieutenant knew that as a piece of the slab was raised it would likely catch on something and slide into a new position requiring another adjustment of the forklift. Twenty feet was far enough away to allow them to wrestle the slab without potentially hurting the chances of someone else in the process.

Lt. Davis had a plan and stooped down next to the two people looking into the void. "You, kid, what's your name?"

"Uhh, Brad."

"Brad, this is what I need you to do. I need you to bring it over here. I need you to create another small opening down here with one of the forks," Davis said calmly. He pointed to a separation of the slab and the steel beam. Brad looked at a V-shaped gap between the top of the steel beam and the bottom of the slab.

"If you can get one fork into that opening and one into the opening here, we might have enough leverage to lift it up. It might give us a chance to pull her out."

"Okay."

Brad scaled the pile and jumped to the atrium floor. The physical movement of his arms and legs filled him with hope – he felt like he was doing something. Climbing into the seat he reached for the gear lever. *Oh, shit.* Brad remembered. *How do I get over to the other side?*

The walkway wreckage spanned over the length of the atrium from the steps of the main entrance on the north end to the function block on the south. There was no way for a forklift to run over the pile of steel and concrete and no way for it to ascend the steps. Brad realized that the only option was to drive into the function block and find a way through from there. His knowledge of the 40-story hotel was thorough, but his bellman's job did not take him into the function block of the hotel very often. But he knew that time and the woman's chances were slipping by quickly.

He drove the forklift frantically into the function block and headed towards dusty daylight coming from a hallway on his right. Turning into the hallway, Brad slammed the right fork into the corner of the wall and jerked the vehicle to a stop. Brad turned left releasing the fork and backed the forklift up about fifteen feet. Banging the gear lever forward, Brad punched the accelerator down and careened towards the sunlit hallway. Once the forklift was even with the hallway and without slowing down, Brad whipped it to the right, and the fork hit the corner with a loud pop. The drywall covering the corner exploded in a white cloud of dust. On a mission, Brad straightened the forklift and proceeded about towards the glass-paned single door that opened onto the sidewalk. The door might be wide enough to fit through, but its heavy-duty closing device would require someone on the outside to hold it open. Nobody like that here. Backing the forklift to the intersection with the main hallway, he raised the forks about three feet off the floor and pushed the accelerator all the way down.

Beads of tempered glass shot across the sidewalk followed by the forklift and crumpled door frame. The forklift bounced hard, teetering to the left before Brad stopped it from tipping over. He turned the steering wheel to the right and the vehicle lurched down the sidewalk. One hundred feet down, Brad slowed down to peer through the tinted windows to determine the location of the lieutenant and the dust-covered man. As the exterior light reflected off the tinted windows, Brad tried to see more than shapes inside the atrium. Suddenly four loud thumps shook the glass in front of Brad. He saw a shadow wearing a fireman's helmet confirming that this was the right spot. Staring down the sidewalk for an entryway in the atrium's west wall, he saw nothing up to the corner of Fourth and Main Streets. That would put Brad into the lobby of the hotel, which would only allow him to get the forklift as far as the main entrance to the atrium. Still, that wouldn't do him any good since the wreckage would still be blocking his path.

Fuck it.

Brad spun the forklift to face the glass where the shadow on the inside had banged on the glass.

The west wall of the atrium was composed of a curtain wall -- a glass and aluminum covering attached to the structural frame of the building. The glass curtain wall on the west side of the atrium began about a foot above the sidewalk. Below the glass was a polished granite sill that Brad hoped was for aesthetic purposes only. He lowered the forks to about an inch off the concrete sidewalk, angled the forks upwards slightly and stepped hard on the accelerator.

The forklift impacted the granite sill with a loud crack, and Brad felt the front wheels of the forklift lift off the sidewalk momentarily while his body rocked forward. Instantly the sill gave way and buckled into the aluminum curtain wall. A waterfall of glass rained down on his head as the glass pane shattered. With the resistance of the sill and frame no longer an obstacle, the forklift bounced into the atrium with the crackling of glass under its wheels.

"That's one way to get here," Lt. Davis declared.

Brad seemed slightly flustered and out of breath.

"I just… I thought… I figured this might be the easiest way to get here. I already broke the door down on the other side."

"No, no. That's good. You got it here. That's the main thing. Get it over here and let's try to open it up," said Davis, who now had shed his thick coat.

Brad positioned the forklift close to the vertex formed between the steel beam and slab. He angled the fork slightly upward and positioned it about a foot away from the point where he was aiming. If the fork hit this intersection correctly, an opening would be created to provide enough leverage to lift the slab. He hit the accelerator and the fork banged first against the top of the beam, producing a screeching sound until it hit the concrete. A few small pieces of concrete chipped off, but both men were expecting more success.

"Back up. Angle the fork up a little bit more. If you hit the concrete right where it meets the steel, I think you will have a better chance," instructed Lt. Davis.

He was being easy on the kid knowing that he was doing his best amid all the chaos. Brad backed and made the suggested adjustments and tried again. This time the fork's impact sheared off two large chunks of concrete which scattered across the floor.

"That's it! Do it again," yelled Davis.

After two more attempts, Brad opened a hole that would allow the fork to penetrate. With the help of the lieutenant and the dust-covered man Brad backed up, and carefully positioned the forklift with the left fork aligned with the newly created space, and the right fork aligned with the void where the person was trapped. Lt. Davis was kneeling on the floor giving Brad his instructions.

"There's only about two feet in there before we get to her. So you don't want to make it any worse, okay?"

Brad nodded. He noticed that his hands were sweating and his heart was pounding. *We are finally there. We can get to her.* The lieutenant peered into the space with the flashlight. He raised his left hand, his palm facing the forklift.

"Slowly, slowly...slowly."

Finally, his hand clenched quickly into a fist and Brad hit the brake hard enough, he thought, to put a hole in the floor board.

"There, that's good," barked Lt. Davis.

The dust-covered man nodded in agreement. The lieutenant shuffled his boots and noticed that the water was pooling up on their side of the wreckage. Instantly he became worried. Water seeping out from under the debris raised the possibility that its depth could be several inches inside the heap of twisted steel and broken concrete. He shuddered at the possibility that those trapped could live through the collapse only to die from drowning.

"Johnson, this is Davis. Get somebody to turn off the water to the goddam broken sprinkler pipe. Now!"

Brad looked past the mast of the forklift at the situation in front of him. The concrete slab was not perfectly flush with either fork, but there was enough contact to give the men hope. Lt. Davis knelt down again and spoke into the opening.

"Ma'am we are going to try to lift the slab up a little to give us some room to get to you. Move your arm if you understand that." A second later the fireman saw an arm move towards him again.

Lt. Davis stood up and wiped his forearm over the sweat on his forehead. Turning to Brad, he yelled, "Lift it."

Brad grasped the middle lever on the forklift's steering column and pulled it back. This simple action engaged the control unit raising the forks. Brad felt the forklift shudder slightly as the steel forks began to bear on the concrete. Although concrete is a rock-like material, it is softer than steel. The whine of the hydraulic actuator grew louder as the concrete slab began to lift slightly. The hopeful anticipation of success began to swell in all three men. Suddenly the whine from the forklift decreased in intensity, and Brad felt his seat rotate forward. He knew instinctively what that meant. When lifting a load, a forklift's center of gravity begins to shift forward. If the center of gravity shifts past the front axle, the forklift responds by tipping forward.

"Fuck me," cursed Brad as the back wheels of the forklift lifted off the ground. The weight of the slab was too great to keep the forklift stable. "I'll lower it down and try again," Brad shouted. Lowering the forks, Brad aligned the forklift and pulled the lever one more time.

The hydraulic actuator let out a loud whine which quickly lowered as the back wheels popped off the floor once again.

"Shit."

Lt. Davis shook his head disgustedly.

"This is not working, just back it out. You stay here. I'll see what else we have that could get her free."

Pausing for several seconds, he closed his eyes while considering other options. What the lieutenant realized but did not say was that time was not on their side.

At that moment, one hundred miles to the south of Cincinnati, a kitchen phone rang eight times without being answered. An old married couple was tending to their vegetable garden on this steamy July evening. The garden was an enjoyable pastime for the husband. Working with his hands seemed to relieve some of the stress from running an engineering business.

A few minutes later the phone in the kitchen began ringing again.

8

Friday June 20, 1986
10:00 PM
North of Lexington, Kentucky

Wispy strands of cirrus clouds stretched across the full moon providing just enough light for Nick to make out the silhouette of trees flanking the interstate. Headed north on I-75, the Monte Carlo rumbled over the pavement as the small green sign for Sadieville zipped past. The interstate would normally be occupied by a heavy volume of tractor trailers at this time but tonight traffic was light. The southbound side of the interstate was full of headlights, leading Nick to guess that many belonged to families making their summer pilgrimage to some beach, somewhere, down south. He flipped on his bright lights to make sure no deer were wandering close to the road. His position in the high-speed lane gave him little time to react if one decided to bolt into traffic.

Joe Jones sat ashen-faced in the passenger seat quiet in thought. Nick had just tucked Mary into bed a short time ago when he received the phone call from Joe. He knew right away that it was out of character for the old man to call his employees at home. Particularly on the weekend. Nick remembered listening in stunned silence as Joe told him that there had been a collapse on one of their projects, the Grand Plaza Hotel, in Cincinnati. An inspector from the Cincinnati Building Department reached Joe at home to tell him. He provided a few sketchy details…collapse of walkways in the Grand Plaza ….about 7:00 PM…..dozens of people killed……. cranes brought in for rescue…..still looking for survivors.

Jenny did not say much as he left. Maybe she just didn't know what to say or maybe she just didn't care. A little later he met Joe at the office, and quickly the two hopped into the car and headed north.

Quiet filled the car for long stretches of time almost as if any stray conjecture might make a bad situation worse. The two silent men had worked together on the Grand Plaza project, including the structural design of the atrium walkways. Unlicensed during that time, Nick had worked under Joe's supervision as required by law. The reality of a small engineering firm meant that Nick had performed the design followed by a review by his boss. Nick had earned Joe's trust quickly as the high workload made it expedient for Joe to do this.

Nick's silence was part of a stoic façade which stood in contrast to a mind that was running in overdrive with hypotheticals about the collapse.

What failed? All three walkways? Just a part of one walkway? Which part could fail? A beam? The concrete support at the end of the walkway? Was it a design error? Could it be a material defect? Was it not built correctly?

Although he would have liked to ask these questions out loud, he knew that only an investigation could find the answers.

Joe was also thinking about those questions and many others. He had spent a lifetime in engineering and had built a strong reputation along the way. Turning design calculations into a set of construction drawings for a host of contractors was a daunting task but one that Joe had done a thousand times before. The complexity of applying the science to create a design on paper to become an actual building was something most people could not begin to comprehend. The design of a building was different for each new project – different project site, different contractors, and different materials. He knew that every project was unique. Joe gazed out the passenger-side window remembering a professional conference where the speaker was lecturing about the similarities between the processes of construction and manufacturing. The speaker argued that both manufacturing and construction contained both inputs and outputs and therefore could be controlled and improved using statistical process control theory. Joe thought this guy was bat-shit crazy.

This dimwit has never stepped onto a construction site. Construction isn't an assembly line. How does your stupid model account for the weather? Last time I checked General Motors wasn't making cars on an assembly line that had six inches of snow on the ground.

Although he hadn't eaten for several hours, Joe felt sick to his stomach. People take for granted that the bridges they drive on will stand up, that tunnels they drive through won't collapse and that dams will protect them from flooding. Engineers know the expectations of public safety and shoulder these responsibilities in their daily practice. Although the scope of the failure in Cincinnati was unknown, the reports of fatalities made Joe's chest tighten. He knew that he had failed. He was afraid that this would wash away the good work that he had accomplished over his career.

"How much longer?"

"Fifty minutes or so, I suppose," Nick replied.

"Was there anything on the walkways that you...that we missed? Can you think of anything that was different on this?"

Nick was a bit surprised by the old man's question. Their relationship was close but tonight was a night to reconsider everything. He was not exactly sure what his boss was thinking. *Was this my error? One that wasn't caught?* Even without evidence, he felt guilty of something.

"I can't think of anything, Joe. I mean, the project was on a tight schedule and had to be fast-tracked. But the walkways were simple – just concrete on a metal deck. Lightweight concrete too. The steel rods connected to the roof supported the beams and walkway. It was all fairly basic."

Joe slowly exhaled as if trying to relieve the pressure inside his body.

"Can you remember any shortcuts taken during construction? Were there any issues with the concrete or steel?"

Nick put his right hand at twelve o'clock on the steering wheel and scratched his head with the other.

"I can look back at the inspection reports, but I don't remember anything being out of the ordinary. The steel came from Asia I believe. Japan,

China, Korea maybe. The owner has hotels all over the world if I remember correctly," Nick replied.

It was becoming increasingly popular to import steel from overseas as the cheap production cost outweighed the cost of shipping it thousands of miles. Asia now produced twenty-five percent of the steel in the world. China was particularly aggressive in the steel market as it had doubled its production over the last ten years. Growing its steel industry not only provided its people jobs but also generated hard currency for its communist government. That was one reason why the slogan "Buy American" was resonating through the country over the last few years.

"Any contractor issues? Were there any problems with the labor?" asked Joe. His chest tightened some more.

"Not that I recall. The contractors were all decent, I think. The unions didn't like the prevailing wage waiver, but there have been plenty of projects built using non-union labor."

Nick was right about this. Although trade unions would argue that their trained workforce resulted in higher productivity, many owners were pushing for non-union labor that provided lower upfront costs.

"Okay...okay. I guess we will find out more soon. I don't know what we will be getting into when we arrive, but we need to get a few things straight. Number one let me answer any questions. We want to make sure there is only one source of information on our end. Number two no talking to reporters, TV, newspaper, no one. Number three snap as many pictures as you can and take notes. You need to write down everything. This could be critical for you later on."

"Got it," Nick said nodding in agreement. That made perfect sense. As he drove on Nick also felt an overwhelming sense of failure, as if he had let the old man down. This feeling was coupled with a new anxiety as he noticed his boss's use of the word 'you' instead of 'we' in the last several minutes.

9

Friday June 20, 1986
10:00 PM
Cincinnati, Ohio

Brad's arms shook violently, and his ear drums exploded with the noise – ra-ta-tat-tat-rata-tat-tat. He was too busy to think about the sheer luck of getting the three jackhammers from a contractor working on a sidewalk replacement project outside the hotel. Stopping to check his progress he glanced through the windows at the activity outside. Fire department personnel were scampering around the crane setting it into place. Brad thought it looked close to being ready. Sensing a new urgency, Brad got back to work breaking up the slab.

The fire department's approach was steady and methodical. Lieutenant Davis had put Brad to work about forty-five minutes ago and sent over a paramedic who assessed the woman's condition. *Pulse is weak. Elevated heart rate. In shock probably due to blood loss. Won't know more until we can get to her.*

With rescue personnel in short supply and the lieutenant needed at other rescue points, Brad continued to make progress opening an access hole in the walkway. Brad got the hang of it after a few minutes and by the time the lieutenant checked on him again he had made a cutting gesture with his hand in front of his throat. Brad stopped.

"You are pretty much through the first slab. I'll pry the pieces out and take over from here. Why don't you take a quick break? Grab a drink," said the lieutenant.

Brad was worn out and nodded in agreement without saying a word. Wandering across the atrium to get a drink, Brad stepped over chairs and tables that were thrown around as if some tornado had touched down for a moment and left. White sheets lined the north side of the atrium floor. People with clipboards were moving from sheet to sheet as if they were pieces to a gigantic board game. Brad's stomach tightened when he realized that this was a makeshift morgue and that the sheets covered bodies of the dead. Walking quickly to the bar on the south side of the atrium he sat down at a temporary rest station. Hours before people had lined up, four deep, waiting on an array of martinis, whiskey, and chardonnay. Now the bar sat vacant, forlornly occupied by cans of soft drinks and bottles of water. Brad grabbed a Coke and took a long sip.

Brad's body ached as he stared blankly at the floor. The sights and sounds that bombarded him over the last several hours dulled his senses. Completely soaked with water, a mixture of dirt and debris caked his uniform pants. Brad's bony knees, now cut, bloodied, and bruised, protruded out from his ripped pants. His knuckles and forearms were in a similar condition -- raw and bleeding. His right hand involuntarily quivered as he sipped from a can of Coke, undoubtedly the result of jackhammering for the first time in his life. Not wanting to think about anything right now, he tucked his chin to his chest and closed his eyes.

Hail Mary, full of grace the Lord is with thee. Blessed art thou among women.

Finished with his prayer, Brad picked his way through the jumble of tables and chairs. Bouquets of colored balloons, still anchored to the tables, seemed to draw a boundary line between heaven and hell. Those behind the cordon of helium-filled latex were safe and alive while those on the other side were either dead, almost dead or in a still-to-be-decided struggle with death. As he walked towards the wreckage, Brad noticed the heavy crane outside the windows of the west wall. Good – it should be ready soon.

His feet hurt as he climbed over the rubble and found Lt. Davis lying on the fourth-floor walkway reaching down into the hole that Brad had opened earlier with the jackhammer.

"What's going on?"

"I broke through the second-floor walkway. Don't want to go any further because we are right over her, I think. Just trying to break the concrete free with the pry bar and hammer."

The lieutenant, his hands raw from scraping against the concrete, grunted with each swing of the hammer. The process was simple – drive the pry bar in, wiggle it to loosen the concrete, remove the pry bar and repeat until the chunk of concrete was free. As he drew the hammer back, his radio spit out a static-filled request.

"Lieutenant, Johnson here. We need you outside by the heavy crane ASAP. Please respond."

Davis put the hammer down and placing his palms on the edge of the hole, hoisted himself up into a kneeling position. Trying to catch his breath, he removed the radio from his belt and held it in front of his mouth.

"This is Davis. What do you need?"

"The crane is ready. The operators think it's best to punch through the fourth level of windows and position it over the walkways but..."

The lieutenant knew the words that were coming next.

"...that will mean removing all rescue personnel from the walkways."

Brad's heart sank when he heard this. Although the heavy crane could remove significant portions of the slab quickly, it still required time to determine which pieces to remove first. Then cables would be wrapped around and anchored to the concrete. That was time they didn't have. It was time she didn't have. Running on instinct and adrenaline the awkward teenager had stepped up over the last three hours to save the anonymous person trapped beneath the walkway. The force of gravity that had acted so easily in bringing the walkways down seemed to be resistant to lifting them back up. Still, he was not stopping now when they were so close to opening up an access hole.

"Right sir. Could you come outside? We need to make sure the crane operator is on the same page as us."

"Be out in a minute."

The lieutenant knew that soon he would be forced to give the command to have the crane break through the windows. An order for all nonessential personnel to leave the atrium would immediately follow this decision. Once in position, the lifting operation would cause portions of the slab to twist and slide, dropping chunks of steel and concrete. While the process would allow quick removal of victims and bodies, he knew it would undoubtedly jeopardize some of those trapped.

Davis looked at Brad with a stern intensity.

"You have ten minutes. Maybe. Work quickly and keep your fingers crossed."

Brad understood and silently nodded while he took the hammer from the lieutenant. He lay down on his stomach and began pounding on the pry bar.

Drive, wiggle, remove. Drive, wiggle, remove.

Finally, it happened. The impact on the pry bar produced a different sound than those previously. Instead of rebounding back, the hammer followed the pry bar as it slid about two inches. Brad had broken into the void space under the second-floor walkway. Buoyed by the real hope of breaking through, Brad's heart began to race, and the intensity of each hammer blow increased. A small hole about the size of his fist opened, and placing the hook of the pry bar underneath he applied his full weight onto the other end. This leverage broke another rectangular piece of the slab free, and he took his flashlight and pointed it into the void. The light illuminated a sliver of fabric covered with dust and seemingly wet.

Brad yelled into the hole, "I am almost there. Hang with me. Okay?"

Brad continued to hammer the pry bar into new crevices. Hammering, prying, pulling – piece by piece the concrete veil was lifted slowly revealing the human mosaic below.

The hole that Brad was making was slightly north of the void space where they had first caught sight of the woman. As the hole expanded, he noticed that the woman was on her left side with her back to the west wall, where Brad and the forklift had created the original space. Her right shoulder appeared free, and he called out to her to move if she could hear him. A slight tremor occurred in her shoulder which was significantly weaker than her response several hours ago. Brad pressed on.

Hammer, wiggle, pry.

Pulling a larger piece out and then another, Brad gasped. He was stunned by the brutality of what his eyes were telling him. The woman's right leg was bent backward at a grotesque angle with her foot lying underneath her left hip. Brad retched. Her foot was puffy and bruised, a shade of dark blue like the night sky just before dawn. A steel beam was visible below her right leg where a pool of water, dust, and blood formed a sickening background.

Brad steadied himself on the edge of the concrete opening and took a deep breath.

He stood and yelled.

"I have somebody! I have somebody! Get me some help!"

A paramedic rushed over and took her vital signs.

"I can't start anything but saline right now. Her heart rate is too low. It doesn't look good."

Out of ignorance or optimism, Brad ignored the paramedic's assessment and continued on his work, talking to the woman and imploring her to hang on. After prying out another chunk, he observed that her left leg had disappeared under the steel beam. Dark red droplets splattered the beam. Crying now, he continued talking to the stranger, reassuring her that she would soon be out. He pulled another chunk of concrete up and froze as he saw it – a bloodied and broken arm with a silver charm bracelet. The rounded belly. The pregnant woman he had seated only hours ago. The stranger who had made him feel so comfortable.

Brad let out an audible groan, a primal sound borne of the physical and emotional exhaustion.

His voice choked with sadness.

"Ma'am, it's Brad from the hotel. Hang in there. We have help coming right now."

Brad reached down and grasped her right hand, which was cold and damp. He looked at the charm bracelet and not her broken body.

"Ma'am, squeeze my hand if you can hear me. I have some help here, and more is coming. Squeeze my hand, please."

Brad thought he felt the faintest movement of her thumb and tears flowed down his wet cheeks. Her hand went limp.

Brad called out again, "Squeeze my hand if you can hear me. There's help coming."

Brad waited and called out again. This time there was no response. He looked over at the paramedic. The paramedic would not look back at Brad. Instead, he mournfully shook his head side to side.

10

Saturday June 21, 1986
11:00 AM
Cincinnati, Ohio

Nick unlatched the window and let the fresh morning air blow into his stuffy room. The city's air currents always seemed to move faster as the distance above the ground increased. Nick knew this was just nature following basic engineering principles. Wind speeds increase as a function of height above the earth's surface. That's why wind loads are typically taken at thirty-three feet above the ground surface. His view from the fifteenth floor was well above that thirty-three-foot level.

Nick squinted as the bright sunlight etched sharp lines across the office buildings in the downtown business district. In the shadows below, groups of people massed together on the sidewalk outside the hastily erected barricades. Hood to hood, police cruisers were parked along Main Street blocking traffic from moving south on Fifth Street. Nick could see uniformed officers preventing pedestrians from walking on the sidewalk south of the intersection as well. Several curious onlookers walked up to the officers standing behind portable orange barricades, exchanged words for a few moments, then turned and walked away. Nick saw this same scene repeat itself several times within the span of fifteen minutes.

The city had closed down all traffic in a two-block area surrounding the Grand Plaza Hotel to facilitate rescue operations. From his room, Nick had a clear view of the heavy crane standing in the middle of Main Street with its boom extending horizontally into the hotel.

Jesus, how bad is it?

Based on the local TV reports that had been broadcasting non-stop all morning, Nick was quickly getting an idea of just how bad it was. When he'd checked into his room last night, the local news was reporting that three walkways had collapsed with over fifty dead and 100 injured. Nick listened to the facts change over the last few hours, finally reaching a degree of uniformity among the local and national media outlets. Now almost every station reported that two walkways had collapsed, one on top of the other and the death toll was approaching one hundred and expected to rise.

He fought off nausea that tightened his stomach, and tried to prepare for what he would find when they were allowed into the hotel. He turned and looked blankly around the room, eyes finally fixating on an impressionist-inspired print of a vase of lilies. Lilies were Jenny's favorite. He thought that maybe he should surprise her with some soon.

Nick walked over to the unmade bed and unrolled a set of structural plans to the hotel project. The stack of twenty-four-inch by thirty-six-inch sheets contained the sections, notes and details for the atrium construction.

Two walkways, one on top of the other. That would mean it's the fourth-floor walkway and the second-floor walkway.

He studied the plans and made mental notes regarding the walkway configuration. Steel rods threaded through the box beams supported each walkway. The box beams, made from two channels or 'C' shaped members, were placed together and welded down their entire length. Nick glanced down at the title block in the lower right-hand corner which contained the typical information found in all engineering drawings. The title block is the headline of the engineering company who produced the drawing. In this case, it showed the J. B. Jones Engineering logo, which had a script 'J B' made from a line type that resembled a roadway – a black line with a white dashed line down its center. Nick stopped his mental note taking, as his eyes dropped to the bottom of the title block where three boxes contained the following information – 'Designed By', 'Checked By', and 'Date'. Inside those boxes, blue lettering noted the following: 'NRK', 'JBJ', and '2/15/85'. Seeing the letters, 'NRK' made Nick sway slightly. He backed up and sat on the other bed. The TV caught his attention as a local station cut to their reporter on the ground.

> *"Bob, I am outside the police barricade on Fifth and Main Streets but have confirmed from a source in the coroner's office that the Grand Plaza walkway collapse has claimed the lives of at least one hundred and five people. General Hospital, Sacred Heart Hospital, and St. Ann's Hospital have reported treating another one hundred and eighty-five individuals with at least a dozen in critical condition and several dozens more in serious condition. Lieutenant Jim Davis of the Cincinnati Fire Department confirmed that they lifted the last portion of the walkway slab an hour ago and that the Department's response has shifted from a rescue to a recovery operation."*

Nick's mind drifted away from the reporter's voice. He began to wonder what a person thought about after jumping off of a tall building. People always say that in the moments before death a person's life flashes before their eyes, but Nick wondered if it is their actions or regrets that occupy that time. Maybe some just want to make the pain go away, while others want to escape the fear of impending consequences. He assumed that all might want to escape an overwhelming hopelessness. Jumping off a 400-foot tall building would give a person roughly five seconds to think about something. Or maybe it would allow them a few seconds to think of nothing at all. Maybe the freefall is peaceful because they have handed control over to the laws of physics.

The darkness of that thought caused Nick to exhale several times quickly as he tried to compose himself. His face had a blank look pasted across it. Engineers probably think of nothing in those final seconds – only that their freefall is a transient state of instability. Maybe the ground is the final solution to this instability. Maybe it's a way to restore equilibrium.

Nick got up and walked over to the window considering the relation-ship between equilibrium and the ground. He pushed on the window, opening it wider and allowing more fresh air to blow into the room. He peered out at the street below. The phone rang and jarred Nick out of his thoughts. He quickly turned around and walked to the phone sitting on the nightstand between the two double beds.

"Hello."

"Nick, it's me." The voice on the line was easily recognizable.

"Yeah, Joe. What is going on?"

"I talked to the Building Department and the news reports now seem to be right. The walkways in the atrium, fourth and second floors col-lapsed. People were on the walkways and underneath them when it hap-pened, lots of dead and injured. The fire department has been there all night, and they finished lifting all of the walkway pieces. They have re-covered all the bodies. It's just a matter of identification now," reported Joe Jones in a raspy voice, one that belonged to a person on the verge of complete exhaustion.

"Any more news about the dead and injured?" Nick inquired as if there was some possibility that all the news reports they had heard since last night were somehow inaccurate.

"Last I heard was a hundred and five, and a hundred eighty-something injured. But some of those injured are in bad shape so….," answered the old man reluctant to utter the obvious end of his sentence.

"When will we be allowed to get in there?"

The young engineer felt as if he had been in a purgatory for the last twelve hours, caught in a place full of questions and unknowns. If he could at least see the scene then maybe answers would begin to satisfy the many issues that rattled incessantly in his head.

"The owners of the hotel called in their lawyers, so nobody other than rescue teams and some media are allowed in right now. They have their people along with the fire department recording the location and condi-tion of everything. I think they want to make sure their asses are covered for liability and such," Joe stated as his voice grew raspier with each sen-tence. "That should wrap up within the next few hours I suppose."

"So maybe we can get in by one or two o'clock?"

"It's going to be later than that. It seems that the mayor wants to make sure there is an independent investigation, so it doesn't look like the city is hiding something. They asked the feds to head the investigation. We are only allowed access after the federal team gets here."

"Is the federal team from OSHA?" asked Nick, who was familiar with the government's Occupational Health and Safety Administration from many of his projects.

"No, it's not OSHA. It's a team from inside the National Bureau of Standards. The long and short of it is that we won't be getting in there until the hotel and fire department have cataloged everything and the team from Washington gets in there," Joe said.

"So we just sit around and wait," asked Nick dejectedly, already knowing the answer.

"Yep, that's right. Sit tight. Keep reviewing the plans and files on the project. Make sure we have enough film in the camera. I will let you know when I hear something."

Nick hung up the phone and stared at it while letting his mind float away from the uncertainty that lay ahead. Sunlight shone through the window and creeped along the carpeting in the room until it stopped halfway up Nick's right leg. Its warmth relaxed the young engineer, who was numb from the events of the last fourteen hours. Being numb was a good thing, a defense mechanism against the guilt, uncertainty, and anxiety that he felt when the exhaustion waned. He thought about Jenny, Mary, and Robby and wondered what they were doing on this Saturday morning. He wished he could rewind the clock and find himself back home. He walked over to the window again and closed it, hoping the team from Washington would arrive soon so that he could stop the torment of this waiting game.

Five hundred miles to the east of Cincinnati, Nassir Yassim walked up to the ticketing counter at Washington's National Airport. Checking one suitcase, Nassir presented the gray-haired Delta agent with his driver's license.

"Destination is Cincinnati, Ohio?" asked the woman as she stared down at the screen in front of her.

"Yes, that is correct," replied Nassir as she handed his license back.

"Business or pleasure?"

"Business, today," he said tucking the license back into his wallet.

"Very good. Your plane will be at gate B-21. Have a nice flight," she said smiling at him.

"Thank you."

The young man turned and began walking towards the gate where he would meet others who were heading to Cincinnati on the 12:40 flight. He was excited to be on the team investigating the collapse although he realized his inclusion was more a function of availability than expertise. Nonetheless, it was something different from the stacks of data and reports that the young Palestinian waded through on a daily basis. He walked hurriedly through the waves of people moving through the terminal. As an engineer, he appreciated the number of systems that had to work in harmony to move people from one city to another in such a small amount of time. He admired the quality of infrastructure in the United States which was head and shoulders above that in his homeland. Looking up at the clock, he realized that he had enough time to grab some lunch and began to walk towards the food court.

11

Saturday June 21, 1986
6:00 PM
Cincinnati, Ohio

A muscular patrolman moved the barricade to the side allowing the two men to continue their walk down Main Street. The evening was once again humid, and Nick noticed the old man heavily perspiring as they walked briskly on the hard concrete sidewalk. The sound of their steps eerily echoed as they marched on. Tonight, in the middle of the city, they were the only people out on this stretch of sidewalk, a sidewalk that would be packed with people on a regular Saturday evening. Less than a day since the accident had occurred, they were now inside the police cordon which effectively sealed the hotel from the rest of the world.

The two men walked up to the portico of the Grand Plaza and walked through the revolving door. Transformed into a command center by the Cincinnati Fire Department, the lobby of the hotel buzzed with activity. Metal tables flanked both sides of the lobby with fire department officers and other first responders sitting behind stacks of boxes, manila folders, and telecom equipment. The clack-clack-clack of a typewriter intermingled with the buzz of voices talking on phones and walkie-talkies. Off to Nick's right the hotel's offices had been re-tasked into a media room which was monitored closely by the public relations liaison from the city. Local government officials recognized the grave nature of this event and were doing their best to provide information to the public.

Joe edged in front of his young partner and walked up to a table, where he asked a middle-aged official where he could find Lieutenant Jim Davis. Nick stood behind Joe and felt the straps of his backpack digging into his shoulders. Loaded with cameras, film, notebooks, file folders, measuring tapes, chalk and spray paint, Nick had stuffed the backpack with almost everything that they would conceivably need. Collecting information was his highest priority while Joe's number one job was communication. Each man understood the seriousness of this event and the consequences that it could have on their livelihood.

Glancing past the line of metal tables, Nick saw the entrance to the atrium in the distance. Although still a good fifty yards away, the activity inside signaled that this was indeed the eye of the storm. Nick looked back as the fire department official picked up his walkie-talkie and said something into it while Joe nodded his head and turned around to stand next to Nick.

"He'll be here in a minute," said the old man.

"Okay."

A minute later, a fifty-something-year-old fireman walked towards the two engineers. He wiped his gray hair, matted from sweat and debris, across his forehead and he hitched up his brown insulated pants as he approached them. The white cotton shirt that he was wearing the night before had been replaced by a gray cotton tee shirt with a blue "C.F.D." over the left breast pocket. The man's gait was awkward and favored his right side.

"Hello. I'm Jim Davis of the Fire Department. You two the engineers?"

"Yes. Hello, Joe Jones from Jones Engineering," said the old man as he extended his hand to the lieutenant. "And this is Nick Kremer."

The three men perfunctorily shook hands.

"Well, the team from Washington arrived a little while ago, and I guess you know they will be leading the investigation. The city and the hotel felt that it was best to get someone independent in here for this," said the lieutenant in a terse but professional manner.

"Right, yes, that's what I understood was happening," said the old engineer. "We are here in a support role, to provide the team any insight they need on the design."

Lieutenant Davis nodded and began to walk towards the atrium. He stopped and turned quickly towards the two engineers. "Remember, you can look around, but you need to ask before you touch anything. Recovery operations are complete, but that doesn't mean that we have cleaned everything up."

"Understood. Not a problem," said Joe nodding to the lieutenant as they continued to the scene of the collapse.

Nick's eyes flooded his brain with images as he stood on the top step of the atrium entrance. The incoherence of the space shocked Nick's engineering senses. Broken walkways were lying on the floor. Broken windows with the crane boom still hovering silently over the atrium floor. Steel handrails, twisted and broken, but still attached to the walkway in some locations. Chairs and tables upturned and scattered across the space. A row of fresh white sheets in the corner by the bar. Nick's body swayed as a current of fresh, humid air blew in through the broken windows in the west wall.

The three men walked down the steps to the atrium floor with the lieutenant leading the way. The broken chunks of the walkway sat in two rows in the middle of the atrium like a jigsaw puzzle with no hope of fitting back together. Nick's gaze drifted from the walkways to the ceiling, where he noticed the six steel rods hanging down near the west side of the atrium. These steel members seemed lonely to the young engineer, structural orphans no longer with any purpose to serve. Glass, debris, and water still littered the floor, and Nick reconsidered his decision to have worn dress shoes instead of boots.

Several dozen people were working in various parts of the atrium. Four of the people standing near the broken walkway were wearing orange safety vests with "NBS" stenciled in black across their backs. The lieutenant led the two engineers directly to the tallest person in that group.

"Chuck," called the lieutenant, "I would like you to meet the engineers who worked on the project."

Chuck Swenson, a stern-looking fifty-year-old associate director from the National Bureau of Standards, turned his tall and slender frame towards the two engineers. Fifteen years ago he had landed a position with the National Bureau of Standards as a quality control specialist and, being a nose-to-the-grindstone kind of guy, he'd quickly climbed the federal bureaucracy ladder. His office oversaw various federal laboratories and late last night he had received the order to assemble a team to come to Cincinnati.

"Hello, Chuck Swenson."

"Hi, Joe Jones, from Jones Engineering in Lexington," replied the old engineer as he clenched the associate director's hand. "And this is Nick Kremer."

Nick responded in a similar fashion, keeping his words to a minimum and remembering to let Joe do the talking.

"We're here to do whatever we can do," offered Joe.

The associate director said as he scratched the back of his head and glanced around the atrium,

"Well, the job here is quite straightforward. We are here to collect all the information necessary so that my people in D.C. can determine the cause of the collapse. My team secured plans to the atrium upon arriving, and we really won't need you for too long. Just maybe if you could confirm and clarify a few things for us."

"Sure. That would not be a problem," answered the old engineer. His answer belied a good deal of uncertainty, however, as Joe assumed that there would be more than a few clarifications that would require their presence. "Nick, let me get the project file out of your backpack…here I will get it."

Before Nick could get the strap off his shoulder, Joe pulled Nick around to be between him and Associate Director Swenson.

"Start taking pictures and notes. Take as many as you can," he whispered to Nick. "Here, I got it," chirped Joe. Clutching the accordion-style folder, the old man wobbled back towards the D.C. bureaucrat. "What do you need to know?"

"Well, first, let me get the research person from our engineering laboratory over here," he replied as he motioned to a twenty-something to join the group. Chuck Swenson proceeded to introduce the two Lexington men to Nassir Yassim. Nick studied the young man from Washington who was not much older than him before asking about the closest restroom. The associate director pointed Nick towards the lobby.

"First, we would just like confirmation on the composition of the involved walkways. It looks like the two walkways over by the wall collapsed, and we assume that they were suspended in some fashion by those rods." He pointed to the remnants of the steel rods, which were still swaying from the atrium ceiling.

"Right," said Joe as he began to discuss this with the men.

Nick slowly wandered towards the lobby and, once far enough away from his boss and the two men, he retrieved his camera and a notebook from his backpack. Following Joe's orders, he proceeded with the process of taking a photo and then scribbling down notes.

Photo 1 – Hangers suspended from roof, 4th-floor level

Photo 2 – 4th floor west bearing; steel bearing plate intact, concrete edge cracked

Photo 3 – 4th floor east bearing; steel bearing plate deformed; concrete edge cracked

He turned and walked towards the center of the atrium where the broken walkways were lying. Looking down at the tiled floor, Nick saw dried dark swirls in no particular pattern. He knelt down and ran his finger across a swirl to further inspect the residue. His eyes watered slightly as he became aware of a slight floral smell. As he rubbed the residue between his thumb and forefinger, a wave a nausea swept over him again.

Blood and disinfectant.

He stood up, placing his hands on his knees to steady himself. He glanced over at Joe, who was now pointing to something in a file folder that appeared to be of interest to the group.

Beads of glass crunched under Nick's shoes as he walked toward the wreckage and the process of walking made him feel slightly less sick. Looking towards the bar, he saw Lieutenant Davis talking to a group of men in white jackets holding rolls of dark fabric under their arms. They were standing next to four white sheets arranged in a row next to the wall.

Two of the men bent down next to a sheet and unrolled the dark roll of fabric and pulled on a zipper. Nick turned his eyes away as they reached to lift the white sheet away. *A body bag. Don't look.*

The young engineer approached the rubble and stopped outside the ring of yellow caution tape wrapped around orange traffic barrels every thirty feet or so. From this vantage point, Nick immediately noticed a distinct difference between the two walkways -- the concrete slab of the closest walkway shattered as if subjected to an explosion. He took out his camera, hurriedly snapped several photos and recorded a series of notes.

Photo 10 – Walkway; extensive fracturing of concrete slab

Photo 11 – Walkway; extensive fracturing concrete slab; significant distortion support beams under slab

Photo 12 – Other walkway; mild fracturing of slab; less distortion of support beams under slab

Nick quickly surmised that the walkway with more damage was the second-floor walkway. With the fourth floor walkway impacting it from above and the atrium floor impacting it from below it made sense to him that it would have virtually exploded under the competing forces. Nick studied the fourth-floor walkway carefully. News reports said witnesses saw the fourth-floor walkway fall onto the second-floor walkway and, although accounts are not always accurate, Nick sensed from his initial assessment that this was correct. If the fourth-floor walkway fell first, it had to be a failure at the connection.

Six connection points occurred in the middle of each walkway, three on each side. His design called for steel rods that were hung from the atrium roof and attached to a rectangular steel beam that ran across the walkway – in essence forming a trapeze. The steel beam was composed of two "C" shapes facing inward and welded together. The rod extended from the roof through the rectangular beam and was secured using a nut and washer at the bottom of the steel beam. The second-floor walkway had a similar design with one difference – the end of the rods extended through the beam, secured with a nut and washer at the top of the steel beam. Nick's design initially had called for one rod to extend down from the roof to the second floor at each of the connections points, but the contractor had asked to separate the rod into two pieces at the fourth floor to expedite construction. Nick remembered thinking that the split rod arrangement detracted from the overall aesthetics of the structure but, with so many other things on his plate at the time, he had approved it without hesitation.

All connections were outside of the concrete walkway and could be viewed rather easily even while lying on the atrium floor. The young engineer stared intently at the three connection points that faced him. His heart began to race as he saw the piece of the structure – the piece that he had designed – the one that likely had failed. His hands trembled as he focused the camera and snapped several more photos. He let the camera hang by its strap and recorded a series of notes.

Photo 13 – Fourth-floor beam-rod connection (north end); channel flanges distorted, weld broken; rod pulled through

Photo 14 – Fourth-floor beam-rod connection (middle); channel flanges separated appx. 1", beam pitted where rod pulled through (rust?)

Photo 15 – Fourth-floor beam-rod connection (south end); channel flanges separated appx. 1- ½", beam pitted where rod pulled through (rust?)

Based on the distortion of the steel beam coupled with the steel rods that were still hanging from the atrium roof, Nick grew convinced he had found the component that had failed. The steel rods had pulled through the rectangular steel beam. Breaking the weld between the channels and bending the bottom. That would allow the rods to slip through.

Still, there was something out-of-place with the broken connections that bothered him. Lost in his thoughts, he edged closer to the caution tape which surrounded the perimeter of the laydown area for the walkway rubble.

Forgetting the instructions that Lieutenant Davis had given him before they entered the atrium, Nick pulled the caution tape up and ducked under to get a closer look. He knelt down at the first connection point and noticed that the amount of rust was more severe than he'd thought a minute ago. He pulled a small plastic ruler out of his shirt pocket and held it up against the bent steel beam. The piece of steel was supposed to be one-quarter inch thick but was significantly smaller than that at several locations due to corrosion. Nick fumbled with his camera and adjusted the focus. Holding the camera with one hand, he edged the plastic ruler down along the area of the steel beam that was showing areas with severe rust.

Photo 16 – Fourth-floor beam-rod connection (north end); corrosion at channel flanges; 50% reduction of flange

Photo 17 – Fourth-floor beam-rod connection (north); corrosion at channel flanges; 60% reduction

Corrosion of steel is both an electrical and chemical process requiring iron atoms in steel to give up both ferrous ions and electrons in one area of the steel called the anode. Steel at the anode is eaten away while the ferrous ions and electrons re-form at another location called the cathode. At this location, ferric oxide, also known as rust, is formed. What perplexed Nick was that normal corrosion typically requires an electrolyte, like water, to act as the pathway for the electrons and ions to move. Water did not make any sense being that the walkways were inside. Even if it was water, how could this much corrosion take place in a little more than a year?

Nick put the plastic ruler back in his shirt pocket. He reached into the open end of the box beam and probed the broken edges of the steel with his fingers. The distorted edges of the steel shapes were colder than the warm, stagnant air that was now blowing into the atrium. The young engineer became aware that his shirt was now sticky with sweat. As he continued to reach farther into the inside of the beam he experienced an unfamiliar sensation. Cold and slippery. Removing his hand from the beam Nick wiped his fingers on top of the beam to get the gooey coating off.

Nick took several pictures of the paste and jotted down more notes.

Photo 18 – Residue found inside box beam on broken flanges (north side); unknown film (black) and paste-like substance

Photo 19 – Paste-like substance on top of beam near connect (north side); sludge with embedded granules

Nick stood up and walked down to the next connection. He realized that the beads of glass that he was stepping on were most likely the remnants of the panels that had been attached under the chrome hand-rails. Stopping at the middle connection, he bent down to inspect it close-ly. The same distortion existed where the steel rod pulled through the beam as before. The corrosion appeared to have produced a section loss of approximately fifty percent on the bottom of the beam. Engineers find comfort in consistency. They design based on principles where the resul-tant behavior is predictable. This failure – his failure – was on full public display. Now, for the first time in the last day, he was absorbed by what was in front of him and comforted by the consistency in what he was seeing. Understanding this similarity could lead to an understanding of the cause of the collapse.

Nick started to move onto the next connection when his foot bumped against the steel beam. A piece of the steel rod rattled inside the steel beam and had become dislodged by the force of Nick's shoe. Curious, Nick picked it up and examined it. Roughly three inches long, the piece still had the hardened washer and nut attached. The edge of the washer was deeply pitted from the corrosion as Nick had previously noted with the beam. Without much thought, Nick slipped off his backpack and opened it. Retrieving a plastic bag from his backpack, he dropped the piece of steel into it and marked it with a felt-tipped pen.

"Rod/nut @ middle connection, 4th fl. 6-21-86"

He progressed down to the next connection point and continued his work. Absorbed in his work Nick was not aware of Joe's location anymore. Suddenly, Nick was startled by a light touch to his shoulder.

"Hey, you shouldn't be inside the caution tape," said Nassir Yassim in English that bore only a hint of his foreign heritage. "Our team should be the only ones in this area."

"Oh, okay. I am sorry about that," said the young engineer in an apolo-getic tone. Standing up, he faced the Palestinian. "I was trying to see if I could see what exactly happened."

"Well, that is our job."

Nassir's tone was forceful and direct. Being on the team had given him confidence in dealing with outsiders, a confidence that he hoped would be noticed by his superiors. Although not entirely comfortable

with the American way of communication, he was shrewd enough
to know that the young engineer might have some valuable insight.
This insight would make the research associate look even better to his
superiors.

"Since you are here, tell me, what are you thinking so far?"

Nick was pleased that his expertise could be of some assistance.

"To me, it seems likely that the steel rods pulled out of the box beams.
Almost as if the rod bent the top of the beam causing it to lose support,"
said Nick as he kneeled down and pointed towards the bottom of the
beam.

Nassir squatted down and looked at the bent flanges.

"I see what you mean. But why would that happen?"

"At this point, I don't know. There was a change during
construction – from a single rod to a split rod arrangement. They wanted
to do that to speed up the building process," said Nick forgetting Joe's
instructions to say very little to anyone.

"What was this change all about?" asked Nassir.

"Well, originally a single steel rod was to extend through the box
beams on the fourth floor and straight down to the second floor," Nick
explained.

"And the contractor wanted it changed because…?"

"They thought it would be easier to have two sections of shorter rods.
That way they could complete the fourth floor first and then construct the
second-floor walkway below."

"That makes sense. Anything else that you have noticed?"

"There is a good deal of corrosion on the steel beams which just seems
odd," Nick said as he motioned to the Palestinian to follow him.

"Odd?" asked Nassir a step behind the engineer.

They stopped at the nearest connection and Nick knelt down followed
by Nassir. Nick took his flashlight and directed its beam towards the inside of the beam's void space.

"See how the steel is pitted. It just doesn't make sense that there would
be that much corrosion on a building that has only been open a little more

than a year. Especially on the inside of a building." Nick emphasized the word *inside*.

"Yes, that does seem a little unusual. Maybe the steel was corroded before it got here," hypothesized Nassir as he shifted from kneeling into a crouched position.

"Take a look here," Nick instructed as he pointed his finger in the direction of the light. "The other thing that I noticed is that all the corroded areas have a residue."

"I see. I will make a note of that. I will see if our laboratory can determine what that is."

"Your laboratory?"

"Yes. Our laboratory in D.C. The wreckage is being shipped there so we can study it further and report on the probable cause."

The research associate eyed Nick carefully, unsure how he would react to what he was about to say next.

"Hey, I am sorry, but it is my job. I saw you taking photographs, which is not allowed per our rules. The city put us in charge of all evidence collection. So I will need you to hand over the photos," he said gesturing towards the camera hanging from a black strap around Nick's neck. "I will include those as evidence as our laboratory develops our report."

Nick's face was expressionless as he absorbed the words from the research associate. Evidence. The walkways were now evidence. He was now acutely aware that this was a quasi-crime scene. Evidence would be collected to determine the cause of the collapse. He had a sinking feeling that the investigation would point to J. B. Jones Engineering and their newest partner.

"Okay," Nick said as he advanced the film in his camera to the end. He popped open the back of the camera and pulled out the roll of 35mm film, and handed it over.

12

Saturday June 21, 1986

10:30 PM

Lexington, Kentucky

Jenny tilted the wine bottle straight up making certain that all of the Chardonnay found its temporary place in her glass. The stress of the Saturday, alone with her two children, made her eager for an escape at the day's end. Well into her third glass, she felt warm as the stress disappeared and her body sank lower into the overstuffed leather couch. The bottle wobbled awkwardly on the end table as it slipped from her fingers and she grabbed it just before it fell. The last thing in the world that she wanted right now was to drop something that would cause her kids to awaken.

The TV was on, and although she stared at the screen she wasn't watching. She kept the volume low and closed her eyes as her body relaxed and her cotton sundress slid up on her thighs. Closing her eyes, she began to drift off, but her alcohol-fueled mind jumped fitfully from thought to thought. She thought about her kids. She thought about Nick. She thought about sleep. She thought about how she wanted more. She thought about how she wanted her thoughts to go away.

The ringing of the doorbell was loud. Much louder than the voices on TV. She sat there, semi-conscious and eyes still closed, wondering if the doorbell was real or part of some dream. A few seconds later the doorbell rang again.

It's real.

Struggling to her feet, Jenny swayed a bit before placing a hand on the wall.

Damn it.

She walked in an unsteady gait through the kitchen and down the hall, keeping a hand on the wall for balance.

"Coming," she said in a whisper. "Hold on."

She flipped on the front porch light and pulled on the sheer curtain covering the sidelight to see who was trying to wake her kids. Her neighbor, a contract attorney from up the street, was standing there in swim trunks and a polo shirt taking a swig from a bottle of imported beer. A gold bracelet glistened from the porch light, and his Panama Jack tee-shirt was drenched with water. Although in his late thirties, Bob Jensen was still in good shape and his carefree attitude was something that Jenny certainly wished she had. Jenny pushed her blonde hair back over her ears and steadied herself on the door frame before opening the front door.

"Bob? What are you doing here?" Jenny said making an effort not to slur her words. Her cotton sundress moved slightly in the humid night air.

Bob was a successful man as his late-model Mercedes, luxuriously decorated house and jewelry would attest to. The gossip around the neighborhood was that he had made a fortune by winning a multi-million dollar damage award against a famous horse breeder in a class action suit. As Jenny understood it, the breeder had a champion stallion that demanded an enormous stud fee but produced a string of live foals that had severe genetic defects. In front of the Kentucky Supreme Court, her neighbor had successfully argued that the breeder had an obligation to produce not just live foals but non-defective live foals. The legal judgment and subsequent eight-figure settlement had cemented his reputation throughout the state.

"Hi, Jenny. I just wanted to see if you and Nick wanted to come on down to my house for a little late night get together with some of the neighbors – Joan and John, Amy and Dan and a few others," said the lawyer, who was not concerned with slurring his words. "Sit at the bar, take a dip in the pool, and just relax a little." He took a final swig of his beer and smiled. "Maybe drink just one more beer."

Although Bob had heard about the walkway collapse on the news and knew that Nick was a structural engineer, he didn't know Nick was *that* engineer.

"Oh, the pool sounds nice, but Nick is out of town, and the kids are asleep," Jenny said.

The wine was making the pool and everything sound good to her. She did miss the carefree days that used to occupy her time. Although a young mother of two, her size three frame could still fit nicely into jeans, skirts or even yard clothes. Having children had even filled out her body with womanly curves, and she made sure to wear items that accentuated each and every one. She liked the attention she received from the men in the neighborhood and did not care what their wives thought. Tight clothing with an extra button or two undone seemed to maximize that attention. The looks that Jenny received made her feel a little like she was back in college.

"I really wish I could, the water and a drink would be great. But..."

"Hey, I am dry right now so how about a drink for the road?" Bob interrupted, shaking his empty bottle and flashing a smile. Jenny's gaze lingered on him.

"Sure, Bob, I think I have one for you. Come on in. But you just have to be quiet. The kids are upstairs sleeping," she said tapping her fingers on his chest and letting them slide slowly down his chest.

"You can be quiet, can't you?"

Bob looked at her excitedly.

"Of course."

The wine and Bob's appearance at her front door made Jenny forget about her day. She liked the power she still held over men, especially men like Bob. She walked to the kitchen quietly with Bob following behind her. Her bare feet made a light smacking sound on the hardwood in contrast to the clacking his loafers made. The kitchen was relatively dark; the only light in the space was coming from a small lamp in the adjacent family room. As she opened the refrigerator, its light revealed her body's silhouette through the cotton dress. Jenny hesitated before asking, "What do you want?"

Bob stepped forward and squeezed his body against Jenny's rear end and closed the refrigerator. He wrapped his left hand around her waist and pushed her hair back while kissing her neck.

"You," he whispered.

He slipped his right hand under her dress.

"Bob, I don't think we should," Jenny whispered.

Her words were not a protest but rather part of a negotiation. She knew all about control and she liked being in charge. It was a feeling that she had not had in quite some time.

"We should," Bob said. "I can take care of you."

Caressing her he could feel the tension in her body subside. He continued to kiss her neck slowly.

"No one will know," he said as he lifted her dress and pushed against her harder. As he pulled her closer, Jenny arched her head back. He turned her around and kissed her lips.

"Let's go in here," she said leading him into the family room.

At that moment, one hundred miles north of Lexington, Nick nursed his third vodka and tonic at the hotel bar. He stared blankly into his glass as the alcohol helped his mind escape from the events of the last day. He listened to the clinking of the ice cubes as he swirled the glass trying not to think about the responsibilities of engineers, sons, husbands and fathers. He just wanted to be numb for the time being. Although the future is always uncertain, he was glad that he had his family to fall back on.

13

Wednesday October 1, 1986

10:00 AM

Washington, D.C.

The morning sun pierced the slats of the wooden shutters which elegantly occupied the four large windows that looked out onto a bend in the Potomac River. Chuck Swenson sat behind his expansive desk, his right hand thoughtfully rubbing his gray hair and staring at the report in front of him. His desk was neat and orderly. Framed personal photos, file folders, phone, calendar and Rolodex all were correctly positioned for maximum efficiency. He expected as much from his employees as Nassir Yassim was well aware. He breathed softly and squirmed quietly in a straight back mahogany chair directly across from the associate director. The young research associate had spent the last several months directing his laboratory's efforts to determine the probable cause of the walkway collapse. It had been over three months since the disaster in Cincinnati, and Nassir knew that his boss was coming under intense pressure from Congress to deliver a report. Likewise, the pressure was building on Nassir to produce a report that spoke to the facts but also would enhance his standing with the man sitting on the other side of the desk.

"Okay, I think I understand it. The investigation shows that the change during construction from a single steel rod connection to a split steel rod was the primary cause of the collapse. Is that right?"

"Yes, sir. It was a primary cause," said the young research associate.

"I will have to explain this to the media, politicians, and public in no-nonsense language," stated Swenson, his tone direct and forceful. "So tell me, in simple language, what this means," he said dropping the report in a loud smack on his desk. "Make it brief."

Nassir squirmed again in his seat, thinking about how he would respond to the director. His boss challenged him with heading up the investigation and he knew bigger things at the NBS could be in store for him – as long as he didn't screw up. It isn't easy explaining scientific principles to the average person, and with English not being his native tongue Nassir knew it was even easier to get lost in language differences. He cleared his throat.

"Sir, when the design of the walkways used the same single rod, the connection to the beam at the fourth floor carried only the loads from the fourth floor. When the design changed to the split rod connection, the beam at the fourth floor took the loads from the fourth floor as well as the loads from the second floor. The fourth-floor connection wasn't able to carry all of those loads and because the beam experienced some corrosion at the connection, the connection failed."

He exhaled, not knowing how many sentences he had used, and waited nervously for the associate director's response. Rubbing his forehead, Swenson looked up at his ceiling fan trying to picture himself behind a podium at a press conference at the report's release. He hesitated before looking at Nassir.

"That was pretty good. I can sell them that. The only part that I don't like is the part about the corrosion – it doesn't wrap this up neatly. I mean it puts too many questions in people's minds. They want to know what caused it and they start to ask – are there other corroded walkways out there? That could generate questions that we don't have answers for."

"Yes," said Nassir meekly.

"Was the corrosion a significant contributor to the failure and do we know why the corrosion occurred?"

Up to this point, the investigation had not focused on the cause of the corrosion, only the amount, and location where it occurred. The film in the corroded areas was known to contain a type of bacteria, something the lab had called Thiobacillus. His lab techs told Nassir that this was strange and they were still at a loss for how it got there. Without definitive answers, Nassir thought the relationship between the corrosion and the collapse was severe enough to continue looking at it.

Hoping to say the right thing, Nassir swallowed hard.

"There was significant corrosion in the area of the beam connection, but we don't know why or how it got there. We found a film, a biological film, near the areas of corrosion. We tested the area, but we don't know if that had any impact on the amount and rate of corrosion."

Swenson's jaw tightened, and he leaned up in his chair, his elbows now resting on his desk. "Well I fucking can't explain that to the public, can I?" he asked sarcastically. The director's use of the expletive made Nassir clench the arms of the chair.

"I need to have this goddam report wrapped up with a nice little bow on it and the best you give me is *the source of the corrosion is unknown.*"

"Well, I, I mean....we were working on it and..."

His boss interrupted and pointed his index finger at the man across from him.

"You have been working on it for over three months. Let's get serious for a moment. One hundred and thirteen people died, and another one hundred and eighty people were injured in this collapse," The director emphasized this number again, "One hundred and thirteen. The biggest structural failure in the history of the country and I have people – senators, representatives, the White House – climbing up my ass for answers."

He pushed himself off the desk, paused for a moment and then slumped back into his leather chair. There was an extended period of silence between the two.

"Nassir, I know you have been working hard on this report, and I am glad to see bright young people come to this country to improve their life.

I expect all the people here at the NBS, especially those here on the H-1B visa program, to work hard for our country.

Swenson's dark eyes looked directly at the research associate.

"So, if we don't know what caused the corrosion, how can you know if it was a contributor as far as the collapse is concerned? What I am asking is would this failure have occurred without the corrosion?"

Although Nassir lacked a mastery of soft skills, he was very aware of the nuanced threat his boss had just made. Loss of his job meant a one-way ticket back to Egypt. He hated being put on the spot like this, and he knew that his position at the National Engineering Laboratory and his future at the National Bureau of Standards hung in the balance. He weighed the certainty requested by his boss versus what he currently knew. He believed the corrosion was significant, but he was uncertain about its causal relationship to the actual collapse. The actual corrosion lacked uniformity and therefore the actual condition could not be replicated in the lab. Any analysis on its exact relationship to the collapse would be approximate. If laboratory testing could not simulate the actual condition of the corrosion on the steel beams, then he could not say for certain that it had caused the failure. Nassir contemplated what he did know for certain. The NEL's testing and analysis did show with certainty that the change to the arrangement of the rods had been a major factor in the collapse.

"Sir, we cannot say that the collapse occurred because of the corrosion on the steel beams," stated the research associate. "Right now the testing and analysis show that the primary cause of the collapse was the change for the steel rod connection made during construction."

"Okay, now we are getting somewhere," said Swenson as he sat up and leaned forward. "So if you cannot say that the corrosion was a cause of the collapse I guess then it really doesn't need to be mentioned in the report, right? I mean we don't need to mention all the possible contributors to the collapse. It would give people the wrong idea. Am I right?"

The young Palestinian knew the answer he needed to give to this question.

"Yes, sir," he replied submissively.

"So the report should indicate the change to the connection was the cause of the collapse." Swenson paused as he paged through the report. "I thought I saw somewhere in here that your analysis showed that the loads on the fourth-floor connections essentially doubled because of the change."

"Yes, sir. That is correct."

"Make sure you highlight that. That is easy for people to understand. Who was it that approved the change to the connections, anyway?"

"Who?" asked Nassir not sure if he understood his boss's question.

"Was it the engineer or just the contractor?"

"Well, the contractor approved it and passed it along to the engineer for their approval as well. The project was being fast-tracked and so....."

The director cut him off immediately and glared at him.

"I don't care about the rest of the story. Just make sure that you mention that the engineer approved it. Mention them by name."

"Sir, our policy is to refrain from identifying companies or individuals in a technical report like this," replied Nassir in a soft and mild tone.

"This isn't a fucking typical report, you idiot," yelled Swenson. "I want the report to say the engineer approved the change to the connection and I want everybody to be clear on who that was. Do you understand?"

"Certainly, sir."

"Then get the hell out of here. I expect the revised report on my desk by four o'clock, do you understand?"

"Yes," said the research associate.

Swenson's phone rang and he grabbed the receiver but before answering he looked at Nassir and said, "By the way, if you want to stay employed here it might be good if all the stuff about the corrosion disappeared."

The director picked up the phone and waved the Palestinian away. Nassir was so lost in thought on his way back to his office that he didn't even notice the changing colors of autumn on the trees that lined the street. Once in the laboratory, he walked down a long corridor of pale yellow concrete block walls and a dirty linoleum floor. He walked past the testing lab on his right before he entered his office and closed the door. He knew the changes that he had to make in the report but did not feel good about them. He felt weak and helpless. The veiled threat that Swenson used against him was weighing heavily on Nassir. Sitting down at his desk, he started to revise the report.

Executive Summary

This report presents the findings of an investigation into the collapse of two walkways in the atrium of the Grand Plaza Hotel in Cincinnati, Ohio on June 20, 1986. The collapse occurred at approximately 7:05 P.M. causing one hundred and thirteen deaths and more than one hundred and seventy injuries. The team from the National Bureau of Standards completed an on-site inspection of the walkways in the aftermath of the collapse and collected evidence to conduct physical and analytical testing at the National Engineering Laboratory (NEL) in Washington, D.C.

There were two walkways in the atrium involved in the collapse at the Grand Plaza Hotel. The second-floor walkway was located directly underneath the fourth-floor walkway and was supported by the fourth-floor walkway through the use of 1-inch diameter rods. The fourth-floor walkway was similarly supported by steel rods which were attached to the roof framing of the building. As the collapse occurred, both walkways fell to the floor crushing many people, with the fourth-floor walkway ending up lying on top of the second-floor walkway.

Based on the results of this National Engineering Laboratory's investigation, it is concluded that the ~~most probable~~ cause of failure was the lack of support for the beams where they were supported by the steel rods. Observed distortions of steel beam near the rod connection ~~strongly suggest~~ indicate that the failure of the walkway system initiated at a connection on the fourth-floor walkway's middle box beam.

~~Two~~ One primary factor~~s~~ contributed to the collapse: the change in steel rod arrangement during construction ~~and the corrosion that occurred on the steel box beams near the connection. The change to the steel rod that~~ essentially doubled the load on the connections at the fourth-floor walkway. As originally approved for construction, the design called for a single set of steel rods being attached to the roof framing and passing through the fourth-floor walkway beams and on through the second-floor walkway beams. As actually constructed, two sets of steel rods were used, one set extending from the fourth-floor box beams to the roof framing and another set from the second-floor box beams to the fourth-floor box beams. (Added) *This change was initiated by the contractor but approved by the engineer of record, Nicholas P. Kremer, and the firm of J. B. Jones Engineering from Lexington, Kentucky.* ~~The second primary factor that was a probable factor in the collapse was a significant pitting of the steel beams that occurred at each walkway connection. This pitting was the result of corrosion that in some instances resulted in a significant loss of steel in the connection area. At this time the proximate cause of the corrosion is still being investigated.~~

Based on the physical and analytical testing performed by the NEL, it is concluded that had the original single rod arrangement not been changed, ~~and the steel beams not been subject to severe corrosion,~~ the load carrying capacity of the walkways would have likely prevented the collapse. [1]

14

Tuesday October 21, 1986
10:30 AM
Columbus, Ohio

Nick nervously tapped his fingers on the metal arm of the chair in the lobby outside the offices of the Ohio State Board of Registration for Professional Engineers. He counted the seconds passing on the antique-styled wall clock while he waited for Joe to arrive. Anxious about being summoned by the State Board to review the walkway collapse, Nick had known that this day would come as the public was demanding accountability. Today's hearing was inevitable after a complaint had been lodged alleging that the design of the walkways was grossly negligent.

Nick was pale and gaunt, as the last four months had drenched him in a tidal wave of sleepless nights and troubles with Jenny. Since the walkway collapse, business at the firm had suffered dramatically. Current clients raced to cancel contracts, and prospects disappeared as J. B. Engineering was now a pariah among structural engineering firms. The profit sharing that Nick was counting on to make ends meet vanished as receivables dried up. Things were so bad that all employees were asked to take a twenty percent pay cut.

Talking to Jenny about this new financial reality had caused a series of heated arguments, full of name-calling, blame, and accusations.

Emotionally estranged, Nick spent his days at the office doing very little work but knowing he did not want to go home either. It broke his heart that Mary was a witness to many of their arguments and he thought it was best to limit his time at home. At least this would shield her from the anger between her parents.

Joe Jones walked through the door at 10:40 and gave the young engineer a slight nod as he made his way across the carpeted office. The old engineer was wearing a navy blue pin-striped suit which was tight around his chest. A set of construction drawings was tucked under one arm while a leather briefcase occupied the other. Nick knew that the old man was not a suit-wearing type of guy but the importance of today's meeting called for it. The old man was out of breath and slightly groaned as he sat down.

"Sorry I'm late. I was in a phone call with our lawyer before I left. It took longer than I thought," said Joe sucking in air several times mid-sentence.

"That's no problem. I got here a little early. I thought traffic would be heavier," said Nick turning to look at his mentor. The old man's face had aged considerably in the last few months, and the size of the bags under his eyes looked almost cartoon-like.

"What did the lawyer say?"

"Not a lot. Something to the effect that this meeting would outline the Board's investigation to date. They would probably tell us where things stand and give us an opportunity to clarify anything that needs to be cleared up."

"Is he on his way? I thought he would be coming."

"To tell you the truth, Nicky, I asked him not to since he thought it would be pretty straightforward today. I didn't want to pay him for a full eight hours. I really can't anymore," said Joe turning away from his protégé.

Nick felt a veil of disappointment envelop him as he looked at the old man who had been such a friend and mentor to him. He thought it was ironic that sitting there in a suit and tie, Joe looked more pitiful to him than the countless days on which he would walk into the office, untied muddy boots, faded blue jeans, and shirt tail hanging out. Clothes make the man – what a bunch of crap.

The two men sat there alone in their thoughts until a middle-aged office assistant emerged from a wooden door near the rear of the reception area. Her hair was jet black and pulled back tight into a bun, which gave her facial features a stark and cold appearance. Nick thought she might be a good fit as a prison warden.

"Mr. Jones and Mr. Kremer?" she asked in a nasal tone.

"Yes," the two men responded in unison.

"Hello. I am Ms. Cornish, and the Board is ready for you now. Do you have anyone else with you today?" she asked. Nick felt uneasy as he interpreted 'anyone else' as 'your lawyer.'

"No just the two of us," answered Joe, wheezing as he stood up.

"Okay. Why don't you follow me to the main board room," she said, turning around and striding forcefully back to the door in the rear of the lobby.

Nick let Joe walk behind her. His pace was slower than normal, and he was favoring his right side. Nick figured the normal aches and pains of old age probably had been exacerbated by the stress he had been under. Nick knew how the last few months had worn him down and he was pretty confident that they had a similar effect on Joe as well.

The office assistant led the two men into the board room and down a center aisle flanked on each side by rows of padded folding chairs. Nick guessed that the chamber might have been big enough to seat eight people. Ms. Cornish continued towards the front of the room where two oak veneered tables sat on either side of the aisle. Each table had three leather chairs and a microphone positioned in front of each seat.

"Do you have a preference for which side you would like to be on?" Ms. Cornish asked.

"Doesn't matter," said Joe attempting to sound pleasant. The two men chose the table on the right and sat down. Joe passed the set of plans to Nick, who rolled them out on the table in front of them. An arc-shaped, maple bench on a raised platform with eight seats stood twenty feet away. Each seat had a microphone placed in front of it, although Nick wondered if they would be needed at today's meeting. A large blue and gold emblem of the Ohio state seal was affixed to the front of the bench, an engraving of the sun rising over a river and a plowed field with a sheaf of wheat and a bundle of arrows. Nick remembered from American history that the seals of many states contained symbols representing something from their past but also a symbol of the Sun representing hope and prosperity. Waiting in silence, Nick pondered the meaning of the bundle of arrows in the emblem when the door behind the bench opened and seven people, five men, and two women, walked in and took their places.

The older man with a white beard and wire-rimmed glasses, sitting on the center-right seat, was the first to speak. Clearing his throat, he leaned forward in his chair.

"Good morning, gentlemen. I am Amos Greenwich, the chairman of the Board of Registration for Professional Engineers. To my right, I have Mr. Peter Burg, a board member. To his right is Miss Betsy Rogers, who is also a board member. Finally to her right we have Mr. Clark Smith, our board investigator for disciplinary actions. To my left is Matt Kensett, a board member. To his left, we have Thomas Studer, who is also a board member. Finally, last but not least we have Miss Amy Menkhaus, our administrative assistant for the board." The bespectacled board chairman paused for a moment.

"And could you introduce yourselves for the record, please?"

Joe placed his elbows on the table and slid forward to speak into the microphone.

"Hello. I am Joseph B. Jones, President of J. B. Jones Engineering."

Nick paused for a moment seemingly frozen as fourteen eyes stared at him. Finally, he stammered slightly into the microphone, "Hello. I, um, I am Nicholas Kremer, partner with J. B. Jones Engineering."

Mr. Greenwich adjusted his glasses.

"Okay, thank you. Is there anyone else who will be joining you today?"

Joe responded, "No sir."

"Then let's get started," intoned the chairman. "Today is a meeting of the Board's disciplinary committee in response to a complaint filed against the two engineering registrants that are with us today. As noted in the State Board's by-laws this is a closed session, although Miss Menkhaus will take minutes. Per Section 4733 of the Ohio Revised Code, the State Board has a duty to investigate any registrant after a complaint alleging fraud, gross negligence, incompetency, or misconduct is filed against them. In the case before us today, complaints have been filed against the registrants, Joseph B. Jones and Nicholas P. Kremer. The business entity, J. B. Jones Engineering, the holder of a certificate to practice in the State of Ohio has had a separate complaint filed against it."

The seriousness of the chairman's statement made Nick nervous. The last four months were an emotional hell as they reviewed the design on the Grand Plaza walkways. Poring over his calculations, Nick became his own harshest critic as he tried to absorb the guilt of all the deaths and injuries he had caused. The young engineer knew that there was room for criticism of his actions. Still, this was different, and it made him tense. Now a board of his peers would sit in judgment of his actions. He tugged at the collar of his shirt and wiped his hand over his forehead that had suddenly become damp with sweat.

The chairman continued, "We are here today because the Board has determined that there is cause to believe that registrants before us today have performed engineering services that are grossly negligent relating to the walkway collapse at the Grand Plaza Hotel in Cincinnati on June 20, 1986. The registrants will provide testimony as part of the adjudication process. Is that all understood?"

Both men somberly agreed with a nod.

"Good. Then I will turn it over to Mr. Smith, the Board's investigator on disciplinary actions."

"Thank you, Chairman Greenwich," said the investigator as he inched closer to the microphone. His gray suit framed a fold of excess skin that hung over the collar of his white shirt.

"Our initial review into this incident determined that there was enough evidence to proceed with an investigation, and today we will present our findings and allow you a chance to clarify or respond to these findings. Although this is an administrative proceeding all of the statements will be recorded. Is that understood?"

"Yes, sir," responded Joe. Nick followed with a nod of his head.

"As you know, the walkway collapse at the Grand Plaza Hotel killed one hundred and thirteen people and injured another one hundred and eighty. Your company, J. B. Jones Engineering was the structural engineer responsible for the design of the walkways, correct?"

"That is correct," responded the old engineer.

"The design is shown on sheets S101 through S104 of the contract drawings produced by your firm, is that right?" said the investigator.

The pages he referred to were a few of hundreds that made up the full set of project drawings for the hotel.

"Yes, sir, those are the pages detailing the Grand Plaza walkway design."

"To the panel members present there is a copy of these sheets in front of you. Mr. Jones would you explain the walkway rod connection design that is shown on the plans then?" asked Mr. Smith.

The other board members stared intently at the two men before them as the administrative assistant scribbled shorthand onto a legal pad.

"Nick, do you want to handle this?" the old man asked his young partner.

Nick adjusted his body and sat up straight as if to shake the words from his throat. He had expected the investigator to ask about the change to the walkway connection and the part it played in the collapse. Nick slid the plans over in front of him and opened to the proper page.

"Sure. Umm… the beam-rod connection shown in sheet S101 through S104 is a one-inch diameter steel rod attached to the roof framing of the atrium as shown in detail two of sheet S103."

A crinkling sound permeated the room as he folded another page over and glanced at the title block.

"The rods are attached to six points on each walkway, three on each side as shown in the framing plan on sheet S102. The rods attach through a steel box beam which is made from two steel channels, or C-sections, that are welded together, shown in detail three."

Nick had reviewed these sheets so many times since the collapse that he could recite what was on each sheet with his eyes closed.

"Mr. Smith, I would like to ask a few questions now if you don't mind," interrupted the chairman.

A brief nod from the investigator signaled the chairman to continue.

"Mr. Kremer, can you please address the rod connection in detail three," bellowed Chairman Greenwich.

"Yes, sir. The steel rod extends through the box beam attaching on its underside with a nut and washer. The washer is a hardened washer."

"As shown?" asked the chairman.

The young engineer was flummoxed by the interruption as he did not immediately understand the question.

"I am not sure I understand your question."

"The steel rod goes through the box beam, as shown, Mr. Kremer but it was constructed in a different manner. Wasn't it?" snapped the chairman in an accusatory tone.

Nick looked over at Joe for support, but his friend only looked at the drawing in front of him. The young engineer felt he now understood the chairman's previous question.

"Sir I think you are asking if the original design called for a single rod and, as you can see in detail three, the connection was initially supposed to be a single rod that extended through the fourth-floor walkway down to the second-floor walkway."

"And was that the way it was constructed?" asked the chairman with a scowl etched across his face.

"No, it wasn't. Ultimately during construction, we used two pieces for each rod. The contractor wanted this because it would be easier to build," replied Nick.

His stomach turned as he was acutely aware that the panel was about to make sure his mistake became part of the public record. The admission of his error was bound to come up at some point in today's hearing, but he found himself overwhelmed by the reality of this moment.

"Please explain how this change from a single rod to a split rod occurred. Also please describe for our panel the process of how this change was approved," replied the chairman.

"Well, the contractor didn't ask us for approval, they had their steel fabricator submit a shop drawing showing the split rod arrangement," explained Nick as he looked across the panel of board members. As you know, contractors routinely use shop drawings to show the exact length and other characteristics of structural elements. The fabrication process requires that the steel fabricator produces shop drawings, as a set of plans for their shop personnel."

"So the contractor did not ask for approval?" asked Mr. Greenwich. His tone seemed to be composed of equal measures of disgust and sarcasm.

"The contractor didn't call us on the phone or anything like that," explained Nick.

"But the contractor did submit the shop drawings to you, didn't they?"

"I did not remember it specifically at the time, but after reviewing our files over the last few months, yes they did submit a shop drawing," stated Nick.

Nick was not trying to sound intentionally vague because the truth was he did not remember the change to the split rod on the walkway connection. On a big project like the Grand Plaza, an engineer might get dozens of shop drawings a week to review for some months. Nick, like every other practicing structural engineer, would look over these in a cursory manner. There was no special request made on the shop drawing showing the change to the connection but it had been submitted, and Nick had reviewed it.

"You reviewed it?"

"Yes, I did," replied the young engineer.

"And did you approve it?"

"Well, I…"

Nick stopped and looked blankly at the panel. He knew the time that he had feared was at hand. The chairman smiled at Nick from his seat on the bench.

"Fellow members, this is a copy of the shop drawing, sheet SD-12, from Miami Valley Steel Fabricating showing the detail in question," said the chairman, holding up a plan sheet folded in eighths. "Mr. Kremer, are you familiar with this shop drawing?"

"Yes."

"Does this shop drawing contain a stamp from J. B. Jones Engineering on it? And does that stamp show a status for that drawing and does it have a signature line on it?"

Nick swallowed hard. His voiced cracked slightly.

"Yes."

"What is the status indicated on the shop drawing and whose signature is on it?"

"Its status is 'reviewed and approved' and the signature is mine, Nicholas Kremer," answered the twenty-seven-year-old engineer.

"Mr. Kremer, explain to the Board what this change did to the fourth-floor beam connection," directed the chairman.

Silence permeated the room waiting on Nick's answer; however, his mind was not thinking about responding at this time. It wasn't thinking about anything. Joe looked at his young friend and placed his hand on Nick's arm.

"Without any other changes to the connection, the change from a single rod to a split rod at the fourth-floor connection would essentially double the load on the connection," replied the old man.

"So, I am not a structural engineer but let me see if I can explain this in simple terms. The steel rod is sort of like a rope. This rope is hanging from the roof of the atrium, and there are two people hanging from that rope," began the chairman shifting his glasses up to the bridge of his nose. He had the full attention of all the others in the room. "The two people represent the walkways; one person above the other. As they are hanging from the single rope, the person that is higher up the rope does not feel the weight of the person below. The weight of the lower person is transferred completely through the rope. Am I making sense so far?" he asked turning his head to the left and right.

The other panel members nodded in approval. Nick rubbed his forehead nervously as he knew exactly where the chairman was going with his explanation.

"But in this change, this approved change, I split the rope and tie the lower end of the rope to the foot of the person who is higher up the rope. What happens? The rope on the foot of the person above feels the full weight of the lower person. Mr. Kremer, I know this example might not be a perfect explanation but wouldn't you agree that it is what happened to the walkways?"

The time had now come for his admission of fault. Nick felt the room seemingly closing in on him.

"Well, I guess......yes."

"Fellow members," continued Chairman Greenwich, "I think we can agree that the ultimate responsibility for the safety of the public lies with the engineer of record, J. B. Jones Engineering and its two representatives before us today. I believe we should go into executive session and discuss our decision in this case."

Regaining his senses, Nick blurted out, "But there were other factors as well. You need to know about the corrosion of the steel."

The panel members stared at Nick, most with a look of surprise on their faces.

"Listen, I know that I bear responsibility for approving the shop drawings and that I should not have overlooked this change. But that wasn't the only factor at work in the collapse. The steel on the walkways was corroded and had a significant loss of section and..."

"Hold on right there, Mr. Kremer," growled the chair, his face growing red. "We have investigated this, talked to the various parties involved and we have seen nothing that indicates that corrosion was a factor in this collapse. Isn't that right Mr. Smith?"

The board investigator tugged at the collar of his shirt and said, "That is correct, Mr. Chairman. We have seen no evidence indicating that corrosion was a contributing factor in the failure."

Chairman Greenwich knew that the National Engineering Laboratory had possession of all the physical remnants of the walkway and that they had studied and analyzed the walkway before sending him an advance copy of the report, which was being released to the public next week.

"That's just not true," countered Nick in a raised voice. "I was there in the atrium the day after it happened. I took pictures of the connections. I gave them to the investigator from the federal laboratory. I have his name here somewhere."

Nick riffled through several file folders containing his notes.

"His name was Nassir Yassim – from Washington."

"Mr. Kremer we can only present to you the facts as we have them. And the facts from the National Engineering Laboratory say nothing about corrosion. Nothing. Maybe there was ..."

"That can't be. I showed him the corroded areas; he has my photographs, plus I have notes here, and..."

"Enough is enough, Mr. Kremer. These are the findings from the federal laboratory," Greenwich said, holding up the advanced copy of the report. "This two hundred-page report, soon to be released in a few days, is an exhaustive analysis of the collapse. It says, and I quote – 'One primary factor contributed to the collapse: the change in steel rod arrangement during construction essentially doubled the load on the connections at the fourth-floor walkway.'"

The Chairman slammed the report down on the table in front of him for emphasis.

"What we have heard here today is that you approved that change. So I think we have what we need. The adjudication process will continue to determine the status of your license to practice engineering. Bear in mind, that the practice of engineering carries significant responsibilities and that your errors led to one hundred and thirteen deaths. We will notify you once we make our decision. Is there anything else that you would like us to consider?"

Nick looked over at Joe, who seemed much smaller than the barrel-chested boss he had come to know over these past four years. Ashen-faced and emotionless, the old man stared out somewhere in front of him. Nick felt angry and alone. The hearing today was little more than a formality before the State Board took away his license to practice. It appeared that the report coming out from Washington placed the blame squarely on Nick's shoulders.

"Yes," Nick said standing up and walking to the front of the table. "You don't want to hear about anything other than the change to the connection. Fine. I approved it. It was a mistake. I am sorry, and I will live with that forever. But the corrosion was a factor. I know it."

"Stop, now!" yelled the chairman. "You should have spent more time thinking about the approval you gave for the connection change.

Maybe there would be one hundred and thirteen people still alive today."

It is often said that dying people see their death from a detached vantage point floating somewhere overhead. Nick felt something similar to this as he seemed disconnected from his body as he floated to the maple bench in the front of the room. Nick saw himself grabbing the chairman by the neck and pulling him over the top of the bench and throwing him to the floor. Time slowed, and Nick felt peaceful even though he could hear himself speaking.

"Fuck you, you son of a bitch, fuck you." As the chokehold caused the chairman's eyes to bulge out, Nick felt a remarkable sense of serenity.

"I am going to make it an even one hundred fourteen," Nick said as his hands squeezed harder around the chairman's neck.

Then, with a blow from a security guard's nightstick, his world went black.

As Nick was being handcuffed and dragged out of the conference room, his house in Lexington was unusually quiet for a weekday. The kids were spending the day at the babysitter's giving Jenny a break. Upstairs in the bedroom, Bob lay on his back as his hands rubbed slowly along her waist. Jenny shivered slightly as she positioned her body to be perpendicular with his. Jenny's muscles tensed as she closed her eyes. Her breath quickened and curls of blonde hair fell in front of her face. She glanced forward at a framed picture of Nick on the shelf over the headboard of the bed. Taken during a weekend they had spent camping with college friends; the image captured the essence of happiness. She bit her lip and closed her eyes wiping remnants of the past from her mind. It was good to feel wanted again.

15

Monday December 1, 1986
4:00 PM
Washington, D.C.

Nassir looked at the white envelope with the blue emblem of the National Bureau of Standards occupying its top left-hand corner. His name was neatly typed and centered along its face. He turned the envelope over, as he had done a dozen times before, and slowly pulled a single sheet of paper out. The thickness of the paper gave the letter a feel of authority, and he studied it again, trying to absorb its contents and what it meant for him.

> *Dear Mr. Yassim,*
>
> *This letter is to notify you that your position with the National Engineering Laboratory (NEL) will be eliminated. As such, your employment with the NEL and the National Bureau of Standards will be terminated as of Friday, December 5, 1986.*
>
> *As you are a beneficiary of the H1B visa granted by authority of the United States Citizenship and Immigration Service (USCIS), we have contacted USCIS regarding your termination. By statute, we have requested the withdrawal of the original petition made in order*

to hire you. This action will lead to the automatic revocation of said petition and result in your deportation from the United States. Please contact the USCIS with questions that you may have regarding this.
Sincerely,
Charles L. Swenson
Director, National Bureau of Standards

Although committed to memory, the words still left him paralyzed with a mixture of shame and uncertainty. Shame at a job lost and uncertainty about his future. His mind seemed untethered as the same questions raced through it.

What do I do now? What do I say to my family? What did I do wrong?

The last question particularly infuriated the young Palestinian as he thought he had dutifully fulfilled his superior's request. Still learning the subtleties of departmental politics, Nassir was confident that he had performed his duties in an adequate, if not extraordinary, manner. Asked for a reason for the termination, the human resources department offered none. Being an at-will employee meant that no reason had to be provided. Still, Nassir found the threat made by the associate director weeks ago to be prescient. A smirk crept across his face as he read the title below the signature line. Promoted, Swenson was now the Director of the NBS. Undoubtedly the new Director's political contacts were pleased with the outcome of the walkway report. And why not? It had effectively ended the national discussion on building safety which had boiled in the media for months.

Nassir, without a visa, would be sent back to Egypt. *What will I do there?* Palestinians in Egypt could not find work – any work – as his family had found out firsthand. Thinking about this caused him to become angry, and he shoved the letter back into its envelope and threw it back on the desk. He picked up another letter, this one from his mother, and opened it.

His hands shook as he began to read. A mixture of sorrow, helplessness, and guilt over his family's life back in Rafah swept over him.

Nassir,

Since I last wrote you, things have changed considerably. With all of the Sinai being turned back over to Egypt in a few months, the feeling is that things will not improve for us here. We have sold most of our belongings and have little left. Your brothers, Fayad and Jamal, have gone to Gaza through the Rafah Crossing hoping to find work as laborers. Your father and I are staying here for the time being, but if your brothers find employment, then we will likely cross over to be with them.

Although the Jewish state has caused great disruptions in our lives, their withdrawal from the Sinai is making it less safe here for us. The building of the border crossing through the middle of Rafah was the last straw for many Egyptians in this territory. The crossing has separated Egyptian families on each side and has given them another grievance against us as refugees in their land. I am afraid that it will become more dangerous as the final steps in the turnover of the Sinai occur next spring.

I hope that you are in good health and your job is going well. Your father and I are so proud of your accomplishments, and we are so thankful for the good fortune bestowed on you. Please stay in good health and advance far in your career. Please take care of yourself and ...

Nassir's back stiffened upon reading about his mother's pride, and he wrestled with the thought of their struggles. Returning home might relieve the guilt of separation but would be accompanied by the shame of a lost opportunity. He sat there at his desk considering his options. His thoughts were interrupted by a soft, but steady, knock on the door. He got up from his desk and opened it. Maggie Jones, the newly hired forty-something secretary, stood there fidgeting in a wool skirt that hugged her hips more tightly than it should have.

"Mr. Yassim I heard about what happened to you and I want you to know I don't think it was right for them to do that," she said in a smooth Georgia drawl.

Nassir looked at the woman in front of him and momentarily left his anger and guilt behind.

"Thank you. It caught me off guard. I don't know why it happened but thank you for saying that," he said.

She was shorter than him, and as he looked down at her, he found his eyes drifting from her round painted face to her ample breasts under a blouse with blue embroidered flowers on the collar. The blouse, like her skirt, was purposely tighter than it needed to be and Nassir took notice.

"I just want you to know that if there is anything I can do or any help you need please just call me. Okay?"

"I appreciate that," Nassir said, his eyes coming back to her face. "I need to start packing things up today. I could use some help."

16

Nick rubbed his hand over his face and looked out the front window. The roughness of his two-day-old stubble was in stark contrast with the airiness of the new snow swirling around the For Sale sign. It was not unusual to get some snow in Lexington, although this year had been the snowiest that he could remember. There was a scheduled showing today, and Nick hoped it would result in an interested buyer. He wanted the house, which he could not afford, sold. At least that piece of his life would then be wrapped up.

His slippers made a clacking sound as he shuffled into the kitchen to see if any remnants of the morning coffee were still left over. His days passed in a slow fog since J. B. Jones Engineering had closed its doors for good. After all, it is hard to run an engineering business after your business permit has been rescinded. Nick's spirits slightly lifted as he saw a dark layer of liquid still residing in the bottom of the coffee pot. He grabbed the handle and poured the contents into his coffee mug, watching the steam's tendrils rise briefly before disappearing. The mug warmed his hand as he looked around the kitchen in a quasi-hypnotic state. The place was empty now – no toys, crayons, cribs, or baby bottles – in general, no mess that accompanies a house with two small children.

The ringing phone snapped Nick back into reality. He trudged the four steps across the kitchen and picked it up.

"Hello."

"Nick, it's me," said a voice he recognized immediately.

Nick gripped the phone tighter as he felt his body come to attention. Things between them had deteriorated since the summer and had boiled over in the last few months. Nick knew that she was having an affair. Jenny did not deny it, and Nick was hurt more by her non-denial than if she would have just lied about it.

The weeks of yelling between the two had ended when little Mary interrupted a late-night fight telling them through a tear-stained face she was sorry and she would try to 'do-gooder' if they would stop fighting. Realizing that a change had to happen Jenny suggested that she would take the kids to live with her parents while they sorted things out. Nick agreed and with no income coming in they both decided that selling the house made sense. Jenny and the kids had been with her parents for about three weeks, and the house had been up for sale for almost that long.

"How are the kids doing?" he asked.

"Okay," she answered. "How are you?"

"I'm all right. Couldn't be better," said Nick unable to curtail the disdain that he felt for his wife. Although he had agreed to the separation, he still seethed about her affair and could not shake an overwhelming sense of abandonment. He had tried to be there for her, to give her what she wanted. Now, when he needed someone to lean on, she was gone.

"O…kay," she responded. What about the house?"

"We have a showing in about forty-five minutes," Nick said. "A young couple with kids. The realtor thinks they are serious about finding something in this area."

Nick winced as he remembered the first time they drove into the Whispering Hills subdivision. They'd been the young couple with kids once upon a time.

"That's good. Make sure that you straighten up. Dishes in the dish-washer, clothes hung up in the closet, vacuum the carpet. You know all the typical stuff."

"Yeah, I know. That's what I've been doing for a long time. I do see things around here."

Those last six words seemed to hang in the air for a long time.

"Don't start, Nick," Jenny spit back. "You don't have to go there."

"All I'm saying is I'm not an idiot, I know how to pick up after myself," said Nick, his voice beginning to rise.

"All I am saying is that a clean house might be easier to sell. I'm just trying to help. Don't be such a prick."

That pushed Nick over the edge as he felt his contempt for Jenny boil over into anger.

"You're the expert on selling, aren't you?"

Nick's words formed easily as he was well past the point of worry-ing about consequences. "Don't worry about the house selling, Jenny. I know what my sales pitch will be…This is a great house for a young family. Great rooms, great yard, great neighbors. Everything will be great until your wife screws around on you. Here let me show you where that happened."

"Fuck you, Nick. I am tired of this bullshit. We both know it's over. Sell the house, don't sell the house, I'm…I want a divorce," Jenny's voice hesitated as she caught her breath. "It's been over for some time."

Silence permeated the phone line until Nick spoke, his voice steady but searching, "Is that really what you want? I mean what about the kids – do you really want a divorce?"

There was no hesitation.

"Yeah, that's what I want, Nick. You know when we met, we were two kids. I was young, we both were young. I wasn't sure what I wanted – a career, travel, a family. But then I was pregnant. Any decision on what my life was going to be was not in my hands anymore. I guess I always wondered what could have been. I needed you to take care of me, Nick. I deserved to be taken care of."

"Is that why you cheated on me? You wanted to be taken care of?"

"I don't know," said Jenny as she choked back some tears. "It just happened, Nick. I'm sorry, but it felt good to be more than just a housewife. It felt good to be taken care of again. I tried to hold it together, but you were wrapped up in your job, it seemed like I was an afterthought. And then with the collapse. I just needed more."

"So when you saw the opportunity you spread your legs," snapped Nick. "Is he still doing you?"

Jenny, disgusted with her husband, did not wait to answer.

"Yeah, Nick. The first opportunity I got. You are such a prick."

"And you're a fucking whore!" yelled Nick.

"We are done here, you goddamn loser. I want a divorce. Good luck with your job. Oh, that's right you don't have one." She hesitated before delivering the verbal blow, "It's tough to be an engineer after you killed all those people."

His anger quickly dissipated into a stunned silence as he contemplated the truth that her words held. On the kitchen window sill sat the plastic sandwich bag that held a small piece of steel rod that Nick had picked up from the walkway wreckage last June. He didn't know why he kept it, maybe to remind him of the wrongs that he had committed. He regularly moved it from here to there but always kept it in plain sight.

A flash of red distracted him from the bolt and he looked out the kitchen window at a cardinal that had landed on the split-rail fence in his back yard. It sat there alone, its head tucked into its breast feathers trying to protect itself from the harsh winter wind. Nick always appreciated the persistence of the cardinal, a bird that spends its entire life close to where it was born.

"And one more thing, Nick," her voice now drawn with a hardened edge.

"Yeah?"

"He did me better than you ever did."

The phone line clicked as Jenny hung up. Nick stood there so numb from her taunt about the collapse that he did not even process her closing salvo. He looked out at the cardinal still sitting alone, now nestled down more deeply into its feathers. He wished that he could stay nestled in place but knew the realtor would be there within minutes. He opened the pantry and found a pint of bourbon. Walking to the closet near the front door he opened it and kicked off his slippers. Grabbing a dark brown leather jacket, he placed the bottle into the inside pocket and slipped it on.

The cold January wind greeted him immediately as the front door slammed shut. Pulling his collar up, Nick walked gingerly down the snow-covered sidewalk towards the Monte Carlo parked in the driveway. For a brief moment, he thought that he should have shoveled the sidewalk, but that thought quickly left. He slipped a little on some ice, but he steadied himself and opened the car door. Grabbing an ice scraper he got out and started to clear the windows on both sides of the car quickly. Before getting into the car he looked at his mailbox, where another cardinal was perched atop the wooden post that anchored the metal mailbox to the ground. This one was also a male, and its red feathers were slightly more faded than the one he had observed minutes earlier. He looked at the bird, sitting alone, tightly compacting itself into its protective layers.

Nick got into the car and placed it in reverse. He backed up to the mailbox and stopped. The cardinal had flown off, and Nick reached in to retrieve his mail. With his car idling, Nick shuffled through several bills and advertisements until his eyes fixed upon an envelope from the Ohio State Board of Registration. He opened the envelope and pulled out a single sheet of paper.

> *Dear Mr. Kremer,*
>
> *A complaint alleging gross negligence was filed against you based on engineering services you provided on the Grand Plaza Hotel, specifically the walkway collapse which occurred in Cincinnati on June 20, 1986. This incident was investigated by our office per section 4733 of the Ohio Revised Code. An adjudication meeting was held on October 21, 1986, to collect testimony from you regarding the aforementioned incident.*

Based upon our investigation and careful consideration of the evidence, the Board of Registration has unanimously voted to permanently revoke your professional engineering license in the State of Ohio.

This revocation is final and cannot be appealed. You must cease all engineering activities immediately, and any evidence that you are still engaged in the practice of engineering will result in criminal prosecution. The State Board is required by law to publicly notify all other states of this decision and allow them to pursue their own action if desired. Please feel free to contact the State Board offices if you require any further explanation.

Sincerely,

Mr. Amos Greenwich, PE

Chairman, Ohio State Board of Registration

Nick had been preparing for this final shoe to drop. He knew it was only a matter of time before he lost his license to practice, given what had transpired. The finality of the letter was just another punch that had pounded him since last June. No family, no job, no career. He reached into his coat pocket and unscrewed the cap on the bourbon and took a long, slow gulp. The discomfort in his throat from its burn actually soothed him. He took another gulp and screwed the cap back on. He backed his Monte Carlo out into the street and drove slowly down Proud Clarion Lane for the last time.

Part II

Newton's First Law of Motion:

An object that is at rest will stay at rest unless an external force acts upon it.

PART II

Seeking Equilibrium

17

Thursday December 10, 1987
6:30 PM
Alexandria, Virginia

Nassir sat rigidly in the leather recliner, his eyes transfixed on the evening news. The town of Jabalia, several miles north of Gaza City, was aflame with rioting. Several days earlier a truck from the Israeli Defense Force wrecked into a car and killed four Palestinians. Sparked by this event an uprising, an intifada, was unfolding throughout the occupied territories of Gaza, the West Bank, and East Jerusalem. Young Palestinians, angry at the two decades of Israeli occupation, were confronting Israeli security forces on patrol to restore the peace.

Sitting in his comfortable chair, Nassir watched today's news of a 17-year-old boy shot by an Israeli soldier after throwing a Molotov cocktail. Images of rock-throwing youngsters, roads blocked with burning tires, and throngs of protesters being dispersed by baton-wielding soldiers flooded across his television screen. The scale of the uprising was astounding, and the news media highlighted areas where excessive force was being used to quell the violence. The reporting made it easy to be sympathetic to the plight of the protesters, and the scenes stirred more than sympathy in Nassir as he knew what it felt like to live as a Palestinian in the Middle

East. Whether it be in Egypt, Israel, or Lebanon, to Nassir Palestinians had forever been the outcasts searching for, but never finding, stability.

Growing up in Rafah, his family had welcomed the Israeli occupation of the Sinai but now, aided by the guilt accompanying his Western life, his feelings had shifted.

"Sweetie, dinner is ready. Pull yourself away and eat before it gets cold," called Nassir's wife in her syrupy Southern accent.

Maggie flipped her brown, shoulder-length hair behind her ears as she piled the noodle casserole from the stove directly onto two plates. She was happy and content with her life as Mrs. Maggie Yassim. At forty-two she was no wide-eyed teenager, but marriage agreed with her after being unattached for so many years.

"Wait a minute. I am watching this," shouted her husband.

Nassir was happy that Maggie had knocked on his office door about a year ago. Her sympathetic ear had provided him an opportunity to explore a romantic solution to his deportation problem. Although they were from different cultures, he enjoyed her companionship and had settled into the rhythm of married life. Although she was almost fifteen years older, Nassir's needs were satisfied. Like Maggie, he had wondered for years if he would find someone. Never having developed a broad circle of friends, he was grateful that he had Maggie.

Maggie had used her contacts in the Washington bureaucracy to secure Nassir a new position with the Federal Highway Administration (FHWA). As a field specialist in the FHWA's Research, Development and Technology Transfer Program, he now helped states prioritize planning for various transportation projects. Nassir had been in his new position only six months, but he found it both challenging and enjoyable. His team spent time visiting each state to review their upcoming highway projects to maximize the amount of construction work completed. The job also gave him the opportunity to travel across the country and see more than just D.C.

Maggie sat at the kitchen table waiting for her husband. Her Southern manners were deeply rooted and she knew it would be bad manners to eat before Nassir was present. Waiting was particularly challenging of late because of her new diet. Maggie had struggled with her weight for as long as she could remember although she had never thought much about it growing up on a chicken farm outside of Macon, Georgia. Maybe her parents had sheltered her from the sex, drugs, and self-indulgence of the 1960s or maybe they'd loved her unconditionally, but they had never talked about outward appearances. As Southern Baptists, they had believed that one's eternal reward was dependent on one's spiritual, rather than external, appearance. Faith, family, and friendliness – that is what her parents had stressed to the young Maggie. Although she had not been back since her parents had passed away almost two decades ago, the ideals they had raised her with were still a large part of Maggie Yassim.

Nassir made his way to the kitchen a few minutes later, smiled at his wife and sat down. His plate of noodle casserole was still warm, and he began to pick the carrots out immediately.

"Looks good," he said automatically.

"I should remember that you are not a big fan of carrots. It's just that the vegetables are all frozen together in the bag."

She began to eat quickly to calm the hunger pangs her diet had wrought. She consciously told herself to eat slowly, as a co-worker had told her, so as not to overeat. She looked up at Nassir.

"So what is the news saying about what's going on over there?" Maggie had learned to use the phrase 'over there' as the generic substitution for anywhere in the Middle East. She never really fully understood the countries, politics, geography or history that made up her husband's background. Although he had discussed his life in Egypt on many occasions, the description from Maggie's perspective was superficial at best. Egypt, Israel, West Bank, Palestinians, Rafah – these were all words with very little context to the daughter of a Georgia chicken farmer. Once she actually had gone to the library to check out a book on the region's history but quickly lost interest as it was both hard to read and boring. She did know a few things about her husband's background. How he had fled to Egypt after a war, how he had lived a decent life as a child, how things had changed prompting him to come to the U.S. for a graduate degree, and how his family had recently moved from Egypt back to Gaza. That was about it.

Nassir's faced hardened as he looked at her.

"The Israelis are killing children who are demonstrating in the streets. God damn it," he cursed in a voice tense with anger.

Maggie stopped chewing her food and swallowed.

"Oh, that sounds terrible. Why is that?"

"Because they are on our land!" he barked.

His balled-up fists crashed down on the kitchen table and shook the plates. Maggie recoiled as the silverware rattled on the table top. Deep down she knew that there was much about her new husband that she didn't know but this anger was new. Her parents had always told her that any relationship grows and changes over time and she thought this might be an opportunity to learn more about her husband.

"Nassir, didn't you say that Israel had actually made life easier for you and your brothers when you were growing up?" she asked.

Nassir's brown eyes stared at his wife. He grabbed Maggie's wrist tightly and squeezed hard.

"Remember what I am telling you now. The Jewish state is the cause of my people's problems. We need to have our homeland returned."

Maggie winced as he squeezed her wrist and she quickly pulled away once he let go. She returned to eating her casserole, now quickly, forgetting her dieting advice.

As midnight approached in the town of Jabalia in the Gaza strip, Jamal Yassim waited silently sipping a soft drink, inside a shallow alcove of a repair shop. The alcove bordered a narrow alley that dead-ended about one hundred feet from where Jamal stood. The night air was still thick with the acrid smell of burning tires and Jamal intermittently wiped the tears from his eyes.

The days of rioting had led to a curfew throughout Gaza, a curfew enforced by the Israeli Defense Force, who patrolled the streets in groups of four. From his location, bathed in the shadows, he watched soldiers walk down the main thoroughfare approximately seventy feet from where he stood. The patrols seemed to occur every fifteen minutes and had calmed things down from earlier in the day. He heard the muffled voices of another squad approaching from the north on the street in front of the store. The sodium vapor security light on the road turned the three soldiers and their equipment a ghostly shade of orange as they walked past. Jamal saw one of the soldiers turn around and yell something down the street as they continued to walk with their American-made M16A2 rifles in front of them. Thirty seconds later, Jamal saw who the Israeli patrol was yelling at moments before. A lone soldier, the missing fourth soldier of the squad, was in a half-jog to catch up with the others.

Jamal reacted instinctively and hurled a bottle towards the back of the alley. As the bottle shattered the noise echoed in the narrow alley, awakening a nearby dog, which started to bark. The fourth soldier stopped and yelled something to his squad before turning towards the alley. He crept down the dirt path slowly, and the flashlight mounted to his rifle scanned in a left to right fashion repeatedly. Jamal's heart beat faster as he backed up farther into the shadows, watching the light draw closer to where he was standing. He closed his eyes and held his breath. When he opened his eyes again, the soldier had just passed within five feet of him. In one fluid motion, he launched himself towards the soldier, plunging the six-inch serrated blade into the side of his neck. His other hand grabbed the soldier around the face as he repeatedly drove the knife into his victim. As blood covered his arm, his hand fell limp as a volley of bullets tore through his head, chest and legs. He collapsed onto the dead soldier, as the sound of yelling and the thumping of boots drew closer.

18

Sunday February 28, 1993

11:00 PM

Louisville, Kentucky

The old man shifted his weight from one side to the other in an unsuccessful attempt to relieve the chronic back pain that was now just a fact of his seventy-year-old life. The cushioning on the worn chairs in the detention center lobby lacked the comfort of home. It had been five years since his own business had closed and the old man always took note of the way other businesses operated. He was a firm believer in the principle that people should be comfortable while they waited, a belief that the Jefferson County Department of Corrections apparently did not share.

As Joe Jones waited, he glanced at the TV situated behind the young deputy seated at the glass-enclosed check-in desk. The deputy was intensely involved in reading and, dressed in his crisp blue uniform, seemed oblivious to the constant chatter coming from the Sunday morning news show. Joe assumed that the deputy's intensity probably was directed at an official report, but little did he know that the twenty-five-year-old was intently "reading" the newly released *Sports Illustrated* swimsuit issue.

The clock behind the desk read eleven o'clock and the next Sunday morning show led with the latest update on the bombing which had occurred in New York two days earlier. Joe squinted, but his deteriorating eyesight prevented him from identifying the exact news program that was on the TV. He listened to the latest information anyway.

"Federal and local law enforcement officials are continuing to investigate Friday's bombing of the World Trade Center in New York City. Authorities have determined that a truck bomb detonated in the parking garage under the North Tower at approximately twelve-fifteen carrying over one thousand pounds of explosives. The bomb blew a hole approximately one hundred feet wide through several levels of the parking garage, killing six people and injuring over one thousand. With electricity cut off to the building, firefighters had to work methodically to evacuate the building.

Investigators from the FBI and the ATF, as well as authorities from the New York City police department, are combing through the wreckage for clues. An anonymous source has told this reporter that a letter claiming responsibility for the bombing was mailed to the New York Times. The source has said that letter warned of additional actions against American targets unless the United States ended interference in Palestinian affairs and severed diplomatic relations with Israel."

The seventy-year-old shook his head in disbelief as he listened. Although New York City was culturally a million miles away from Kentucky, the news of a bombing on American soil stirred emotions in the old man. Emotions that he hadn't felt since serving as a grunt liberating Europe from Hitler. He did not understand Middle Eastern affairs like he understood engineering principles but recognized the continual unrest that flowed throughout that part of the world was not good. His eyes moistened as he listened to the end of the report when the names and images of the six people killed scrolled across the screen. He knew that the names were just names to ninety-nine percent of the people who heard them but to some brokenhearted souls they were fathers, mothers, sisters and brothers.

"Goddam shame," he muttered under his breath.

The names of those killed in the Friday bombing were also lost on the young deputy as he slowly turned the magazine page. His eyes studied another bronzed model with her arms stretched over her head, seductively pulling the wrap-around swimsuit tightly around her svelte frame. Although he was one of the ninety-nine percent of people who did not feel any connection with the names on TV, his heartbeat quickened as the images stirred more primitive thoughts of other activities on a sun-drenched beach. The deputy stiffened reflexively as his thoughts were interrupted by the ringing phone. He quickly buried the magazine under a stack of folders and answered the phone. Joe noticed that the deputy spoke sporadically in a quiet voice and then hung up, the plastic receiver making a dull thud on the phone cradle. Standing quickly, the deputy looked out at the old man in the lobby.

"Sir, you can see him now. Please go over to that door, and I will buzz you in."

Joe nodded his head.

"Okay."

He used his arms to push himself out of the uncomfortable chair and limped over to the door, which led to the visiting area of the detention center. A small rectangular window allowed someone on the other side to identify the person waiting in the lobby. Joe noticed the closed-circuit camera mounted on the wall with its lens directed at the area in front of the door. A hollow metal click sounded as the door unlocked from the inside and opened slowly, revealing a much larger, more muscular deputy standing on the other side.

"Sir, step over here please and place your hands over your head," he said.

Joe followed his instructions and looked forward as the deputy firmly patted him down starting with his shoulders and advancing over his body and down each leg. The old engineer knew the importance of safety was an overarching concern in any correctional facility.

"Okay. You can follow me please."

Joe followed the broad-shouldered deputy down a corridor lined with painted block walls that seemed brighter as the light reflected sharply off the speckled linoleum floor. Joe hobbled to keep up with the young deputy, grabbing the wall for support as they turned and approached another security door. The deputy pushed a button, followed a few seconds later by the same hollow clicking noise as the door again unlocked from the inside. Once inside this door, they walked twenty more feet, where the deputy opened a standard office door for the old man.

"You have twenty minutes."

Joe limped into the room and saw Nick Kremer sitting across the table. It was the first time he had seen his friend in almost five years. The person who sat in the hard chair across the gray table looked much older, more worn than a man in his early thirties should look. The stubble that ringed his jawline fit well with the man's close-cropped haircut. This look, however, was at odds with Joe's recollections of the young engineer he knew. The old man studied Nick's face, which seemed much thinner, making his pale blue eyes stand out more. The two men stared at each other for a minute before a word was spoken.

"Nicky, it's been a long time," said Joe in an almost half-whisper.

Nick nodded slightly.

"It has been. It seems like it has been a lifetime."

Joe walked over and sat his large frame down into the chair across the table from the man he once considered as almost a son. The awkwardness should have been expected as their once-upon-a-time closeness had been one more casualty of the Grand Plaza collapse. Lost licenses and lawsuits have a funny way of destroying not only businesses but also careers. Joe drew a deep breath and wiggled in his chair in the unending attempt to relieve the pain that radiated up and down his back.

"Nicky, it's good to see you again. I know a long time has passed. I just wanted to see how you are doing."

The length of their separation left both men trying to think of what to say next. Joe broke the stalemate.

"I just want you to know that I am sorry about the way things turned out for you, for us."

Nick studied the old man as he spoke, hearing his words and interpreting whether he was talking about what had transpired five years ago or what had occurred since then. Although the events that had followed the collapse were painful, he had come to terms with the separation from his mentor as the end of just another relationship. The anger he had once felt had been replaced with a sense of inevitability. Life happens. Sometimes the bond between two people just doesn't survive. At least that's the way it had been with Jenny.

"Yeah, I guess we all wish things could have been better," said Nick as he clasped his pale hands together on top of the table. "At least you haven't killed anybody since then."

The victim in Nick had nurtured a sarcastic side to his personality. A part of him that presented itself frequently now in jail.

Joe fidgeted again, but this time the discomfort was not in his back. The man across the table was the reason Joe had driven from Lexington to Louisville to see his old business partner. Losing track of his protégé had made the old man unaware that Nick spent the years after the collapse drifting from one alcohol-fueled binge to another. He hadn't known that Nick was in the middle of a week-long bender when he signed his divorce papers at a fleabag interstate motel. A motel that Nick called home at the time. The old man remembered the sickness he'd felt as he read the story in the Lexington Herald several months ago.

Ex-Engineer Charged with DUI Convicted of Manslaughter

A Louisville man has been convicted of manslaughter while driving under the influence in the death of a mother and her three-year-old daughter last year in Jefferson County. A circuit court jury convicted Nicholas Kremer, age 31, on two counts of manslaughter and sentenced him to serve two concurrent fifteen-year sentences. Police said Kremer was driving a Chevrolet Monte Carlo on Manchester Road just south of the Watterson Expressway on September 12th of last year. Police tested his blood after the accident, and the results showed his blood-alcohol level to be about 0.21, which is more than twice the legal limit of 0.10.

Kremer had been arrested two other times on DUI charges in the last four years in the Louisville area, and had been convicted of assault in a confrontation which erupted

at a hearing to revoke his engineering license. Kremer
was the engineer of record in the structural collapse at the
Grand Plaza Hotel in 1987 which killed 114 people.

"I know. I read about that. That's why I came down to see you," mumbled
the old man as he searched for the right words. "You know…with all that
happened I think I just concentrated on getting my own life together."

Joe gazed up at the dirty metal grids that diffused the light from the
fluorescent bulbs above. He took a deep breath and looked at Nick.

"I wish things could have gone along as they had before and that none
of this damn stuff would've happened. I want you to know that I am here
for you, praying for you."

Nick stared back at the old man. His sarcasm faded as he was aware
that Joe was here because he cared. Nick unclasped his hands and placed
them on his lap. He remembered the old man's 'God is first' creed and
respected someone who could still believe in a benevolent God after all
that they had been through.

"I think you probably have a better chance of being heard by Him
than I do."

Joe's eyes moistened.

"I don't know about that, Nicky. I think He listens to us all and works
in different ways." He looked down at the table and said, "He is still there
for you, he forgives you."

Without the numbing effect of alcohol available in jail, Nick had
learned to compartmentalize his thoughts. The bad choice that had killed
another two people could occupy every moment of the day if he did not
learn to wall that off and think about other things. He only allowed himself to think about that young mother and her daughter at night, alone
while trying to fall asleep. Joe's visit and his message of forgiveness caused
those thoughts to re-surface in the light of day.

"I'm glad He forgives me because I am not sure the family does. I sure
can't forgive myself," he said, his voice now soft and calm.

"Nicky, you can't bring them back, any of them back, by hating yourself. I spent a long time in a bad place myself, trying to dig myself in

deeper. Trying to hide from the world. I was wrapped up in hating myself, blaming you, just being pissed at my situation."

"Well, the good news is I have fifteen years to think about it," replied Nick.

Stung with the sarcasm Joe was silent for a moment until his fatherly side came out.

"Look, if you don't get out for fifteen years, that's the way that it is. Fifteen years is a long time, but it isn't a lifetime. Life's just really a series of changes that you choose to adapt to or not. We don't realize it as it is happening because just when we are getting comfortable, then lo and behold, life changes on us again. That's just the way it goes."

Nick stared at his old friend for a moment. He knew what he was saying was the truth although it did little to change the past.

"Well, the changes life has given me over the last few years have really sucked," he said without looking up.

The self-pity in Nick's words was easily detectable.

"Get your head outta your ass, boy. Spend your time healing, improving, make amends. Just don't spend it feeling sorry for the past, it's over. Don't go feeling sorry for yourself. Look to the future. God has a plan. He'll help you through."

Nick sat there silently. He was not as sure as Joe was about the Almighty's plans for him but knew that Joe's advice about not changing the past was true.

Three short knocks on the door preceded the guard saying tersely, "Time's up."

The two men stood, exhaled and smiled at each other. Both felt relieved that their time together had accomplished something. For Joe it was a reconnection to the past; for Nick it was a recognition of a pathway forward. Joe embraced the young man and sharply patted him on the back.

"Remember, I will be checking in on you," said Joe.

"I know," replied Nick.

The old man turned and began to shuffle towards the door. Nick watched him, and before Joe reached the door, Nick called out.

"Hey, I never asked what you are doing these days anyway."

"You aren't going to believe me, but I am teaching at WCC. In the engineering technology department," replied the old man.

Nick recognized 'WCC' as Winchester Community College.

"No shit," Nick said smiling. "Damn, so you are educating America's next generation. It sounds like you'll make them as happy as a woodpecker in a lumber yard."

Joe chuckled at the young man's attempt to use some back-home saying as he had so often in the old days. He smiled back at Nick and winked.

"Damn right, God help them."

19

Saturday June 1, 1996
2:00 PM
Kunar Province, Afghanistan

Fayad stared out of the window at the young boys, maybe eight years old, playing in the dirt courtyard. Needled-shaped flowers withered in gray clay pots behind the house and the boys instinctively knew better than to play too close to those. He thought about his brothers, Nassir and Jamal, and how they had played many years ago in Rafah. He smiled to himself at the memory of how their playing would go from rough-housing to hard-nosed wrestling until their mother intervened with a scolding. A long time had passed since those days, and the smile slowly disappeared from his face.

The afternoon sun beat down on the village tucked into the rocky hillside that rose from the bottom of the narrow valley. It seemed that the construction of the houses here – thick mud walls and wood timbers from the nearby hillsides – did not provide much protection from the variability of temperatures in this region. As Fayad waited for the others, an old woman who had greeted him upon his arrival brought a pitcher of water in and placed it on a wooden table.

Hearing a door slam from the other side of the house, Fayad turned anxiously, his eyes fixed on the arched entrance to the room. Five men, clad in beige linen robes, entered quickly. Two of the men, the first and the last, carried Russian-made AK-47s, and around their waists wore leather bandoliers which were heavily laden with bullets. The gun-toting men fixed their eyes on Fayad as did the two others who were surrounding the eldest man in the middle of the group. Fayad could feel the deference given to the old man, a sure sign that he was the one Fayad had traveled to see – Gazin Kumal. The old man's flowing gray beard and heavily creased face spoke of a lifetime spent in the elements. His appearance was fitting of a Pashtun tribal leader, especially one who had fought during the entire Soviet occupation. The Palestinian stood quietly as Gazin sat on a floor cushion until the old man finally motioned him to take a seat across from him.

"You have traveled far. Why is it that your people have sent you?"

"Most respected one," began the Palestinian, "your reputation is well known. Your great heroism in fighting the Soviets is legendary. Like your country, my country is similarly occupied. What we ask for is very simple – your help so that we may free my country from the Zionists."

Gazin stroked his beard as he listened to Fayad's request. Many did not understand that the Afghan resistance to the Soviet invasion, the "mujahedeen," had been a collection of tribal warlords and other guerrilla factions formed to protect their separate interests. The United States and other Western powers had funded the resistance to defeat the Soviets. In the process, the tribal warlords had amassed great power in the form of fighters, weaponry, and money. Gazin Kumal was one of those tribal warlords. In the Korengal Valley, he was known as 'the holy fighter' and was currently helping the Taliban smuggle U.S. arms from Pakistan. With this weaponry, the Taliban had already taken over many large cities and had their sights set on the capital of Kabul. Gazin believed it was only a matter of time before Kabul fell and, with that, the Taliban would effectively rule the country.

"My friend, I understand your desire to break the shackles of an occupier. I respect your willingness to fight. Our forces, however, are here in this valley. We cannot travel as mercenaries to your land."

"Forgive me, most respected one, I have not been clear in my request," Fayad stammered. "What I ask is that you train me and others in the tactics of war that you have used so successfully."

The old man looked at the Palestinian for a few moments, which seemed like an eternity to Fayad.

"Your request is reasonable. Although we are different – Pashtun and Palestinian – we both share similar interests. My people do not directly provide such training, but I know those that can give you what you want. I will talk to those and see what arrangements can be made. How many men should I tell them you will bring?"

"We would like to send twenty," said the Palestinian.

"Remain here in this domicile. I will meet you again the day after tomorrow."

Fayad bowed touching his face to the ground in front of the old fighter.

"Thank you, most respected one."

20

Friday June 1, 2001
6:00 PM
Tel Aviv, Israel

Leah pushed the black curls out of her face and adjusted her pink head-band as she walked quickly down the street holding a small gift. The air was warm but not oppressive due to a stiff breeze blowing in from the west. Leah's heartbeat quickened as she eyed the recreation center where her friend Haya was having a birthday party. This Friday night marked the beginning of summer, the end of the school year, and a chance to celebrate with Haya and her other classmates. It also gave her an opportunity to see Andrew, the American in her class. The object of her first serious crush.

Her pastel cotton dress swished across her legs – legs that were becoming more womanly as she approached her fifteenth birthday. Leah thought of asking her parents if she could have a birthday party also. It would be another excuse to see Andrew again although she didn't know if she could wait that long. Andrew had been in school since fall semester, and she had become intrigued with him right away. Everybody was intrigued by him, an American whose father did some work for the university. Since coming to school, Andrew had done his best to fit in, not in a showy way that many teenage boys do, but in an understated manner. Maybe it was his maturity or maybe it was the flood of hormones in his body that gave definition to his arms, or maybe it was the way he looked at her lately, but in any event, tonight's party gave her a chance to be around him again. She felt an attraction, and if tonight went well, maybe it would be the start of something. Maybe she would have a boyfriend this summer.

Leah's parents were oblivious to the potential for their daughter's budding romance. Like most parents in Israel that summer their thoughts were pre-occupied with the unrest that had spilled over from Gaza and the West Bank. The continued construction of Jewish settlements and failed peace talks had given way to a new round of Palestinian rioting. Israeli security forces had recently replaced rubber bullets with live ammunition to quell the unrest in many areas. However, this had caused an increasing number of Palestinian deaths, which in turn had led to the kidnapping of Israeli soldiers, citizens and even children resulting in brutal murders. The pressure was building for the government to quell the uprising.

That summer, most adults in Israel carried on with their daily lives under a veneer of normalcy which belied the fact that the routine of their daily lives had been turned upside-down. Leah had other things, teenage girl things, on her mind and did not notice her parents' increasing anxiousness. Her home in Tel Aviv was less than thirty minutes from the West Bank enclave of Ramallah, but the security presence blanketing the city made the unrest feel like it was a thousand miles away. At least it felt that way to a fourteen-year-old girl excited about the end of school and the possibility of her first summer romance.

Leah reached the door of the recreation center and was greeted by Haya's eleven-year-old brother, Yousef, who was fully engaged in his job as the official greeter of his sister's party. He checked Leah's name off the list and pointed her to the upper floor. Her long legs took her quickly up the half-flight of steps and around the corner to a large multi-purpose room where the party guests were gathering. Ribbons and balloons adorned the tables arranged in long rows on the left side of the space. Leah paused and sized up the situation. About thirty people milled around the room – mostly her classmates, Haya's parents, and some others she didn't know. Being fourteen and walking into that room, or any room with people in it, made Leah immediately self-conscious. With her teenage anxiety bubbling to the surface, she saw Haya who, in turn, saw her and gave an animated wave. Knowing she would soon be safely ensconced within Haya's group made her feel better immediately.

Leah approached, and the two girls embraced.

"This is for you," Leah said. "I hope you like it."

Haya's smile stretched across her face. "Thank you, thank you soooo much! Tonight is going to be soooo much fun."

Hardly able to contain herself she blurted, "You know Andrew is coming this evening. I think he's coming just to see somebody I know!"

Leah's cheeks started to turn a shade of pink which quickly intensified to red. Once again she felt that she was the focus of everyone's gaze.

"Shhhh," Leah said in an almost whisper. "That's not true. He's coming for the party, to see you, to see everybody."

"And to see youuuu," giggled Haya, almost unable to control her laughter. "By the way, he is not here yet. In case you didn't know that already."

Haya could not contain the pleasure in teasing her friend. Leah rolled her eyes and sighed. The two girls coalesced back into the larger group as Leah made sure she was facing the room's entrance.

Outside, a late model Volvo pulled up across the street and parked. Andrew jumped out of the passenger side and re-tucked his polo shirt into his jeans. He reached back into the car for the gift as his father unbuckled his seatbelt.

"Dad, what are you doing?"

Andrew's father, Don Cartwright, stepped out of the car and pushed the door closed. Smiling, he uttered the words that sent a wave of fear racing through his son's fifteen-year-old body.

"I'm going to walk you in. You know, introduce myself."

"Dad, no, don't. I can walk myself in," pleaded Andrew in a deep voice that had only completely changed a few months earlier.

"Son, I know you can walk yourself in, but it's the polite thing to do. We are still getting to know people. Believe me, parents appreciate when other parents stop in and introduce themselves."

He looked closely at the humiliation etched on his son's face.

"I will be in and out. Just a couple of minutes, I promise. Maybe short-er if they don't like me," chuckled Andrew's father.

Don and his family had moved to Tel Aviv almost a year ago. As a senior project manager of the global security firm FMI, he did not usually consider assignments that involved relocation. However, Don Cartwright had begun to think about this job when FMI landed an eight-figure con-tract from the Israeli Ministry of Defense. He had found himself house-hunting in Tel Aviv when they tripled his salary and promoted him to a vice president.

What Andrew's father was working on was a well-kept secret. Even his wife did not know the exact nature of this project and he felt it was best to keep it that way. FMI had agreed to locate, map and monitor the network of tunnels used by the Palestinian resistance in Gaza. The nature of his work was not going to endear him to ninety-nine percent of the populace in the Middle East. The tunnel network had been started as a conduit for Palestinians to smuggle contraband from Egypt to Gaza, but after the turmoil of the first intifada, the tunnels had significantly expanded in size and now ran throughout Gaza. FMI had already mapped several tunnels that terminated inside of Israel. Those were the ones that worried the Israelis the most.

The Israeli government was under mounting pressure to act as the tunnels were suspected in several high-profile kidnappings of soldiers in-side Israel, as well as re-arming the Palestinian resistance. Solving the tunnel problem was FMI's job. The private security conglomerate had de-veloped a proprietary technology – Whisper – that the Israelis believed could do just that. The Whisper system released airborne dust particles into the tunnels, then subsequently tracked those particles using ground-penetrating radar systems mounted in non-descript pick-up trucks that crisscrossed Gaza. The data collected was linked with a global positioning system to determine coordinates and produce an exact tunnel map. Upon completion of this mapping, the Israeli military could take the necessary action to eliminate the tunnel problem.

Both FMI and Israel knew there was one drawback to the system — the airborne particles blown into the tunnel contained depleted uranium.

Theoretically, using a high enough volume of particles, the complete tunnel system could be mapped very quickly. However, this would potentially contaminate the soil and water inside Gaza, which would then be a public relations disaster. The Israelis opted for a lower concentration to limit both the risk and detectability. Don Cartwright was FMI's man in charge of the operation to slowly saturate the tunnels with depleted uranium, thereby leaving a signature that could be easily mapped. He figured that the slower process would take approximately thirty months. Enough time that he should put in the effort of getting his family acclimated to life in Tel Aviv.

Andrew walked across the street quickly with his father trailing a few steps behind. Although he wasn't happy about his father's insistence on introducing himself, the teenager hoped that the unwanted intrusion would be quick. He pulled on the front door and flung it open and Don caught it as the arc of its swing reached its apex. Haya's younger brother was still enjoying his job as the 'official greeter' and found Andrew's name on the list, and placed a checkmark next to it. He looked up at Andrew's father, who looked a little old to be on the list.

"Are you here for the party too?"

"Only for a few minutes," answered Don Cartwright, smiling at the boy. "I am Andrew's father. I just wanted to introduce myself to Haya's parents."

Andrew cringed with those words. *It will only be a couple of minutes.*

"Haya's my sister," the young boy eagerly responded as if Andrew's father would certainly be interested.

"Well, it's a pleasure to meet you, young man," answered Don as he extended his hand to the boy. "Can you tell me where I could find your parents?"

Pleased with the recognition and feeling important, Haya's brother smiled broadly at the American.

"Follow me."

The young boy quickly made his way towards the half flight of steps that led to the multi-purpose room. Andrew's father followed him with Andrew lagging several steps behind. Turning back to his son Don teased,

"Better catch up, so you can introduce me to all your friends." Andrew wanted to die.

Outside, around the corner from the recreation center, a rusty Honda Accord parked in the partial shade of a lemon tree. Fayad looked over at the brown-haired boy who sat with his eyes closed in his passenger seat. The brown jacket that he wore seemed bulky, but that was the best that Fayad could provide. The boy's lips moved quietly repeating something, and Fayad looked at the young boy with a pleasant smile.

"Adeeb, we are here. The party is right over there in that building."

The boy looked back at Fayad and smiled weakly.

"Thank you for bringing me."

The car door creaked open, and Adeeb got out. As he trudged his way up the sidewalk, he could hear the tires of the car crunching the loose asphalt some fifty feet behind him. Even at this time of day the air was warm and he looked forward to getting into the air-conditioned building to cool off. Fayad, seeing the young boy walk into the building and knowing he was safely inside, stopped at the intersection and then turned left.

Adeeb looked at the small table with a legal pad of handwritten names, almost all with check marks next to them. The pad was the guest list that Haya had given her youngest brother, the guest list that he had momentarily abandoned to walk Don Cartwright to meet his parents. The young boy looked down at the guest list and searched the list of names. Finally, he spotted a name that stood out – Andrew Cartwright. No one was there to welcome him, so he decided to go and find his way to the birthday party. Up the steps, he trudged, his eyes cast downward, as a boy and a girl approached him giggling and pre-occupied with each other. Once they passed, Adeeb's pace quickened and he arrived at the entrance to the large room. The music, balloons, and people disoriented him for a minute, and he held on to the door frame to get his bearings.

Don Cartwright smiled broadly as Haya's mother thanked him for coming in and introducing himself. Haya's father stood in the background and let his wife do most of the talking, which Don surmised was not uncommon in their relationship. Don related the story of Andrew's displeasure with being walked into the party, and both of Haya's parents laughed as they were all too familiar with that particular teenage embarrassment. Don thanked her parents again and turned to begin to navigate his way across the room. He looked for Andrew and spotted him in a group of five other kids, talking and laughing. His noticed Andrew was standing next to a long-legged girl with curly black hair and a pink headband. Must be his girlfriend. Don smiled to himself. Maybe I should go over and give him a hug goodbye.

At that moment, Don noticed a young boy about thirty feet away from Andrew's group, standing alone and wearing a brown coat which was obviously too large for him. Although he couldn't put it together right away, Don Cartwright's training told him something was wrong. Young. Alone. Coat. Big. Summer. Then it clicked. Andrew's father ran full speed in his son's direction.

The young Palestinian reached into the pocket of his coat and pulled out a trigger with a red cord that was attached to the belt of explosives around his waist. The guests were too busy to notice the American man sprinting towards the boy standing by himself. Even Andrew barely recognized his father as he raced within five feet of where he was standing. Don Cartwright launched his body forward at his target.

"Death to Israel! Death to America!" shouted the uninvited guest as his finger gripped the trigger. Simultaneously Don Cartwright's hand grabbed Adeeb's brown coat.

The concussion rocked Fayad's car back and forth. He looked in the rearview mirror and saw the fireball billow out and then collapse back in on the black cloud that followed. The sounds of glass and debris cascading over the street sounded like a hard rain on a metal roof. Fayad started the car again and drove off.

"Thank you, Gazin," he whispered to himself.

21

Tuesday June 20, 2006
9:00 AM
Louisville, Kentucky

It was twenty years ago today.

Nick hummed the melody to the Beatles' classic. Smiling, he remembered how his older sister had loved this song and was in love with Paul McCartney. She had made sure that their music was a daily constant in the Kremer household as it echoed through the halls for hours on end in 1967. He had been fascinated by the box-like Dansette record player that his sister had in her bedroom, the bedroom walls plastered with magazine clippings of the Fab Four. Mom had always worried that the tape would peel the paint off, but she didn't push the issue. Keeping a pre-teenage girl happy went a long way towards making everyone's life a little more enjoyable. If that meant listening to Beatles albums 24/7 or dealing with a little wall repair, so be it. Nick's mother was a smart lady.

Sgt. Pepper taught the band to play.

Today marked the twentieth anniversary of the walkway collapse. Nick wasn't sure what made him think of the song today, two decades after the collapse, but he didn't put any extra significance in the fact that it rattled around in his head. Perhaps it had been the letter his sister had sent him last week. Perhaps it was his release date that was quickly approaching.

Or maybe he was thinking about Joe's offer to do some teaching at WCC when he got out. From felon to faculty. Now that would be interesting. Fifteen years in prison had changed him, he thought, but was he the right person to change others? He rubbed his hand on his brow as he considered that question. His past sins were not forgotten, but he had actively started to think about his future purpose. The static nature of his time in jail would soon be over, and he would need to find his way out in the real world. Equilibrium had both a short-term and long-term perspective, and he hoped for long-term stability to grow out of the short-term changes that were about to happen.

They've been going in and out of style. But they're guaranteed to raise a smile.

He glanced around at the various outdated magazines strewn across his cell – *Sports Illustrated*, *Scientific American*, *Popular Science*, and *Time*. Among the magazines were several of his favorite books – Kurzweil's *The Age of Spiritual Machines*, Drexler's *Engines of Creation*, and Hawthorne's *The Scarlet Letter*. On the table, next to his bed rested a worn Bible given to him by Joe. He walked over and collected the books and stacked them on the small bench next to his bed. The Bible might not be stylish for some, but it was a fairly popular reading choice in jail. Nick did not consider himself born again, but he did find an application of its stories to his life. The books by Kurzweil and Drexler interested him because of their focus on the intersection of technology with the future. The potential for good and perils of being misused. He knew something about potential and perils. Still, he was aware that the world would rely on technology to produce bigger and better things.

He had tried to keep up with the advancements of materials, processes, and tools that were changing healthcare, banking, and business. Technology was always at the forefront of changes to society as men would use technology to gain greater control over their world. Technological progress, a human characteristic, was accelerating such that technological tools were changing at an exponential pace. Evolve with technology or it will leave you behind. Nick hoped that his time in jail had not changed him into a dinosaur of sorts.

So may I introduce to you, the act you've known for all these years?

Nick looked around the space that he had called home for the last thirteen years and knew he would only get to call it that for a little longer. Thinking about the past did not make him anxious as he believed the events of his past were just threads in the fabric of his being. Churchill had a saying that resonated with Nick. The farther back you can look, the farther forward you are likely to see. He resolved to remember his past failures but knew that others would remember as well.

Maybe that is why he had a particular fondness for Hawthorne's classic. Nick could relate with the public nature of Hester's sin and her loneliness she was forced to endure. Although the State Board was not composed of seventeenth century Puritans, the loss of his license and banishment from the engineering profession gave him a unique insight to Hester's public humiliation. Just as Hester had hoped for the reverend to come forward with the truth, so Nick wished that the National Engineering Laboratory would have mentioned corrosion as a possible catalyst for the collapse. Nick closed his eyes and knew that a different report would not have brought back any of those who were killed. He opened a clothes drawer in his cell and pulled a plastic bag from under some underwear and socks. It was the piece of steel that he had taken from the atrium the day after the collapse. Still there, the jagged piece of cold steel was a part of him, as much a part of him as the color of his eyes or the creases starting to form on his cheeks. He shoved the bag back into the drawer and closed it.

In spite of his weaknesses, he found hope in Hester's story. She had changed the public perception of the scarlet letter over time. Aided by the passage of time, the letter meant to be a symbol of humiliation was looked upon with reverence. He did not know how his story could be changed, but Hawthorne's tale gave him hope. Maybe the world isn't always fair, but he was determined to go forward with a purpose, some purpose, to give his life some meaning.

Next to his pile of books, he picked up an old photograph. Mary, Robby and him holding them in a recliner. Nick fought back the tears and bit his bottom lip. They were just another casualty of his drinking, the alcohol-fueled stupor that had provided him the opportunity to be an absentee father. He had not heard a word from them during his years in jail. Mary would be twenty-five, and Robby twenty years old now. The loss of contact with his children was a pain that he hoped to heal one day.

Sgt. Pepper's Lonely Hearts Club Band.

22

Saturday February 10, 2007
1:00 PM
Ramadi, Iraq

Fayad Yassim stared out of the second-floor window of a three-story concrete block building that stood several hundred feet west of the Euphrates River. Sweat dripped off his forehead as he lifted the binoculars up and continued watching the movement of American forces across the river. A task group comprised of Army infantry and Navy SEALs was in the midst of an offensive in East Ramadi aimed at clearing Al Qaeda from the city once and for all. Ripples of heat reflected off the pavement and coupled with the sweat irritated his eyes, preventing him from observing their movements for extended periods of time. He made sure he stepped away from the window before he wiped his eyes as the Americans had deployed some snipers throughout the city in preparation for the U.S. surge.

Fayad looked at his watch and knew that he would have to leave soon. He was not happy about the current state of the fight against the U.S. and its coalition allies. A year ago Ramadi, Fallujah, and other cities had been controlled by Al Qaeda and forces loyal to the insurgency. Car bombs followed by small-arms fire and the occasional RPG had proved successful in pinning U.S. and coalition forces into an unending series of skirmishes. Fayad and the others in the insurgency knew that a stalemate would ultimately be a victory as the U.S. and its allies would not have the stomach to endure the continual drip, drip, drip of casualties.

Fayad leaned against the block wall and wiped his eyes. He knew that things had changed over the last several months. The American president had unexpectedly ordered tens of thousands of new troops into Iraq with the goals of isolating the insurgency and protecting the population. The stage for political reconciliation within Iraq could occur if this happened. Fayad and others were apprehensive about the American strategy. Up to now the local population in many cities had left or remained disengaged, fearful of choosing the wrong side. But the U.S. gambit was stabilizing parts of Ramadi, and with the help of local security forces, had begun to clear and hold area within the city. Fayad was dismayed at the progress made by the U.S. forces in the last several weeks and felt that his brothers in the insurgency had to adapt or risk defeat. The Palestinian remembered what it felt like to be an outsider from his boyhood days in Egypt. If the U.S. forces could convince local Iraqis that they were the key to winning the fight against the insurgents, then their days were numbered.

He started to pace around the second-floor room making sure to stay away from the window. Fayad hoped that the council meeting this afternoon would generate new ideas to thwart the Americans. Waiting a few more minutes, he became impatient and decided to make his way towards the river.

The dust on the main avenue seemed to be hot like everything else baked by the midday sun. The Palestinian held his breath as the heat radiating from the buildings enhanced the stench from the garbage lying along the sides of the road. Fayad intermittently swatted the swarms of flies that were feasting on the decomposing trash as he made his way closer to the river. A minaret visible over the buildings served as his guidepost as he shuffled through the street.

Walking past a police station, he nodded to the two officers slouching on either side of the front door. Smoking cigarettes, they nodded back at the Palestinian from behind ill-fitting sunglasses. He continued walking and turned down an alley that opened after several hundred feet to a dirt path that pointed directly towards the minaret. Tall grasses swayed with more frequency as the breeze from the river caught hold of them. The air seemed to cool ever so slightly as he walked into an open area with copses of scraggly willow trees. Although the location of these council meetings changed on a regular basis, Fayad had been to this small mosque before. It was a good place as the American rules of engagement prevented intrusions into mosques and the local security forces were not brave enough to violate its boundaries.

The perimeter of the mosque was guarded by a concrete block wall several feet taller than the Palestinian, and covered in a beige colored stucco. He walked to an opening guarded by an iron gate made of thick square bars running vertically, with wide bands of metal intersecting the bars at even intervals along their height. Fayad picked up a short steel rod, perhaps stolen from a construction site, from the weeds on the right side of the gate and smacked the iron gate four times in quick succession. The noise summoned an old man who was wearing a whitish sackcloth and gray vestment to the gate.

"Asalaamu alaikum," the old man said to Fayad in a gravelly voice.

Fayad nodded as the gate swung open.

"Wa alaikum salaam," he replied stepping into the compound.

The irony of their greeting "Peace be with you – and peace be with you" was lost on both men as they walked past the main entrance to the rear of the mosque. There the old man reached down and pulled open two wooden doors revealing six stone steps that led to a storage cellar. Fayad nodded again in appreciation and gingerly made his way down to the meeting area. As he reached the final step, he ducked his head to clear the door framing, and the old man quickly closed the doors over him.

The cellar air was cool and seemed almost hopeful as opposed to the stagnant air outside. The cellar was a barren space measuring approximately thirty feet by forty-five feet with a dirt floor, and wooden floor joists above. The area was lit with bare incandescent light bulbs hung from the framing above, creating stark shadows that arched across the room. Fayad walked over to an open floor mat exchanging a series of greetings with those he passed. Inclusion in this group was tightly controlled for security reasons and specifics on each member were kept to a minimum. The Palestinian took his place and quietly waited for the leader of the council to arrive.

A few minutes later the door to the cellar opened, and Abu al-Yasin descended the steps in a stiff and methodical fashion. He wore a full-length gray linen tunic, and a black and white shemagh wrapped around his face and head. Fayad believed that al-Yasin was a high-level administrator in the Finance Ministry before the invasion, and had spent the last five years on the run from coalition forces and the new Iraqi government. Although he did not know everything about al-Yasin, he respected anyone who had evaded the U.S. troops for that long. Today's meeting, like most recent meetings, would discuss strategies in Ramadi and surrounding towns.

"Fellow believers," the former Iraqi official said in a nasal tone, "reports from across the Euphrates indicate that the Americans are having some success in driving our fighters back. Successful IED attacks by our people inside East Ramadi are down. So, too, are reports of American casualties. We must think of ways to stop the invader's progress. Let me hear your thoughts."

A Syrian known only as "the Scar" spoke first.

"We need to draw the American forces away from Ramadi. By inflicting casualties on the local populations, in Hit or Habbaniyah, we can trap them on the roads as they make their way there."

Heads nodded around the room and the cellar hummed as people spoke back. A Sunni Iraqi from Nasiriyah cleared his throat.

"I agree. Americans want to be heroes. Like their movie stars, they want to come to the rescue. We can ambush them as they try to rescue innocents. But I am not sure that we should target civilians. Remember we want to turn people against the Americans. Bombings should target the Iraqi police and military – the Shiites who conspired with the Americans in the first place."

Another milling of voices took place for a minute before al-Yasin quieted them.

"We can get our people and the necessary equipment into these cities. Habbaniyah has a training center for new police recruits. Bombing it would send a message to all security forces in the area as well as any others that want to take up arms against us."

Fayad listened to the exchanges regarding money, men, and material needed to carry out the attack in Hit. He listened patiently to suggestions of using chlorine bombs, taking Americans hostage, and further IED attacks. He listened to several other ideas that held tactical potential, but he heard nothing of a larger strategy. The council leader scanned the room and noticed Fayad sitting quietly on his mat staring aimlessly at the earth floor of the cellar.

"My friend from Gaza, I have not heard your thoughts yet. Do you have anything to add?"

Fayad stroked his beard and hesitated for a moment.

"My esteemed brothers, what I have heard so far are plans for waiting out the Americans. These are well-considered. We all agree that over time the Americans will grow weary and leave. That would be a victory here in Iraq and for our cause. But I come from a land oppressed by those who have been supported by the Americans for decades."

He stopped and surveyed the council. A quiet spilled over the cellar and all eyes looked at him. His words were the only sounds that pierced the cellar air.

"The key is not just to stop them in Ramadi or Nasiriyah or Baghdad. The key to defeating the Americans is not just to drive them out of Iraq or Afghanistan. The key to stopping our enemy is to drive them out of the Middle East, then Africa, and then Europe. The American people have little stomach for the death of their soldiers, but they have no stomach for the deaths of their friends, their neighbors, or their children."

His voice had strengthened, and his tone became more urgent as he pounded the dirt with his fists. "We must take the fight to American soil and strike at the heart of their world like our brave brothers did in New York."

The room remained quiet as everyone considered the Palestinian's words.

"My friend," al-Yasin interrupted, "I hear what you say. But our resources must be directed at the fight that is in front of us. Your vision is

strong, but the Americans have hardened their homeland since our success in New York. They have made it very difficult to plan, much less
implement any attack there."

Fayad frowned as the council's leader spoke. Resources from al Qaeda
or its affiliates were not directed towards strategic planning, and this frustrated the Palestinian. He saw the battles being fought daily not as discrete
events but instead as events with a larger purpose. As he was thinking of
how to respond, a voice to his left broke the silence. An Iranian, known
only as Saeed, leaned forward out of the shadows and into the incandescent light. A middle-aged man with wire-rimmed glasses perched high on
the bridge of his nose looking more like an accountant that an insurgent.
Fayad suspected that Saeed was an agent linked to Iran's security forces
but his exact background, like everyone else's in the room, was anything
but certain.

"Our council leader has good judgment, and we must not take our eyes
off the battle in front of us. Giving the Americans a victory here is bad for
our cause but also is bad for the region as well." The Iranian cleared his
throat before continuing.

"But our friend from Gaza has a valid point as well. Many of us have
gathered skills from a variety of places scattered over several continents.
These skills have caused our adversaries to change their approach, and
we similarly must consider changing ours. While mortars, machine guns,
and RPGs remain crucial for our immediate fight, the Palestinian speaks
of other strategies which should also be considered. Technology has made
America and its allies vulnerable and weak. They rely on items built upon
technologies that control every part of their lives. Many in my country
believe that striking at these, interrupting these, and ultimately destroying
these will bring our enemies to their knees."

"What do you propose?" said al-Yasin.

"If my friend from Gaza would like to work on larger strategies to
fight the American state then I can put him in touch with others who are
similarly interested," said Saeed looking first at al-Yasin and then over at
Fayad.

The council leader looked around the room.

"Does anyone have an objection to this?"

The people around the room shook their heads indicating approval of Saeed's request.

"It seems you have our approval. Would you like to leave the fight here in Ramadi and work on the larger plans of which you spoke?"

The Palestinian tried to control his excitement.

"With your blessings dear leader, yes, I would."

23

Thursday March 1, 2007
8:00 AM
Washington, D.C.

Nassir struggled with his keys. Unlocking the door to his office while holding the cup of hot coffee and his briefcase in his other hand was a precarious skill at best. Finally, getting the tumbler turned and the door unlocked, he quickly walked in and set the coffee down. He shook his hand a couple of times trying to get rid of the sting caused by the heat. He surveyed the stacks of folders which were arranged in orderly rows as he walked around the other side of the desk. Sitting down at his desk, his body weight sunk slowly and then stopped as if the leather chair had a setting on it specifically for the Director of Materials Procurement for the Federal Highway Administration (FHWA). After two decades with the FHWA, Nassir had progressed into a directorship which oversaw the approval of all construction materials used on federally-funded highway projects. Since ninety percent of highway projects were funded by federal money Nassir's department had veto power over the materials used on these projects. Nassir knew he had a full day in front of him. Congress and their constituents had pushed through "Buy America" provisions aimed at ensuring that American highways would use American products. This legislation was a headache for Nassir as it required a review on any project with a budget of over twenty-five million dollars. Just another layer of regulation that gave him another job to do. March 1st signaled the semi-official start of the construction season in most states, and the folders in front of him today contained projects that needed him to certify that the "Buy American" requirements were met so that federal dollars could start flowing. Northern states found this certification process especially important as the active construction season only lasted six months. Without the release of federal dollars in the next week, materials orders would not occur on-time, and thereby would delay these projects.

As he looked at the stack of folders the cell phone in his pocket began to vibrate. Only his personal cell was set to vibrate. Pulling the phone out of his pocket, he recognized his wife's number immediately. It was not unusual for her to call him several times a day about anything that she deemed worth talking about. It had taken Nassir a while to get used to her need to talk, but after almost twenty years he had grown fond of her reliance on him as a confidante.

"Yes dear," he said.

"Nassir, honey...I have a surprise for you," replied Maggie in her southern drawl that persisted even after all these years in Washington. Her request to not worry made Nassir feel better as she had been recently diagnosed with Type II diabetes. The thought of getting a call saying something was wrong worried Nassir. Maggie had started insulin shots to keep her blood glucose levels in check, but her taking shots worried Nassir. An insulin overdose would cause hypoglycemia, a condition where a person could have symptoms from dizziness to seizures.

"A surprise...really, what is it?"

A pause occurred for several seconds and Nassir thought for a moment that the call had been dropped.

"Your brother is here. He came to see you."

The blood drained from Nassir's face as he struggled to understand. He sat upright and leaned forward placing his elbows on his desk, bracing himself from the shock.

"My brother?" he asked. "Fayad?"

He had not spoken to his brother in almost two decades, and the fact that he could be in D.C. was hard to fathom.

"Nassir, it has been a long time," a gravelly voice said.

"Fayad? I can't believe it," Nassir said as his voice trailed off into almost a whisper.

After relocating to Gaza, Nassir's parents had kept in regular contact with their son in the United States. Now that they were up in their seventies, Nassir rarely asked about Fayad because he did not want to get them upset. He knew that his brothers were involved in something – smuggling, drugs, something that made his parents uncomfortable. Nassir's parents rarely spoke about his brothers and, when they did it was only to offer some vague and deflecting tidbit. Even when they had told him of Jamal's death, they had said Israeli security forces had insisted it was a case of wrong place – wrong time. Nassir knew better after researching online accounts of his brother's death.

"It's been such a long time, and I wanted to see you and meet my sister-in-law after all these years," replied Fayad.

Nassir felt overwhelmed as if someone had just dumped a jigsaw puzzle out of the box and asked him to identify the picture contained within.

Struggling to control his thoughts, Nassir cleared his throat.

"That's good. I would love to see you. Why don't you and Maggie come down to my office? I will clear my schedule this morning."

A pause was all that Nassir heard for several seconds.

"It would be too much to ask – to have her drive me around. I have already delayed Maggie from work, and with her condition, I think it might be better if I waited for you here."

Nassir's heart raced, and a queasiness in his stomach grew knowing that his brother, out of contact for all these years, was in his house with Maggie. *Her condition? Did he mean her diabetes? How could he know that?* The picture in the jigsaw puzzle was still unknown, but Nassir had a feeling he may not like it once he knew why his brother wanted to meet him.

"Okay. I can be home this morning. I am not too busy. Maybe see you in thirty minutes," Nassir replied.

"Really? That sounds very good. I feel that I have already been a nuisance to you and I don't want to make a bad impression on my new sister-in-law."

Fayad hung up and placed Maggie's cell phone on the kitchen table in front of them. Smiling at Maggie, he reached inside his blue wool coat and felt the handle of the hunting knife from the holster that he had over his left shoulder. The kitchen light reflected off Maggie's face, which she hadn't had time to thoroughly make up before being interrupted. Fayad looked at his brother's wife.

"I am sorry if I have inconvenienced you. You have been so kind to me. My brother is a lucky man."

Maggie smiled. She thought her husband's brother was a little creepy, weird, or both. She wanted to be hospitable to her guest, but Maggie's Southern charm was being put to the test this morning. A family member she had never met, showing up unannounced, was making her reconsider the many times she had wished for having family who lived close by. Through her discomfort, she continued to smile pleasantly.

"Well, aren't you just the charmer. Thank you."

Nassir jammed his car keys back into his coat pocket and threw open his office door. His beige trench coat flapped around his back as he walked past the curly-haired blonde receptionist.

"Gina, something has come up. I am leaving for a little while, please mark my calendar as out of the office. I will give you a call if it's going to be more than a few hours."

She noticed that the Director's coat was not buttoned, which seemed unusual for a man who was meticulous in his appearance.

"Yes, Mr. Yassim, I will do that. Have a good morning."

"I hope so."

24

Thursday March 1, 2007
8:30 AM
Winchester, Kentucky

The green and orange cubicle walls and the industrial-grade carpet squares lining the office floor smelled of air freshener and disinfectant. Nick swiveled his chair in a cubicle that was one of an array occupying space in Room 210-M in the Technology Building on the campus of Winchester Community College. He squinted as the early March sunlight beaming through the office windows overwhelmed the fluorescent lighting above his metal desk.

Welcome to the ivory tower.

"You ready for your first class, Nicky?" the familiar voice asked.

Nick smiled as he looked up from his textbook and saw his old friend standing in the doorway. Joe Jones was pushing eighty years old and had transitioned from the salt and peppered stage of twenty years ago to a slightly thinner and fully gray head of hair. Although still a stocky man, his frame was noticeably smaller, and his shirt had multiple folds above where it was tucked into his pants. The ever-present plastic pocket protector holding two mechanical pencils, a six-inch plastic ruler, and a gold Parker fountain pen still resided in the old man's shirt pocket.

Some things never change.

"You know it. I want to make sure that I impress the dean on my first day. Maybe they will keep me to the end of the semester," said Nick, leaning back in his chair and clasping his hands around the back of his head. Most ex-convicts had a hard time finding work after being released from jail. Being forty-seven years old and no longer an engineer did not enhance Nick's marketability. He was thankful that his old friend had reached out to him about the teaching position. As the interim dean of the Engineering Technologies Division Joe was highly respected by the WCC administration. Although advanced in age, Joe brought stability to the department, and the college had told him he could work as long as he wanted. When he had approached administration about hiring Nick, there was no hesitation.

End of the semester.

Those words were anxiety-producing, to say the least. Nick had zero teaching experience, except for a few computer workshops during his years in prison. Teaching inmates and teaching eighteen-year-olds are not the same things, and Nick had considered turning down Joe's offer at first. The old man had reassured him that it wasn't unusual for new instructors to lack formal teaching experience. Nick chuckled as he remembered how his old friend had tried to allay his fear using his folksy way of reassuring someone.

Boy, just get your ass in the classroom and do it. You ain't teaching a bunch of rocket scientists. Most of these kids could throw themselves at the ground and miss. You'll be fine.

Nick knew he couldn't turn his friend down with an argument like that. Plus being a mid-semester substitute was an excellent way to get one's foot in the door should a permanent position become available. Nick was filling in for someone out on emergency medical leave, and Joe mentioned that he thought there was a good chance that the medical leave might lead to a retirement. Finishing out his classes this semester would allow Nick to gain some teaching experience should a full-time position open up.

"What's your first class today?"

"Properties of Materials," replied Nick tapping the textbook on the desk in front of him. "I haven't seen some of this stuff since I was in college. And that was a long time ago."

Joe laughed.

"Boy, ain't that the truth. I remember my first semester here. I had to teach some stuff that I hadn't thought about since my college days."

"Back when you took classes with Sir Isaac Newton, right?"

"That's right, smartass," replied Joe with a chortle.

It felt like they were back in the old office, the mentor and his mentee, talking about the world, the past, the present and life in general.

"Anyway I remember my first lecture. I was so afraid of forgetting something that I spent the first ten minutes of class writing on the board without turning around. Finally, when I turned around to ask for questions half the class had their heads lying on the desks and the other half looked like they were having seizures."

Nick grinned.

Don't give them seizures, I will have to remember that.

"So what's the topic for today anyway?" the old man asked.

"Some chemistry stuff. Le Chatelier's Principle," said Nick.

"Le Chatelier….let's see if I remember. The equilibrium law for chemical reactions?"

"Yeah, that's right. I need to talk about changes made to a reaction, and how the reaction changes to restore that equilibrium."

"Until something else changes the reaction," replied Joe.

"Bingo. If something changes the condition of two reactants, Le Chatelier says the reaction must change to restore that equilibrium. Maybe more products are created, perhaps different products are created, something like that," the professor-in-waiting said. "At least that is what the textbook tells me."

"Geez, Louise, it sounds like we have us a real chemistry professor here," the old man deadpanned in his exaggerated Appalachian accent. "Don't worry, Nicky, I won't tell anybody. We don't want the chemistry department stealing you away from us."

"Thanks, boss," Nick said as he looked at his watch. "Eight fifty. I better get packed up and get going to my class. Don't want to be late on my first day."

"That's right. Remember you only get one chance at a first impression. Don't make me look bad," Joe cackled.

"Will do."

As Nick watched his friend turn around to head back down the hallway, he stopped him.

"Joe...," Nick said as he watched the old man stop and turn around. "Thanks...for everything."

A slight smile, restrained with memories of their past, came across Joe's face. Looking at the man he had known for a quarter of a century, thinking about what they had been through, the old man stood a little taller.

"Sure, no problem."

Nick quickly gathered his lecture notes, textbook, and class list and shoved them into the same brown leather briefcase he'd had since his graduation decades ago.

Some things never go out of style.

Rushing out of his cubicle into the hallway, he navigated his way through the mass of students scurrying to their nine o'clock classes. Jostling his way through the sea of people, he felt the comfort of anonymity. People passed by, unaware of his past, providing Nick a refuge of sorts. The kind of refuge he had previously sought through a bottle.

Anticipation and excitement competed against each other as he made his way towards his first class. Nick felt a sense of direction that he hadn't felt in a while. He was starting to look forward, something that Joe had told him to do a long time ago. Today's lecture on Le Chatelier's principle had him thinking about more than chemical compounds and reactants. Like a chemical reaction, people's lives seemed to be journeys to different points of equilibrium which exist for a while until a change occurs. Life change disrupts the balance and causes the establishment of a new equilibrium, one where people and their surrounding environment are once again stable. Nick thought that maybe his new role in this new environment, Winchester Community College, would mark a re-establishment of equilibrium. At least he hoped that was the case as he walked towards the Science Building and his first class.

He paused outside the classroom door for a few seconds, then inhaled deeply and opened the door. He was purposely a minute early hoping that would give the class an impression that he had done this a thousand times before. Walking in from the rear of the room, he offered a perfunctory "hello" on his way to a table with a small metal podium at the front of the room.

He laid his briefcase down on the table, opened it, and arranged the textbook, his notes, and the class list in front of him. It was show time.

"Hi everyone," Nick began as he surveyed the room from left to right. Eighteen students, most of whom looked so young.

"I am Nick Kremer, and I am going to be teaching you for the remainder of this semester. "Who knows something about Le Chatelier's Principle?"

A twenty-something girl with straight brown hair that seemed still wet from her morning shower raised her hand. Nick saw the other seventeen students turn their gaze towards her outstretched arm.

Good, no seizures so far.

25

Thursday March 1, 2007
9:00 AM
Alexandria, Virginia

Traffic was cooperating as Nassir drove hurriedly past the Lincoln Memorial towards the Arlington Memorial Bridge. The gray skies of March made the stone arches more muted than normal as the flag to the Arlington House waved to drivers approaching the Virginia shore. This went unnoticed by the materials procurement director as he made his way back to his two-story brick and stucco home in the Aurora Highlands neighborhood. He did not notice the skies or the flag as his mind was pre-occupied with possible reasons his brother would show up after all these years. The feeling of excitement at seeing Fayad was overwhelmed by a sense of foreboding that his appearance was bringing bad news of some sort.

As the minutes passed more questions filled Nassir's head. His grip tightened on the steering wheel as he turned right at a stop light and continued driving. Wanting to go faster, Nassir resisted that temptation and kept the car at the mandated twenty-five miles per hour down the tree-lined street. The trees, still bare from winter's onslaught, stood at attention reaching their spindly branches out over the pavement. Early March mornings left the neighborhood empty as kids were already at school and their parents already at work.

Pulling into his driveway, Nassir noticed only Maggie's car and instant-ly he thought that maybe this was just some dream that he would wake up from soon. The absurdity of Fayad showing up at his house clashed with the reality of Maggie's car still in the driveway. He knew at this time of day it should be sitting in her parking spot at work. Nassir stepped out of the car, and a cold March gust met him which confirmed he was not part of some dream.

His fingers trembled as he tried to insert his key into the deadbolt. After a second he was successful and swinging open the door, he stepped inside.

"Hello, I'm home?"

"In the kitchen, sweetie," a delicate Southern voice replied.

As he walked down the hall, his brown leather wingtips echoed lightly on the hardwood floors, announcing his arrival to the kitchen occupants. Entering the kitchen Nassir glanced first at his wife and then looked at his brother with a blend of amazement, anticipation, and angst. Both men did not speak for several seconds, as if trying to absorb the existence of each other in the same place after all this time.

"Fayad," said Nassir in a quiet voice, "I can't believe it is you."

Looking at his brother, whose hair was now streaked with white from the temples around to the base of his neck, Nassir walked closer as if want-ing to inspect him before going any further.

"Nassir, my brother, it is so good to see you."

Both men stood there a while longer before they simultaneously threw their arms around each other.

Nassir released his brother and stepping backward looked at him. For a moment all his trepidation passed.

"It has been too long. I still can't believe it. What brings you here?"

"Business. I arrived in town this morning. I wanted to see you as soon as I could."

Fayad was not entirely truthful. He had arrived in New York City more than a week ago as a guest of Iran's U.N. mission in New York. His trip was taken at the request of an institute affiliated with Tehran University. The nine-o'clock train last night had brought him to Union

Station early this morning. After getting a hotel room for a few hours of sleep, he had caught a taxi over to his brother's house, arriving just before eight.

"I was trying to surprise you. I didn't realize that you got such an early start to the work day here in the U.S."

"You did surprise me. I would have waited if I had known, but I typically leave for work by six thirty. But I am glad that you stopped by my house. We both are happy you stopped by," he said, nodding at Maggie. "So what business brings you here after all these years?"

Fayad looked awkwardly at his feet.

"I had an opportunity to come here to America. It is a long and boring story. But I knew once my plans were finalized that I had to see you while I was here."

Nassir was happy to hear the word 'opportunity' coming from his brother's mouth. Given the downward spiral of the Middle East, he had suspected the worst out of his brother.

"Well, we are glad you did," replied Nassir reaching out and putting his hand on his brother's shoulder.

Fayad smiled warmly at his younger brother.

"Me too. We can spend time catching up. But there are some matters that I needed to discuss with you sometime. Privately if I could."

Maggie saw this as the perfect opportunity to excuse herself.

"Let me leave you two boys alone to catch up with each other. Fayad, please make yourself at home. I told work I was coming in late and they will be happy to see me a little early. Fayad, it was nice to meet you. How long will you be in town?"

"Just until tomorrow. As soon as I get my business completed I will be off again."

"Well maybe we can see you before you leave," Maggie said, half hoping that his schedule would not permit it.

"Maybe, that would be nice. I will let Nassir know."

She reached over and hugged him and turned and kissed her husband goodbye.

The anxiousness that Nassir had felt upon his brother's unexpected arrival had dissipated, and he motioned to Fayad to have a seat at the kitchen table.

"I still can't believe you are here, in front of me, after all these years, my brother," said Nassir smiling warmly. "You needed to talk to me about something...what is it?"

"First, let me say how sorry I am about being out of touch. For many years I was involved in things that I have come to regret. I wish I could have changed things. I wish I could have protected Jamal," said Fayad in a voice filled with slivers of distress. "I stayed out of touch to shield the people I knew from any consequences of my actions. But I have changed. Now I am involved in things that I feel very excited about. That's what I wanted to talk to you about before I left."

Nassir looked at his older brother, happy that he was here and happy that he had kept him in the dark about his past deeds. With the last two decades spent away from his family, Nassir longed to reconnect with his only remaining brother.

"What is it, Fayad? What do you want to talk to me about?"

"I have been working with a German company, Einfall AG. They specialize in industrial coatings. Coatings to protect storage tanks, process piping, exhaust liners, and those types of things. Recently, they started a branch of their business that focuses on incorporating nanotechnology to be used in their coatings. Have you heard of this before?"

With a background in materials science, Nassir was somewhat familiar with nanotechnology – a new field aimed at improving materials by adjusting their composition at an atomic level. The concept had been around for decades but only recently had technology allowed researchers to begin to work on the 'nano' level – there are more than twenty-five million nanometers in an inch. The federal government had a number of projects devoted to improving materials by changing them at the smallest scale possible. Nassir recalled just reading about a nanotechnology to remove pollutants from drinking water using a rust-based nanoparticle. It was fascinating how the rust-based nanoparticle attached itself to pollutants allowing them to be extracted using a simple magnet. The research amazed him, and it seemed that hundreds of other breakthroughs were coming in this field.

"Yes, I am somewhat familiar with it. Not industrial coatings but, in general, yes."

"Well, then you know about as much as I do. My company partnered with a research institute and developed an anti-corrosion coating. It is a paint that uses zinc nanoparticles modified with cobalt atoms and some other things. The idea is that this paint adheres so tightly to a metal that it completely blocks corrosion from occurring," explained Fayad.

Nassir's scientific mind was absorbing the content. He knew that zinc coatings had long been used to protect steel by providing a physical barrier against corrosion. He also knew that cobalt was also readily used as coatings. Embedding these on an atomic scale would be more efficient if the production costs were controlled.

"Interesting. That would seem to make a lot of sense."

"We believe so. That is part of why I am here – to promote our product. We think there is an opportunity for our coating in new markets. If we can prove it to be successful, it could help us expand into other areas as well"

"It sounds promising, but I don't understand why you are telling me about this," responded Fayad's younger brother.

The older brother shifted in his seat anxiously.

"I came here to ask if we could get our product, the anti-corrosion paint, on the list of approved materials for the bridge projects that you oversee," said Fayad.

Silence shrouded the kitchen as Nassir looked down at the table and considered his brother's request. Seconds passed like minutes.

"I don't...I don't know if that is possible, Fayad. We have 'Buy American' rules in place now. These rules prohibit the use of federal funds unless all materials used originate in the United States. I want to help, but your product would have to be produced here before I could begin to consider it."

The older brother buried his face in his hands and rubbed the sides of his face in a semi-circular motion as if trying to wipe away his disappointment. He considered how to respond to this obstacle and felt the holster holding the knife on the inside of his coat. He didn't tell his brother that Einfall AG was a shell company acting as the prime distributor for the product which was being developed by the Institute for Science and Technology housed at Tehran University. Fayad knew that the problem of the "Buy American" legislation was compounded by the existence of the Iran Sanctions Act, which prohibited the importation of any goods or services from Iran. He pondered the problem a few seconds longer.

"Nassir, I did not realize there were such restrictions in place. I understand your position. My employer will be very disappointed by this. I might have overstated our relationship, but that is of little consequence. I am sure they will understand. I will just have to work harder to find other markets for it."

Pangs of guilt filled Nassir as he looked across the kitchen table. His older brother, who had only existed as a memory for so long, was asking for his help. A nanotechnology coating could, in theory, be a cost-effective tool for a nation whose infrastructure was quickly falling apart. The recent "Infrastructure Report Card" released by the Federal Highway Administration had estimated that the average age of the nation's bridges was 43 years and that more than 30% of these had exceeded their design life. A more sobering statistic was that almost 25% of all bridges were categorized as structurally deficient or functionally obsolete. Everybody was looking for a magic bullet to help extend the lifespan of bridges with a minimum of capital investment. Nassir contemplated the situation before looking back at his brother.

"There might be a way that we could pilot your coating on a project or two, maybe as a demonstration project. Part of the 'Buy American' legislation allows a waiver for public interest purposes. I could apply for a waiver on a project or two with a justification that your new coating could be a breakthrough technology."

"You could do that? For me?"

Nassir's eyes gleamed with contentment upon finding a possible solution that satisfied him on both a personal and professional level.

"If you can get me the technical specs we could pilot it on a project this summer. You will want to get me that quickly because approving materials for projects takes place this month."

Fayad jumped up, leaned over and embraced his brother.

"Thank you, thank you. You don't know what this means to me. I don't know what to say…I think you will see that this will be a great step forward."

Smiles and kind words flowed freely between the two brothers. Nassir was happy that Fayad was involved in legitimate work – work that had brought the two together after all this time. He wished they could spend more time together and felt a bit sad as Fayad told him he had to be going. After his brother had called for a taxi, the two men talked about their past, their parents and about Jamal.

"I wish he would have never gotten involved in the intifada, Fayad. I wish he would have stayed out of it. He would still be with us today."

Fayad looked at his younger brother with a stern expression.

"My dear brother, it is probably hard for you to understand being here in America. Jamal fought for what he believed to be a just cause. A cause that still exists even to this day."

"One day I hope it changes," Nassir said to his brother.

"I think it is already changing."

Realizing it was better to end their visit on happier thoughts, the two brothers engaged in small talk until the horn honked. Saying their good-byes, they promised to see each other soon. Fayad walked down the steps and got into the taxi and waved as it pulled away and headed north. As he watched the leafless oak trees parade past, Fayad smiled at the thought of his successful visit. Although he had never been to the research institute entrusted with producing the anti-corrosion coating, he had no doubt in their capabilities to succeed as well.

Sixty-three hundred miles away, a chemist swiped her identification badge through the card reader. A metallic buzz sounded indicating that she was unable to open the windowless, unmarked door. The laboratory the chemist entered was technically part of the Institute for Science and Technology, the IST, but access to this section of campus was off-limits to regular university personnel. Walking into a holding area which served as the portal to a large space containing both research and production facilities, she slipped her ID badge into her coat pocket. The chemist took off her standard lab coat and poured her slender frame into a white sterile gown, and tucked her long black hair up into a hood before donning a facemask and goggles. Isolating possible contaminants on her body from the clean room was standard protocol before entering. The chemist walked over to another door and placed her thumb on a biometric scanner, which beeped. The door unlocked, and she briskly walked inside.

Several workers moved about pushing carts, some with electrical meters, others with glass plates covered in plastic. The chemist walked to the far end of the lab and approached a stainless steel cylinder that ran almost the entire length of the lab. The front part of the structure housed several silver vats perched on top of tubular framing. The elevated vats contained a circular orifice currently discharging separate streams of blue and red liquid into a mixing compartment which blended the components. A low hum became more intense as she approached and picked up a clipboard with sheets of data. As she carefully reviewed the data a technician, almost anonymous in his clean room apparel, approached the chemist.

"Captain, I have the ductility and toughness tests on the embrittlement samples that you requested."

Captain Jarireh Reza was known as Professor Reza in the university but within this laboratory was addressed using her military title. Very few people beyond the walls of this compound knew that she was part of a research branch of the Iranian government. Her specialty involved the nano-science of doping living organisms into materials. The process of inserting organisms into things was nothing new. The mold used to produce bacteria-killing antibiotics had been around for almost a century and Captain Reza was now extending that work at an atomic level.

"Have we reached the desired levels of ductility and toughness in the steels?"

"The samples coated with the primer exhibited a twenty-five and thirty-three percent reduction in ductility and toughness after thirty days. This decrease is higher than previous tests run on the same sample two weeks ago," replied the lab technician.

"Good. Schedule a round of testing on the same samples in another two weeks. I want to know if there are further changes. Also, check the results of the corrosion samples at that time. Keep me informed of all progress. Do you understand?"

"Yes, captain," said the technician as he turned and scurried away.

Captain Reza finished reviewing the production data and walked across the lab floor and exited the clean room. Once outside, she pulled off her gloves and removed her facemask. It felt good to breathe air unencumbered by the clean room restrictions. She retrieved a cell phone from her pocket and texted the following message.

> General Assam
>   Coatings with embedded bacteria are reducing properties at faster than expected rates. Corrosion testing ongoing. Production of coatings is continuing. Ready for trial shipment if desired. Please advise.
> Jarireh

She pressed 'Send" and then removed her sterile gown. Putting the white lab coat back on, she brushed her hair with her hands and walked through the door heading towards the university. Professor Reza had a lecture to give.

26

The regular thumping of the joints in the concrete pavement finally stopped as Joe Jones steered his Crown Victoria into the slow lane of eastbound I-94. The eighty-year-old would normally not be driving during rush hour but today was not a normal day. Driving through traffic was a small price to pay to have dinner with his granddaughter, Aimee, a finance major, who was working in Minneapolis this summer on an internship. Joe was looking for the exit to I-99N, which would take him past the Metrodome and across the Mississippi River to her apartment near the university. Ever cautious, he was happy to let other drivers, who might be more familiar with the highway, pass him. This way the old engineer could keep a good distance between his Crown Vic and the car in front of him. He had called Aimee from a rest stop a few hours earlier and told her to expect him by about six thirty and, although traffic had slowed in the city, he was still on track to meet his projected arrival time.

Joe had always loved traveling with his wife, talking about the regular things that occupy the time shared by two people navigating their way along a highway. The scenery, the weather, the kids, the grandkids, the garden, the highs, the lows – all composed the full list of topics thoroughly covered by the couple. Joe loved the decades of summer driving trips with his wife. These became easier to plan since Joe had started his second career in higher education. Summer was a time where life at the college slowed down considerably, allowing time to get away for a week without returning to find thirty people waiting to see him.

Now the summer trips were quiet without his wife. Since her passing five years ago, silence and the radio occupied the time he spent on the road. It was different taking trips without her, more solitary, but he still enjoyed the drive. It gave him time to think about the longer journey that he was still on. Joe knew that all in all life was a series of trips. Trips that had a beginning and end, each one temporary in its own right. One trip, when added to the others, made up the permanent record of one's existence. Although the trips with his wife had reached their end, the trips to see his children and their children still needed to be taken. Although he missed her greatly, Joe was comforted that this trip to see his granddaughter was a legacy of the time spent with his wife on their journey together.

He was especially happy today. Nick had applied for and accepted the full-time faculty position at WCC. The old man knew that Nick enjoyed teaching and was glad that he had agreed to fill in as a substitute a few months ago. Joe thought his one-time protégé would be a good fit and that the teaching would add some needed stability to Nick's life. Family and a job were two anchors that kept people from drifting towards bad habits. Joe had seen what the absence of these anchors did to his friend two decades ago, and worried that he might re-discover old habits without something to fill the space of daily life. Teaching could be that filler. The routine and the students would keep him busy – and out of trouble.

The lines of cars slowed down, a sure sign that he was close to crossing over the Mississippi River. The predictable reaction of drivers still caused a sense of wonder in the old engineer. The same patterns repeated themselves no matter where the old man drove. Gawking at a car wreck, ignoring the 'lane closed' sign until the last moment, and slowing down when crossing a body of water were all predictable behaviors no matter where he drove. The brake lights told Joe the Mississippi was approaching and he also guessed that there might be some construction ahead as well. The interstates in Minneapolis, and all over the country, were in the summer construction season. The building of new lanes, the repaving of driving surfaces, the maintenance of deteriorated components were all activities that repeated themselves every summer. As Joe continued towards the bridge, he could see the closure of a lane ahead as some cars started to merge over. The cautious octogenarian thought this was a good time for him to do so as well. Some drivers roared past him after he merged over, seemingly oblivious to the 'lane closed 1500 ft.' signage. A caustic smirk crept across Joe's face.

People.

The approaching bridge had a design familiar to the old man, who had worked on similar bridge projects over the Ohio River in his younger days. The bridge he was now approaching was just one of many bridges constructed as the interstate system expanded during the building boom of the 1960s. The I-99N bridge measured almost two thousand feet and consisted of three trusses that crossed the river. Driving more slowly Joe recognized this particular bridge as a deck truss, a bridge where the actual structure sits below the roadway and allows drivers an unobstructed view of the river as they cross. Traveling at forty miles per hour Joe could not see much of the actual structure, which arched gracefully towards the abutments on opposite sides of the Mississippi. The separate pieces of the steel truss provided a simple elegance when viewed from the overlooks and parks that dotted each edge of the riverbank. These pieces were connected to each other by steel plates, called gusset plates, which provided the connections that held the spider web of steel together.

Although the bridge was forty years old, it was the newest of all the bridges that crossed the Mississippi in the Minneapolis area. The thought of bridges filled Joe with satisfaction. Out of all the structural work he had performed, the old man felt most fulfilled from his work designing bridges. The creation of a structure that would serve as a conduit for connecting people over a river, valley, or an interstate gave him an incredible sense of fulfillment.

As he steered the Crown Vic towards the river, orange barrels stood as sentries alerting passers-by of construction work that was well underway this summer. Two of the four northbound lanes were closed off, causing the flow of traffic to be funneled to the remaining two lanes. Piles of sand and gravel arranged inside the line of barrels passed by the passenger-side window along with a water truck, cement tanker, and portable concrete mixer.

The removal of several inches of the concrete bridge deck from the lanes in the closed-off area, along with the material and equipment, was a sure sign that the bridge was in the midst of getting a new roadway surface. Concrete contractors love construction season.

After another several hundred feet, he passed a snooper truck parked on the approach with a mobile painting truck parked next to it. He was familiar with these two pieces of equipment from his years working with the Kentucky Transportation Cabinet. The combination of the truck and equipment was a sure sign that cleaning and painting operations were also ongoing, most likely in areas showing evidence of deterioration. The snooper truck had a twenty-foot-long work platform attached to a series of reticulating arms. These arms allowed the truck to sit on top of the bridge and lower a crew under the bridge for inspection, sandblasting and painting. The system eliminated the need for hanging or erecting a series of platforms under the bridge and allowed for a rapid movement from point to point, which allowed the contractor to work quickly. Spot sand-blasting of rusted steel followed by painting in a particular area was a standard maintenance technique that allowed the state to delay the full-scale painting of the bridge for a few more years.

Red brick buildings with metal roofs sprawled over the landscape on the other side of the river. From this distance, the buildings seemed typical of so many Midwestern university campuses – brick-clad structures of steel and concrete sprouting up amongst the greenery of the urban cityscape. The old man glanced down at his watch and was satisfied that he would definitely be picking up his granddaughter by six thirty.

Joe continued over the bridge at a steady speed keeping his eyes fixed on the car in front of him. Deck truss bridges are unique because the truss, sitting below the roadway, goes unnoticed by those that drive over it. In spite of this obscurity, these trusses are constantly at work transferring loads back and forth, from member to member. The pushing and pulling on the individual members in a truss will typically place forces on those members of several hundred thousand pounds or more. At the end of each member, there are large steel gusset plates perforated with dozens of holes. These holes line up perfectly with the holes in the truss members that frame into that area. During construction, the holes are lined up, and bolts are installed making the gusset plate responsible for transferring the forces from member to member. Today was a typical day in the life of the I-99N bridge until a crack initiated at a steel gusset plate which had been given the designation U10 when designed back in 1964.

This gusset plate and several others in the main span had been sandblasted, and spot-painted six weeks earlier. Like a zipper unzipping, the crack in the steel gusset ran quickly to the adjacent bolt hole and then to the next. At five minutes after six o'clock, the four hundred and fifty-six-foot main span of I-99N plummeted down one hundred feet into the murky Mississippi. One hundred and eleven vehicles collapsed with the bridge including Joe Jones' Crown Victoria.

A mop-headed boy playing on a swing set in an adjacent park heard a loud metallic rumble similar to the low growl of a slow moving train and turned around. He looked in the direction of the noise and saw the south end of the span drop downwards, quickly followed by the deck and cars. The cracking of concrete and the screeching of the steel did not scare the little boy, who was transfixed with the huge tongue of water arching upwards almost seventy feet until it effortlessly fell back into the river. Smiling as a huge splash of water sprayed outwards, the little boy clapped his hands together before running back towards the swings.

Joe Jones did not hear the rumble as the bridge collapsed beneath him. A feeling of lightness, similar to the feeling one gets on a roller coaster after it crests a hill, was the first sensation he felt. Subsequently, the old man felt his body sinking back into the driver's seat as his car pivoted backward. Many say that in situations like this one's life flashes in front of them; Joe had a slightly different thought.

Oh shit.

The depth of the Mississippi River at that location stood at only fifteen feet thanks to the dry summer throughout the state of Minnesota. Broken pieces of the bridge's roadway rested at or above the water line, sitting on the crumpled steel framing of the bridge, which had been driven into the bedrock of the river channel. Some cars sat perfectly in their lanes as if frozen to a time only minutes earlier. Others cars sat at odd angles, arranged like toys on the floor of a daycare center. Joe's car sat on its side near the edge of a broken slab, close to a school bus which leaned precariously over a concrete barrier. School children, quiet at first, began to cry as voices of adults sought to reassure them. Car doors opened, followed by people staggering out – a bloodied young woman in a business suit, a pony-tailed musician limping on an injured leg, a construction worker doubled over outside his pickup truck. A hundred feet above the river people began to gather on each end of the bridge approaches. They pointed and screamed at those below, but the old engineer and the others below could not hear them. The fire and smoke from several cars sent an acrid black smoke drifting across the crash site and began to enshroud the victims below. The smoke, like the children on the bus, also did not bother Joe.

Within minutes the woman in the business suit waved her arms frantically as two helicopters began buzzing the wreckage, looping back and forth in an apparent attempt to relay information. Within another minute three water rescue craft roared into view accompanied by a medevac helicopter, which circled once before descending to land on the approach slab. The rescue craft pulled into an artificial inlet created by the wreckage of the steel truss, maneuvering close enough to allow its personnel to grasp the bridge railing. The boats were quickly tied off, and first responders began piling out with their trauma kits, backboards, splints, and stretchers. Once on the broken bridge deck, they fanned out scurrying from vehicle to vehicle, reporting back via two-way radio to the temporary command center located on the watercraft. Each responder's primary job was to determine the number of injured in each vehicle and then assess their condition. They placed a strip of adhesive tape on the windshield of each car – one strip of tape for each person inside. The color-coded system was set up to ensure that the paramedics were prioritizing treatment. Red tape indicated a critical injury requiring immediate attention, yellow tape a serious but non-life threatening injury and green tape a minor injury that could wait until later. After assessing the situation, the first responder would spray paint a large fluorescent orange circle on the windshield around the tape.

A burly paramedic with a close-cropped crew cut finished taping the windshield of a minivan. The two green strips of tape indicated two people with mild injuries which were not life-threatening. He jogged unevenly over to Joe's car, attempting to avoid pieces of concrete and glass scattered across the debris field. He could see that Joe was leaning against the driver's side door, which was resting on the bridge deck. He called out to the old man, who did not respond. Needing to get inside, the paramedic decided that the easiest access to the old man was through the front windshield. He retrieved a small screwdriver from his shirt pocket and punched the handle of the tool into the bottom corner of the windshield. The glass shattered instantly into a thousand pieces. He kicked the windshield with his boot, and it folded inwards allowing the paramedic to grab it and peel it back. Talking to the old man, he put a pair of gloves on and reached up to feel for a pulse in his neck. He looked back and went back to his trauma kit. He retrieved a roll of tape. Without a windshield anymore he placed one strip of tape on the hood of the Crown Vic.

He drew a fluorescent circle around the strip of tape. A piece of black tape. No need to spend any more time here. He packed up his trauma kit and moved on to the next car.

27

Wednesday October 3, 2007
10:00 AM
Winchester, Kentucky

The beautifully furnished provost's office stood in contrast to the other offices around campus. The walnut-trimmed wingback chairs, upholstered with floral print looked to be new, or at least unstained with the grime of countless students. The chairs seemed to help the back aches that had become more prevalent as Nick coped with middle age. Several framed prints adorned the office walls – one of a Victorian garden, another of a lighthouse overlooking a roaring ocean, and a third of birds sitting on a branch. Nick studied these intently and came to the conclusion that all the prints were by the same artist. The same illegible signature in the lower right-hand corner was the final piece of evidence. The only framed items that hung on the walls in the technology department were the college's mission statement or some personal item from the staff. Nick liked the one that was on the secretary's desk in his office.

ANSWERS PRICE LIST
Answers - $1.00
Answers requiring thought - $2.00

Answers that are correct - $4.00
Intelligent answers without sarcasm - $5.00
Dumb looks - FREE

The person occupying the chair to Nick's right fidgeted continuously while gulping down coffee as they both waited for the provost, Dr. Lucinda Wills, to arrive. Nick's companion this morning, Tim James, was there to make sure that everyone followed due process rules per the union contract. Tim held a doctorate in Medieval History and had the typical look of a thirty-something college professor – a black button-down oxford, blue jeans, black leather loafers, and hair longer than a thirty-something-year-old should wear it. Nick was still in the process of learning the players at the college but knew that Tim had been at WCC for about ten years and was involved in many governance committees at the college. He was both liked and disliked which, in Nick's estimation, meant he was doing something right. Tim could be, at any one time a combination of articulate, contemplative, outspoken and irreverent. Nick liked the fact that Tim had the ability to cut through all the bullshit that people liked to spew out. He remembered his first committee meeting when Tim brought a quick end to the debate over whether WCC should spend money on new laptops for the college administrators. His statement "you must be fucking kidding me. Exactly how the piss does getting the Athletic Director a new laptop enhance student success?" was met with stunned silence and a quick adjournment. Nick found Tim's characteristics refreshing, or at least different, from the straight-laced demeanor of his engineering colleagues.

The new professor felt awkward sitting there with Tim, imagining what his predicament must look like to this veteran. New guy gets hired on full-time with the help of the dean. Fucks up when the dean dies.

"I think you have the record, dickhead."

"What?" replied Nick, wondering for a moment if he had correctly heard his colleague sitting to his right.

"I think you have the record. The engineering boys don't get called into this office all that often," said the history professor pointing to the closed office door of Dr. Wills. Through the glass sidelights, both men could see the room was still dark.

"Definitely not within the first three months after being hired. It's a new record – you're special."

A smile crossed Tim's face as he adjusted his tortoise shell glasses.

"Well, I strive to make a first impression," said Nick sarcastically. "Besides the chairs up here are comfortable – good for my back."

The smile grew wider on the history professor's face as he let out a laugh.

"Keep that sense of humor, my friend. It will come in handy around here."

He looked down at his coffee, and his demeanor grew serious.

"Look, I know you and Dean Jones were friends and I know what happened was a shock to everyone around here. Especially you. I will remind her of that so maybe she will be inclined to go light on you."

Nick absorbed the words of the grievance officer, satisfied that Tim did not know how right he was in his assessment. Joe's death was a crushing blow which had left Nick untethered for weeks. Nick had to force himself to get out of bed in the morning for weeks after the death of his friend, and was hopeful when classes finally started. Still, he seemed preoccupied to those in the department, which was a correct assessment. Nick was spending his weekends up in Minneapolis trying to put his engineering mind at rest by finding out why this tragedy had happened. Most of the time during these visits was spent sitting on a bench in the same riverside park where the little boy had been playing at the time of the collapse. He passed the time watching the removal of debris and the work preparing for a replacement bridge. When he wasn't staring blankly at the collapse site, he pored over information about the bridge that the Minnesota Department of Transportation had made publicly available – inspection reports, maintenance records, timelines of major rehabilitation work. The information he wanted – design plans and specifications – would be sealed until any litigation ran its course. The need to find an answer as to why his friend died drove Nick forward. Now he knew exactly how those families of the victims in the Cincinnati collapse felt – bewildered, angry, searching for someone to blame.

"Yeah, it has been rough. Joe was always there for me. He gave me my first job out of college, helped me get this job," replied Nick. He didn't want to expand on their relationship much more than that because, although his history was public record, he did not want to advertise it. "It hurt to lose him like that."

"No doubt. I am sorry about it…I really am," said the history professor as he nervously tapped his shoes together. Nick could tell he was sincere. One more reason he liked Tim.

"Thanks."

"But Nick, I have to tell you what you did to that student in your class was, well…it was way over the line."

Tim was referring to an incident that had happened last week in Nick's Structural Design 2 course. Nick remembered most of the event well, at least his version of it. In his short time teaching, he had started to realize that students basically fell into one of two categories – those who wanted to learn everything they could and those who wanted to learn the bare minimum required to pass. At WCC, the latter group greatly outnumbered the former. Although he tried to use different learning strategies in class to help engage the 'just get by' crowd, he had quickly realized that some students were never going to change no matter what he did.

Kyle Ellison was one of those students. A tall, beefy kid with slicked-back black hair under a worn out Boston Red Sox baseball hat, he carried an air of confidence or arrogance, and Nick thought that he might be slightly older than most of the others in the class. Kyle had a penchant for asking questions or adding comments that were usually unrelated to the topic. His participation was more of an attempt to produce a few laughs from the other students. Kyle always sat in the same place – last row of tables in the back of the room. The chair on the end of the row.

Nick had immediately noticed that Kyle never took notes. Instead, he had spent his time in class with his hands clasped behind his head, tipping his chair backward and trying to balance himself on the back two legs.

Still new to the teaching game, Nick had not come across a student like Kyle and, still reeling from the loss of his mentor, was not really in the mood to put up with the antics of a classroom wise guy. Still, for the first month of the semester, Nick had absorbed Kyle Ellison's stupid comments, minor disruptions, and lack of interest in an attempt to keep the waters calm. That had changed last Monday.

The topic that day had been the role of building codes and how they are used to determine the loads needed to design a building. Nick had talked about the history of codes and different types of loads when a recognizable voice from the back of class interrupted.

"Who's at fault for the bridge collapse up in Minneapolis the other month? Is somebody going to jail for that?"

Nick turned around and gave the prick a half-smile.

"Mr. Ellison, it is always good to raise your hand to be recognized before interrupting. But to answer your question: Usually, individual governmental bodies will send people to the site to investigate, gather information, and ultimately write a report to make their finding public. Most of the time."

Leaning back in his chair with his hands clasped behind his head, the young man started to balance his chair on its back two legs.

"Sounds all well and good but by the time that report is out those engineers will be long gone. They need to throw them in jail today and make them pay."

The bluntness of his statement opened an old cut in Nick's psyche, one that would never actually heal.

Yeah, dickhead, I never had to pay.

Nick remembered turning towards the last row and becoming irritated.

"It's not like that, Kyle. If the engineers are at fault, they are held accountable. Believe me, they are accountable."

"Yeah, right. Once they get their professional licenses, the system and their lawyers protect them. Nobody is ever held accountable."

Nick remembered seeing Kyle's contempt-filled face.

"You don't know anything, Kyle. Plenty of engineers have been held accountable for their mistakes. In fact, the standards they are held to are much higher simply because of the public safety involved."

"I bet the old dude from here that died in the collapse wishes there would have been a little more attention to public safety. But, I guess it was fitting that he was an engineer. No great loss there."

At this point, Nick's memory became a bit fuzzy. Sometimes adrenaline, anger, and sadness combine, making certain things difficult to remember later. Kyle said that his professor had kicked the chair causing him to flip backward and bang his head hard on the floor. Nick thought maybe the student's balancing act had failed on its own and that it was more a case of bruised ego rather than a bruised head. In any event, that is why Tim James was sitting with him in the office of the provost this morning.

"I don't know if it was crossing the line or not, Tim. That student is a real asshole."

"You will find out that a lot of students are assholes. They are always trying to push your buttons. You just have to learn to shake it off. You want some advice?"

"What's that?" asked Nick shrugging his shoulders.

"No confrontations, just go with the flow. You are not trying to save the world."

"Got it – no confrontations," answered Nick stoically. He thought about the list of what not to do.

No seizures, confrontations, or saving the world. Geez, this list is getting long.

Dr. Wills finally walked into her office a few minutes later, dressed in a navy blue business suit and wearing a noticeable amount of perfume.

"Gentlemen, sorry I am late," she said in an unapologetic manner. "Please come into my office."

Both men followed her and took a seat as she closed the door behind them. Dr. Wills was business-like while she presented the student's complaint against Nick and asked him to respond. Nick told her his recollection of the events was not exactly as the student had stated but that he was sorry it had happened. The provost lectured him sternly on the seriousness of this matter and his responsibilities as an educator. Being untenured meant that the range of disciplinary actions she could take was long, ranging from dismissal to a letter of reprimand. Tim gave a passionate defense of his new colleague, reminding her of his good teaching evaluations and willingness to help his department. He also reminded her the loss of Dean Jones had affected Nick more than others because they had known each other for decades. Tim emphasized this last point, and the provost seemed sympathetic as she, like everyone at WCC, had a great respect for the old man. There was a period of silence among the three as she seemed to ponder her next words.

"This is what I am going to do. Nick, I want you to apologize to the student. Remember you have eight weeks left in the semester, so I expect you to be on your best behavior, okay?"

"Yes, certainly."

"I also want you to enroll in our Student Outcomes and Academic Responsibilities program. Have you met Dr. Walsh from the chemistry department?"

"I don't think so."

"Well, Professor Walsh started our SOAR program last year. It promotes higher student achievement through better faculty engagement. Many new faculty, like you, have a great deal of specialized knowledge but have no real background in teaching. Learning about things like student achievement, assessment, teaching strategies and classroom management will really benefit you. The program meets three days a week, a couple of hours each day. You'll be doing it for the rest of the year."

Tim looked at Nick and a saw mixture of confusion and resistance in his face. Tim was anxious about how Nick would react. Nick scratched his head and exhaled loudly.

"But I think that…"

Tim quickly cut him off in mid-sentence.

"I think that sounds like a good plan, Dr. Wills. Who can argue with something that recognizes the vital role that faculty play in student success. Hell, Nick, you might be teaching me a thing or two by the end of the year."

Tim smiled as he glanced at Dr. Wills and saw her nodding affirmatively.

Nick thought the training sounded silly, but feeling outnumbered, he decided not to push back on the decision. He sat quietly as Tim and Dr.

Wills discussed a few more items before the three stood up, shook hands and said their goodbyes.

Once in the hallway Nick grabbed Tim's arm and spun him around.

"What the hell was that all about? I mean, I teach engineering. I practiced as an engineer for years. I think I know something about achievement."

The history professor exhaled as he pushed his tortoise shell glasses back to seat them higher on his face.

"Listen, ass-for-brains, you got off with a slap on the wrist. I could think of worse things to do than spend six hours a week learning about success strategies. Besides you'll like Katie Walsh, she's pretty good. Her SOAR program is not too bad as well."

Nick shook his head. With shoulders slumped, he turned and trudged down the hallway and thought about his list of teaching rules.

No seizures, no confrontations, don't try to save the world, listen to what Dr. Walsh says. The list was getting longer.

28

Monday October 15, 2007
8:00 AM
Washington, D.C.

Nassir sat at the small wooden table watching the steam rise from his coffee. Lost in thought, he did not seem to notice the hordes of people who were streaming into the shop waiting to get their caffeine fix before heading off to begin their day. His stomach had been hurting for months, and he knew that drinking more coffee was not the smartest thing to do; however, his recent inability to sleep forced him to drink more.

The chatter of patrons didn't distract him as he considered what the preliminary report on the I-99N bridge collapse might say. It was due out later this week for departmental review and, as the Director of Materials Procurement, he would be kept 'in-the-loop' on its contents. He had not spoken to his brother since that day in March and could not help but fear that someone would uncover his approval of the nano-coating. The collapse had sent shockwaves through the agency and Nassir suspected that everything related to the bridge, including the materials used in the rehab work, would be reviewed. He knew how bad it would look if someone found out the real reason for his waiver. It could be bad enough to put his job in jeopardy. The pains in his stomach returned as he thought about this.

He sipped some coffee and thought about the manila envelope that had shown up on his porch last Tuesday. The envelope contained a burner phone with a note that read 'Turn on at noon.' Later that day he turned the phone on and opened the following text message:

<u>Meet Thursday. Coffee house. Connecticut near
DuPont Circle. 8am</u>

A familiar voice jolted Nassir out of his thoughts.

"My brother, it is good to see you again."

Nassir looked up at Fayad, who was wearing a wrinkled gray hoodie, and a baseball cap covering his hair. Nassir looked only somewhat surprised to see his brother standing before him. Having appeared out of nowhere last March only to disappear for six months, his reappearance today in this coffee shop was not out of the possibilities that Nassir had considered.

"Fayad, hello. What are you doing here?"

The question was hardly a question, as Nassir knew there was zero probability that his brother and the text message were unrelated. A feeling of suspicion now replaced the happiness he'd felt when first seeing his brother last March.

Putting a hand on his brother's shoulder, Fayad smiled at him.

"I came to see you, Nassir. Can't brothers get together now and then?"

Reluctantly Nassir nodded his head and gestured to the chair next to him.

"Certainly, have a seat. I was expecting to meet someone here, but I think that person may be you."

"You are correct, Nassir, it was me. Sorry about the phone and the envelope. In my business we have to be careful, you know, trade secrets and all," he said sitting down at the table. After getting situated, he leaned forward and placed his elbows on the table.

"I did want to talk about what happened with the bridge."

Dread cascaded over Nassir's body as he knew the feeling of foreboding about his brother was about to be validated. Drops of perspiration broke out under his arms as the pain in his stomach moved to his head.

"What about it?"

"First, thank you for getting the waiver for the anti-corrosion paint on that Minneapolis project. My employer, Einfall AG, is very grateful for that opportunity, Nassir. It was a real tragedy, but sometimes things like that just happen."

Nassir stared at his brother with scolding eyes.

"Just happen? They don't happen like that here. Not in this country. Not with me."

Fayad sat back in his chair and crossed his arms tightly across his chest. He looked at his brother as a little brother again. Just a little brother who needed to be set straight just like they were kids in Egypt again. The older brother took off his baseball cap and ran his hands through his graying hair.

"You know the infrastructure in this country is getting old and people take it for granted. Linking the paint to what happened in Minneapolis would be bad for my benefactors. You see, we are still working to improve it and at this stage of development we wouldn't want any publicity that could prevent it from reaching its full potential."

Nassir stared at his brother in disbelief.

"If my agency finds out that I pushed through a product waiver to help a family member I will be in big trouble, Fayad. It could cost me my job. The only thing worse would be if the paint actually..."

Nassir's voice trailed off as if he thought saying the words may make them true. He forgot completely about the pain in his stomach.

"The paint didn't have anything to do with the bridge collapse. Did it?"

Fayad leaned back in his chair again pulling away from his brother. His face grew stiff, and he looked around to observe those who were within earshot.

"I guess there could be an infinite number of possibilities as to why that bridge collapsed. You will know what happened well before I will. Aren't you getting a preliminary accident report in a few days?"

"How did you know about that?"

"My company makes me aware of many, many things. You would be surprised at all the things we know about you, your job and your family," said Fayad, pulling on the sleeves of his hoodie. He sneered across the table feeling a sense of satisfaction at the look of confusion on Nassir's face.

"What do you mean?"

Smiling, Fayad asked, "How much would you like me to tell you?"

Nassir felt sick to his stomach as his worst suspicions seemed closer to being realized. He had shrugged off the sudden appearance of his brother at his house after a decades-long absence. He had considered Fayad's request for help with the nano-coating as a legitimate request. But with the appearance of the envelope, the cell phone, the text message and his brother sitting in front of him today, Nassir knew he was about to find out something very different.

"Who is *we*?" asked Nassir, clasping his hands together in front of his mouth trying to shield himself from what he didn't want to know.

"Technically, *we* is my employer, Einfall AG, the distributor of coating products."

"Technically?"

Nassir clenched his hands tighter, realizing how quickly he could be identified as a co-conspirator in his brother's plan.

"What you don't know is that the manufacturer of the coatings are the people that made it possible for me to visit you."

As Fayad said this, he reached into his coat pocket and took out his passport and slid it across the table. Nassir felt numb as he looked at the burgundy-colored passport with the Iranian coat of arms, under which were printed the Persian words and below the Persian words their English translation. The **Islamic Republic of Iran.**

Those words made Nassir's heart beat hard enough that he was certain that others in the coffee shop could hear. He wished he could slink away unnoticed and go back to a time before Fayad's appearance last March. The fact that his brother was working for Iranian benefactors was bad enough, but he knew that allowing the pilot program made him guilty by association.

"So, I still don't understand. What do you want?"

"My brother, you know our history – our family and our people. You know that the root of our problems starts with the Jewish state," said

Fayad in a whisper hoping not to be heard above the din of the endless line of people.

"We have been thrown out of our land, our homes, and our businesses by the Zionists."

Fayad looked at the line of people who waited for their morning coffee wistfully. Getting their order filled correctly was their biggest concern. However, the concern on his brother's face did not seem to be about the coffee.

"I have spent my life trying to take back what is rightfully ours. Take it back for our family, take it back for our people. There are many of our people who have given their lives in this effort." Fayad's voice cracked just a bit as he thought about Jamal. "There are many other struggles besides just the Palestinian cause. But the common thread is America. If America is defeated, then its support for the Jewish state will cease. The achievement of our cause and the causes of our friends will be realized."

Nassir listened without expression. He sympathized, in part, with what his brother was saying but realized that the years had widened the gulf between them. Still, he did not understand the nature and scope of his brother's pursuits.

"Fayad, we have been apart for so long, and I don't pretend to know what you have experienced, but I still don't see why you are here. Why have you sought me out?"

Fayad shifted around in his seat as if pausing to consider his words carefully.

"Some of our people are interested in the fights that take place on the streets back home. Others believe in sending bigger replies to the West's bombs and planes. My benefactor believes America must be turned inward to make them address the needs of their citizens. Needs like infrastructure."

His brother's last words caused Nassir to squirm in his seat. He began to realize what his brother was talking about.

"The pilot project for the coating wasn't meant as the only one. You want me to approve it on other projects," said Nassir.

"That's right. We would like to see it on other bridges, water supply systems, dams, floodwalls and the electrical grid too. Think of how dependent Americans are on these things."

Nassir knew that he was right. Six trillion dollars of goods was carried by trucks in the U.S. annually. A couple of bridge collapses here and there would grab headlines but the after effect of frustrating delays and higher prices would cause an uproar from the American people. Pushing foreign affairs to the backburner would happen. Nassir knew that even a few disruptions would be sufficient to make this happen. He also knew that he was inextricably involved.

"So you used me to get your coating on that bridge. Did it have something to do with the collapse?"

Fayad continued to speak in a voice barely more than a whisper.

"We knew you could use your authority to get our coating on a project. Did it actually cause the collapse? I don't know, but it seems like quite a coincidence, doesn't it?"

The younger brother wanted answers, not for the sake of finding the truth but more to measure the depth of his troubles.

"I don't understand. How could it cause that?" asked Nassir.

"I am no scientist, but nanoparticles can be used to do many things. Things like help prevent corrosion, right?" asked Fayad.

"I guess so."

"Then I guess it would be possible for nanoparticles to *cause* corrosion or at least provide conditions that *favor* corrosion. Isn't that logical?'

Nassir contemplated the question. Nanotechnology made it possible to alter the composition of materials at the atomic level to improve properties. The technology made materials lighter, stronger, and more durable. Improving materials was the economic engine driving this new technology so why couldn't the opposite be true as well? He knew that the largest supporter of nano-research in America was the Department of Defense. He rubbed the stubble on his chin and pondered if military research centered only on improvements.

"Sure. I guess so."

"Look at me, teaching my younger brother something," said Fayad as a broad grin crossed his face. "Anyway, that brings me to the reason

I wanted to see you today. We are not sure about what role our coating played in the collapse. So I need you to do two things."

Nassir's stomach tightened, and he winced in response.

"What?"

"The first item involves the preliminary accident report. Should the report mention the nano-coating, you must do what you can to minimize it as a contributing factor. Okay?"

Nassir sat up reflexively as if defending his territory at the table.

"I can't do that, Fayad. I am just a reviewer," answered Nassir, incredulous.

"Reports can be changed before a final one is issued. Just like in Cincinnati," said Fayad with a nod towards his brother.

Nassir sat there frozen in stunned silence.

"How did you….."

"Know?" interrupted Fayad. "Like I said before, we know a lot of things about you, Nassir. We have been watching you for a very long time."

This revelation caused Nassir's mouth to become so dry that it became hard to force words out past his lips. The National Engineering Laboratory report on the Cincinnati collapse was ancient history as far as Nassir was concerned. How could anyone know how he had shaped that report unless they had somebody else working in the department at that time. Paranoia crept over him as the possibilities were too numerous to consider.

"I will see what I can do. What else do you want?"

"We need a sample of the bridge. We need to determine how the nano-coating performed," said Fayad.

Nassir shook his head.

"I don't even know what happened to the wreckage," said Nassir in a raspy voice.

Fayad leaned over the table and patted his younger brother's shoulder.

"We have that covered. A barge took it down the river to a warehouse, where it is being stored by the state's transportation agency. I am sure that you will know somebody that can get you samples."

"And what if I can't?"

"Nassir, you don't want that to happen. Believe me do these things or else…"

"Or else what?' demanded Nassir.

Fayad looked at his brother and coolly reached into his pocket and pulled out his smartphone. He tapped and swiped its screen several times. Smiling, he turned the phone to face his brother. Nassir looked at the screen for several seconds as his mind tried to process what his eyes were seeing. Finally, the younger brother shrank back into his chair. The grainy video was a live feed from someone who was following a woman as she waited at a crosswalk. The woman turned briefly and then proceeded to cross the street. The small image jumped back and forth on the smartphone screen, but Nassir could see the woman's curly gray-streaked hair falling over a colorful scarf. As the seconds passed, he recognized the woman on the screen.

Maggie.

He turned away and looked out the window at countless people with no idea of the situation he was involved in.

"Or else things will end up badly. You don't want that to happen."

Part III

Le Chatelier's Principle (aka The Equilibrium Law):

Changes applied to a system in equilibrium cause the system to move to a new state of equilibrium thereby counteracting the effect of this change.

PART III

Equilibrium Found

29

Wednesday October 24, 2007
3:05 PM
Winchester, Kentucky

The VCT flooring made his shoes squeak as Nick walked casually down the hallway of the Science Building looking for Room 102A. He had taught several classes in this building before but never on the first floor. Already late, the new professor was dreading his first SOAR session – the penance handed out by Provost Wills for his sins. Hands in pockets, he shuffled along glancing at the bulletin boards stuffed with flyers of all sorts. Apartments for rent, cars for sale, deadlines for scholarships and announcements for student activities of all sorts. He noticed one flyer promoting a band called Flogging Noggins playing at the Student Union this Friday night. At least he thought it was a band but, the more he thought about it, he wasn't sure.

God, I must be getting old. Flogging Noggins? That sounds like a bunch of people getting smacked in the head. Just what my students need.

After a few seconds, he gave up thinking about the musical tastes of today's generation and continued towards his destination.

He opened the door and walked into the back of the room, seven minutes late. Room 102A was a nondescript room like dozens of others on WCC's campus. Four walls of institutional concrete block painted in semi-gloss oyster shell white. Twenty-four desks with their polished steel frame supporting a plastic seat and a beige laminate surface. There were two other people sitting in the front row while the facilitator, with her back to the room, was in the midst of writing on the whiteboard. Nick moved stealthily forward in an attempt to take a seat without being noticed, but stopped suddenly as the woman at the board continued to write.

"Is that Professor Kremer that I hear coming in?"

"Uh…yes. Yes, it is," replied, Nick embarrassed that his tardiness caused him to be the focus of attention.

As she turned around, the young woman looked calm but serious.

"Did we get lost on the first day or do you make it a habit to be late to your classes?"

A second later the seriousness faded from her face replaced with a smile.

"Just kidding, I wanted you to feel like a student again. Glad you could make it. I'm Katie Walsh from the Chemistry Department. Here we have John Gibbs from Humanities and Laurel Jackson from the Math Department."

"Thanks, I'm Nick Kremer from Engineering."

Nick acknowledged the other two people as he sat down before turning his attention to Professor Walsh in the front of the classroom. Kathrine Walsh was young, maybe thirty, and filled the room with an air of confidence. As she moved out in front of the podium, her long black hair cascaded over her shoulders onto the white WCC warm-up jacket she was wearing. The contrast of black on white framed her shoulders and her noticeable athletic build. The form-fitting warm-up jacket flattered her fitness as well as her curves. Zipped three quarters of the way up, the opening at her neck revealed a thin gold chain holding a cross. Curls of her long hair fell out of place and momentarily obscured her face. She casually brushed it back over her shoulders revealing dark eyes and makeup-free cheeks which accentuated her Midwestern girl-next-door beauty.

It surprised Nick to notice so many things about anyone. Ever. Much less in the first few seconds. He was not into noticing things about people, at least not at this point in his life, and his observations about the young professor occupied all of his thoughts at this moment. Whatever his prior expectations had been of the Student Outcomes and Academic Responsibilities sessions, he knew that the young chemistry professor was in the process of changing them quickly.

"Well, Nick. Why don't we start off with a little ice-breaker. Tell us a little about yourself and why you are here."

The words 'ice-breaker' caused a wave of anxiousness to sweep over the engineering professor, as he was comfortable discussing the 'how's' in life but less so discussing the 'who's.' Especially if the 'who' was himself. Since prison, he had struggled with how many details of his past he should share. Thanks to Joe the new professor was fairly confident that his manslaughter conviction was a well-kept secret at WCC. Sitting there, he contemplated how to answer Katie Walsh, who again was pushing strands of wayward black curls across her shoulder.

"Well," started Nick, as he crossed his arms together, hoping that the fire alarm would ring. Hearing no alarm bells ring, he took a deep breath and cleared his throat.

"I received my engineering degree a while ago and worked as a design engineer on a lot of different building projects. Projects that I worked on were in many different sectors – hotels, commercial buildings, and retail, bridges and some other things. Besides that part of my life, I like music. You can consider me a recent convert to country music, but I enjoy classic rock as well."

He paused for a few seconds and a sheepish grin began to curl the sides of his mouth.

"I also want to end world hunger, cure cancer, educate the uneducated – even the kids who are lost balls in tall weeds. Really, I guess I am all about helping people. That's why I am here at WCC."

Nick hoped that his attempt at humor in his answer deflected possible questions over how he had spent the last twenty years of his life.

The two other professors in the front row chuckled at his introduction, and Katie Walsh smiled as she walked a few steps in his direction. She knew bullshit when she heard it and began to try to read this guy in front of her.

Was he trying to be funny or was he just trying to be a dick?

It was refreshing to have someone from engineering who was different at least. Most of the engineering professors were somewhat rigid and task-oriented, an absolutely boring combination. This guy was a little different – he actually tried to be funny. Still, there was something else about him that made her curious. The non-verbal signal of crossing his arms as he spoke told her that he was keeping something to himself. There was more to his story than he was willing to share.

"Those are noble aspirations indeed, Professor Kremer," she said smiling.

Feeling good that he had caused that reaction, he noticed a slight fragrance as she stepped closer. It was not perfume, and that made sense. She didn't strike Nick as a 'perfume at work' type of woman. It was something else – maybe her shampoo or maybe her clothes.

"I don't know if these sessions will do much for world hunger or cancer, but I hope we can make some progress on the education front."

"Me too," he responded. "Let's hear something about yourself. Turnabout is fair play, right?"

Katie brushed her hair effortlessly over her shoulder.

"It sure is. Let me see. I double majored in chemistry and psychology as an undergrad. I chose to go the chemistry route for my graduate degrees. After my Ph.D. I worked at a large research-intensive university for a few years. I didn't like the focus on research instead of teaching. I saw an opening here at WCC and decided to come because this is a place that values teaching. Or as you might put it – finding the lost balls in tall weeds."

Nick smiled and nodded his head.

"Oh, by the way, I have a life outside of the college also. I like to bake, rock climb, play softball, and fundraise for cancer research."

Nothing surprised Nick about what she said.

"What we are going to do here, however, is focus on becoming better teachers by understanding that how we teach can affect student learning. A simple concept. Our focus is on teaching or, as Nick put it, educating the uneducated."

His blue eyes were focused entirely on her as she stepped closer to him and looked directly at him.

"Did I get that right?"

"Yes, you did," said Nick.

"Good, then. Let's get started."

She walked over to the podium and brought up a slideshow titled 'Teaching and Learning.' Katie looked at the screen and then back to the three seated in the first row.

"Let me ask you – how do students learn? How do they take in the information presented to them?" Katie asked her three professor-students.

Feeling like he was back in his freshman engineering class thirty years ago, Nick looked around to see if anyone was eager to answer. It seemed that he was not in a class full of straight-A students, so Nick knew it was up to him.

"With a pen!"

Katie again considered the funny versus dick question as she tried not to smile. Nick was more of a challenge than a typical engineering faculty member. But then again the engineering folks usually did not get sent to her SOAR sessions by the provost. She smiled at him.

"They write information down with a pen. Yes. But how do students process it?"

Nick slid slightly down in his chair.

"Seeing it," replied Laurel.

"That is one way. Other ways are by hearing and doing. Students typically have a mixture of styles that they prefer. Parts of the human brain specialize in different types of learning. Your right brain focuses on visual-spatial learning while your left brain is more suited for verbal learning."

Nick watched Dr. Walsh present the information with the enthusiasm of an expert. He didn't know much about her but could sense there was something that he liked about her. A connection, of sorts, that replaced the dread that Nick had felt only minutes earlier. He made a mental note to thank Tim James the next time they bumped into each other.

30

Thursday November 1, 2007

1:00 PM

Tehran, Iran

Jarireh Reza took off her lab coat and poured her body into the sterile gown. She tucked her long brown hair up into the hood before donning a pair of goggles and entering the production lab. The biometric scanner unlocked the door after identifying her thumbprint, and she walked in with short, forceful steps. Equipment hummed behind a bank of computer monitors. She picked up a clipboard and began reviewing several pages of data, then made her way across the lab to a windowless door hidden in a small alcove.

Once inside, she shut the door and proceeded to take off her hood and goggles, letting her brown hair fall down across her forehead. The room was much smaller than the production lab and contained a variety of testing equipment scattered chaotically here and there. The randomness of this place stood in stark contrast to the sterile precision of the production facility. She motioned to a middle-aged man dressed in jeans and a cotton t-shirt, and he dutifully proceeded to walk towards her. As he drew close, the stubble on his face obscured but did not entirely hide the long pink scar that zig-zagged the olive-colored skin of his right cheek.

"Captain Reza, nice to see you again," said the man. Although she was still wearing the sterile gown, the man's eyes made their way up and down her body. "How can I help you today?"

Jarireh Reza seemed immune to the creepy looks that she received from the men at the university. Even though she was an accomplished chemist and had achieved the rank of captain, she still had to endure being objectified. Even by a lowly lab technician like the one before her.

"Hello, Tariq," she said brusquely. "I want to see the data on the Minneapolis samples that we received. The toughness testing specifically."

"Yes, we have that over here."

The lab technician turned and walked to a table near some other pieces of equipment. Although Captain Reza was not an expert in material science, she knew all about the impact test that was performed to measure the toughness of metal. This test would be a key tool in helping her determine if the nano-coating used in Minneapolis had decreased the toughness of the steel as she had predicted months earlier.

The lab technician took a brown accordion file off the table, pulled out several pieces of paper, and handed them to her. She studied the pages intently.

"Is this all the data we have?"

"Yes."

She exhaled audibly as her eyes returned to the data. Finally, exasperated, she threw the paper down on the table. The captain's explosive temper was well-known, and Tariq backed up to give her some room.

"The sample size is too small. It's not enough to confirm whether a significant decrease in toughness occurred," she growled. She knew the lab technician did not understand her use of the word 'significant' to refer to a statistical difference in values, and not just a numerical difference. "I will need to get more samples for testing. Let me take a look at a sample in the SEM."

She followed the technician to the far corner of the room, where the scanning electron microscope or SEM was located. The microscope by itself was rather unimpressive in appearance – a white box-like machine with a twelve-inch diameter tube protruding from its top, and connected by cords to three computer monitors.

"Put the first sample into the chamber," ordered the captain.

Without hesitating, the lab technician walked to a metal cabinet and unlocked a drawer. Removing a plate from the cabinet, Tariq went over to the box-like apparatus and opened the door to the lower chamber and placed the sample inside. The sample was a thin square piece cut from a gusset plate of the I-99N bridge sent to the lab.

Captain Reza punched several keys on the keyboard, which began the transmission of electrons through the magnetic lenses onto the sample below. The scanning electron microscope detected leftover electrons emitted from the sample after being bombarded by the electrons transmitted by the microscope. The scan created a three-dimensional image of the sample at a size of two nanometers, or about the thickness of a single piece of hair – divided into one hundred thousand smaller pieces. Successive clicks of her mouse provided different perspectives of the sample on each of the three monitors. She studied the vivid images, which looked like the surface of some alien planet, looking for crack patterns within the steel. The SEM was the perfect tool for determining the morphology of any cracking that might be present in the sample. Looking for areas similar to a watershed where small cracks would lead to a confluence of larger cracks, which would be a precursor to a catastrophic crack in the plate.

After a few minutes, the captain jotted down some notes on the clipboard and looked at the black and white images on the screen.

"That is all I need to see for now. You can remove and store the sample."

She stood up and clutched her clipboard. Without another word, Jarireh walked out of the room and back out into the production area. The impact of her shoes on the concrete floor echoed under her quick strides although there was no one there to notice. Entering the dressing area, she removed her goggles and hood before unzipping her gown. She noticed her body was wet with perspiration as her white blouse was sticking to her chest and back. Unbuttoning her blouse she fanned it repeatedly in an attempt to dry off. Feeling better, she buttoned up her top and tucked it back into her navy blue slacks. She retrieved a cell phone from her pocket and texted the following message:

> General Assam
>   Samples with the XT001 coating show reduced hardness.   15 percent lower than the control sample. Need more samples to confirm. SEM review of samples shows cracking initiated at coating-steel interface. Request more samples before XT001 production scales up. Select next project for shipment.
> Jarireh

The captain pressed 'Send" and placed her hair up onto the back of her head, and fixed it in place with bobby pins. She thought about not putting on her white lab coat because of the heat, but relented and slid it over her shoulders. She once again became Professor Reza as she walked out of the production facility.

31

Saturday November 17, 2007

9:00 AM

Washington, D.C.

Nassir looked out at the fall sky, shrouded in clouds, floating north across the Potomac. The grayness of the sky matched his mood as he considered the latest text message request that had shown up on another burner phone. He remembered a time, not so long ago, when he had dreamed of the satisfaction that would come with an office overlooking the river. Now as he was a director in the FHWA, that office with a view was his but instead of satisfaction, he felt as if he had fallen into an abyss. He shook his head thinking about the mess he was in. He had been talked into using a corrosion-resisting paint on a bridge which had subsequently collapsed. Afterward, his brother, involved with factions tied to Iran, had insisted that Nassir skew the preliminary accident report away from any linkage to the paint. Now those factions had threatened his wife, forcing him to be a pawn in their plans which he still didn't fully understand. Every time Nassir talked to his brother the abyss became deeper and blacker.

He pulled the burner phone from the inside pocket of his suit and stared at it. He had continued to receive the manila envelopes containing a new burner phone every few weeks since the first one arrived. Nassir had found this one on his front porch two weeks ago. It had remained silent until this morning when it had pinged just over an hour ago.

> Need more samples from test project at fracture points. Need on or before 11-27-07. Overnight ASAP. United Nations, Office of Humanitarian Affairs, East 42nd Street, New York, 10017.

Acid inside his stomach ate into his ulcer. The more he thought about the consequences of his actions, the more his stomach hurt. Fumbling through his desk, he found a bottle of antacid and gulped down a mouthful.

Nassir's mind raced, thinking about how he might get out of this situation. He could turn himself in to the FBI and confess everything but, for all he knew, his every move was being watched. A meeting with the FBI would set off alarm bells, possibly putting Maggie's life in danger. Whoever Fayad was working for might get to Maggie before federal agents could put her into protective custody. As he rejected that option, the thought of suicide crept into his mind. That would get him out of this hell on earth, but the thought of having Maggie find his brains splattered somewhere was more than he could handle. Suicide was an easy way out but not for Nassir. He finally accepted that he had little choice but to do what his brother wanted for a bit longer. Just a little longer, he told himself.

Sitting in his leather chair, the chair of a director, Nassir retrieved his wallet from his pants pocket. Opening it, he grabbed a slip of paper which held a name and phone number. He paused for a minute as his mind drifted to a space void of thought. It was as if his body had pressed a pause button, putting him in a stupor-like state which protected him from doing what he was about to do. The pinging of the burner phone shook him out of his stupor. Filled with anxiety, he retrieved it from his coat pocket. He looked at the black letters on the white screen.

Can you get the samples?

Holding the phone in his lap, he tapped out the reply.

Will try.

He looked at the phone number on the slip of paper and glanced out the window at the gray clouds still marching north across the river. His burner phone pinged again.

Need to do more than try.

An attachment icon accompanied this text message. Nassir clicked to open it and waited several seconds as the image buffered. Nassir could feel the muscles throughout his body tense in unison as it opened. It was a picture of his wife walking out of their house wearing a brown wool skirt and a tan colored coat. Nassir recognized the coat as her autumn coat, the one she wore before the cold winds of winter settled in the District of Columbia. He knew that they had him where they wanted him.

He pulled his personal cell phone out of his pants pocket and punched in the number written on the slip of paper lying on his desk.

"Yeah," answered a gruff voice on the other end. "Pampling here."

Ray Pampling had managed security at the National Bureau of Standards when Nassir started decades ago. As a foreigner directly out of college, Nassir found him interesting, to say the least. Chain-smoking, hard-living, and foul-mouthed, Pampling was ex-military with a penchant for drinking and gambling. As a young man, Nassir knew very little of drinking and gambling but had found in Pampling someone that actually talked to him. The young Palestinian had found Pampling's stories of his military, drinking and womanizing exploits fascinating. The old military man, in turn, liked an audience and had engaged Nassir in conversation every time they saw each other. Not exactly friends, they had developed a casual relationship over time. Pampling had retired from the federal government several years ago to become a security contractor for the FHWA, specializing in protecting federal equipment and office trailers located on project sites. His security business was decent at first, but with his gambling and other vices, Pampling was always looking for other income.

"Ray, this is Nassir."

"Yeah, what do you want?"

The hardness of his tone still intimidated Nassir.

"I need to get a few more samples from the warehouse. I would like to fly up there on Tuesday," said the director, wiping small beads of perspiration from his forehead.

A vacant warehouse located in an industrial park several miles downriver from the collapse site held the steel of the collapsed I-99N bridge. Pampling's company was responsible for controlling access to the warehouse although FHWA specialists were in the final stages of the on-site study. Still, the wreckage needed protection in case the investigators wanted to see anything for a second or third time.

"You want more samples," the ex-military man growled, emphasizing the word *more*. "From the same plates as before?"

Although he was asking the security contractor to tamper with evidence in a federal investigation, Nassir knew that Pampling was willing to bend the rules. For the right price.

"Right, from the same gusset plates. The plates marked U10 are the ones I want," replied Nassir.

"I guess I could cut those out for you. I assume you want the same rectangular strips as before. How many?"

Nassir thought about it, realizing he didn't want to go back to Pampling for a third time.

"As many as you can take off the plates without making it obvious."

Since the gusset plate had broken apart, the investigators were most interested in the portion of the plate that had fractured. Pampling could remove samples from the edges without detection as investigators would not be looking at this area of the plate.

"That might only be three or four samples," replied the old man. "But you will need to come and get them. I'm not around Tuesday. You do know Thanksgiving is next week, don't you?"

"Yes, I know. How much are we talking about?" asked Nassir.

"It will be a thousand. Being the holiday season and all."

Anger boiled inside Nassir. Pissed that the price had doubled since the last month, he knew that this was not a negotiation that he could walk away from. He paused to collect himself.

"Okay, a thousand. I can get to the yard around three-thirty Tuesday afternoon. Will that work?"

Pampling lit a cigarette and took a long drag before responding.

"People could still be around in the afternoon, dumbass. You'll need to come later, after they lock up. Make it in the evening, maybe eight-thirty, okay? You can get in through the gate on the back side of the building. The office door will be open. When you get to the office, leave the money in the mailbox outside the office door. I will pick it up the next morning. Leave the money, get in and get out. Got it?"

"Okay. Since you aren't going to be around could you bag the samples and put my name on the outside of the bag? I don't want to spend hours looking for them."

"Yeah, no problem," replied Pampling. "I'll put them in a bag and tape them to the back of a member. I will keep them out of view. Panel U12, right?"

"No, panel U10," responded Nassir shrilly.

"I know, dickwad," laughed Pampling. "I just wanted to yank your chain. They'll be waiting for you Tuesday night at eight-thirty. Remember – money in the mailbox. I would hate to have to tell the FHWA folks that somebody had broken into the warehouse. You know what I am saying?"

Nassir wanted to respond with something that had the words 'fuck you' in it, but he paused to regain his composure.

"Yeah, I know."

Nassir hit "End" to hang up. Being threatened by someone else made the pain in his stomach intensify once again. He knew Tuesday was not a good day to travel, but it would be better than the Wednesday before Thanksgiving. He would tell Maggie that he needed to go out of town on business. Opening the desk drawer, he grabbed the bottle of antacid and took another swig. Just then his burner phone pinged again. A dull ache pounded from one side of his head to the other. He retrieved the phone and took a deep breath before looking at the text.

<u>Meet Monday. Coffee house. 4:00pm</u>

32

Nick put the red pen back in the top drawer of his desk and organized the stack of newly graded tests. Opening the spreadsheet software to enter these grades would be his last task for the week since the college was closing on Wednesday for the Thanksgiving break. The plan was to leave early tomorrow morning and spend several days in Minneapolis. He was relieved that the long holiday weekend would give him a little more time to recuperate from the eleven-hour drive each way. The frequent visits to the site of the collapse were taking a physical toll, but Nick needed to figure out why Joe had died. He felt he owed that much to his friend.

Rubbing his forehead, he stared at a copy of the preliminary accident report. He had collected a significant amount of information about the bridge and had reconnected with an old college friend who was now working for the Minnesota Department of Transportation. He told his friend that he was developing a class assignment on 'lessons learned from engineering failures' and, although the report was not yet public, he had received a copy yesterday. He picked up the report from his desk and re-read the executive summary for the twentieth time.

Executive Summary

On Wednesday, August 8, 2007, the eight-lane, 1,900-foot-long I-99N bridge in Minneapolis, Minnesota, experienced a catastrophic failure in the main span of the steel truss over the Mississippi River. Approximately 400 feet of the steel truss fell 95 feet into the river. Over one hundred vehicles were on the bridge at the time of the collapse and as a result thirteen people died, with many others injured.

On the day of the collapse, roadway work was underway on the I-99N bridge, and sand and gravel were delivered and stacked in the two closed inside southbound lanes. The equipment and aggregates were used for a concrete pour that was to take place on the evening of August 8th.

At approximately 6:05 p.m., the I-99N bridge collapsed and fell into the river. The National Transportation Safety Board investigated the collapse and has determined that the probable cause of the failure was the inadequate load capacity of the gusset plates at the U10 joint. The failure was due to a combination of the concentration of traffic and construction loads on the bridge as well as corrosion that may have compromised the aforementioned gusset plates. Contributing to the accident was the inadequate attention given to the corrosion of the gusset plates which was not noted during previous inspections. [2]

The words on the page danced in front of him as he considered what they said and also what they didn't say. Nick knew firsthand that reports sometimes fail to tell the complete story. The Cincinnati report had completely disregarded the potential contribution of corroded steel in that collapse and had pointed the finger of blame squarely at him. He understood enough about the I-99N bridge to know that the design was fairly typical for a 1960s-era bridge. He guessed that there might be dozens of similar bridges built from that era and found it hard to fathom that this one, the one that Joe was on, had collapsed. The Cincinnati collapse had taken his friend's career, and now the Minneapolis collapse had taken his friend's life.

The gusset plates on a truss bridge were critical because they were the elements that tied a number of the other members together. If a member failed, there was the possibility that other members could carry these loads, but when a gusset plate failed, it left all the members connected to it with no support. Engineers called such members 'fracture critical' and designed them with extra precautions to prevent their failure. As he read over the summary, he was bothered by the fact that corrosion "was not noted during previous inspections." This oversight seemed hard to understand. Bridge inspectors were notoriously thorough, especially on major interstate bridges. When visiting the DOT office on a previous trip to Minneapolis, he had been allowed to review a 2006 inspection report for the bridge but couldn't recall any mention of corrosion on the steel truss or its gusset plates. Nick didn't consider himself to be a corrosion expert, but he believed that it would be hard for the steel to go from a fully functional state to a state of imminent collapse in just a little more than a year.

He paged through the report again to see if there was something he had missed. Maybe it was his own past or maybe it was because his best friend had died, but he was far from being at peace with the report. He wanted more information about the bridge's gusset plates. His friend from the DOT had mentioned in passing that the wreckage of the bridge was being kept in a warehouse located in an industrial area several miles downstream.

The warehouse would be a good place to look for more information.

A short series of soft knocks on his office door interrupted his thoughts.

"Nick are you busy?"

Swiveling his chair around to face the door, he brushed his hair with his hands.

"No, please come in."

The door opened, and Nick's eyes widened as Katie Walsh poked her head inside.

"Are you sure you're not busy?" she asked.

"Not at all. Come on in and have a seat. To what do I owe the pleasure?" replied the new professor as a broad smile arched across his face.

Katie's blue jeans hugged her strong legs as she took several long strides over to the wooden chair that faced Nick's desk. As she walked in, his attention was drawn downward by a smacking noise coming from the floor. Flip-flops. In November. He noticed the paint on her toenails – some colorful design of blue and yellow. He felt self-conscious that he was staring at her feet.

She might find that a little weird.

"Little cold outside for those, isn't it?" Nick asked pointing to her feet.

"Well, I guess it is. But I have to attend a Student Activities function today – we are having a Thanksgiving Beach Party today in the Commons. Hence the flip-flops."

Her black hair fell over a long-sleeve button-front blouse, and she ran her fingers through it brushing it back over her shoulders. The combination of casual jeans with a business style shirt accentuated her comfortable beauty.

"Sort of late in the year for beach weather, I would think," said Nick knowing that Winchester had not seen the sun in more than a week.

"I know, right? It's just an activity to let them blow off some steam. To help stave off the depression that comes from not seeing the sun for months at a time. Maybe it will help them make it through the last couple weeks of the semester," replied Katie as she eyed the spreadsheet open on the computer screen behind him. "Anyway, I stopped by to ask you something."

"What's that?" Nick asked in a tone slightly higher with anticipation.

"How have you liked the SOAR sessions so far?"

Nick leaned back in his chair, relieved at the generality of the question.

"Well, to tell you the truth, I was kind of dreading them at first. I always thought teaching was a one-way process. You know, turn on the fire hose and deliver the material. But, I have to admit that I have learned a few more things about the teaching process and what I can do to help them learn."

"You must have a good teacher," chuckled Katie.

"I have a *great* teacher," said Nick.

His face felt slightly flushed after he said those words.

"Well, great. I am glad to hear that," said Katie as she adjusted her body in the wooden office chair. "There's a proposition I have for you."

She paused as if to gather the courage to speak. Nick sat up in his chair, not knowing what this could be about.

"I am leaving on a sabbatical next fall semester, and I have been thinking about who I could get to cover the SOAR sessions while I am away. I thought it might be good to get someone new, someone, different to run the program. I thought about you."

Katie eased back in her chair knowing that it was a big 'ask' for someone that only a month ago she had thought might be a dick. Over the past four weeks, she had seen that Nick really could be exciting and, when he tried, engaging. He did seem to care about teaching, plus he was an engineer. She had been hoping that she could drum up interest in the SOAR program throughout the college, particularly among the engineering and science faculty. Nick Kremer could be just the person to help her do that.

"Well, I…um, I don't know. I'm still sort of new here," Nick stuttered.

Caught off guard by this request from the chemistry teacher, Nick was happy that she had asked him. He loved working with her but questioned his ability to deliver the program with her level of expertise. She was a teacher's teacher. She knew not only the 'what to teach' but also the 'how to teach' and the 'why to teach.'

"I'm not sure if I could do the job the way you do it," he said.

Nick's hesitancy to accept her offer was reassuring to Katie. If he accepted with a quick 'yes,' that would have set off alarm bells. She had seen plenty of her colleagues who overestimated their abilities. She appreciated his more thoughtful consideration of her proposal. "Professor Kremer," she said smiling, "you don't have to teach it the way I teach it. Everybody finds their own way of delivering material. Just like students find their own way of learning. You would have almost nine months to prepare you and I have been impressed by your work in the sessions so far."

Nick turned slightly pink as her recognition sent a wave of embarrassment through him. It was an unusual feeling for him. In the years since Jenny had left, Nick had walled himself off emotionally with the primary aim being to get from one day to the next. Being in prison had made it convenient for him to live this way. Joe's friendship had pushed Nick out of the past and made him see the opportunities waiting in front of him. Now he could feel the young chemistry professor pushing him in a new direction as well. Although his personal inertia was keeping him in the same space, Katie's confidence and charm were proving to be hard to resist.

"Well, can I think it over?"

"Absolutely, take your time. But in the end, you will have to say yes," she said with a wink.

Nick wasn't so sure he deserved her confidence, but it made him feel good.

"Well, I appreciate your belief in my abilities. By the way, what are you doing on your sabbatical?"

"It's an interesting project with a company in Virginia. Not to get too geeky but they are doing work on underground pipelines. They are studying the corrosion mechanisms that cause failure in their transmission lines. I want to analyze the failure process so that they can develop preventive strategies," she said as she played with the top button of her white blouse.

The word *corrosion* caught Nick's attention to the extent that he didn't even focus on Katie's fingers playing with the button.

"That's not geeky at all, in fact, it sounds neat. Very practical. I didn't think chemistry teachers got into something like that."

She smiled thinking about the natural rivalry between those in the basic sciences and those in the applied sciences. Engineers, falling in the applied science realm, were always looking for practical applications and sometimes skeptical of research without a direct application.

"Nick, don't sound so surprised. Not all chemists spend their time in ivory towers. Some of us work on problems to find real-world solutions. Corrosion is a big issue in industry. Many companies are exploring measures that can be used to prevent it from occurring."

"That sounds interesting," said Nick.

"Yeah, it's almost as cool as engineering," chuckled Katie. "So, anyway…. since my sabbatical is going to have real-world applications I assume you are going to say 'yes' to my offer. Right?"

Nick squirmed in his seat trying to buy some time before answering the charming professor in front of him.

"Well, you are making it hard to resist but could I think on it a few days before I give you a definite answer? Maybe after the Thanksgiving break?"

"That would be great. As long as you are planning to come back after the break. You don't have any plans to overdose on turkey and stuffing – do you?" Katie said with a giggle. "What are you doing for Thanksgiving anyway?"

The thought of long-ago Thanksgivings with Jenny and the kids brought a sense of loss that Nick fought not to externalize. His jaws clenched slightly.

"Going out of town for the break, spending some time in Minneapolis. I am checking on an old friend. What about you?"

"Going to my parents' place, a little north of Indianapolis. They have my sister and her family over. My mom puts on a big spread for us – like something right out of *Good Housekeeping*."

"That sounds nice," replied Nick.

A pause interrupted their conversation as they looked at each other. A mild awkwardness ensued as each waited for the other to say something and when silence still continued both simultaneously looked at the floor.

"Well, I should be going. I have my Beach Party to go to," said Katie. Standing, she ran her fingers of each hand over the top of her jeans to make sure that her blouse had not become untucked. She tossed her head backward and most of her black hair fell back across her shoulders, and what remained she brushed back with her hand.

"Stop on by if you get a chance."

"I'm not sure I am properly dressed. I forgot my flip-flops."

Her dark eyes sparkled mischievously.

"I never took you for a flip-flop kind of guy," Katie said. "I thought all engineers wore gym shoes and black dress socks on the beach."

"Not all," smirked Nick. "I wear black socks with my flip-flops."

"I knew you were special," replied the young chemistry professor, rolling her eyes. "That's why I asked you to fill in for me. You will let me know next week, right?"

"I certainly will."

She stepped forward and leaned over his desk, and grabbed a pen and jotted some numbers down on a legal pad sitting under his coffee cup.

"Just in case you want to talk more about my proposition over the holiday here's my number."

Turning to walk out, Katie gave him a little wave goodbye which Nick returned. The click-clack of her flip-flops faded as she walked down the hall. They both knew that her push was overcoming his inertia and that his 'maybe' was getting closer to a 'yes.'

33

Monday November 19, 2007
4:00 PM
Washington, D.C.

His chest felt tight as he sat at the small wooden table staring blankly out the window. Traffic streamed up Connecticut Avenue non-stop as rush hour started. The tightness he felt would normally worry a man in his late forties, but Nassir had grown accustomed to it lately. A cup of coffee sat in front of him, untouched, waiting for the tightness to subside. Small beads of sweat made an appearance on his forehead only to be swept off by a shaky hand moments later.

The coffee house was slow that time of day; a few people trickled in to pick up a bagel or a sandwich to go. The aroma of coffee soothed the patrons scattered quietly at tables around the establishment – an old man reading a newspaper, a college-aged woman surfing on her laptop, a salesman in a suit and tie looking at his phone. Nassir sat there, in a state of quasi-engagement with the coffee house community, waiting for his brother. He knew that Fayad wanted additional samples from the I-99N bridge, but knew something else was going on. *He wants something else*, he thought to himself. He fiddled with the coffee cup as the tightness in his chest eased slightly.

The coffee house door opened and banged shut as a man walked in and approached the perky, blonde barista at the counter. Nassir looked at his coffee sitting there, untouched, and then returned to watching the traffic which was starting to build. A deep voice shook him out of his thoughts.

"Is this seat taken?"

Nassir looked up at the man. It was the same man he had noticed walking in only a minute ago. Close-cropped hair, light beard, and square-jawed, the man was dressed in business casual attire. His close-set eyes and piercing stare conveyed a persona that intimidated the FHWA director. Without waiting for an answer, the man pulled the chair out from the table and sat down. Nassir, taken aback by the forcefulness of the man's actions, finally mustered the strength to speak.

"I am waiting for my brother."

The man's cold eyes bore down on Nassir. Without blinking, he replied, "I have been sent in his place. You will see him later."

Although Nassir was not looking forward to seeing his brother, the appearance of this stranger sent a wave of anxiety through his body.

"Then I guess you will tell me why I am here today? I told Fayad that I would be getting additional samples in a few days. Is that what you came here for?"

The small beads of sweat transitioned into larger beads on Nassir's forehead. The man leaned forward and flexed his broad shoulders before resting both hands flat on the tabletop. Slowly and deliberately he rubbed his hands on the table in small circles.

"Yes, we know that. You will deliver them by the twenty-seventh." The man paused before continuing. "However, I was sent here today with another request."

Although Nassir knew there had to be another reason for today's meeting, the absence of his brother increased his foreboding of the imminent request. He nervously eyed the man and saw on his left hand a gold ring with crossed swords and crescents which, along with his accent, gave Nassir the impression that he worked for his brother's benefactors.

"What do you want now?"

"Besides the samples, we are looking for another project to test the coating on. It is important for our special paint to be placed on another project while we test the samples from Minneapolis."

An incredulous look plastered itself on Nassir's face.

"That's impossible. I have already signed waivers for a bridge project in Kentucky. Now you want another project?"

Nassir regretted having signed the waiver allowing the use of the coating on the Minneapolis bridge, but fearing being blackmailed he had signed one for a bridge carrying I-275 over the Ohio River in Cincinnati. Now they wanted another project. He wiped the sweat from his brow as he realized that these requests would become more and more frequent.

"Someone will find out. I will lose my job or...."

"or worse," said the stranger as he completed Nassir's sentence.

Nassir looked at him speechless.

"That is what you were going to say, right? I will lose my job or worse."

The man clasped his hands together and glanced down at the ring. He unclasped his hands momentarily while twisting the ring on his finger. He wanted to make sure it was facing Nassir so that his table companion could have a good look at it.

"I think you must ask yourself what could be worse. A lot of things could happen if someone found out about your involvement in this matter. I don't think that it is an exaggeration to say that they would be bad things, Nassir. Bad things for you, bad things for your wife, or.....," said the stranger. He fished a phone out of his pocket and proceeded to tap the screen several times before sliding the phone across the table.

Nassir picked up the phone and tilted it upwards to avoid the glare of the lighting over their table. It took Nassir several seconds for his eyes to focus and process the image in front of him. What he saw was a man, his head covered with a black hood and his arms suspended by ropes of some kind so that he was close to the ground but not touching it. The man's limp body was shirtless, and his feet were hanging down into what looked like a metal basin of some sort. Almost like the party coolers that people use to store their drinks on ice in the summer. There seemed to be another rope draped over the right side of the basin. At that moment another man walked behind the basin and stood next to the wall immediately behind the hanging man. Looking directly into the screen, the man reached for a light switch and flipped it on. The hanging man's body shook violently as his head whipped back and forth under the black hood. Nassir recoiled as the phone's audio picked up a guttural scream. The man standing at the light switch flipped it off and walked towards the hanging man, whose body was at once limp again.

"Okay, okay. I have seen enough," whimpered Nassir as he put the phone down and began to slide it across the table. The stranger reached out and pushed the phone back towards Nassir.

"Take another look."

Nassir slowly picked up the phone and looked. The video was now shaky as if someone was holding the camera with their hand. A hand reached into the screen and grasped the black hood and pulled it sideways. Rivulets of blood dripped down from the man's nostrils and his spit-covered chin glistened in the lighting. The camera zoomed out slightly, and Nassir's eyes grew wide, and his mouth opened as if to say something, but no words came out. Finally, the stranger broke the silence. Reaching over and taking the phone from Nassir he said, "Say hello to your brother. I told you that you would see him later."

Nassir sat there trembling and unable to speak. If they would do this to Fayad, they would most certainly not hesitate to do worse to Maggie.

"So, just to make sure you know what we need – samples and a new project for our coating by the twenty-seventh. Identify the project in the same package with the samples. Is that clear?"

"Yes," replied Nassir catatonically.

The stranger tucked his phone back into his pocket and stood up. He glared one last time at the shrunken man across from him.

"Remember, everything by the twenty-seventh."

Nassir nodded, and the stranger turned around and walked away. The FHWA director sat there for several minutes trying to let his head clear. Finally, he reached into his pocket to get his phone. Pulling up his calendar, he confirmed his flight for tomorrow.

<u>Depart DCA Flight 867 – 4:32 pm. Arrive MSP – 6:55pm</u>

Traveling the Tuesday before Thanksgiving was not easy but at least he would secure the additional samples from the I-99N bridge tomorrow. *One thing at a time*, he told himself.

34

Tuesday November 20, 2007
7:30 PM
Minneapolis, Minnesota

Soreness shot up Nick's right leg as he got out of his Ford pickup truck and began to shuffle towards the warehouse. As he walked out the pain, his eyes began to water as a cold gust of wind met him head-on. A few more awkward steps over the asphalt and the pain began to ease, changing his gait from a hobble to something resembling a normal stride. He started to look more like a forty-seven-year-old instead of a sixty-seven-year-old.

The eleven-hour drive through the bare corn fields of the Midwest left Nick with the firm belief that flying would be a better option next time. Although he liked the peacefulness of the harvested land, its emptiness coupled with the unyielding gray skies of November always made him feel a little lost. He was pleasantly surprised that traffic had been relatively light on the Tuesday before Thanksgiving, and he was doubly grateful that the weather had cooperated. Being a life-long Midwesterner, Nick knew that snow and ice storms were a common occurrence over the Thanksgiving holidays in this part of the country.

He looked at the security fence forming a perimeter around a thirty-foot-tall concrete block warehouse inside. This area of the industrial park was quiet and, as his eyes surveyed the property, Nick wondered if that was due to the time of day or the fact that the holiday weekend was starting. Pointing his flashlight on a large double gate, he noticed a chain and padlock that linked the two sides together, preventing it from being opened. He pulled out a piece of paper from his coat pocket and checked the address that his old college friend had given him.

8723 Medallion Street

He waved his flashlight over the green metal plate affixed to the top rail of the fence. It bore no company name, only the numbers 8723. He was at the right place; this was the place that held what remained of the I-99N bridge. The warehouse was two hundred feet wide by three hundred feet long and its proximity to the collapse site made it an ideal place to keep the wrecked structure. He knew firsthand the need to collect evidence after a collapse so that an official review could be completed. Government officials felt duty-bound to provide an explanation for why something bad happened. The public assumes structures will stand up and when they don't, people need reassurance that their government knows the reason, and can take appropriate action.

Holding the flashlight under his arm, Nick grabbed the padlock and yanked on it, which caused the chain to rattle against the fence. He thought he just might get lucky that someone, rushing to get home, might have forgotten to lock the gate. That optimism faded quickly as the hardened shank did not unlatch from the body of the lock. Nick turned the lock over and looked at the key slot. It did not appear overly complex, and he thought it might be able to be picked, given his vast experience in watching this occur on television. Realizing that he had no paperclips, he quickly gave up on that idea as well.

He ran the flashlight over the top and bottom of the fence, looking for a place to slip through, continuing down the property line between the warehouse and the building directly to its south. Going over the top was out of the question as the inclined metal arms holding strands of barbed wire were not an inviting choice. He realized that pushing underneath would not be possible as the fencing at the bottom extended past the bottom rail. Feeling less optimistic he continued searching around the fence's perimeter. As he made his way to the rear of the warehouse, his flashlight illuminated a small fenced off area outside the main perimeter fence. Woven through the fence openings in this area were dark green privacy slats. It was a weak attempt to conceal the two large garbage dumpsters inside. Nick chuckled to himself thinking about the need to hide dumpsters in an industrial park.

He walked over to the gate and pulled a simple slide latch, which allowed him to swing the two halves of the gate open. Walking around the dumpster, he noticed a single gate on the perimeter fence was unlocked. Within a couple of seconds, he was inside and walking quickly towards the warehouse. Dodging the orange glow of the security lights that were affixed to the eaves of the warehouse, he walked briskly towards a darkened corner. Pausing in the shadows next to the warehouse, he considered his options to get inside. Nick didn't think there would be much security in this industrial park, but he did not want to draw attention to himself by doing something stupid. Creeping slowly through the shadows, with the flashlight pointed towards the ground, Nick came to a single nondescript door with the glow of a fluorescent light shining through the window panel running horizontally across the top of the door.

With his back pressed up against the wall of the warehouse, Nick reached over and grabbed the doorknob and began to turn it. Expecting to feel the resistance of the locking mechanism, he let out a small sigh of disbelief as the knob turned freely. He held his breath as he pushed the door open a couple of inches and waited, expecting an alarm to go off. Seconds passed and, hearing nothing, he inhaled and walked inside.

The office inside appeared to be fairly standard. Concrete block walls partitioned the room from the rest of the warehouse. Desks with pictures, phones, files, and computers splayed across the surfaces. A row of metal filing cabinets lining the one wall. A framed picture of smiling people standing in front of a long haul truck. A table with a small coffeemaker seated next to a bowl of creamers and Styrofoam cups perched precariously close to the table's edge. Wooden cabinets along the other wall hanging above flat-top tables with plans and papers. The smell of stale air freshener. The lighting that Nick noticed from the outside was actually several small recessed lights affixed to the underside of the cabinets.

Nick had one goal – to get a firsthand view of the corrosion on the gusset plates mentioned in the preliminary accident report. Like twenty years earlier, the disgraced engineer could feel himself being pulled towards the information contained in the wreckage that was lying just outside the office. His desire for information was personal. Drawn to the misfortune of others most people gawk at the scene of a wreck; Nick needed to understand what happened in Minneapolis for his sake, for Joe's sake and the sake of the people in Cincinnati many years ago.

The dim security lighting bathed Nick in a yellowish light as he entered the warehouse. Stretched out in four neat rows was the somber wreckage of the I-99N bridge. Hesitating for a minute, Nick stopped breathing as the image of the cold, lifeless steel lying in front of him brought back memories of the hotel atrium two decades ago. The gray sections of the bridge truss were lying on their sides, stacked across the floor of the warehouse. As he began to walk down the pathway between the second and third rows of steel, Nick noticed that certain sections were completely intact while others were twisted, bent and broken. This difference didn't surprise him as he knew that structures were much like the human skeleton – the actual fracture acted to relieve the build-up of stress allowing the rest of the frame to remain intact. The difference was that while the human skeleton could have its frame reset by a physician, a structure's life ended once it failed.

Shuffling only slightly as the stiffness in his legs eased, Nick noticed the laminated placards that were taped to the concrete floor every twenty feet or so.

L53. L52. L51.

Immediately he knew the alphanumeric identifiers on the cards were naming the panel points of the truss. "L" stood for a lower chord or the bottom of the truss, and the number was just a progression so that everyone had a common frame of reference.

Panel point U10 had been singled out in the preliminary accident report as the location where the collapse had started. His shoes made a hushed thumping sound which seemed in harmony with the dim security lighting, giving the entire warehouse an ethereal quality. The row of wreckage seemed to stretch out forever in front of him, and he continued walking the gauntlet of steel.

L24. L23. L22.

He turned right, walked several feet and then turned right again starting down another row. His stride quickened almost to a jog as the anticipation of finding U10 grew. He paid little attention to anything else except the placards.

U20. U19. U18.

Finally, he found it. Nick stood there silently for quite some time allowing his brain to absorb the mangled debris lying before him. Panel point U10 bore all the characteristics of being 'ground zero' of the bridge collapse. The point was on the top of the truss and had five steel members joined by two gusset plates. The gusset plates acted like pieces of bread in a sandwich – half-inch thick plates holding the five members together with rivets. The plates were rectangular, approximately eight feet wide by four feet deep, their bottom edges clipped off to fit the diagonal members which framed in from below.

Nick made mental notes of what he saw. Both gusset plates had fractured in a V-shaped pattern along each diagonal member. The crack had left a portion of the gusset plate still attached to the upper ends of the diagonals, almost as if someone had extracted a tooth from the plate. These V-shaped pieces were bent, indicating that there had been a substantial amount of lateral displacement when the bridge broke apart. The three other members remained attached to the rest of the gusset plate although they bore various dents and scrapes where debris tore into them during the collapse. Looking at the culprit of his friend's death, the engineer in Nick searched for answers in the tangled puzzle before him.

Was it overloaded? Was it a problem with the plates? The rivets?

Nick ran his hand along the edge of the fractured plate. The cracked surface was smooth to the touch and looked almost as if it had a salt and pepper type of grain structure under the beam of Nick's flashlight. The smooth surface indicated that the steel had broken in a brittle manner with the crack progressing quickly through the member. As the light bounced off the rivets at the connection, Nick saw what looked like brush strokes in the paint covering the gusset plate. The brush strokes seemed odd as the paint of a massive steel structure like this would typically be applied using a spray gun. Looking farther away from the fractured plate, Nick saw that the marine green paint around U10 was a lighter shade than the adjacent steel.

Possibly a touch-up the contractor was doing on the project.

He stepped back and walked down to U11 and then U12 observing the same color difference that occurred systematically at the panel points.

Definitely touch-up painting.

Back at U10, he stepped onto a steel beam to see if he could look behind the cracked plate. Holding onto a diagonal piece of steel he contorted his body under the diagonal, only to have his forehead strike something hanging off the diagonal steel member joined to the gusset plate. His rear end banged hard into the steel truss as Nick bent his body backward attempting to let his eyes focus on the object as a small red scratch appeared on his forehead.

What the hell? A bag?

With a swift jerk, he ripped the bag from its perch and slowly wiggled his body back through the steel until he was standing upright again. The bag was a typical clear freezer bag, one with a zip-lock top that had been pressed closed. Nick could clearly make out several rectangular pieces of steel approximately four inches long by two inches wide. Staring at the metal strips with a puzzled look on his face, he assumed they were from some part of the bridge.

Why had they been put in such an inconspicuous place?

Stepping up on a steel beam to examine U10 with the hope of answering that question, he again wriggled his body past the front gusset to get a better view of the panel point from the rear. Shining his light from underneath, he saw something. On the right edge of the rear gusset plate, Nick observed the unpainted edge of gray steel that was left exposed after a saw cut. The cut was neat, clean and well-hidden. It was also at U10 — the initiation point of the bridge collapse. Taking samples from the gusset plate wasn't odd, but it was confusing why the samples were still there after the preliminary report was already out. Any mechanical testing performed by governmental agencies would have already been complete months ago. Cutting pieces for testing and then not needing them was a possibility that crossed his mind. That thought satisfied him as he slid them into the pocket of his winter coat. The steel strips might shed some light on the cause of the collapse, but he would have to get them analyzed. Happy that he had something tangible to take home, he began to think about the trouble he could get in if caught inside a warehouse being leased by a federal agency. Since he had entered through an unlocked door, what he was doing could not be considered breaking and entering, although it was definitely entering. Maybe even trespassing or at least enough to get him in trouble with his probation officer. The thought of going back to jail made him realize that he had overstayed his welcome here.

Retracing his steps back to the office, Nick could smell the staleness of the warehouse air. His pace quickened as his anxiety grew. Somehow he didn't think the administration at WCC would stick with a first-year teacher who was sitting in a federal prison on trespassing charges. Especially after his little incident with Kyle Ellison.

As he made it to the office, Nick looked over the room again. Knowing that he would never be back to this place, he paused to think if there was any other information that he needed. A set of bridge plans sat on the table in the corner, but their bulk would make it impossible to conceal and carry to his car. He approached several sets of stackable plastic trays and pulled out an assortment of crème-colored file folders.

Timesheets. Purchase Orders. Correspondence.

Everything seemed to be of a mundane nature until he came across a file folder with the label *Corrosion Protection*. The preliminary accident report had pointed to corrosion as a possible initiator of the collapse, and the label on the file piqued his interest. He paged through the folder until he stopped at a sheet of paper with the imprint of the Federal Highway Administration occupying a prominent position on top of the page. Illuminated by the flashlight, Nick's pupils widened to absorb the light as he carefully began to read.

March 8, 2007

Re: Waiver to Use Anti-Corrosion Coating

Dear Sir or Madam,

This letter is to notify you that the specified paint product to be used on the steel truss portion of the I-99N bridge rehabilitation project in Minneapolis, Minnesota should be replaced with the approved substitute, XT-001 Anti-Corrosion Coating manufactured by Einfall AG Inc. This product is considered a breakthrough technology and, as such, is to be incorporated as a demonstration product. The coating will be considered by the FHWA as being non-available through U.S. manufacturers and therefore you will not have to petition the administration for its use. The FHWA is, therefore, waiving the requirements of the Buy-American legislation per 49 U.S.C. 5323(j)(2)(B); 49 CFR 661.7(c).

If there are any questions about this please do not hesitate to contact the divisional office at (202) 465-1321.

Sincerely,

Mr. Nassir Yassim, Director

Materials Procurement Division

Federal Highway Administration

He sat down considering the touch-up paint that he had seen on the steel inside the warehouse. Knowing he had been away from the engineering world for quite some time, Nick was not current with the latest materials or their procurement on federal projects. Nonetheless, his mind raced with questions.

What is a breakthrough technology? Why does the FHWA consider this a breakthrough technology? How does this coating work? Could those previous inspections simply have missed the corrosion problems? Was corrosion the initiator of the collapse?

At that moment Nick stopped asking questions. Answering that last question first was the key. He reached into his pocket and ran his fingers over the plastic bag filled with cold steel.

Feeling as if he had missed something, Nick sat there and re-read the memo one more time. His concentration was broken as light from outside the warehouse pierced through the rectangular glazing at the top of the office door. Nick froze, and he held his breath as the light moved at a steady pace along the office wall. A car's headlight he thought. A sense of foreboding fell over him as the car lights faded. Stuffing the memo into his pocket, he knew that he needed to leave and placed the file folder back into the plastic tray. Nick stood up to make his way back to the car and was caught off guard by the stiffness in his legs, which caused him to stagger on his first step. Stumbling, he thrust his right arm down to the desk to keep from falling. Focused on regaining his balance, Nick sat back down and caught his breath.

A cold wind greeted him and forced him to pull the collar of his coat tightly around his neck as he walked out to the perimeter fence. Looking each way for the car that had passed by only a minute ago, he was relieved to see only the shine of the security lighting bouncing off the pavement. He walked quickly and slid through the gate by the dumpster, stealthily making his way past the two large metal containers. The green privacy slats woven through the fencing around the dumpster made it darker in this area, and Nick stepped cautiously making sure he didn't trip on something. Although his vision was limited, his hearing was not. The sound of footsteps walking down the pavement froze him instantly. As the clicking of the footsteps grew louder, Nick's heart began to race.

The squeaking of the slide latch as it rose seemed to take forever, and suddenly the gate swung open. The sense of panic in Nick's brain overwhelmed any other options. Rushing forward and lowering his shoulder he barreled into the shadow in front of him. He felt little resistance as his shoulder hit the man's chest squarely, indicating he had surprised his target. The blow staggered Nick as well, and regaining his balance he looked down at the man sprawled out on the pavement. A man about his age. A man dressed in business attire. A man who looked to be in pain. That was all Nick could process before running off down the parking lot.

Nassir Yassim looked up at the cold November sky and tried to catch his breath. Not sure what had happened he told himself not to panic as his short, unsatisfying gasps for air would soon pass. After a minute he rolled onto his right side, sat up, and closed his eyes again as his head began to throb. Running his hand over the back of his head he realized he must have smacked it on the pavement. Collecting himself on the ground for another minute he achingly stood up and reached his hand into his pocket. Still feeling light-headed, he was thankful that the envelope of Pampling's money was still there. Nassir trudged towards the warehouse to collect what he had been sent here for.

The cold air helped clear some of the fuzziness in Nassir's head, and he became more sure-footed with each passing step. Soon he was at the office door and, as promised, it was unlocked. Nassir paused for a moment before reaching into his coat pocket for the bank envelope with ten one hundred-dollar bills in it. As agreed upon with Pampling, he dropped it into the black metal mailbox outside the office door. He was familiar with the warehouse, so once inside he quickly passed through the office making his way towards the wreckage. Without spending time in the dimly lit office, Nassir paused while his eyes took a while to adjust to the dim haze from the security lighting, before he continued to panel point U10.

He walked north looking at the placards on the floor, trying to keep focused on the task and away from the enormity of the debris which stretched out to all corners of the facility.

U25. U24. U23.

The pain in his head was subsiding the closer he got to U10. Finally, he was standing at his destination. Nassir wished Pampling would have left the bag of samples sitting out in the open. Now he would have to wiggle his body behind the twisted steel to find the bag, which he hoped wasn't hidden too well. The FHWA director approached the panel point and stepped onto the same steel beam that had supported Nick only a short time ago. He shuddered to think about the destructive potential of the nano-coating if it had in some way contributed to the collapse. As a tinge of guilt crept over him, Nassir told himself to focus on Maggie and her safety.

Retrieve the samples, that's all you have to do right now.

He lifted his right arm and grasped onto the broken diagonal, and ducked his head while swinging his body under the diagonal. This movement caused him to gasp as a jolt of pain shot through his back. Gritting his teeth Nassir now realized that the fall on the pavement must have hurt more than just his head. He slowed his breathing while straightening himself up. Stepping carefully off the beam, he slowly looked for the samples and stepped onto something resting on the warehouse floor. Nassir pulled a small flashlight from his pocket and ran its light over the floor. Hoping that it was the samples he stepped off the object and reached down to identify it.

Rectangular. Soft. Leather. A wallet.

Big f-ing deal.

Sticking it into his coat pocket, Nassir continued to run the flashlight's beam over the gusset plate. He lowered the flashlight and ran it up and down the steel diagonals in a methodical fashion. Nassir's back was tight, and his head was starting to pulsate with each heartbeat, but those were the least of his worries right now.

No samples.

He looked around for another minute before carefully backing his way out from behind the gusset plate. Standing in front of the gusset plate, he looked down at the placard on the floor to confirm he was at the right location. Thinking that maybe Pampling had misinterpreted his directions Nassir walked over to the U11 panel point and maneuvered himself behind the twisted steel once again. Frustration boiled inside him as he continued to search for the samples. He quickly searched panel point U12 and then U13 and U14. Still finding nothing he pulled out his cell phone and pulled up Pampling from his contact list.

"Yeah, Pampling here," answered the voice on the other end.

"Ray, it is Nassir. I'm here at the warehouse, and I can't find the samples. Where the hell are they?" asked the FHWA director with no attempt to hide his exasperation.

"I put them right where you told me. In a plastic bag, taped to the back side of the gusset plate we talked about," replied Pampling.

"At panel point U10?"

"Yeah, the one we talked about."

"It's not fucking here. Where the fuck is it?' barked Nassir into the phone. He was not prone towards cursing but the stress of the day, really the stress of the last six months, had taken its toll on him. He consciously decided to not think about what would happen if he missed the deadline.

"How the shit would I know. Listen, asshole, I cut out the samples for you and I put them where we talked about. You sure you are looking in the right place?"

Nassir looked hopelessly on the floor to confirm what he already knew to be true. The placard read *U10*. He rubbed his eyes and then looked back down again at the placard. It still read *U10*.

"I'm at the right place, Ray. They aren't here," he replied in a voice tinged with equal parts resignation and despair. "Who would have taken them?"

"Shit. I don't know. I'm the only one that knew. Besides that, they were well hidden. Nobody would have known to look there," answered Pampling.

"Can you get me some more?"

"Maybe after the holiday. Saturday or Sunday at the earliest. That's the best I can do," said the ex-military man.

Nassir knew that he would be cutting it close to the deadline. The deadline set by those who had tortured Fayad. Reluctantly he accepted knowing that he couldn't make it back up to Minneapolis again.

"Make it Saturday. And express them to me. Okay?"

"I told you I don't want to get caught up taking government property out of a government warehouse. That's just too much risk," came the reply through the cell phone.

"Come on, Ray. How much will it take?"

There was a pause on the phone for several seconds as Ray Pampling thought about the fair reward for his risk. Then he multiplied it by four.

"It will cost you another three grand."

"Shit, Ray, you got to be kidding!" screamed Nassir.

"Hey, take it or leave it. You are the one asking me to put my balls on the line. That's not a comfortable position to be in."

There was another pause on the line while both men considered the offer that was on the table and potential counter offers that could be made. Nassir rubbed his hand over and over across his forehead.

"Okay. Three thousand. Total. And I need them expressed to me. I need them in my possession by Sunday. Sunday afternoon at the latest."

"I can do that. Send me a cashier's check by Saturday. Overnight it if you have to."

Nassir put his phone away and headed back towards the office. His flight back to D.C. departed in the early afternoon, and he hoped to find a hotel room close to the airport. His back, legs, and head began to ache in unison. One of his shoelaces started to flop progressively more with each step but bending over to tie it was too much for him in his condition. Once in the office the shoelace came completely untied, and he decided to take care of it before going outside in the dark. Another fall on the pavement might not be easy to get back up from. He walked over to the chair and sat down to tie his shoe. Sitting up, he removed the wallet he had found in the warehouse from his pocket. Staring at the black leather wallet for several seconds, he finally opened it to find seventy-eight dollars.

Not enough to pay off Pampling.

He reached into the wallet's pocket and pulled out a stack of cards – driver's license, insurance card, two credit cards, one AAA card, and a college ID card. He casually read the name on the license – Kremer, Nicholas P. He paused as the name seemed familiar to him.

Nicholas P. Kremer.

Electrochemical pulses fired through the neurons in his brain as the retrieval process of a distant memory began.

Nicholas P. Kremer.

The memory began to build like a wave in the ocean. Almost imperceptible at first and then, at a point closer to shore, it became more and more apparent.

Nicholas P. Kremer. Cincinnati.

The wave of his memory was now crashing on the shoreline.

Nicholas P. Kremer. Cincinnati. Walkway. Engineer.

The memory had finally come ashore, and a blanket of disbelief shrouded the Palestinian.

It can't be.

His fingers fumbled through the cards and stopped at the college identification card.

Winchester Community College
Nicholas P. Kremer
Assistant Professor

He remembered the long-ago meeting in the hotel atrium with the young engineer, and the report he had authored laying blame on the young man's company. Missing samples that no one else knew about. *Coincidences like this just don't occur,* Nassir told himself.

35

Wednesday November 21, 2007
7:30 AM
New Lisbon, Wisconsin

The daylight parading through the dirt-streaked window of the Mayfield Motor Lodge revealed another cold, gray day in the Upper Midwest. The events of last night had pumped enough adrenaline through Nick that he'd thought about driving straight back to Kentucky. That plan had changed on I-94 outside of New Lisbon when the sound of the rumble strips on the shoulder of the highway kept him from crossing through the median into incoming traffic. That scare was enough for the forty-seven-year-old to realize that he had reached his limit of driving for a single day.

Turning away from the window he went over to the small blue gym bag resting on the bed he hadn't slept in. To say he packed light was an understatement. The gym bag contained mostly soft drinks and snack bars, a change of underwear, a raincoat, a sweater, and a small wad of money. *Thank God I always bring some extra cash with me and this motel was reasonable.*

Nick chuckled thinking of the adjective 'reasonable'. *This place is just a step above a crack house.* Pissed that he had lost his wallet, at least he had found somewhere to crash for a few hours and still had enough extra money to make it home. Nick pulled the sweater out of the bag, a cable-knit pullover that looked every bit like the close-out piece of apparel that it was. Slipping it over a white tee-shirt caused him to wince as a sharp pain shot through his left shoulder.

Must have popped something during my Ray Lewis imitation last night.

He took the sweater off his head and pulled the sleeve up over his left arm first before putting his head through. The pain seemed to be kept at bay if he kept his arm angled below his shoulder. Searching through the side pocket of the gym bag, he found several foil packets of pain relievers, which he ripped open and gulped the pills down with some bottled water.

Nick eyed the plastic bag with the pieces of steel sitting next to the blue gym bag. After all his trips up to Minneapolis to gather information on the collapse, he felt that these small pieces might contain something he needed. If nothing else they might give him some peace of mind that the officials were investigating the entire body of evidence, not just a subset to give them an easy conclusion. Cincinnati and its aftermath had jaded him on bureaucratic investigations. Both he and Joe had come away from Cincinnati with the unshakable feeling they were only parts of a convenient story.

He combed his hair back over his forehead and thought about his next steps. Without a doubt, the pieces of steel, specifically the coating mentioned in the memo, had to be tested. He was knowledgeable enough to perform testing to determine the strength, hardness and type of steel on his own. But testing the coating and the corrosion on the steel was a different story. The mention of corrosion as a possible cause in the accident report made the memo found at the warehouse all that much more bothersome. Finding out more about the coating would require testing that fell beyond the realm of his expertise but it would be essential to rule it in or out. He walked over to the window and exhaled loudly. He knew the call that he had to make. Reaching into his pocket, he retrieved a folded piece of paper with a phone number on it. He hesitated briefly before punching the numbers into his cell phone.

His breathing quickened, and he pre-emptively cleared his throat. It rang two and then three times with no answer and Nick was about ready to leave a message. Halfway through the fourth ring, a clear, familiar voice answered on the other end.

"Hello, Katie here."

"Hi…Katie. It's Nick. Did I catch you at a bad time?" replied Nick as he looked around for the bottle of water to quench the dryness in his mouth.

"Nick, why hello. No, no, it's not a bad time. Just give me a second, okay?"

Nick waited while he heard some muffled voices and what may have been the closing of a door. Finally, she was back on the line.

"Okay, that's better. Just wanted to get out of the kitchen. You know how inquisitive parents can be, right?"

"Well, sure, I guess," answered Nick. "It's been a while since I thought about that." It seemed it had been a lifetime ago when a young Nick worried about keeping his private life out of view of his parents. Or in his case, parent. "Are they getting everything ready for tomorrow?"

"Nick, it's over the top. The silverware is polished, the gravy boats are washed, and the turkey is soaking in the brine. This year my mom made origami turkeys for the centerpieces. OR-I-GA-MI, Nick, origami, do you believe that?" replied Katie, her voice tinged with happiness.

"Well, yes, I can. It's nice that they go all out," replied Nick as a slight smile crept across his face. Her happiness made him feel happy, at least for the moment.

"So what's going on? Don't tell me – you are calling to take me up on my offer to lead the SOAR group. Am I right?" said Katie quickly. Her voice showed obvious excitement at the possibility that Nick would say 'yes.'

Nick had not thought about her proposal since she had left the office on Monday afternoon, and he immediately felt bad that it had slipped his mind. Caught off-guard and not wanting to disappoint her, Nick stumbled into his reply.

"Well, I was thinking, umm, about it and…"

"Just go ahead and say 'yes' Nick," said Katie. "I know you will sooner or later."

The certainty of her voice instantly alleviated Nick's indecision. He had felt the pull of her gravity the first time they had met, and that pull felt good. It felt nice to be in orbit around someone who believed in something so strongly.

"Yes," he replied.

"I knew it," squealed Katie with a fist pump. "I knew you would do it."

Nick smiled at the happiness embedded in her words.

"Well, I guess you know me pretty well. Maybe you should add mind-reading to your list of skills on your resume."

"Who says it's not already on my resume," she responded playfully. "You'd better watch what you think when you're around me."

"Thanks for the warning. Hey, I have a favor to ask you too, if you don't mind."

"Ask away," she said.

"I am sort of working on a project and I know how you mentioned that your sabbatical research was focused on corrosion and such. I wanted to analyze some steel samples. They are corroded, and I would like to find out more about the corrosion. You know, about its composition, the progression, and so on," he replied, not wanting to get too far in front of himself.

"Sure, that's no problem. We could do that in my lab back at the college. Put them in the electron microscope, and set up the spectrophotometer. That would give us some information on the chemistry of the corrosion, their molecular energy levels, and so on. How does that sound?"

"Like Greek," deadpanned Nick. He smiled again when he heard Katie giggle on the other end.

"Well, let me take off my chemist hat for a minute; I forgot I was talking to an engineer."

She smiled as she heard a laugh on the other end.

"The microscope just bounces electrons off things, which creates an image of the sample. It shows us things ten thousand times smaller than a strand of hair."

"That's pretty small," interjected Nick.

"Yes, it is. The spectrophotometer, sorry about the big word, uses a known wavelength of light off a solution made from a sample, and measures how much of the light is absorbed. It provides a spectral analysis which tells us about the composition of the sample. Does that make sense?"

"I think so," said Nick. He knew he would be grateful for any help Katie could give him. "When would be a good time to do this?"

"Well, tomorrow is Thanksgiving. Then my mom and sister and I go out shopping on Black Friday; it's sort of a tradition."

"So you're one of those people," Nick responded in an exaggerated tone.

"Yeah, I'm one of those people, Nick. It's a girls' day out of sorts. Coffee and pastry, shopping, late lunch. It's all fun, and my mom really enjoys it." Katie paused a moment. "I am planning on coming back Friday night. I could meet you Saturday morning at the college if that works."

"That wouldn't ruin your weekend?" asked Nick. "I don't want to take you away from time with your family – origami turkeys and all."

"Not at all. I have been up here since last night. My brother and sister and their kids will be arriving later today. Believe me, by Friday afternoon I will be ready to leave. I love my family but, you know, after a couple days of sharing a bathroom with eight other people I am ready to get home. So Saturday will be fine."

"How about noon?" asked Nick.

"Noon it is. Just meet me at my lab in the Science Building, okay?"

"It's a date," replied Nick.

As the last word left his mouth, he cringed. It had been so long since he had even been on a date, much less used the word in the company of a woman, he didn't even know if the word *date* held the same meaning as it had thirty years ago. She was just a colleague helping him out. Still, he couldn't deny the attraction he felt for Katie, and worried about crossing some line. "Okay, it's a date. See you Saturday at noon," replied Katie in her self-assured voice that made Nick feel better.

"Sounds great."

"Nick," Katie said, "have a nice Thanksgiving."

Nick looked out of the window of his room at the Mayfield Motor Lodge to see the uncollected leaves swirling around the cracked pavement.

Being in prison for the last fifteen years had almost made him forget about holidays with family. In prison, the holidays shared a sameness with every other day.

"Yeah, thanks, Katie. You too," he replied. "Have fun sharing that bathroom."

Katie smiled and wiggled her toes inside her fuzzy slippers.

"Oh, you have no idea how much fun I will have. See you later."

"Take care," said Nick as he hung up.

He looked around the motel room and thought he should begin to pack up. He still had a nine-hour drive ahead of him, and traffic could be bad on the Wednesday before Thanksgiving. He began to put his few items into the gym bag including the samples. His shoulder still throbbed so he sat down to let the pain ease before he left.

36

Wednesday November 21, 2007
11:30 AM
Minneapolis, Minnesota

Gate B-24 in the Minneapolis-St. Paul Airport was the definition of chaos as travelers moved in all directions trying to make their way to somewhere for Thanksgiving. The airport buzzed with conversations, announcements and equipment creating a constant noise. Sitting at the gate, Nassir became more aware of how bad he felt, and reached into his coat pocket in search of some pain relievers. He frowned when his search came up empty but he was too exhausted to give up his seat and walk to find some.

The masses at his gate engaged in various activities – talking, gaming, reading, eating – and he knew there was one that needed to be taken care of before he boarded. He had delayed notifying his contact, trying to sort out what had happened last night. The missing samples sickened him, but Pampling could get more by Tuesday's deadline. The wallet found in the warehouse belonged to a college professor with the same name as the engineer in the walkway collapse twenty years ago. He wasn't one hundred percent certain if the name on the I.D. and the engineer were one and the same but it seemed at least a possibility. Before leaving the motel this morning, a search of the Winchester Community College's website had a Nicholas P. Kremer listed in the faculty directory. His biography was brief, but it did list that he was an engineering graduate in 1983 from the University of Kentucky. That graduation date would seem to fit with the young engineer he had met in the atrium of the Grand Plaza Hotel.

He retrieved the burner phone from his coat and began to text.

<u>Problem retrieving samples in Minn.</u>

Nassir looked at the TV attached to the column several rows away. He watched but was unable to hear it because of the airport noise. Maybe the sound wasn't necessary due to the young, blonde anchor with a low-cut black dress who occupied the screen. He scratched his head and waited, wondering if any response would come. After several minutes of staring at the TV anchor, he was startled back into reality by the ping of his phone.

<u>Problems?</u>

The Palestinian contemplated how to respond. The last eight months had wrecked his body physically and emotionally. He didn't want to endanger himself or his wife, and wanted to put as much daylight as possible between his culpability and the missing samples.

<u>Samples were stolen. My contact will get more by the deadline.</u>

The announcement for boarding all first-class passengers came over the gate speakers. Listening for his flight to be called, he continued to watch the TV anchor in a back-and-forth with a reporter on site for some parade. He was letting his mind drift but had a feeling he would not be waiting long.

<u>You sure? By who?</u>

His fingers tapped the keyboard of his phone. Concentrating on his texting, he missed the announcement for first-class and zone 1 passengers. People seated in his area were beginning to place items into backpacks and carry-ons. Nassir didn't notice them, but he did notice that even his fingers hurt now.

Contact put them in the warehouse. Not there when I arrived. Found wallet in the warehouse. Not sure if related to samples.

Nassir leaned back in his seat and stretched after hitting 'send.' He considered telling his contact about the person he had encountered fleeing from the warehouse but thought better of it. The line of people forming at his gate was growing longer, and the boarding announcement made a call for all first-class, zone 1, zone 2 and zone 3 passengers. He retrieved the boarding pass from the inside pocket of his coat. Zone 2. With only a small bag to carry onto the plane, he decided against standing in line just yet. After a minute his phone pinged again.

Wallet. Whose?

The gate area was thinning out quickly. Nassir flipped the strap to his bag over his shoulder carefully and inched forward on the seat before standing. His chest and legs seemed to resist this decision, but Nassir moved forward taking short steps towards the back of the line. Stopping behind an older lady who smelled of cigarettes and too much perfume, Nassir texted back.

Nicholas P. Kremer. Professor. Winchester Community College.

He shuffled forward three steps and waited a few seconds before he shuffled forward a few more.

Did he take them?

The twenty-something gate agent was quickly scanning the tickets given to her, and the line dwindled to only a few people in front of Nassir. A family with a baby in a stroller would buy him a little more time.

<u>Don't know. Just found the wallet.</u>

After a minute he was almost to the gate and his phone pinged.

<u>We will check.</u>

A lump formed in Nassir's throat as he knew what these people were capable of doing. He wasn't certain if this Nicholas Kremer was the same person from Cincinnati, but he was certain that the people he was texting would stop at nothing. The image of his brother still haunted him, and he hoped for Mr. Kremer's sake that he didn't have the samples. Nassir swallowed hard.

"Your ticket, sir," the gate agent said.

Her voice snapped Nassir back from his dark thoughts.

"Oh, yes. Here it is," he replied.

"Thank you. Have a good flight."

Nassir smiled weakly and trudged down the jetway towards his plane. The chill of the Minnesota weather inside the metal tube caused Nassir to walk faster. Although it was a full flight, Nassir was relieved by the warmth of the plane. He was also relieved as he turned off his cell phone. He would have some degree of peace for the next three hours.

37

Wednesday November 21, 2007

2:30 PM

Cincinnati, Ohio

Leno Kraznek dangled his legs off the scaffolding thirty feet above the bridge deck of the I-275 bridge and pulled off his respirator. His head pounded, and his mouth was dry, both remnants of his drinking binge which was now in its third week. It was warm for the end of November, which pleased everybody working for the AGA Painting Company. It gave them an opportunity to work a little longer until winter's deep freeze shut them down for the year. Scratching his scruffy beard, he unzipped his coveralls and popped some acetaminophen into his mouth followed by a swig of water from his bottle. He needed to unclog his paint sprayer for the umpteenth time today. His dry, cracked hands removed the intake screen quickly and dipped a sponge into a bucket of solvent whose fumes made his head hurt. He had done this so many times today he could do this in his sleep. Leno's skill at troubleshooting the equipment came from his years of experience working on the paint crew, although the new paint used on this project was especially frustrating. The incessant clogging of the sprayers was a problem no one had quite figured out how to solve.

This new paint sucks. Fucking Buy American next time.

The job was behind schedule and would undoubtedly stretch into December. Inside the paint shroud, Leno listened to the steady stream of cars drive by at slower speeds than normal. Congestion caused by the shutdown of the lane immediately under him was even further amplified due to the holiday traffic. He wasn't personally worried about traffic this holiday as a trip back home to Beaumont, Texas was too far to make it back to work on Friday. Bummed at the thought of not seeing his mom on Thanksgiving hurt Leno, but the money he was going to make was too good to pass up.

There will be other Thanksgivings.

Sitting there on his platform, he looked forward to spending Thanksgiving relaxing on his motel room bed with a bottle of vodka and football to keep him company. At least he wouldn't have to smell the stench of solvent for a day. That was something to be thankful for tomorrow.

He reattached the clean intake screen and brushed off the nozzle to his sprayer, and climbed back into position in front of the steel gusset plate. The canvas shroud covering this portion of the bridge undulated with the breeze and Leno was happy that he wasn't able to see the entire expanse of the structure given his compromised condition. Not that the bridge was extraordinarily long or high; it was the lack of food and the excess of alcohol that made Leno feel a little sicker than normal. The I-275 bridge stretched over three main spans, totaling more than twenty-four hundred feet in length. He had been on bridges like this in the past. Bridges completed in the 1970s, made of steel and spanning a river in the middle of the country. This bridge was indiscernible from the multitude of bridges built in this time period and, due to age, was in need of a face-lift.

Leno looked at his watch and knew that the last hour of work would be agonizingly slow. He sucked in one last gulp of air and placed his respirator over his face and began to spray. A light green film covered the bridge, which had been power-washed down to bare steel. The hum of the sprayer and the rattle of the pump were the only sounds that Leno could now hear. He moved his right arm back and forth falling into an almost hypnotic state as he watched the green mist cover the steel.

Finally, it was over. His watch showed it was a little past four o'clock. Leno sat on a five-gallon bucket sipping water and slowly removed his coveralls, which were moist with sweat. He looked out over the Ohio River to the Coney Island amusement park, silent and showing no signs of life as winter approached. The pounding in his head had eased significantly, and he considered what he would do tonight. The thought of spending all night watching TV in his motel room was not too appealing. He disconnected the intake line, removing it from the tank marked with a white production tag labeled Einfall AG – Berlin, Germany. He paid little attention to the label; instead Leno's thoughts focused on having a day off tomorrow. The fresh air made him feel even better as he cleaned the sprayer one last time before trudging over to the tool shed to put it away. He noticed that the traffic was lighter and moving faster now as it was getting late in the day. That would make it easier to get back to his motel and decide upon his plan for tonight.

Several miles north of the bridge as the sun began to break through the clouds, Nick Kremer passed Exit 59 for Hillsboro, Ohio. He had never heard of Hillsboro, Ohio although he had never heard of many of the small towns that were just names on exits off the highways that crisscrossed the country. He wondered now, like he had so many times in the past, about the nature of this unknown city – the people, the stories, and the secrets it held. Would it be a good place to live or a good place to get lost? Was it a place where nothing special ever happened or a place of people leading special lives? He squinted as the sun, low in the autumn sky, began to make his eyes water. He pulled down the visor to help with the glare. Traffic was slowing, which was predictable given the appearance of the orange signs reading 'Construction Next 8 Miles.' He merged into the slow lane and dutifully assumed his place in the line of cars that drove steadily down I-275 towards the Ohio River.

A few minutes later he saw the bridge looming in the distance like a sentinel allowing the chosen to pass. Nick smiled knowing that the bridge meant that he was that much closer to being home. The first thing he wanted to do was ice his aching shoulder. He glanced at the shroud which was draped over the eastern truss of the bridge, flapping like a ship's sail in an ocean breeze. Keeping his eyes on the car in front of him he thought about how pleased the contractor must be with the warmer temperatures this year. Approaching the Kentucky side of the bridge, the shroud over the steel ended while a line of compressors, trailers, and tool sheds were focal points of activity as another day of work came to a close. As he passed under the blue and white 'Welcome to Kentucky – Unbridled Spirit' sign a scruffily-bearded painter with his coveralls pulled down to his waist strolled towards a tool shed. Nick wondered for a moment if the painter was like the towns he passed but never drove into. Did his life fall into the *special* or *nothing special* category? That thought passed quickly as the cars ahead of him were speeding up, a sign the roadway construction was ending. He would be home in Lexington shortly after sunset.

38

Nassir's hands shook as he fumbled with the keys to the front door. He exhaled deeply when he finally stepped into his warm house. He was thankful to be home after driving Maggie to the airport. The first shopping weekend of the holiday season was not a good time to be on the roads around D.C. but driving to and from Reagan National on I-395 was a real test of patience.

Throwing his keys on the coffee table, he walked to the kitchen hoping there was coffee left over from this morning. His footsteps shuffled along the hardwood floor in the house, which seemed much quieter without his wife. He was relieved that she was visiting her family in Georgia for the next week. She would be safe there. He hated the fact that his involvement with Fayad had put her at risk – a risk which she wasn't even aware of. Although he missed her when she was away, a week alone might give him a chance of figuring out how to get out of this mess.

He saw the black remnants of the morning's brew in the bottom of the glass carafe and estimated that there were at least a couple cups left. Filling his cup, he placed it in the microwave then turned to the refrigerator to retrieve the half and half. Pausing before opening the refrigerator, he glanced at the photos Maggie had hung with magnets over the refrigerator door. His wife enjoyed seeing reminders of the people she loved, and she decorated the kitchen, living room, bedrooms and hallways with mementos of her parents, her sisters, and Nassir. Smiling as he gazed at the refrigerator door, seeing all the pictures that Maggie loved. Maggie and him on a bench in Myrtle Beach, Maggie and him at Niagara Falls, Maggie and him at her cousin's wedding in Georgia. Scratching his beard, he let out a wistful sigh, remembering simple times unencumbered by the considerations he now faced.

The beeping of the microwave snapped Nassir back into the present and told him his coffee was ready. The coffee soothed his nerves, and he inhaled its aroma deeply before setting the cup down in front of him. Picking up a large manila envelope stamped with "FHWA – INTRADEPARTMENTAL MAIL" in black letters at the top, he unwound the red string from the clasp and removed the stack of papers from inside. He read the cover letter.

November 20, 2007
Mr. Nassir Yassim, Director
Materials Procurement Division
Federal Highway Administration
Re: 2008 Project Review – First Round
Dear Mr. Yassim,

Per your request, I have attached the summary of the construction materials being used for bridge projects that are slated to start next spring. The projects listed are budgeted to exceed $25 million and pursuant to the requirements of the Buy-American legislation (49 U.S.C. 5323(j)(2)(B); 49 CFR 661.7(c)) a statement of the origin of the materials being used is supplied by the general contractor on each project. Please note that these projects represent only the first round of your review and others will be forthcoming as we receive them. Your timely review and notification that these projects satisfy the aforementioned requirements regarding the use of materials will be necessary to keep the construction schedules on track.

If there are any questions about this, please do not hesitate to
contact the divisional office at (202) 465-6687.
Sincerely,
Ms. Laura Bertram, Director
Construction Administration Division
Federal Highway Administration

Seventeen projects scattered across the country were in the envelope awaiting Nassir's review. His analysis was simple – make sure that the steel, concrete, reinforcement and other materials used on these projects originated in the United States. He rubbed his eyes anticipating the weariness which would come after several hours examining certificates of origin for each bid item on every project submitted. The certificate was relatively simple, consisting of general project information, the contract number, bid item name, item number, the name of the supplier and whether they were domestic or foreign. If a contractor would request to use a non-American supplier, then Nassir would need to check the waiver request, which documented the justification for use.

Nassir's usual process was to separate projects into two piles – those that had no waiver requests and those that did. Those that had no waiver requests were given fast-track approval while Nassir would scrutinize those requesting waivers more carefully. Waivers were either approved or rejected, and the contractor notified of that decision. Of course, Nassir had the power to require a public interest exception as he had done before with the anti-corrosion paint. He was about to do that again. Stomach gurgling, Nassir now thought the leftover coffee was a bad idea. He found two antacid tablets in his pocket and popped them into his mouth.

The normal process of sifting through the project data now had another level of detail as he looked for another bridge project to satisfy the demands of those who held his brother. His right leg bounced up and down nervously as he knew that he had to give them some project. Nassir looked for projects that listed a bid item for the painting of structural steel, preferably projects that required the painting of steel trusses as these had a larger number of individual members than other types of bridges. The larger number of members might provide more redundancy and prevent a catastrophic outcome.

After some time he narrowed his search to five bridges, two of these being truss bridges. He looked at the summaries of the two bridge projects that sat in front of him and rubbed his eyes before exhaling deeply. Based on the Minneapolis collapse, he had the excruciating feeling that his choice was like handing out a death sentence. He hated himself again for being in this position.

He pulled out his burner phone and texted a message.

New project. I-65 in Louisville. Over Ohio River.

He hit send and then stared blankly at the walls of his kitchen. The black hands of the clock ticked rhythmically and soothed Nassir's anxiety for a short time. This respite ended as the burner phone pinged. He pulled the phone close to his face and read the reply.

Good. Start date? Status of samples?

He knew he had to get to the bank and get the cashier's check and overnight it. Pampling wasn't shipping anything until he had his money. Nassir still thought he could get them by the twenty-seventh as requested. He texted back.

The project starts in March. Will have samples by Tuesday.

Nassir wearily got up from his kitchen table and slowly made his way to the living room, where he picked up the car keys and put on his coat. The house seemed emptier now than it had only a short time ago. He didn't want to go outside in the cold again, but it was just another thing that he was forced to do.

39

Even though he was not a believer, the Christmas decorations on the streetlights and storefronts at the West Haven Town Center made Nassir forget about his troubles. There was something about the colored lights, music, and decorations that gave a sense of hope that better days lay ahead. If anyone was walking the stores of the West Haven Town Center who needed a sense of hope on the official start of the Christmas shopping season, it was the frazzled-looking FHWA director.

With the check for Pampling in his pocket, he shuffled along into the swarm of people looking to make that big score to start off the shopping season. Normally, Nassir wouldn't be caught dead in a mall the day after Thanksgiving but the anonymity it provided comforted him today. The smell of fresh-baked cookies blended with the holiday music wafting through the air to calm the shoppers trading nudges as they traversed from store to store.

Growing tired, Nassir walked outside and pushed his way down the crowded sidewalk to a storefront which housed a post office. He walked up to the counter, decorated with silver garland, and took out a cardboard envelope used for overnight delivery. His hand trembled as he fished the cashier's check out of his coat pocket and stuffed it into the envelope. Placing Pampling's name on the outside of it, he walked up and stood in line for a few minutes, spoke sparingly with the USPS clerk, paid his $14.95 and walked out the door.

After starting his car, Nassir paused for a moment and pulled out his phone. His thumbs slowly pressed on the keypad.

<u>Check sent. Overnighted it. Need samples quickly.</u>

He put his phone back in his pocket and turned the heater on full-blast. He didn't like cold weather and this year it seemed as if winter was making an early statement. A light snow began to fall as Nassir sat there before heading home. With the car finally warm he unzipped his coat a few inches as his body began to relax. A minute later his phone pinged, and gingerly he retrieved it and gave it a quick glance.

<u>Okay.</u>

Driving onward, Nassir sighed as Black Friday shoppers coupled with the snow slowed traffic down to a crawl. After an hour, with daylight beginning to fade, he finally pulled into his driveway and turned off the car. Stepping out, he slipped on the blanket of new snow and he reached to steady himself on the car. Then he cautiously made his way up the sidewalk, where he saw a package sitting by the blue and white ceramic planter on the porch. A lump developed in his throat as he stared at the box. Picking it up, he swallowed hard and unlocked the front door.

Nassir took off his coat and threw it over the back of the couch. His body still ached from having gotten knocked down three days earlier, and he groaned as he sank into the couch. Ripping open the package, he pulled out another burner phone from inside. He sat there looking blankly out the window as the light snow began to intensify, cloaking the tree branches in the first real snow of the season. The peacefulness of the white storm outside helped distract Nassir from the phone that sat on the couch next to him. The world always seemed to slow down with a good snowfall as the people sought refuge inside their homes to wait it out. Nassir liked that about snow.

He closed his eyes and within a minute his head began to drop as the earliest stage of sleep began to overtake him. His head snapped upright, and he blinked several times as he offered only minor resistance to the oncoming slumber.

40

Saturday November 24, 2007

11:30 AM

Winchester, Kentucky

After a restless night, Nick rose early to read the paper, check his email, and to tinker around his apartment. The long drive back from Minneapolis resulted in a rather lethargic Thursday and Friday of Thanksgiving week interspersed with football, pizza, and naps in no particular order. He wasn't sure if his lethargy over the last couple of days was a product of too much TV or too much pizza, but today he was amped up about working on the samples. He was also eager to see Katie. The first holiday season since being out on his own again and the loneliness that the prison psychologist had warned him about was real. Seeing his WCC colleague would be a big help in that department.

Driving on I-64 past the fields and pastures dotting each side of the interstate, he glanced over at the bag of samples sitting on the passenger seat. He wasn't sure what he wanted the samples to show him – a correlation between the steel and the collapse or nothing at all. If the testing found the cause of the failure, what would be his next step? Similarly, if the testing did not discern a reason, then how much further could he be expected to go? The more he considered the possible outcomes, the more he decided not to decide.

Twenty minutes later he pulled into the long driveway of Winchester Community College. Past the white split-rail fencing with rows of apple trees behind it, he drove a bit faster than usual today since classes were not in session. The campus seemed much different than normal, the large surface parking lots void of a single car.

Guess my students aren't working on their projects today.

A wry smile appeared on his face. In a few short months, he quickly realized what all college professors know – that no matter how much you urge students to stay ahead of their assignments ninety percent of them will wait until the last second.

A quick walk across the Commons brought Nick to the Science Building, a four-story brick and stone structure that was one of the newer buildings on campus. Without his college ID, which was in his wallet, wherever that was, Nick was relying on the departmental master key to give him access into the Science Building. The front of the building had four sets of double doors and as Nick approached he saw that the door on the far right was propped open with a rubber door stop.

She always thinks of everything.

The building seemed cavernous as he journeyed through its empty halls, the sounds of his footsteps echoing off the walls. He clutched the samples as he walked by the bulletin boards full of 'apartment for rent' flyers, student meeting notices, and ads for the local fast-food eateries that ringed the WCC campus. In this age of social media, which he didn't understand, Nick was comforted that the simple bulletin board remained a timeless tool of information exchange on campus.

The chemistry lab, located in the basement of the building, shared that space with several other science laboratories. Nick winced, and his eyes watered upon opening the door to the stairwell. Fluorescent lighting reflected intensely off the painted concrete block walls and the tile flooring. Closer to fifty than forty, Nick had noticed he was much more sensitive to things like bright lights, loud noise, and disrespectful students. He bounced down the steps and within a minute was standing in front of the double door to the chemistry lab. Pausing, he looked through the glass panel at Katie, who was typing away on a computer. She sat there, with one leg tucked under the other, her black hair pulled into a ponytail and draped over a hoodie. Nick knocked several times and opened the door.

Katie spun around in her chair and smiled at him.

"Come on in," she said.

"Hi, Katie. Hope you haven't been waiting for me," he replied.

Nick knew that he was on time but wanted to say something that wasn't awkward. His comment about this being a date still lingered embarrassingly in his mind. The rectangular tortoise-colored glasses framed her face and with her hair pulled back gave her a professorial look that Nick found even more attractive than he normally did. He didn't want to say she looked amazing but she looked amazing.

"No, no. I got here early to get set up for us," she said. "How was your Thanksgiving?"

He didn't want to tell her that he'd spent the last several days alone watching football, icing his shoulder and taking naps, so he decided on an honest approach. Honesty meant that he was light on the details. "Oh, it was very restful. Watched a lot of football and ate too much. How was yours? Were the origami turkeys running rampant through the old homestead?"

She giggled girlishly.

"They were everywhere. My mom is crazy, but hilarious. We had a good visit. Seeing everyone is always a good thing. But after a couple of days of togetherness, I was ready to get back to my routine."

"I hear you on that," Nick replied. He noticed the gold cross she wore on the outside of the hoodie. It was the same cross that he had seen her wear before. In fact, Nick really couldn't remember a time that she wasn't wearing it. The gold of the cross complemented the embroidered green Notre Dame logo beneath it.

"A Notre Dame fan I am guessing?"

"Oh, yes. Big time," she said with a twinkle in her brown eyes. "Lifelong fans. Living only a couple hours away, my Dad would bring the whole family to a game every year. Plus that's where I did my graduate work. So it's sort of in my DNA. My mom and dad both come from large Irish families. The whole clan really enjoys their sports."

"I see," Nick replied with a bemused look on his face. "I'll have to remember to keep the Irish jokes to a minimum around you. And I won't hold the Notre Dame thing against you either."

"Okay, funny guy," she said with a half-smile. "Just giving you a fair warning that you don't want to challenge me in anything competitive. I was a pretty good athlete growing up. I was a pretty good softball player a few years ago."

"Really? What position?"

"Third base," she replied. "Had a strong arm."

"I'll be on my best behavior, so you won't throw anything at me."

Katie laughed and adjusted her glasses.

"That would be a smart thing to remember. Anyway, tell me, what are we looking at today?"

Nick fumbled awkwardly to retrieve the plastic bag from his coat pocket, and handed it to her.

"I have some steel samples from a bridge project that I wanted to study. I want to find out more about the physical and mechanical properties of the steel. You see that there is a fair amount of corrosion and I thought you might be able to tell me more about that."

Katie slipped on a pair of latex gloves and opened the bag. With the deft touch of someone familiar with lab work, she pulled the pieces out one by one and laid them on a table. The chemist clicked on the lamp of an industrial magnifying glass and slowly positioned the eyepiece over the sample. Nick knew why she wore her hair back today as she began to peer through the eyepiece.

"This only has a three hundred times magnification, but it will let me see the irregularities on the surface."

She took the first sample off the glass and replaced it with the second sample. "These edges have been machine-cut. You can tell by the pattern of grooves on the sides."

Nick edged up behind her attempting to see what she plainly saw.

"Really? I wasn't involved in getting the samples."

She felt his presence over her shoulder, which would usually bother her when she worked. Today Katie wasn't bothered by his closeness.

"Probably an industrial saw, diamond-tipped blade. Running at 4000 rpm, I suppose," she said.

A surprised look arched across Nick's face.

"I didn't know you were a chemist *and* a machinist," he said.

Turning partially around, she looked at him over her shoulder. She adjusted her glasses.

"I am full of surprises, Nick. When I was growing up, we had a workshop in the garage behind our house. My dad would do woodworking, appliance repairs, metal work. A bunch of different things. I spent a lot of time out there. It was a great way to grow up."

"I bet it was," said Nick in a wistful tone. Katie's childhood sounded much different than his – that was for sure. He hoped that she wouldn't ask him about his past.

"Now…this is interesting. There is some type of paint coating the top and bottom of each sample," she said. She took a small metal probe to scrape the surface of the coating and said, "Appears to be rather fresh as well."

Nick hunched over her shoulder and couldn't help but catch a lavender scent from her hair. Struggling to stay focused, he cleared his throat.

"Yes. I believe contractors painted the bridge recently."

Katie continued to pick and probe at the samples and finally clicked off the lamp. Nick watched her fingers work with a precision that came with many years spent in a lab. She turned, her shoulder almost bumping into Nick's face.

"Oops, excuse me. I didn't know that you were so close."

"No, I'm sorry," said Nick, his face turning red as he backed up.

"Well, I guess it's like I told you the other day. I can do several tests which will give you more information about the composition of the samples. The scanning electron microscope will give us a close look at it, but there's a little bit of prep that I have to do. Same with the spectral analysis. Between the two it should give you information on the corrosion products and also the coating."

"That sounds good. What's the next step? What do you want me to do?" asked Nick.

"Well, the prep is a one-woman show. I need to prepare the specimens and then run the tests. Should take me several hours to finish. It will be boring for you standing around here. Didn't you tell me that there was some testing you wanted to do on the samples also?"

Nick looked at the wisps of black hair not caught by her ponytail and knew the last thing he would feel being in Katie's company was bored.

"Yes, I did want to do some strength and hardness testing on these also," replied Nick.

He knew that separating their tasks was the efficient thing to do although he did not want to spend the afternoon away from her. He exhaled audibly and with a tinge of reluctance.

"I could go over to the Technology Building and do those while you stay here and run your tests."

The young chemistry professor couldn't resist the opportunity to tease Nick.

"Sounds like we've been together for ten minutes and already you are in a hurry to leave," said Katie stoically. "Was it something I said?"

"Well, I just thought that…"

Katie laughed, which caused her ponytail to bobble from side to side.

"Just kidding, just kidding. That's what I was also thinking. Here, take a couple of the samples for your tests but realize that you owe me."

An impish smile flashed across her face, causing Nick to laugh as he picked up two samples from the table.

"Oh, I owe you. Believe me, I owe you big time."

"That's right. Big time. Don't you forget it."

Nick knew he wouldn't forget and felt a surge of energy roll through his sleep-deprived body. It felt good working with her, and he felt closer to having some closure on the bridge collapse. More importantly, he also felt that he was moving forward no matter what the results would show. He remembered when Joe had scolded him about living in the past. Now he was moving forward with his life. Things seemed to be working out for him. He liked his new job – the teaching, the students, the college, and Katie. Isolated for so long he wasn't sure what Katie actually thought about him, but he was happy that they were here today.

"I won't forget. I'll surprise you."

"I'll hold you to that," she said.

Nick smiled.

"Okay. I'll see you in a couple of hours."

Placing the remaining samples in his pocket, he turned and headed for the Technology Building.

41

The swinging hammer of the Charpy testing machine made a loud sound as it impacted a rectangular steel sample from the U10 gusset plate. The odd-looking Charpy tester consisted of a black metal box at the end of a three-foot long metal tube with a hardened steel bolt connecting it to the top of the machine. The hammer was lifted and locked into position as a sample was placed into the anvil at the bottom of the device. Once ready, the sixty-pound hammer, released by pulling the lever, fell along its arc striking the sample. The energy dissipated as the hammer impacted the sample would allow an operator to take a reading and determine the toughness of the steel.

The latest impact broke the sample completely and sent two pieces rattling across the concrete floor until they bounced off the protective cage that surrounded the machine. Nick looked at the digital clock on the wall of the lab and realized he had been here for more than two hours. It also told him that the temperature in the lab was 75° Fahrenheit, which was one reason his jacket rested on the desk. He stepped over some extension cords to retrieve the broken pieces. Picking up the pieces, he rubbed the steel sample noticing the smooth texture of the fractured surfaces, which reminded him of fine sandpaper, maybe something on the order of a two-hundred grit. He pulled a small flashlight off the table and studied the sample under its light. Its smoothness told Nick that it had broken in a brittle fashion. The dial on the Charpy tester would reveal that the sample had absorbed very little energy. Nick stepped back across the extension cords and bent down to read the black numbers off of the silver metallic dial on the testing machine.

Five foot-pounds.

Nick stood up and blinked his eyes several times before bending over and reading the dial one more time to confirm his reading.

Five foot-pounds.

"What the hell," mumbled Nick to himself.

He pondered the ramifications of such a low reading. Toughness, among other things, was particularly important in steel bridges because it indicated how fast a crack, once started, would grow. Back in college, he remembered how federal authorities required all steel to have a specified minimum level of toughness due to a bridge collapse in West Virginia back in the 1960s. It had been years since Nick had reviewed the federal specifications, but he knew that the minimum level of fracture toughness had to be at least 20 foot-pounds. Steel with a reading of five foot-pounds was extremely susceptible to brittle fracture. His pupils dilated as the implications of such a low reading settled in. Once the crack had formed in the steel U10 gusset plate, there would have been almost nothing to prevent it from ripping completely through the plate.

Hoping that the sample was an outlier, Nick picked up a second sample and reached down to lift the pendulum hammer into place. Nick groaned, and his shoulder barked with pain as he pushed the hammer up to its locking position. The Charpy tester was a good work-out for a twenty-two-year-old, much more so for a forty-seven-year-old with a bad shoulder. A loud click finally signaled that the hammer was locked. Wiping a few beads of sweat from his forehead, Nick knelt down and placed the second sample into the anvil at the bottom of the tester. Fixing the needle on the dial to the zero, he gripped the lever and, with a quick pull, released the hammer. A metallic thud was followed by two pieces of steel tumbling across the concrete floor until they came to rest after hitting the protective cage. Nick paused for a moment before turning his gaze to the dial.

Three foot-pounds.

"Shit," he said out loud to no one in the empty lab.

He walked over to retrieve the pieces when he stopped in mid-stride as he looked at the digital clock again. He wasn't watching the time on the clock but instead the temperature.

75° Fahrenheit.

The red needle on the silver dial still stood where it had seconds before – three-foot pounds. This piece of data was more alarming as Nick realized that it was reading three foot-pounds in a room that was 75° Fahrenheit. The toughness of steel is sensitive to temperature changes. Low temperatures can cause a drastic reduction of toughness of steel. He again thought back to the bridge failure in West Virginia, which had occurred during a cold December day, and the linkage between the brittle failure of the bridge and those cold temperatures. Nick shivered as if he was bracing himself against a cold wind from long ago. If the steel samples from the Minneapolis bridge showed almost no toughness in the warm confines of the laboratory, how would it have fared on a cold winter morning? He began to collect his items from the table.

A gust of wind caused Nick to tuck his chin down inside his coat, a reminder that winter was approaching quickly even if the calendar said it was still autumn for another month. The keys in his pocket jingled as he quickly cut across the brownish-yellow grass that had quit growing weeks ago. As his boots crunched over the dormant carpet of grass, he was both excited and disturbed about what he had found in the lab today. The sense of proximity to an answer about the bridge collapse had never been greater, and an answer would go a long way towards repaying the debt that he owed to his friend. Tempering his excitement was a fear of the extremely low toughness values. It didn't make sense to him that the steel in the Minneapolis bridge could have existed for decades with such toughness values. Particularly in the cold climate of Minnesota. He knew that mill tests and other documentation required by transportation officials certainly would have stopped construction of the bridge if the steel was defective in some manner.

What changed?

He hoped that maybe Katie would have some answers for him. As he approached the Science Building, he looked at the far right door expecting it to be propped open with the rubber door stop. He frowned upon finding it closed. Instinctively he pulled on the handle thinking maybe it was unlocked. It wasn't.

Maybe she went out to grab a bite to eat or to get something from her car.

Nick glanced at the three other doors of the building, but none of them were propped open either. He reached for his wallet, but felt only an empty pocket. Turning up the collar of his coat, Nick pulled out his cell phone and searched for her in his contact list. Scrolling down, he highlighted her name and pushed the call button. The phone rang, and Nick's anticipation grew. Then it rang a second, third, and fourth time before going to her voicemail.

He paced back and forth in front of the Science Building hoping that his constant movement would help ward off the chilling effect of the northwest winds. The coldness in his hands began to sting so he proceeded to take part in the familiar ritual of shoving his hands into his pockets, pulling them out to blow on them, and rubbing them together. Nick's anticipation of seeing Katie again and hearing what she had found seemed to make time pass more slowly, and make the winds blow harder. He expected to see her walking over the Commons at any time but disappointment set in as the minutes passed. Finally, the cold got the best of him, and he decided to walk around the building to the loading dock, hoping that maybe she would be out there for some reason.

As he walked down the steps and looped around the side of the Science Building, Nick glanced into the classrooms on each level. The classrooms in this part of the campus all had a cookie-cutter type of design to them. Each had the same layout, same style of chairs, and the same computer equipment in them. He had learned early in his first semester that every room had its issues – not enough chairs, broken computers, too hot or too cold, and the occasional stench of poor plumbing from the adjacent restrooms. He remembered it hadn't taken him long to realize that having a restroom right next to your classroom is not necessarily a good thing.

Slightly out of breath, Nick finally turned the corner and walked up the loading dock steps. Three large metal overhead garage doors there were painted white with the blue and gold WCC logo in the center of each. Nick walked past each of these knowing they would be operated from the inside and couldn't be pulled up by hand. Instead, he walked past the garage doors to a gray metal entry door with a sign posted on it that read 'Authorized Personnel Only.' The cold from the door handle seemed to burn Nick's hand as he pulled it towards his body. It didn't move. Pissed and frustrated, Nick grabbed the handle again and yanked on it – hard. A jolt of pain shot through Nick's shoulder as the resistance of the locked door introduced itself to the inflamed capsule of his rotator cuff. Doubled over and waiting for the pain to subside, Nick released the handle and gathered himself by taking several long breaths.

Nick considered making his way around to the front of the building. As he turned around, his eyes caught a glint from something behind the small dumpster used for paper recycling. With his shoulder still barking from his unsuccessful attempt to open the last door, he trudged over to investigate. The recycling dumpster appeared to be flush against the brick exterior wall of the loading dock, but as he approached, Nick noticed that it was angled out. As he walked around the dumpster his spirits lifted when he saw another glazed exterior door. Nick gripped the door knob, sticky with what he hoped was just grease, and began to turn it carefully. Pulling gently, Nick felt a wave of satisfaction as it disengaged from the door frame and opened.

"Finally," Nick said under his breath as he swung the door open until it hit the dumpster.

He walked in and shut the door behind him. Daylight streamed through the door's glass and illuminated the room with a dusty light revealing a maze of carts and boxes strewn haphazardly across the floor. Gray metal shelves lined each wall and contained bathroom supplies – toilet paper, liquid soap, paper towels – as well as a collection of miscellaneous building supplies. On the right side of the room was a collection of paper towel dispensers, air duct diffusers and even several ceramic sinks. The light began to fade as he walked farther into the room. Even in the fading light, he could still make out items – a snow shovel here, some handrails there, a tool box sitting alone on the bottom shelf. Converted into the building's dumping ground for everything that someone wanted out of sight, Nick figured that this space was originally a janitorial closet.

Taking smaller steps, Nick tip-toed over several PVC pipes that stretched across the floor until he made it to a door on the wall in front of him. Reaching out and fumbling with the door handle for a moment, he turned it and stepped into a darkened hallway.

He paused for a moment trying to remember where Katie's lab was in relation to his current position. He knew he was in the southeast corner of the building but he had entered on the dock, so did that make this the basement or some other level of the building? Lights were turned on at the west end of the hallway, and that made his decision easier as he turned and walked toward the yellowish white fluorescent lighting that was about eighty feet away.

Reaching that intersection, he saw the burgundy-colored sign affixed to the crème-colored block wall.

Classrooms 006, 008 →
Classrooms 011, 013 ↑
Biology Lab ↓
Chemistry Lab ↓

The hollow clomping of his boots echoed up the long but lighted corridor. The ceiling tiles showed signs of age as evidenced by the presence of water stains. A step ladder was propped up against the wall under an area of missing tiles to his right. A pipe wrench and a flashlight sat on top of the ladder, probably forgotten by the maintenance staff in their rush to get out and celebrate the long holiday weekend.

The crème-colored block walls changed to blue at an intersecting hallway on the right. The hallway was dark except for the left side, which held rectangular observation windows to allow viewing of the space below.

Although the corridor was semi-dark, Nick could make out the writing on the directional sign about ten feet away.

Classrooms 020, 022 ↑
Biology Lab ↓
Chemistry Lab ↓

The down arrow meant that the dock entrance must have put him on an upper sub-level of the basement and that Katie's lab must be a level down. The warmth of the building and the anticipation of seeing Katie helped him forget about his shoulder.

The light from the observation windows provided some light as Nick walked down the hallway looking for the stairwell that would take him down a level. Glancing through the viewing windows, he looked down at a large lab with chrome-plated cases lining the walls, and black plastic drapes running the full length of the south wall. Colleges were good at partitioning large areas into multiple spaces to be able to schedule more lab sections and accommodate more students. At the center of the first lab area was a metallic rectangular table similar, Nick thought, to an operating table in a hospital. The table was surrounded by carts, some containing metal pans with instruments, while others held towels and a spider web of plastic tubing. Nick continued down the hall, past the black plastic partition, and came to the second area, which was set up similar to the first. Refrigerated cases along the wall, table in the middle, carts with a scattering of equipment. Nick assumed he was seeing the dissection lab and his stomach turned at simply seeing the word *dissection*. The memory of the formaldehyde-soaked baby pig in his seventh-grade science class still made him queasy today. At thirteen years old he didn't know what he wanted as far as a career choice, but he certainly knew that it wouldn't involve anything to do with cutting into flesh.

Still looking for the stairwell, Nick continued. Walking past the second black partition, he glanced down into the biology lab when he felt his heart skip several beats. Katie was there.

Nick stood there as his eyes sent messages to his brain. Messages that he had difficulty processing. Katie was lying on the table with her feet crossed and both arms outstretched and bound by a leather strap. The strap on her right arm looped around her neck and then traveled on to secure her left arm to the table. A man stood over her holding a large knife whose tip was pointing over the Notre Dame emblem on her hoodie. Nick stood there for what seemed to be hours. In reality, it was only a couple of seconds.

He turned and ran back down the hallway.

Running down the hall, Nick could not feel his feet hitting the floor. In his panic, his feet seemed disconnected from his body. Looking for the stairwell down to the lower level, he turned a corner and saw the faint lettering of the sign above the doorway.

Biology Lab ↓
Chemistry Lab ↓

As his hand reached for the door handle, he saw the step ladder he had passed earlier and instinctively snatched the pipe wrench perched on top of it. Scampering down the steps, he became aware of the noise of his footsteps echoing off the concrete block walls. His concern over the noise was only fleeting as his sole focus was to get to the biology lab.

42

Saturday November 24, 2007
5:00 P.M.
Winchester, Kentucky

Fayad Yassim's black eyes stared at Katie as he rested the blade of his knife on her throat and placed his hand over the cloth gag in her mouth.

"Scream and you are dead," he calmly said. "Answer my questions, and you live. Understand?"

Katie's brown eyes were locked on her captor as she gave a slight nod. She didn't remember leaving the chemistry lab when everything went black, but realized from the surroundings that she was in one of the biology pods. The left side of her head throbbed. As her captor yanked the gag from her mouth, she willed herself not to retch as the cold air from the biology lab replaced the sickening taste of the gag.

Fayad leaned in so that Katie could feel the heat of his breath as he spoke. He held the plastic bag of steel samples up in front of her.

"These samples. Why do you have these?"

She sought to control the questions racing through her mind.

What is happening? Why is he here? How does he know what I was doing with the samples?

Although she could feel the flat side of the blade on her throat, the fogginess from being knocked out cold prevented her from processing his question.

"What do you want?"

He pressed the flat edge of the blade into her throat, turning her white skin even whiter around the edges of the blade.

"Listen to me. Why do you have these samples?"

The fear caused by the additional pressure on her throat seemed to clear her mind quickly. Katie became aware that the side of her head, behind her right ear, felt damp and sticky.

"A friend here at the college. He asked me to look at these." She swallowed hard as if the words hurt. "He wanted to study the cracking and corrosion."

However, the mention of corrosion was all he needed to confirm before he commenced with tying up some loose ends. He guessed that the young chemist had found evidence of the XT-001 coating used on the Minneapolis bridge. Still, he wanted to know more about why the college professors were involved.

"And what did you find?"

Katie paused, waiting to string her thoughts together through the pain in her head. Her hesitation was long enough to be both noticeable and irritating to her captor. Fayad pivoted the knife on her throat so that the edge was pressing down onto her flesh.

"I was looking at the samples on the electron microscope. Finding areas of corrosion at the crack boundaries."

Fayad released some of the pressure on the knife, and he could see small droplets of blood appearing on her throat.

"Go on. What else?"

Katie also felt the sensation of a warm droplet of liquid slowly running down the side of her neck.

"The cracking seemed to be caused by an aggressive form of stress corrosion. I found some evidence of hydrogen that was in the samples. Sometimes corrosion is caused by the diffusion of hydrogen."

Katie took a breath and exhaled quickly. Her head hurt even more now, and she decided it was time for a lie.

"But I am not really an expert in that area."

Fayad's brow wrinkled at his complete ignorance of the science that she humbly said she didn't fully understand.

"Okay," grunted Fayad pulling the knife away from her throat, "why are you working with the other professor?"

Preoccupied with the shock of being tied up at knifepoint, Katie had not thought about Nick since she had regained consciousness. Now her captor's question snapped her thoughts back to Nick and what she knew, or maybe didn't know, about him.

"He is just another teacher I know here at the college. He's from the Technology Department a couple of buildings over."

"What did he tell you about the samples? Where is he?"

Katie didn't know much about the samples that Nick had given her. Being helpful was just part of her nature. She found it easy to be helpful when it came to Nick as she found him interesting, or different, to say the least. Learning about someone takes time, as they let you see what they want you to see a little at a time. She had only known Nick for a few months, but her radar was telling her that he was someone worth trusting. Still, lying here bound to a table with a bearded man holding a knife to her throat, she wondered if she knew less about him than she thought. Even with doubt creeping into her mind, she decided that being helpful in this instance wasn't going to happen.

"He said that they were from some project and that he was interested in the steel. He gave me the samples earlier today, and I told him I would have results next week. I don't know anything more than that – you have to believe me," said Katie.

She hoped that he really wouldn't ask any follow-up questions.

Fayad rubbed his beard, still pondering why these two community college professors had inserted themselves into his company's plans to use the XT-001 coating. The young chemistry professor gave answers that seemed believable. Maybe that was all she really knew. Maybe it was the other teacher he needed to find. He looked at her and gripped the knife more firmly. It was unfortunate for her that she represented a complication. A complication he needed to fix. A coldness made its way across Fayad's face as he prepared himself to do what he'd known long before ever stepping foot onto campus he would do – anyone he met would not be leaving alive. Her knowledge of the samples was too much of a risk, and the people he worked for could not take the chance of their plans unraveling. He knew what they were capable of doing to anyone including him.

His work with Einfall AG was finally on the verge of striking a blow to America. A blow that they did not see coming. The thought of achieving victory over the great Satan sent adrenaline coursing through his veins and replaced the coldness in his face with a warm grin.

He liked killing, although he hated the thought of wasting such a beautiful woman like the one sprawled out in front of him. The ropes that wrapped around Katie's wrists rubbed her skin raw, and he liked that. He could feel his heart beat faster as he looked at the drops of blood slowly pooled in the shallow cut his knife had made in her throat. The rope around her left wrist framed a vintage charm bracelet she was wearing with a "K" hanging from it. Fayad's eyes fixed upon the gold cross and chain that hung askew from Katie's neck as he slipped the knife under her hoodie and placed the blade between her breasts.

"Tell me...do you pray right now? Who to? Will he come and save you?"

The state of clarity that she had willed herself into evaporated instantaneously as her body convulsed in anger.

"Go fuck yourself," she screamed as she jerked violently at her restraints.

"Keep screaming while you still can," growled Fayad as he tilted his knife upward and pulled it towards him, slicing through the Notre Dame emblem on her hoodie. He pulled open the two halves of the hoodie and ran the knife slowly from her chest to her navel. He backed away from the table and looked at Katie straining in violent but futile convulsions. He took the bag of samples and threw them on the ground before slipping off his pants and climbing on top of her. He squeezed her breasts and put the knife blade to her throat. Once again she could feel the stench of his breath.

"You'll like it, I promise. It will be the last thing you will ever enjoy."

"Get off me, you fucker, get off," she yelled, arching up her back to resist the weight of his body. Her mind raced as she felt his hands clamp around her throat and squeeze hard. Her airway closed, she gasped for air feeling her resistance fade as her lungs burned. Her eyes closed when he suddenly he pulled his hands away and landed his fist above her right ear. Fayad then slid off of her to the side of the table.

"You didn't want me to kill you just yet, did you?"

Katie's eyes were closed as she let out a feeble gasp. She could feel him unbuttoning her jeans and tugging them down. Reflexively she pulled as hard as she could at her restraints with what strength she had left. Unable to free her hands, she bit her lip and with what little consciousness she had, hoped it would be over soon. In her mind, she saw an image of her family and asked God to watch over them. She could feel her jeans slip down around her knees.

It will be over soon.

A dull crack followed by a louder thud interrupted her prayer. Her right eye opened part way and then her left. Nick stood over her captor trembling with a pipe wrench still in hand.

His eyes locked on hers as he stepped over Fayad's body and bent down so that his face was next to hers. His arms trembled, and a burden of guilt seemed to be preventing any words from coming out of his mouth.

"Oh, Katie. Are you okay?"

"Okay," she mumbled as tears flowed from her eyes. "I'm, okay."

Although her words were reassuring, the sight of his battered colleague quivering in front of him was not. Thinking that she might be going into shock, he reached down to hold her. After several seconds he told himself to act calmly and focus on the task at hand.

"Let's get you out of here," he said as he turned around and retrieved the knife and the bag of samples lying on the floor next to the motionless body. He cut through the rope on each hand and helped Katie sit up, pulling the ripped hoodie together as she continued to shake.

"I think I'm going to get sick," she said.

43

Saturday November 24, 2007
8:30 P.M.
Over the Atlantic
Jarireh Reza looked intensely as the lights of New York glimmered through the blackness of the night. She enjoyed the hum of the jet engines of the government's 747, and leaned her muscular frame into the over-stuffed leather seat. Her mind wandered back to a little girl who grew up in the North Khorasan province, where her family owned fields of wheat and saffron. Located two hundred kilometers from the city of Mashhad, the family farm was so remote that Jarireh remembered how the stars stood out like diamonds in the night sky. At least that is the way a little girl remembered it.

"We are ready to begin our initial descent. Please fasten your seatbelts. We are expecting some turbulence," crackled the co-pilot's voice over the intercom. "We should be on the ground in thirty minutes."

The instructions brought Jarireh back from her memories as she reached over and clasped the seatbelt around her waist. Pushing her jet black hair over her shoulder, she gazed once more at the cascade of lights drawing closer. The luminescence of the city drowned out the pinpricks of light from the night sky. The volume of New York's light seemed to silently proclaim the power contained within this city, which she was about to visit for the first time.

She fidgeted in her seat trying to resist the temptation to be in awe. This trip did not include sight-seeing, and she could not afford to be sidetracked. A rising star among the military's Special Operations unit, she knew that this was another chance to prove herself to General Assam.

Pockets of turbulence bounced the 747 sporadically, but the young captain barely blinked as she thought about her instructions. As the final descent into JFK began she closed her eyes and felt the plane bank to the right and then level out. As the flaps were raised, the whining of the hydraulics signaled the aircraft's speed was decreasing. She kept her eyes closed and steadied herself for the impact of the plane as it touched down on the runway. Though she had been on hundreds of flights, she still hated the feeling in her stomach as a plane landed. She held her breath and then felt the first bounce. Then the second. Finally, she exhaled as the brakes were applied. They would be at the gate shortly.

She opened her eyes and looked out the window. As the jet taxied to the terminal, she turned on her phone to find a text message from Assam.

> Failed to recover samples at college. Whereabouts are unknown. Need to find.

She arched her back, stretching in an attempt to awaken her body, which was stiff from the long flight. She reached into her purse and retrieved her passport bearing the Iranian diplomatic seal. The job was now a bit more complicated, but her training had prepared her to think on her feet.

44

Sunday November 25, 2007
1:00 P.M.
Winchester, Kentucky

The area rugs in the old farmhouse muffled his footsteps as Nick shuffled softly back to the kitchen to fill his coffee cup. Thankfully the generator had gas in it and had started on the first try. That gave the farmhouse electricity, at least in intervals, making it possible for several space heaters to warm the house. The electric generator allowed him to turn on the coffee pot, which coupled with the good fortune of finding coffee and filters in the cabinet, had provided the hot beverage in front of him. At least the coffee seemed to bring a small sense of normalcy to his frayed nerves.

Balancing the cup in his hands, Nick stepped over areas of the floor that were prone to creaking, trying not to disturb Katie, who was still sleeping in the adjoining room. Etched with concern over the trauma she had experienced in the lab, the lines on Nick's forehead seemed permanent. Draped in his fleece jacket, she had barely seemed coherent yesterday as they drove away from campus. He'd been convinced that she was in shock shortly after he had placed her in his car, and she had remained quiet except for mumbling something about the samples before falling off into a disturbed sleep.

Nick worried about what to do next. When he had driven away from the college, he'd considered going to the police and reporting Katie's assault. But what was it really all about? It didn't make sense to him that someone would just drift into campus on a holiday weekend and happen to find and attack his young friend. And why was her attacker interested in the samples? How could anyone even know anything about the samples? What would he tell the police about the samples anyway? The police might be interested in the samples as well. The small detail of how a person, recently released from a long jail sentence, had taken evidence from a federal investigation might be hard to explain. It might also be hard to explain how he had just beaten a man senseless with a pipe wrench.

Felon steals federal property and whacks guy in head — no red flags there.

Nick knew that the scales of justice didn't always seem to consider the entirety of the situation. The option of going to the farmhouse seemed prudent, at least until he had a few more answers or a little more time to think.

He stood at the kitchen sink and looked out the window at the white-gray clouds that rolled into the valley from the northwest. The events of yesterday seemed like a fog in his mind, revealing an outline but no detail. The rustic farmhouse gave him a sense of security which comforted him for the moment. The place had been in Joe's family for decades, and from the looks of things probably hadn't been stepped in for a year. Nick had good memories here. Hunting weekends where the two engineers had discussed everything under the sun. Its placement off State Route 57, north of Clintonville, provided only one access point from the main road. Flanked by a dense stand of old growth hickory, maple, and oak trees, the forest blanketed the house in secrecy from the outside world. If someone was looking for them, that person would be looking a long time before he or she got here.

As Nick looked out the window, he tried again to piece together yesterday's events: The testing, Katie, her attacker — when a streak of color caught his eye. He smiled as he watched two cardinals, a red-colored male, and a greenish colored female twitter back and forth on top of a stack of firewood. He appreciated their persistence in the face of the oncoming winter to stay and not head south.

"Nick?"

Nick's heart seemed to shake in his chest as he spun around to see his young colleague standing there still wrapped in his fleece jacket. Strands of her long black hair were matted down on the side of her head where Nick had applied an ice bag last night. Nick was happy to be seeing her awake.

"God, Katie, how are you feeling? I was worried about you," Nick said as he walked across the kitchen.

"Well, I could be better....but I guess I could be worse too. Where are we?"

"I brought us to a friend's house in the country. I didn't know what to do. I thought it would be safe here."

Katie's brow furrowed as she tried to shake the haze of having been in bed for fourteen hours. The contracting of her facial muscles caused the side of her head to ache from the swelling.

"Ow, that still hurts."

"I put ice on that and woke you up every couple of hours just to make sure you were okay. Everything looked normal, but if you don't start feeling better we might want to get you to the hospital today," declared Nick.

He walked over to the counter, opened a drawer, and found a bottle of Advil. He shook out two pills and handed them to her with a bottle of water.

"Why didn't I go to the hospital *last night*?" asked Katie.

She popped the pills into her mouth. The charm bracelet around her left wrist danced in cadence with the motion of her arm.

"Well, I didn't know what was going on, and I really didn't know what to do. You were more or less out of it, but you did say something about being asked about the samples. I didn't know if that was the only person in the lab yesterday. I didn't know what was happening and I just didn't want to take any chances."

Katie cautiously made her way to the kitchen table and sat down. Nick's words caused the ugly memories of yesterday to seep back into her mind.

"I do remember him asking about the samples. Why would he be asking about that? I thought you said they came from a project you were working on, right?"

Nick watched her dark eyes lock onto him for the first time today. She seemed to be waiting for him to say that it was all some big mistake. He swallowed hard as if the guilt of getting her involved, of almost getting her killed, choked back any explanation. He had felt alone for so many years, and landing at the college had given him a chance at a new beginning. But the blank slate that WCC had offered him had been disrupted by Joe's death. Maybe the slate was never really swept clean. He swallowed hard a second time.

"I don't know who the guy in the lab was or what he wanted. But, I have to tell you some things about me. Yes, I got the samples for a friend. A great friend of mine who helped me in some of the worst times of my life. I am probably going to tell you more than you want to know about me. I don't know how it will make you feel about me but..."

Nick sat down across from her and told her his story. Fifteen years in jail for killing a mother and her daughter in a drunken blackout. The years spent living with the guilt of his actions. The kindness of his friend who had searched him out and supported him even when he didn't want any help. The feelings of worthlessness and despair followed by Joe's counsel. His emotional rehabilitation. Getting the teaching position at WCC. The temptation he had faced after Joe's death to find comfort in drinking again. His mission to find the answers to the bridge collapse, a mission which was keeping him from failing again.

Nick swept his hands through his hair and exhaled deeply as if expelling a poison from his body. The catharsis of telling the story provided him relief but not enough to remove his anxiety about how Katie was receiving it.

She sat and listened politely, nodding her head at various times, and uttering an "oh dear" at different points in Nick's explanation. When he finished, she gazed down at her hands, which were folded together resting on the table. Nick sat there silently as if the silence would help her absorb the pieces of his life which he had laid bare before her.

"Katie, I was telling you the truth. The samples were from a project I was working on for a friend. The samples were not given to me – I found them in a warehouse. I probably should not have done that, but sometimes the real story is twisted, changed or covered up. I really wanted to…"

"Make sure that wasn't happening here," interrupted Katie, finishing his sentence. "You felt that finding out the truth about what happened would repay him for all that he did for you."

Nick's eyes were damp, and now he was the one whose gaze was directed down at the table. He hadn't told her the story of the Cincinnati collapse nor how the report had omitted what he thought were crucial facts, instead placing all of the blame squarely on him. That was another chapter of the Nick Kremer story that he would share with her one day, but at this point, it really did not matter.

"That's right, to repay him. He would want to know what really happened," choked Nick, his voice trembling.

Katie reached over the table and put her hand on his. Her touch made him feel vulnerable and safe at the same time. Remembering Joe's advice not to dwell on the past but to look forward to the opportunities that are right here, right now rang true at this moment. Focusing on the future helped him find a friend in Katie Walsh. Perhaps their work together was about more than just closing a chapter in his life, maybe it was about something else. He stared at her and smiled as she slowly brushed some of her black hair over her shoulder.

"Thanks, Katie. I wish I hadn't gotten you involved in all of this. Whatever this is I am glad that you know about me now. You are really the only person I have left that knows my story."

"Well, I have to say I always thought engineers were boring people. You, however, Mr. Kremer, seem to have broken the proverbial mold. You really know how to show a girl a good time," she replied, rolling her eyes for effect.

"Wait until you see what I have planned for our second date," he replied with a smile.

"Hold on there, Nick. Let's see if we both survive the first date," she laughed.

The laughter sent a bolt of pain through the side of her head.
"Ow."

"I'll get you some more ice," Nick said as he stood up, sliding his hand from underneath hers. He knew that they had other decisions to make, but for the moment he was concentrating on the present.

"Why don't you lie back down and get some more rest. We can talk about what to do a little later."

45

Sunday November 25, 2007
2:00 P.M.
Winchester, Kentucky

Ethan Barstow stood on the step ladder fumbling with the Christmas lights that he was attempting to hang on his front porch. He was under orders from his wife, Mary, to get the outdoor decorations up this weekend before their schedules became crammed with Christmas festivities. The WCC President was glad Mary forced him to stay on top of things as the business of running the college seemed to leave little time to do other things during the work week. After placing the last light onto the last nail, a grimace appeared on his face as his forty-year-old knees balked the descent down the ladder. He shook his head at the irony of a quasi-atheist from Connecticut hanging Christmas lights in the heart of flyover country. Relocating to Central Kentucky had been the next step in his ten-year plan and had checked a requirement in his vitae. University President by the time I am fifty.

"Ethan, how are you doing out there?" asked Mary through a half-opened front door.

Although it was Sunday, Mary was dressed as if she was hosting a photo shoot for the next LL Bean catalog. Her slim figure accentuated her ample bust, which stretched the red cashmere sweater she wore.

Her wardrobe this Sunday was like any other Sunday and gave her the "I live here temporarily" aura. Mary was a perfect partner for an ambitious up-and-coming college administrator. An astute observer of the people, Mary had thrown herself into a plethora of volunteer work – the Winchester Beautification Board, the Association of Helping Hands, the College Scholarship Foundation and several others. Mary believed in community involvement, and she had told Ethan, in no uncertain terms, that it was important to put on a good show for the people of Winchester during the couple's first Christmas here. That meant decorations, hosting parties, and even attending church services at least a couple of times.

"They are up, and they work," Ethan said as his feet finally stood on solid ground. "Am I done?"

"Not a chance," she said as she pushed three boxes of artificial white pine garland out the front door onto the porch. "I need this garland wrapped around the columns, there and there," she said pointing to the columns on each end of the porch. "And the rest of it should get wrapped around the railings in between."

"Really?" replied Ethan in a questioning tone. "Yes, and make it look nice. The Winchester Sun wants to do a story next week on the new college president and his first Christmas in Winchester. I think it would be good for you to say that you did the decorating after they say how good it looks. Or maybe I should say *if* they say that."

"Okay, okay," he replied.

He piled the three boxes on top of each other and trudged over to the far railing. A thought crossed his mind about enlisting the neighborhood kids to decorate next year. His dream faded as he knew Mary would undoubtedly say something about the "bad optics" of paying somebody to do what any full-blooded college president should be happy to do.

The wind picked up, making evenly spacing the garland difficult as he wrapped it around the first porch column. Adjusting it to his satisfaction, he fixed it in place using a roll of packing tape. Starting on the second column, he heard the front door open, and he winced expecting to listen to a critique of his job.

"Dear, the phone in your study keeps ringing. You'd better check it," said Mary as she folded her arms across her chest to protect her from the wind. "It's gone off three times in the last fifteen minutes."

"Okay, thanks."

Although he wanted to finish the task at hand, Ethan was just happy to get out of the wind. He stepped inside, wiping his feet on the doormat and paused for a moment enjoying the warmth of the house. It also gave him a chance to witness the explosion of Christmas knick-knacks, decorations, and artwork that had replaced the traditional décor of their foyer, dining room, and kitchen.

"This is almost enough to get me into the Christmas spirit," he mumbled under his breath.

Walking into his spacious study, he was relieved to see that his print of Monet's "Water Lily Pond" had not been replaced by a picture of Santa. He walked around the mahogany desk and plopped himself in the over-stuffed leather chair. Picking up his phone, he saw that the missed calls were from a 703 area code. He couldn't place the number or the area code but retrieved the new voicemails.

"Hello, President Barstow. My name is Nassir Yassim, with the National Institute of Science and Technology in Washington, D.C. I hate to disturb you on a Sunday, but I have an urgent request. If you could please return my call as soon as possible, I would appreciate it."

Ethan Barstow became intrigued as he listened to the other voicemails repeat the same message. It was not unusual to get calls on the weekend, but they didn't usually originate from outside the college and not from Washington, D.C. His anticipation grew as he hit 'return call' and waited as the other number began ringing.

"Hello."

"Yes, hello. This is Dr. Ethan Barstow from Winchester Community College."

"Yes, Dr. Barstow. My name is Nassir Yassim. I am a director with the National Institute of Science and Technology. Some people refer to us as NIST."

"Yes, I am well aware of your agency."

"Thank you for returning my call," replied the Palestinian, who was sitting at his kitchen table in Virginia. "I know that this is last minute, but we received a request from the United Nations in New York yesterday. I was hoping you could help us out."

The WCC president was already excited about returning a call from D.C., but when he heard "United Nations" and "New York" he sat upright in anticipation of what would come next. "Well, we will certainly try. What is it that I can help you with?"

"We have a delegation from the U.N. interested in developing strategies for use in post-secondary education in technical fields. They are conducting fact-finding trips to a limited number of colleges and universities throughout the country, and the first institution that was scheduled has had to cancel at the last minute. We were hoping that Winchester Community College could take their place."

"Well, that sounds great," declared the WCC president as a smile beamed across his face. He thought that this visit could bolster his credentials and provide another talking point on his next job interview. "What do you need us to do?"

"They want to send out a representative to meet your faculty, tour your facilities, see your campus, etc. They want to focus specifically in the Technology and Science areas. But they want to come tomorrow. I know this is really last minute but do you think you can accommodate that?"

Ethan Barstow smiled, as he knew his programs at the college handled similar requests all the time from politicians, business leaders, and donors. Hosting someone from the U.N. would be a first, but the process would be the same. *Have your best people lead the show, stand back and then take all the credit.*

"I think I can make that happen. There are great things going on here at the college under my administration. We are honored to share them with others."

Nassir shook his head at the consistency of senior management never missing a chance to boast of their successes – real or imagined. Nevertheless, Barstow's acceptance of his request was a great relief.

"Very good, Dr. Barstow. I will email you a tentative itinerary from the U.N. delegate who will be visiting you. I speak on behalf of NIST when I say how deeply we appreciate this. Let me know if you ever need anything from us in the future."

"Oh, I certainly will. Thank you for thinking of Winchester Community College. Do you have my email?"

"Yes, I have it. I will send you the itinerary right now. Thank you again."

Barstow heard the click on the other end and was beaming as he turned to his computer and opened up the browser. He grew impatient waiting for his username and password to be processed by the WCC webmail server. Finally, his inbox opened, and he saw the most recent email. He again waited while the itinerary document opened.

> *UN Delegation at Winchester Community College (Tentative)*
> *8:00 meet at the president's office*
> *8:30 – 9:30 tour the technology facilities*
> *10:00 – 11:00 tour the science facilities*
> *11:30 – 1:00 lunch*

He leaned back in the chair with his hands clasped behind his head. This tour would not be hard to pull off except it was the first day back after the Thanksgiving weekend. He realized if he wanted another highlight on his vitae he needed to make a great impression. With several clicks of the mouse, the WCC president saved the document to his desktop before reaching for a small leather-bound booklet on his desk. It contained his personal directory of key college personnel. He had several calls to make in order to set things up, but his first calls would be to the local TV stations and newspapers in both Winchester and Lexington.

"Never let a chance to promote yourself go to waste," he whispered as he dialed his first number.

Five hundred miles to the east Nassir Yassim sat in his house watching the screen as he made the final few clicks before logging out of his government email.

"Everything is set," he said stoically as if all emotion had drained out of him.

"Yes, it is. Saying you were from NIST was a nice touch. Now you are finished," said an equally unemotional voice from behind.

Two low-pitched pops in quick succession were followed by Nassir's head falling forward and landing on the keyboard. Blood began to fill the two holes in the back of his head and within seconds it started oozing through Nassir's hair and pooling on the kitchen table.

"You can thank your brother for that. Somebody needed to clean up his mess," said the shooter as if offering an explanation to the departed.

Tucking the 9 mm Glock inside her leather jacket, Jarireh Reza picked up the recently delivered samples from the dining room table. Turning around, she rushed through the house and exited through the back door.

46

Sunday November 25, 2007
6:00 P.M.
Winchester, Kentucky

Nick paced around the farmhouse quietly hoping not to disturb Katie. The events of the last week played over and over in his head as he tried to prove or disprove any association among them. The FHWA memo he found concerning the use of the anti-corrosion paint bothered him. Why would they use an anti-corrosion paint on a bridge where previous inspections didn't record any corrosion problems? The timing between finding the memo and taking the samples from the warehouse, and Katie's attack, was hard to shrug off as coincidence. More disturbing was the possibility that the attacker knew that they had the samples and knew where to find them. The longer he thought about this, the happier he was about his decision to come to the farmhouse.

Scratching his day-old stubble, he realized that he probably could use a shower. From his hunting days, he remembered a water heater down in the crawl space that was turned on when they arrived and off when they left. Besides the darkness, the only other obstacle was actually getting his 40-something-year-old body into the crawl space. A cold shower would have to do.

Cold showers and no internet – just like growing up.

He pulled out his cell phone, an off-brand flip phone, and dialed the number to access his WCC voicemail. He was surprised that the cell reception was decent in this area given its remoteness. As he listened to several messages, he slowly composed a text message, the key characteristic of his composition being *slowly*. Texting was a relatively new skill that he was learning, as his clumsy fingers could attest to. Besides the lack of dexterity in his error-prone fingers, there was also the slight problem of his presbyopic eyes, which made it difficult to focus on written words – especially words written on the two-square-inch screen. This required him to hold the phone about a foot away from his face to attempt to review his work.

"We have service up here?"

Nick turned around and saw Katie standing there, and a tinge of embarrassment came over him as he sheepishly hit "send" and closed his phone up nonchalantly. Katie sounded stronger, and her face seemed to have more color than it had several hours ago. Her disheveled hair still had not improved but to Nick just seeing her standing was all he wanted. She could not have looked any better.

"You look like you are feeling better. Yes, the reception is pretty good. I was just checking my messages at the college."

"Is there anything to eat around here?" she asked.

Besides hot water and internet access, food was the one thing in short supply at the farmhouse. Given the events, Nick had not stopped anywhere on the way to the farmhouse and, once there, he had not wanted to leave her alone as she slept. Fortunately, Nick had an answer.

"This must be your lucky day," he replied as he walked over to the stove. Katie's stomach was rumbling in anticipation of what her colleague meant by 'lucky.' Turning around, he walked towards her with his outstretched arms carrying his bounty. His right hand held a bag of snack-size chocolate candy bars, and his left hand a box of chocolate-covered granola bars.

Not the cheeseburger platter she was hoping for, but at least it was something.

"Wow, it *is* my lucky day. I didn't think you knew that I love chocolate!" she said followed by a slight giggle. Her slender hand fished out a granola bar and several candy bars, and she smiled and in an exaggerated tone said, "I hope this weekend never ends."

Nick appreciated her humor after all that had happened in the last day.

"I can tell you are feeling better," he said pulling out a chair for her to sit. "I was really worried." He went over and filled a cup of coffee for her and returned to the table. He watched in silence as she ate her candy and granola bar. Once finished, she slowly drank her coffee.

"You know a woman hates it when a man watches her eat," she said, looking at the cup clasped between her hands.

"I'm sorry," Nick said as he fidgeted in his chair. After what happened seeing you do *anything* makes me feel better."

She glanced up and smiled sincerely at him.

"Thanks. Believe me, I'm glad to be seen."

She took the last sip of coffee from her cup and pulled his fleece jacket tighter around her chest as if trying to keep out a cold wind. "Well, where do we go from here?" she asked.

Nick looked at her and could not help but feel guilty for having gotten her in this situation. The few seconds of silence seemed like minutes before he cleared his throat.

"Well, I think we need to go to the police. I don't know what is really going on here. It seems somebody else is interested in the samples and possibly the bridge. If the samples and bridge are tied together, and somebody knows that we have the samples, I guess going to the police is the best option."

He paused as shadows crept into the farmhouse from the fading daylight outside. A thud on the roof made them both look up and hold their breath in unison, hoping that their stillness would prevent any other unknown sounds from occurring outside.

"It just seems as if something is missing in all this," said Nick.

Katie's eyes grew more intense as she leaned forward in her chair.

"Hold on," she said, trying to pull a memory that was hesitant to be remembered. "The coating, the results from electron scanning and the spectral analysis. The results I found yesterday before…"

"What is it? Did you find something out?"

"Maybe, it's starting to come back to me now. The images from the SEM showed a corrosion boundary in the samples. The boundary had a uniform thickness. It didn't really hit me until just now. These samples came from a bridge so it would seem to me that rusting would occur primarily on the surfaces that were close to the roadway."

"Due to road salt they use to melt the snow and ice."

"Right. Anyway road salt doesn't cause corrosion; it just helps it form faster. Because the salt ions increase the conductivity of the water on the steel's surface."

"Corrosion needs an electric current," said Nick as he leaned forward and cupped his chin in his right hand.

"Correct," replied the young chemistry teacher. "The dissolved salt allows electrons to flow faster from the anodic site to the cathodic site. Electrons are being pulled from where the steel is deteriorating and deposited as rust at the cathodic site. I'm sure you remember all this from engineering school?"

"Geez, that was a long time ago. There's been a lot of water under the bridge since I learned about that."

Nick wasn't kidding about that. His story was a painting that had taken its shape over the canvas of his life. There were a lot of brush strokes behind him now, and the first few seemed harder to remember.

"Okay, I'll slow it down for you. I don't want you getting lost in class now," said Katie with a wink towards her colleague. "Coating the steel would form a protective barrier to at least slow the process down. However, anywhere a coating gets scratched or chipped, a location can form where the salts and water can penetrate and begin to oxidize the iron. And that location is where rusting should start."

"Right, I remember that. So what does that mean?"

"Nick, don't you get it? A bridge has thousands of cars driving across it every day. Conditions are always changing – rain, snow, sun, wind and dozens of other variables. Those conditions are never the same at any two points along the bridge. I mean, you might have some places that stay wet because they are in the shade, some places get more water splashed on them because they are closer to puddles, and other places might get warmer because they have more exposure to the mid-day sun," said Katie as she pushed her glasses higher on the bridge of her nose. "So the thing that finally dawned on me was that the corrosion profile under the protective coating was almost constant. Just about every place I looked, the rust layer was the same," declared the chemistry professor. "I mean almost everywhere."

Nick looked at Katie, his concentration causing his brow to wrinkle above his nose. After a second his eyes grew wider, and he leaned back into his chair throwing his hands behind his head. "You are saying that you would expect the amount of rust to be non-uniform with so many variables in the corrosion process."

"You would think so, wouldn't you?" asked Katie.

Pausing for another moment, Nick posed the obvious question.

"Why would it occur like that?'

"That's the million-dollar question," said Katie, running her hand through her black hair. "Remember I said that corrosion profile was uniform almost everywhere. So I thought I would look for areas of the samples where there was almost no corrosion. Guess what I found."

"What?"

"The sides of the samples which *didn't* have the coating had no corrosion."

Nick rocked forward in his chair and then stood up as if the change of position would help him process Katie's information.

"So you're saying the coating *caused* the corrosion?"

"They seem to be correlated, Nick. My friends that teach statistics have a mantra – correlation doesn't mean causation. So I don't want to say it caused the corrosion, but it seems really suspicious."

Nick's mind spun trying to piece together the information so he could see the big picture. Previous inspection reports had indicated no problems with corrosion of the bridge and yet the FHWA had allowed a special coating to be used. Now it seemed there was corrosion only where the coating was applied.

"Okay, I don't want to piss your statistics people off but let's say the coating and the corrosion are linked together. I don't understand how a protective barrier, a coating, could cause corrosion. I mean how would that even be possible?"

Katie fumbled with her now-empty coffee cup. "Well, again, I am not a hundred percent certain, but the spectral analysis of the samples showed a large amount of diffused hydrogen in the steel below the corrosion boundary."

"Diffused hydrogen. Got it. And what does that mean?"

"Well diffused hydrogen in steel can lead to a condition called embrittlement. Basically, free hydrogen atoms make their way into steel causing it to lose toughness and strength. In some cases, this embrittlement actually causes cracking in steel."

"Are you sure you can say it causes cracking," smirked Nick.

"Okay, Mr. Funny Guy, your point is taken. Typically you worry about hydrogen diffusion as steel is being produced or processed. Quality control procedures are typically in place that would identify excess hydrogen in production, so chances are extremely small that steel could be shipped out with high levels of hydrogen. Plus this bridge has been around for quite some time," said Katie, still smiling at his wisecrack.

"It has been there since the '60s."

Nick's face became serious as several pieces of the puzzle snapped into place.

"You know, my testing of the steel showed greatly decreased values of hardness and yield strength. I mean on the order of thirty percent below what you would expect for that grade of steel. I can't believe that the bridge could function properly over all those years with such poor strength values. So your theory makes some sense."

A silence fell between them as each processed what was being said. Finally, Katie leaned forward.

"So, if it is a case of hydrogen embrittlement then I guess we have to ask ourselves, where did the hydrogen come from?"

"And the answer is?" asked Nick walking closer.

Katie stood up from the kitchen table and began to pace.

"There could be several possibilities. Strong acids could, in some conditions, create enough free hydrogen to do it," answered Katie.

"Now you lost me," said Nick. "First you were talking about free hydrogen getting into the steel and then you are talking about an acid. How do those go together?"

"Acids are found everywhere, and all acids contain hydrogen. They have other stuff too, but they all contain hydrogen. Given the right conditions, an acid can release hydrogen ions. For instance, sulfuric acid is made up of hydrogen, sulfur, and oxygen. If a reaction takes place, you can easily split off hydrogen atoms, freeing them to do whatever."

She looked at Nick and knew that he would just have to take some of this on faith.

Although Nick was not well-versed anymore in chemistry, his mind was trained to follow the logic. "But there has to be a special condition present or this freeing of hydrogen would be happening all the time," he said, searching for understanding.

"That is right, Nick. This doesn't happen all the time. In fact, it's pretty rare. But the analysis did show high levels of hydrogen in the steel. But there is something else that the SEM imaging showed as well."

"What was that?"

The chemist in Katie shied away from speculation. However, recent events made her think that the scientific method might have some limitations when somebody was trying to kill you. The wind whistled through cracks in the frame of the old farmhouse and Katie pulled the fleece jacket tighter around her chest.

"The scanning showed something else at the interface between the coating and the corrosion layer. There is another substance underneath the coating."

"Another substance?"

"I took a scraping of it and put it on a slide and looked at it under a microscope. It's some type of biological or microbial film," answered Katie. "I don't know much more than that. That is the last thing I was looking at before …"

She looked away from Nick, and he understood there was no need to finish the sentence. After a few moments, she continued.

"It would have to be tested but probably is some type of bacteria I assume."

"So it's a safe assumption to think that this is not normal."

Katie gave him a half smile.

"Normal just doesn't seem to follow you around, Nick."

"Tell me about it," he replied.

He stood up and walked over to the window over the kitchen sink. He looked at the dark outlines of the tree-tops being whipped back and forth by the wind.

"So why is this film there? What does it have to do with the samples?"

Katie sighed and exhaled, shaking her head. "I don't really know. Not with any certainty."

He turned and looked back at her.

"I think the certainty ship has already sailed, Katie. I know the science gods always want hard proof, but I think we need to consider all possibilities now. It's my fault that you are involved in this, and I just need to figure this out to keep you safe."

He walked over and held her hands looking into her dark eyes. She smiled softly as the heat from his hands made her feel safe.

"Well, don't tell the science gods about this but I will give you a hypothesis," she replied. "There are types of bacteria called sulfate-oxidizing bacteria. They basically oxidize elemental sulfur to produce sulfuric acid which, of course, is very corrosive. So, possibly, this film might be composed of bacteria which produce an acid that could be the catalyst for corrosion."

The whistling of the wind through the windows became louder, and the skies grew darker outside, indicating a front was moving into the area. Nick paced as his mind tried to put things in order.

"Is it possible that an acid could produce enough free hydrogen to cause steel to lose strength?" Anticipation filled his eyes as he looked at her.

"Hypothetically, yes."

Nick walked over to the kitchen window and watched the trees being shaken more violently. He watched as the outlines of the tree-tops became clearer as faded moonlight broke through the clouds.

"You know, when I took the samples I came across a memo about a new paint or coating being used on the bridge. This was not part of the original specifications for the project. It was given a waiver that allowed it to be used. That seems funny, doesn't it?"

"That seems a little peculiar," replied Katie.

Nick walked back to the table.

"I know someone besides us is very interested in those samples too. I wouldn't be surprised if they have something to do with the coating as well. Hypothetically of course."

Katie leaned towards him with her arms still crossed over her chest.

"I think it would be good to have those samples – if they are still there. Don't you?" asked the chemist.

"Yes. We need to show this to someone."

"We could get the samples that are still in the lab," said Katie. "If he…"

She hesitated and started to tremble.

Nick walked over and put his arms around her.

"Hey, don't worry about that. It will all be okay. I still have samples in my lab and besides that we still have your testing results. We can go first thing in the morning. We can take the information to the police."

"Should we really wait until morning?" asked Katie.

"I think that's best. Whoever that was in the lab yesterday is probably long gone by now. In the morning the campus will be busy with people."

Nick didn't say that by "people" what he really meant was "security." Although the WCC campus security would not be mistaken for the state police, they did offer at least some level of protection. "We can call John Sheldon in the security office on our way in tomorrow, let him know there was a break-in over the weekend."

Katie and Nick looked at each other, realizing they had stumbled into something larger than just the bridge collapse. Although they had more questions now, the coating used on the bridge would be at the center of the answers they sought. They both looked up as another thud came from the roof.

"Must be a branch," said Nick.

47

Sunday November 25, 2007
8:00 P.M.
I-64 Beckley, West Virginia

The BMW handled the curves on this rural stretch of highway to the satisfaction of Jarireh Reza. The solitude of the night was almost as enjoyable as the anonymity of being a ghost. With her true identity left behind in Tehran a day ago, she first was Dr. Navideh Sirzakhani, the Iranian Vice-Director of Education, when she landed at JFK. Now, after making a stop in Virginia, she was Maggie Yassim, the wife of the recently deceased material procurement director of the FHWA. At least that's what her fake Virginia driver's license read. She appreciated the handiwork used by General Assam in counterfeiting the driver's license, as it was indistinguishable from an original. Using the late director's car was a nice touch as it added an additional layer of opaqueness to her identity. Certainly, no one would question a wife driving her husband's car in the event that she was pulled over. Besides, the 9 mm Glock inside her coat could always provide an answer to anyone who questioned her.

On the back seat sat a gray canvas backpack which contained rain gear, food rations, first aid supplies, and the steel samples taken from her previous stop in Alexandria. Picking up the remaining steel samples from Winchester Community College and tying up the relevant loose ends would complete her mission. The fact that General Assam had chosen her to be the fixer in this situation spoke to her dependability, ruthlessness, and background as a scientist. She was different than the other operators in her unit because she was more than just a proficient killer. Jarireh had worked closely in the development of the XT-001 coating, and was intimately familiar with the testing procedures and the data that would be needed. Finding any data on the XT-001 coating's effect on the steel would undoubtedly shed more light on its efficacy, and eliminating anyone who knew anything about its real purpose – well, that would just be fun.

Her headlights illuminated the black roadway as the white lane markings flew by silently. Although her work would be finished tomorrow, she was already anticipating the acclaim within her unit that success would bring. Tomorrow would be the next piece of a journey which she had been on since her time as a doctoral student. Thinking about her days as a student, she often thought how much she owed her advisor, Dr. Aziz Tassani, a well-known academic in the field of bacterial synthesis. Allowing her, a woman, to be involved in his research project involving the neutralization of poisonous hydrogen sulfide gas in sewage treatment facilities, had shown her the promise that he saw in her. Although his research would be beneficial in many industrial processes, Jarireh realized that bacterial synthesis presented a different opportunity as well. Weaponization.

Instead of using a bacteria to neutralize the release of harmful gas, she had theorized that bacteria could be embedded into nanoparticles to cause excessive amounts of gas to be released. The concept was simple – create a coating that embedded Thiobacillus bacteria with nanoparticles of elemental sulfur. The sulfur would act as a corrosion stimulator, and the bacteria would oxidize the sulfur, growing a biofilm that would create sulfuric acid. This corrosion would then release hydrogen sulfide, which in turn produces free hydrogen. If not allowed to escape into the atmosphere, the hydrogen could be forced into steel, leading to the steel's deterioration.

Like any novel idea, it ran into its share of obstacles – both scientific and administrative. Her primary scientific obstacle had been modifying the DNA of the bacteria to work aggressively at low temperatures, while her main administrative obstacle had proved to be Dr. Tassani. An old school academic, he had balked at her proposed research on ethical grounds. Luckily for Jarireh, she had found that a few low-cut form-fitting dresses seemed to help the head of the military's Special Operations Unit, General Assam, take an interest in her work. With such a high-ranking benefactor in her corner, Dr. Tassani had been reluctantly forced to let her pursue this as her dissertation topic. It was too bad that her old advisor had never quite made it to her graduation. University officials were shocked when they found Tassani sprawled out on the laboratory floor, dead from an accidental release of hydrogen sulfide from one of his experiments.

She shook her head thinking about Dr. Tassani.

Such a shame. He had always stressed safety in his labs.

As she drove on towards Charleston, she thought about stopping someplace to rest for a few hours. The temporary Mrs. Yassim was tired after a long day's work, and tomorrow would be another important day.

48

Monday November 26, 2007
7:30 A.M.
Winchester, Kentucky

"And you received the same message from Barstow's office?" asked Katie with perturbation etched on her face. She ran a comb through her wet hair, pulling it straight back over her head. "My hair probably will still be wet."

"Yes, same one. Barstow wants a dog and pony show for some VIP from the United Nations," replied Nick as he drove east on West Lexington Avenue towards the WCC campus. "It will be okay, Katie, we can get the samples and data, meet our VIP and head out to the KSP in Frankfort. He glanced at her and smiled.

"By the way you look fine."

Considering her last forty-eight hours, the young chemist looked better than fine. Showering at her apartment this morning had made her feel almost normal again. The mere state of being clean seemed to help her regain some clarity.

"The Kentucky State Police…you don't want to tell campus security about it first?"

Nick didn't know which was best really. The last few days seemed to be way outside the norm for anyone, and much more so for a middle-aged college professor.

"Well, I think it is better to keep this to ourselves right now. The State Police will get involved at some time anyway. The folks in campus security are good guys but with all that has gone on I just think they are a little out of their league on this. I'm afraid we would spend most of our time explaining why we were on campus when the college was officially closed. They might want to investigate how many lights we turned on."

Katie let out a barely audible groan in agreement. With a fixation on reducing operating costs of all kinds, the college spent a lot of time monitoring paper towels in the restrooms, copier paper in the offices, and, of course, lighting in the labs and classrooms.

"I guess you're probably right," she replied.

They continued, passing Maryland Avenue, the pavement becoming rougher as they got closer to campus.

"What did security say this morning when you called about what happened in the lab?" asked Nick.

"Well, I just said that it looked like somebody had broken into the science labs. They thought it could be a meth-head looking for acetone or something. They told me they would be down to take a look."

That made Nick feel better. Having people around would make campus feel different than it did over the holiday weekend. It might also make the return easier on Katie.

"Good. Just to have security in the area makes me feel better. I am not sure what security will find anyway. I mean whoever was there is long gone. Still, we wouldn't want our VIP guest to be surprised on her tour this morning."

"You don't think Barstow would like the headline *U.N. Diplomat Attacked by Meth-Head at WCC?*" she cracked.

They both chuckled at the thought of the self-serving president having to explain that on his next job interview. They continued for another mile, turning right on College Street, and finally one more right into the faculty parking lot. Nick pulled into a parking space closest to the cluster of buildings ahead and turned off the engine. He turned to get out of the door and pulled on the handle when he realized his passenger was not reciprocating. He looked over at Katie, who sat there staring forward towards the

Science Building, which sat on a slight knoll about one hundred yards to her right. Her face was expressionless, and her chest barely moved with each breath.

"Are you okay, Katie?" asked Nick as he reached over and put his right hand on top of her left.

She paused for several seconds before turning and looking at him, her dark eyes looking for reassurance.

"Yeah, I guess," she replied. "Just so much has happened. I guess seeing campus again…I'm still trying to process it all. It was just Saturday when I was…."

He squeezed her hand and said, "Hey, don't worry. We will get through this. I won't let anything happen to you, I promise."

With a slight nod, she leaned over and hugged him.

"I know."

49

Monday November 26, 2007
8:00 A.M.
Winchester, Kentucky

A slight semi-sweet smell still permeated the third-floor air of Sutton Hall, a three-story rectangular brick building constructed in the 1870s as a tobacco auction house. Gutted and renovated a decade ago, the building's interior now sparkled in high-end mahogany woodwork, original paintings, and glass-enclosed conference rooms – standard adornments for administrative offices in higher education. Jarireh Reza sat comfortably in the reception area outside the president's office admiring the furnishings. She exuded an air of stylish confidence dressed in a black blazer and slacks; her white blouse tantalizingly unbuttoned to show more than enough of her impressive cleavage. The visitor had packed two shirts, and wore the more form-fitting of the two. Its tightness, along with an extra button undone, were an advantage that she thought she might be able to use.

She looked at her watch.

8:02 am.

A middle-aged receptionist faced away from her, checking emails. Jarireh noticed the streak of gray hair that stood out between locks of brown down her neck – a clear sign of someone who colored her hair. Jarireh glanced at the coffee table in front of her, laden with magazines.

Prominently displayed were popular magazines touting expert opinions on sex, fitness, dieting, and the latest celebrity plastic surgery gossip. She considered picking one up as a means of researching the man she would be meeting shortly, and then thought better of it. Displaying magazines like that outside his office and the fact that it was past eight o'clock told her all she needed to know.

Finally, the mahogany door with the gold-plated sign "Dr. Ethan Barstow – President" opened. 8:08 am.

Ethan Barstow stood in the door frame, his three-piece charcoal Brooks Brothers suit and striped silk tie complementing his black horn-rimmed glasses. He hesitated momentarily, looking at the woman seated in the reception area. He was not expecting the beautiful woman in front of him to be the United Nations representative.

"Dr. Sirzakhani," he said as he walked towards her and reached out his hand. "It is a pleasure to meet you. Welcome to Winchester Community College. I'm sorry to have kept you waiting."

Jarireh Reza stood, adjusting her suit and grabbing her leather tote bag off the floor and throwing its straps over her left shoulder in a single fluid motion. She walked forward and shook his hand, noticing that his eyes were glancing downward at her breasts.

"Dr. Barstow, thank you for seeing me on such short notice."

They retreated to his office, where he shut the door behind them and showed her to a seat in front of his desk.

"Can I get you a drink – water, coffee, tea?" he asked.

"No, thank you."

"We are very pleased to have such a distinguished guest here at our college. In fact, we are thrilled. It's not every day that we have someone from the United Nations. But before we get to the particulars of your visit I wanted to give you a small memento from Winchester Community College."

The president stood and reached over his desk to present his guest with a small wooden box.

Jarireh could see his eyes drift again and was satisfied that her choice of the tighter blouse had the desired effect.

"President Barstow this wasn't necessary. The generosity of your time is a gift in itself," replied Jarireh as she leaned forward to accept the gift. She opened the box and feigned some pleasure at seeing a gold pen, pencil, and letter opener emblazoned with the college seal. "Thank you very much. They are beautiful."

"You are most welcome, Dr. Sirzakhani. I hope that your time here will provide you with insights on the education we deliver here at our college. Our focus on excellence, particularly in the technical areas, is what sets Winchester Community College apart."

"That is why I am here. I know my first visit is in a few minutes with the technology programs so maybe we can go over the particulars of my itinerary?"

"Certainly."

She leaned back in her chair and crossed her left leg over her right. Slow enough to make sure President Barstow noticed.

"I was hoping to start with Professor Kremer in the technology area. Would that be okay?" she asked.

A confused look appeared on the president's face. He adjusted his glasses as if to recalibrate his thoughts.

"I show you first meeting with Dean Vignetti. Maybe I have this wrong. She has been at WCC a long time and can provide a good overview of the technology programs. Professor Kremer is an excellent professor, but he has only been on staff a few months. I just think..."

Jarireh interrupted forcefully.

"Director Yassim of the National Institute of Science and Technology specifically mentioned Professor Kremer. I believe they worked closely together many years ago. I wanted to pass along the director's wishes to him personally. Perhaps I can meet Dean Vignetti a little later this morning?"

She looked at the president with hopeful eyes while she fiddled with a button on her blouse.

"Well, I am sure we can work that out," said President Barstow as he reached for his directory. "Let me call Dean Vignetti right now and notify Professor Kremer that you would like to meet."

"That would be nice," said Jarireh, leaning forward in her chair.

She listened for the next minute while the president called his dean and told her of the change of plans. Jarireh opened the wooden box, looked appreciatively at the gift that President Barstow had given her, and softly ran her index finger along the golden pen, pencil, and letter opener in succession. The sound of the phone banging down on its base broke her fixation on the gift.

"Dr. Sirzakhani, I have it all worked out."

"Please call me Navi," she interrupted.

"Okay," he said smiling broadly. "Navi, I have Professor Kremer meeting us in the testing lab in the Technology Building in fifteen minutes. Now, I have to warn you that the testing lab is not the cleanest place on campus. We test building materials – concrete, brick, steel, etc. – in there."

"Don't worry about me. That is exactly what I came to see. I know some tours like to highlight everything that is clean and shiny when showing people around, but I am interested in building technology as well. Your educational processes in this area can be very applicable to many countries around the world. Besides, although you might not know this about me, I don't mind getting my hands dirty," she said, smiling.

President Barstow sat there attracted to the dichotomy that appeared in front of him. Beautiful, stylish, confident. This young woman wasn't afraid to tell someone what she wanted. She wasn't afraid to get dirty. He liked that.

"Well, that's good. Still, I wouldn't want you to get your clothes dirty. We will get you a lab coat and safety glasses."

"Thank you very much. I can leave my jacket here if you don't mind, and come back for it after lunch."

Standing up, she slipped off her suit jacket, enhancing the tight white blouse's effect on her slender but curvaceous figure.

"Yes," he replied as he watched her place the jacket on the back of her chair. "Navi, I was thinking, if we have time, I could show you some nearby points of interest after lunch. If your schedule permits of course."

"I would like that. I am sure we can find the time. Thank you, President Barstow."

"Please call me Ethan."

"Certainly, Ethan. We probably should be going soon. Part of my work will be to write a follow-up report on my visit. I was hoping you can tell me the room number for the technology lab where we will be meeting Professor Kremer?"

"That is no problem," he said, turning his chair around to face his computer. "Just give me a minute. I will pull it up from the facility website."

"Thank you, Ethan. For everything," she replied, walking around his desk. She stood over his left shoulder and bent down to peer at the computer screen as he clicked through the college's intranet. He became distracted by the heat of her body and fumbled with the mouse due to his mounting excitement.

"Here it is," he said.

Jarireh bent down closer to his shoulder. She enjoyed her ability to excite men of his age. As she leaned forward to see the screen he could see her face peripherally as her breast brushed against the left shoulder of his suit coat.

"We will be meeting him in Room 134A in the Technology Building."

"Thank you, Ethan. That is what I needed," she replied softly.

In a seamless motion, her left hand grabbed his forehead as her right hand plunged the letter opener into the base of his skull. Severing the brain stem allowed one to die quietly except for an occasional involuntary twitch. She laid his head softly down on the desk.

"It looks like you won't be giving me that personal tour after all," she whispered.

She walked around his desk and retrieved her suit jacket. Slipping it back on, she checked her tote bag and made sure the two 9 mm Glocks were loaded. She walked out the door, locking it behind her and made her way to the receptionist.

"President Barstow is talking to my director at the United Nations and said that he wasn't to be disturbed until lunch. Could you point me in the direction of the Technology Building?"

50

Monday November 26, 2007
8:25 A.M.
Winchester, Kentucky
"Katie. It's me."

"Don't tell me you miss me already," she giggled.

Although it had only been a few minutes, Nick was glad to hear her voice. The cell phone was a poor substitute for actually seeing her but for now it would have to do. His head was still pounding despite the three-aspirin breakfast he'd had with his morning coffee. With all that had gone on over the last several days, being separated from her just added to his general state of anxiety. He wanted to get done with this tour, pick up Katie, and head to the KSP post, which was about a forty-five-minute drive from campus.

"Is it really that obvious?" he replied. "Are you doing okay?"

"I'm all right. I'll feel better when we talk to the police."

As she spoke, Nick walked over to the MTS machine he had used to perform the tension test on the samples last Saturday. Scattered over the console of the machine were screwdrivers, wrenches, and shim plates now covered in hydraulic oil, which constantly leaked from the manifold. At the end of the console sat a roll of paper towels used to keep the oil from dripping onto the floor. Broken pieces from the two samples tested sat on the table adjacent to the console, along with the print-out of the stress-strain diagram showing the maximum strength of each item.

"Me too. Do they have you doing anything with the United Nations visit today?

"No, they are stopping by sometime, but I haven't been asked to do anything, so I guess I am not involved," said Katie.

"Well, I just found out from Vignetti that the VIP wanted to start in my lab this morning."

"Really?"

"Yeah, go figure, right? They are supposed to be here in a few minutes. Trying to straighten up a little before they get here."

"Nick, that's a lost cause. It would take you a week to clean your lab up," replied Katie.

Nick looked around the lab and agreed. He had concrete, soil and mortar specimens tucked away in every corner of the lab. Long forgotten, he guessed they must have been left over from previous courses or research samples.

"I know. Did you find your samples in the lab?" asked Nick.

The thought of going down to her lab without someone made her feel nauseated.

"I, uh…don't feel like going down there by myself," she whispered. "I just don't…"

"Hey, don't worry about it. I will be done here in a half hour, and then I can come over. We can get your stuff from the lab then. Okay?"

"Sure, that sounds good. It won't take me too long. I just need to pull SEM images off the computer and then will copy the data to a thumb drive after that."

"Sounds good," Nick said reassuringly. "We should be out of here by ten o'clock."

Saying goodbye, Nick walked over to the Charpy tester. Collecting the broken pieces from off the ground he studied the smooth edges of the fracture surface. The ex-engineer knew the samples had broken in a brittle manner indicating very low toughness values. He placed the broken samples into a drawer of an old wooden desk and picked up a yellow legal pad, on which he had recorded his notes.

He unrolled a wad of paper towels and walked over to the MTS to mop up some hydraulic fluid which was dripping down its front panel, when he heard the door swing open at the far end of the lab. The slow squeak made by the door's hinges echoed to the top of the concrete block walls, which stood more than twenty feet vertically. Due to the inability of the low-pressure sodium lamps to power up quickly, the far end of the lab was darker than the area he occupied. Straining to see who it was, he could hear the sound of footsteps confidently striding towards him. Within seconds he could see the slender-framed Iranian.

"Dr. Sirzakhani?" he called out.

As the words left his mouth, she came into full view. Her sharp but delicate features accentuated by her black hair that was pulled back tightly into a bun, surprised him. She was not what Nick thought a bureaucrat from the U.N. should look like.

"Yes, and you must be Professor Kremer," she replied as she strode forward with her right hand outstretched.

"Yes, Nick Kremer. Pleased to meet you."

Her eyes were inviting and hard to look away from, but he glanced past them to the far end of the lab and noticed that they were alone.

"I thought President Barstow was coming, wasn't he?"

"He was stuck in the office," replied Jarireh, smiling as she enjoyed the pun alone. "He told me to come over to meet you and that he would be here when he could."

"Well, okay. Where do you want to start?"

"I trust your judgment," she said in a demure voice. "I came here to your college because I wanted to see firsthand what you were doing. Developing countries might benefit from the community college model used here in your country, as it relates to technology. So why don't you just show me what you do here."

Nick nodded in agreement. Although he was new to the college, he had been involved in tours before and, except for the stature of his guest, this morning was no different than leading a group of prospective students and their parents. Making his way around the perimeter of the room, explaining the nuances of concrete and soils testing, he told his guest how the WCC students were highly sought after by companies for summer internships. Nick provided good answers to several questions, which she seemed to appreciate. As they walked over to the MTS tester he wished that he would have spent more time wiping up the hydraulic fluid, a sheen of which covered the front of the machine. Pointing to the loading frame, he explained how real-time data was relayed to the computer, thereby generating a plot on the computer. Finished with the explanation, he turned around, satisfied that he had provided her with the information she wanted. His eyes opened wider as he found out he was wrong.

"Professor Kremer," Jarireh said in an icy voice, "you have been doing some testing lately, in the last few days. I can see from the hydraulic fluid. I know what you are working on and I will make this very easy for you. Give me the samples and results, and I will be gone."

Nick could feel his heartbeat quicken as he stared at the Glock pointed at his face. He knew Katie's attack was not random and now wished he had heeded Katie's advice to go to the police right away. Nick's instincts told him to buy some time, but his first option was to not get his head blown off.

"Okay, okay," he replied raising his hands above his head. "I will get them. You are talking about the samples from the bridge, right?"

He barely saw her right arm swing until the butt of the gun impacted his skull above his left ear. Pain shot down his neck as he crumpled over with both hands on his head. Eyes watering, he blinked to clear them.

Jarireh stepped hard on his foot with the heel of her black leather pump to regain his focus. "Don't test me, Professor Kremer. Things will end up badly for you and your colleague also," she growled.

Still bent over, Nick stiffened when he heard his visitor refer to Katie.

"My colleague?" he asked, hoping his feigned ignorance would somehow be to Katie's benefit.

"Yes, my good professor. I know all about your colleague from the chemistry department. You didn't think the visit she had over the weekend was random, did you?" She let off of his foot. "Why do you think I am here now? Just get me the samples and results so I can be leaving."

She pushed the muzzle of the gun into his forehead. "Do you understand me?"

"Okay. Okay...I understand." She removed the barrel of the gun from his head and motioned for him to stand.

"First the samples and data from the tension testing," she said as she retrieved a flash drive from her blazer. "Give me the tested samples and download the data on here."

Nick wobbled as he walked over to the MTS tester, his head throbbing. She handed him the flash drive, and he plugged it into the workstation next to the MTS and clicked through several different directories to find the testing data. The flash drive blinked as the data was downloaded.

"Delete the data directory," she commanded.

"What?"

"Delete the directory," she barked, lifting the gun up to his face again.

She wanted all evidence of her linkage to the WCC campus destroyed. His breathing became faster and shallower as he also suspected that the destruction of data would not stop with computer files. He clicked on the directory and deleted it.

"Now the recycle bin as well. Unplug the flash drive and hand it to me."

He did what she asked.

"Now get me the samples. Slowly," Jarireh said, pushing the gun into the small of his back.

He began to walk over to the old desk to retrieve the samples and he stopped.

"What are you doing?" she barked. "I'll kill you right now."

"Listen," said Nick, his irritated voice crackling with fear. He turned slowly with his hands raised towards his shoulders. "Just listen. A friend of mine died on that bridge in Minneapolis. I know enough about it. The coating. The weakened steel. I know it contributed to the collapse. I just want to know why – the collapse, the attack on my friend, you being here today – why is this, all this, happening? I think I deserve to know."

She looked at the American professor with a mixture of anxiousness and appreciation. Her training told her to complete the mission, while his idealistic desire of wanting to find answers in the face of death made her listen to his request. His 'need to know' is so American, she thought to herself. With her gun trained on his forehead, she stared at him silently.

"Well? What about it?" he said. "I guess it's some cover-up. Corporate? Government?"

Nick took a half step towards her until he saw her finger tighten on the trigger.

Smiling, Jarireh backed away from Nick while she thought about ending this conversation once and for all. She lowered the gun, keeping it tucked close to her body.

"I am not certain that you deserve to know, Professor Kremer. As a general rule, I don't believe in granting last wishes, but I am in America."

"So you will?" Nick interrupted.

A wicked smile crept slowly from the corners of her mouth.

"This time I will."

She raised the gun level with his face again.

"Get me those samples, and I will tell you."

51

Monday November 26, 2007
9:00 A.M.
Winchester, Kentucky

Tired of waiting around, Katie went to the lab alone and took a deep breath before forcing herself to enter. The same place she had escaped less than forty-eight hours ago. Approaching the SEM, she turned it on and plugged a flash drive into the console of its workstation. Searching through the directories for the folder containing Saturday's results, Katie waded through the files and one-by-one transferred them from the analyzer and then compressed them into a single zip file.

After ejecting the flash drive, she stared at it as she turned it over in her hand. The amount of information stored on such a small thing always amazed her, but the fact that some of this information was important enough to kill for gave her pause. The more she thought about the information, the more she convinced herself she needed a backup plan. Katie walked quickly across the room and sat down at her workstation. Logging onto her personal email via a virtual private network, she composed an email.

> Dad,
>
> It was great to see everyone last week. I wish I could have stayed longer.

Katie's eyes started to water thinking about Thanksgiving, and she smiled through her pain. The events of the last couple of days had reinforced for her how blessed she was. A family who, for all their nerve-wracking habits, cared about her and loved her without limits. A good career that she found challenging, rewarding, and satisfying. A job that she looked forward to every morning. Well, almost every morning.

> *I have had some things happen here at work. It's a long story, and I don't want to bore you with it now. I have attached some files that I would like you to keep for me just in case I need them in the future. Please download the files to a flash drive and should something happen send them to your friend at the Department of Transportation. Tell him it is information that might be of interest to him.*

Her dark eyes began to glisten, and she blinked them quickly to stem the tears.

> *I hope to see you and mom real soon. No matter what remember I love you so much.*
> *Katie*

She attached the zip file named I99N-Bridge and hit send. Getting up from her chair, she pinched the bridge of her nose and wiped her eyes. She paced around the lab for several minutes before deciding to go to her office to wait for Nick.

In his English Tudor home outside Indianapolis, Bob Walsh was enjoying his decision to take a week of vacation. Halfway through his third cup of coffee, his fingers quivered slightly, turning the last few pages of the morning paper as he sat in his study. Hearing a chime of his computer notifying that an email had arrived, he put the paper down and swiveled his chair to face his computer. Glancing over his reading glasses at the screen, he smiled when he saw that Katie was the sender. As he opened up the email, his smile faded, and his forehead became furrowed with concern.

52

Holding the bag of steel samples in her left hand, Jarireh motioned with her gun for Nick to sit down. She walked behind him and sat on a beat-up metal lab stool.

"So you want some answers?"

"Yes. I want to know about all of this," Nick replied as he started to turn around. He realized that "all of this" could take days to explain, but right now he was just hoping to buy himself a fraction of that.

"Don't turn around," she chided. "Where should I start? I could go back long before you were born if you like. Where I come from, professor, people have long memories. Memories passed down from generation to generation. At its core, the answers you seek are all about making your country pay for what it has done."

Nick squirmed a little in his chair. The coldness of her words echoed in the openness of the lab, which seemed to amplify the evil nature of the woman who was holding a gun to his head. He realized that the answer to his questions involved more than corporate executives looking to preserve the bottom line. Her voice contained bitterness which made her closed to reason. Not wanting to anger her, Nick realized that any geopolitical discussion would provide time for him to think about his options.

It's better to talk than have a bullet in my head.

Without turning around, he cleared his throat.

"What do you mean by *what we have done?*" he asked making sure that he emphasized the word 'we.'

"Oh, my dear professor, where do I begin?" she said almost with a chuckle.

He could hear her metal stool squeak as it slid slightly on the concrete floor. Standing, now she walked around in front of him, her shoes clicking stealthily on the floor.

"Israel, Saudi Arabia, Iraq, Pakistan, El Salvador, Nicaragua," she paused, waving the gun in front of him. "I could go on and on. The corruption you have spread in pursuit of power is disgusting. But that is changing, mark my words."

Nick sat there and let her harsh words pass by him without leaving a mark. He guessed the rant was some branch of extremism whose origin didn't matter. Whether home-grown or foreign, to Nick it seemed that these groups all shared a simple hatred of the Western ideals. He wasn't by nature a political person but, like many people he knew, had grown tired of being blamed for everything wrong in the world.

Victims always need someone to blame. They probably couldn't even explain why they hate us. Although he was inclined to let her words slip away, he realized their potential to buy him some more time.

"I don't understand. How is it changing? I mean, at the end of the day you can't change people through fear alone. That has been tried, right? I mean shootings and stabbings which killed a few evolved into suicide bombers which could kill dozens. Truck bombs which could kill hundreds became planes which could kill thousands. Did that really advance your cause?"

He tip-toed around the word *terrorist* although he knew from her words that it was an apt description of who stood before him.

His words got under her skin. She sneered as the grip on her Glock tightened, and she leaned her lithe body closer to him. "If it hasn't yet, I think it will," she said as her dark gaze bore into him.

Nick sensed the tension in her body and he knew she was pissed off. While he was achieving his goal of engaging his captor in conversation, he still was fully aware of the tenuous nature of his situation. *Get her moderately angry, and she stays talking. Get her too angry, and I stop talking – and breathing.*

Jarireh smirked and walked around behind him.

"I think this time will be different."

"Really? How?"

"Professor, many groups always looked towards the bigger, more spectacular attacks as a way of gaining notoriety. That is why you always see a rush to get in front of the camera after an attack."

Nick heard the clicking of her heels stop behind him and he grew concerned.

"Okay, so how is this time different?"

"We aren't rushing to get in front of the camera. What if you could have the largest attack on American soil without people even realizing that it took place? What if the attacks came in cities, large and small, such that it disrupted the daily life of every American? What if you stopped the flow of goods across America causing millions of people to lose their jobs? Would that be different, professor?"

Nick didn't know what to say. The breadth of her words enveloped him as if he was standing at the bottom of an abandoned well. For the longest time, Nick had looked at events in his life as if they were linked together only by happenstance. With death looking at him through the barrel of a gun, Nick heard the Iranian's words, and they finally converged with the questions he had. Questions not only about the bridge collapse but also of the journey that had placed him here. The arc of his life from Cincinnati to Winchester, from Jenny to Katie, from jail to freedom seemed to make sense to him now. He felt as if her words had finally found him at the bottom of the well. The question now was would he ever be able to tell anyone.

"So the bridge collapse was not an accident," said Nick although he already knew the answer.

"Your words, not mine, Professor."

"And the corrosion-inhibiting paint is causing the steel to weaken?"

"You catch on quickly," the captain said as she stepped closer towards the back of his head.

"But how?"

"That question has a complicated answer. Unfortunately, I don't have the time to explain," she replied, raising the gun to the crown of his head. The skills she had mastered over the years had taught her the cleanest way to perform a kill. A gunshot from the rear in the center of the skull with a Glock angled downward would not leave blood splatter. She didn't want to change clothes before driving back to New York.

"Can you give me the short version, at least?" he asked.

"You ask a lot," she replied releasing her pressure on the trigger. "But I like you. Does the term hydrogen embrittlement mean anything to you?"

Nick realized that Katie had mentioned that at the farmhouse.

"Sure. It causes steel to lose strength."

"Yes, and when exposed to acidic solutions its diffusion into steel is much more effective. Did you know that some bacteria use sulfates to produce acids?"

"Maybe, I am not sure," replied Nick.

"Well, there are some that can. These types of bacteria use sulfates to produce an enormous amount of acid. Hydrogen is a by-product, and either this is released into the air or absorbed into steel. Our coating facilitates this process quite well. Usually, it takes years for steel to absorb a significant amount of hydrogen to deteriorate, but we have succeeded in speeding that up."

Nick blinked his eyes quickly. Biodegradation is what Katie had hypothesized at the farmhouse.

"By how much?"

"Let me just say that the paint is special; we make it with a few special ingredients," she chuckled ominously.

"You used nanoparticles?"

Jarireh's eyes widened at Nick's response. She was surprised by the technology professor's question.

"Professor, I am impressed. Evidently, the community college system is excellent here. Yes, the paint is embedded with nanoparticles of sulfates and a genetically modified microbe. Our microbe has all the sulfates necessary to produce large quantities of acid, and therefore large amounts of hydrogen. Hence, an artificial embrittlement of the steel."

Nick needed to buy time, but the engineer in him was also interested in solving the puzzle.

"But you typically need a positive pressure to get a significant amount of hydrogen to diffuse into steel. Without it the hydrogen just escapes into the air, right? It doesn't seem possible to get that amount of hydrogen to diffuse in such a short span of time."

"It's not possible under normal conditions," she snapped. "But our bacteria grows into a biofilm that is sensitive to the smallest changes in pH. As the pH of the biofilm drops, the acid forms, causing the biofilm to become more impermeable. It creates a biological barrier preventing the hydrogen from going anywhere except into the steel."

Jarireh smiled. She always liked being able to explain science to people who could make the connection between theory and its application. It was too bad that the conversation would have to end on that note. She raised the gun again and positioned it close to the back of his head and at a slight angle.

"Great talk, professor. But I must be going. I wish it didn't have to end like this."

"Hey!" the voice called out from above as a mortar cube sped through the air.

Jarireh wheeled around and pointed her gun in the direction of the voice coming from the storage balcony fifteen feet above and to her right. She squeezed off a shot at the same moment the mortar cube struck her above her left eye. She staggered backward falling into the wooden table as her body struggled to regain control. Covering her forehead with her free hand, she could hear footsteps running away. She became instantly enraged as the warm gush of blood began to flow through her fingers.

Nick recognized the voice and within a second of hearing the shot, scrambled out of the chair and raced towards the exit doors at the far end of the lab.

As he ran, Katie lay on her side with her back pressed tightly against the wall, trying to minimize her profile from the shooter below. Happy that her throwing arm was still in good shape, she couldn't say the same about her left leg. Blood poured slowly from the gunshot wound which had hit her in the outside of her thigh.

Although the balcony was not accessible from the laboratory floor, she needed to get out of the line of fire. She looked anxiously at the storage office, which could provide cover but was thirty feet away. Katie winced in pain each time she placed her elbows in front of her and lurched forward. Her limp leg was leaving a smear of blood in its wake on the balcony floor. The pain was intense, but she didn't feel lightheaded, so she thought it had to be a clean through and through. Still twenty feet away from the storage office, she ducked her head as a loud crack echoed through the laboratory. As the bullet passed above her head, glass from the office windows began raining down all around her. Seconds later another gunshot struck the windows about ten feet away, followed by a third shot still a bit farther down towards the office door. Lifting her head, Katie realized that the shooter had now covered the remaining pathway to the storage room in shards of razor-sharp glass.

Jarireh's anger fixated her on eliminating the person on the balcony. Although Professor Kremer's escape compromised her plan, she still had the samples and had erased the testing information. She would take care of the person on the balcony – the loose end that had allowed the professor to get away.

With no stairs to the balcony, Jarireh considered her options. One possibility was to exit the lab and go through the building to the balcony, but that would allow her target time to make a run for it. Suddenly the captain sprinted towards the corner of the lab, her black hair haphazardly bouncing across her shoulders.

A ladder.

Upon first glance, she wasn't sure if the old wooden ladder would be tall enough to reach to the balcony. She pulled it into a vertical position and placed it towards the balcony about thirty feet away from where Katie lay, and slowly tilted it forward. The top of the ladder fell short of the balcony walkway but rested firmly on the steel support beam below. Resting on the beam would make the transition from the ladder to the balcony a bit more complicated, but it was nothing that Jarireh could not handle.

Katie grimaced every time the glass cut into her forearms and stomach as she pulled herself towards the office door. Now ten feet away, she anxiously looked in front of her when she heard the ladder bang into position on the steel beam. Although not sure what exactly was happening, a thud followed by another and another told Katie the shooter was on the way up to see her. The glass dug deeper into her arms as she lunged towards the office door.

"No sense in going any farther," barked Jarireh as she grabbed onto the metal railing with her left hand while pointing the Glock at Katie with her right. The position of the ladder on the steel beam caused the captain to lean back away from the balcony to see the person lying on her stomach against the wall.

Katie, her arms bloodied from her crawl, lifted her head. As her black hair fell into her eyes, she looked at her shooter and laughed.

Jarireh recognized her immediately.

"Dr. Walsh, I was planning to see you a little later. You look so much worse for wear than your picture in the faculty directory. It's so good that you still have a sense of humor. Usually, that's not the case when I am ready to kill someone."

A measure of freedom comes when facing an end and Katie accepted the apparent finality of her situation. Maybe she was beaten, but the Midwestern girl wasn't giving up.

"Well," said Katie with a strained voice, "there hasn't been anything normal about the last couple days. Have you ever had those days when you keep running into one asshole after another?"

Jarireh was surprised by her spirit. Her victims typically begged for mercy right before she killed them. This time she gets a smart-mouth chemistry professor. It didn't matter to her.

"Well, I'm one asshole you shouldn't have run into."

Instinctively Katie covered her head and closed her eyes. When she heard the gunshot ring out, she thought that death really didn't feel too bad. In fact, the pain Katie felt was similar to the pain that she'd had only minutes ago. She looked up but didn't see the shooter. She dropped her head down to her hands and laughed again as tears started to flow.

Nick struggled to get Dr. Sïrzakhani or whoever this was, off his legs so he could reach the gun. His plan to knock her off the ladder hadn't included her falling on top of him. Although the bulk of her body had not contacted him directly, her legs had hit him behind the knees causing him to fall face-first onto the laboratory floor. Luckily for him, she landed hard on the floor and seemed to be out cold. This was his opportunity to grab the gun resting only ten feet away. He climbed from under her body and staggered toward the gun, thinking that his legs had forgotten how to run. Picking the gun up, he placed his hands on his knees. Relieved that this was over.

Finally.

His head jerked back as a slight but powerful arm locked itself around his neck. His eyes widened and bulged out as air did not make its way in or out under Jarireh's chokehold. Nick dropped the gun and grabbed onto her arm as the involuntary reflex to breathe and his inability to do so sent a wave of panic through his body. His hands searched chaotically to find an opening between her vise-like arms and his neck. Jarireh kicked the back of his knees, which dropped him into a kneeling position and maximized her leverage as she began to pull him back.

Katie, soaked with streaks of blood, made her way over to the balcony railing to see the commotion below. Her body tensed as a tidal wave of fear crashed over her. Moments ago she had escaped death, but now her shooter was moments away from choking Nick to death.

"Hey, up here!" she screamed at Jarireh.

The blood from the gash above her eye was plainly visible as she turned her head and glared at Katie.

"You're next!" she yelled.

Nick's face turned a deeper shade of crimson as he began to see gray spots darting in and out of his field of vision. Katie's feet seemed frozen to the gray concrete of the balcony as she watched Nick's eyes starting to close. With only seconds left she lifted her wounded leg over the balcony railing and then kicked her right leg over. Perched with her feet on the edge of the balcony slab, Katie crouched down and prepared herself to jump on Nick's attacker.

One, two....

A gunshot echoed through the hollowness of the laboratory. Jarireh fell sideways as a ring of blood expanded on her shirt below her clavicle. Three state troopers surrounded Jarireh with their guns drawn as she writhed in pain. Nick rolled over, his chest heaving as he gasped for breath. He coughed several times as the gray spots he had seen moments before began to dissipate.

"Buddy can you hear me?" asked a broad-shouldered trooper as he lightly shook Nick's shoulder. "We have help coming, are you going to be okay?"

He heard Katie burst through the lab doors and heard her light footsteps drawing closer and closer to him.

"Couldn't be better," responded Nick.

53

Monday December 17, 2007
11:00 A.M.
Washington, D.C.
Nick sat at the table next to Ben Jones, Congressman from Kentucky's fourth district, and other assorted dignitaries. His new suit and tie made him feel uncomfortable, not because they were inherently uncomfortable, but because they weren't his usual khakis and button-down oxford. Thankfully he had managed to hold the seat next to him for Katie, so he could be in someone's company that he enjoyed. He swapped small talk with the politicians at his table, scanning the ballroom intermittently for her to arrive.

What's taking her so long?

Finally, he spotted her and got her attention with an exaggerated wave. She smiled and waved back, tossing her black hair over the Christmas-colored stole that she had wrapped around her shoulders. Her strides seemed almost effortless as she walked towards the table as if she was gliding above the floor. The long-sleeve black knit dress silhouetted every curve of her body while the knee-high black leather boots gave her an air of invincibility.

That certainly is fitting.

"Hello," he said as he reached out and embraced her in a friendly hug. "You look… fantastic."

"Well, thank you. You don't look too bad yourself," Katie answered as she lightly put her hand on the lapel of his suit.

"I saved you a seat," he said, turning halfway around towards the table.

"Don't tell me it's the one next to you," she replied as she rolled her eyes in bemusement.

"Unfortunately it is. Sorry, you are stuck with me – at least through the reception."

Introductions were made followed by handshakes and congratulations to the chemistry professor. Nick had gone through a similar experience only thirty minutes before. It seemed that unraveling a plot to use nanoparticle-infused paint to collapse interstate highway bridges across the country was the type of thing that got one noticed in Washington. Nick and Katie had become a national sensation even though they tried to resist most of the offers that came their way.

Nick took a deep breath as he watched Katie. A satisfied smile crept across his face as he thought about the monikers that the media had pinned on them – Angels of the Interstates, Sentinels of Steel, or – his favorite – Professors of Punishment. Looking at Katie, it was easy to imagine her as a superhero.

In the six years since 9/11, the Secretary of Homeland Security had never awarded the Gold Medal Award for Exceptional Service to any civilian. Today he was going to award *two* gold medals. The room quieted down, and people took their seats as a clean-cut young man, dressed in a crisp navy blue suit, stepped to the podium in the center of the room. Nick had heard someone mention that it was the deputy secretary of DHS as he slid into the seat next to Katie. The young man thanked everyone and launched into a rather lengthy history of the department, and the vital role that it played in preventing terror inside the United States. Nick glanced at Katie as she listened to the speaker with her hands clasped on her lap, and he could see the vintage bracelet with the letter "K" resting vertically on her wrist. She seemed to wear that bracelet everywhere. Whether lecturing to students, working in her laboratory, or being given the highest honor awarded by the DHS – that bracelet was a constant companion.

After a few long minutes that seemed much longer, the young man introduced the Secretary of DHS, who stepped to the microphone and gestured for Katie and Nick to join him. Nick hated being the center of attention but at least today he got to share it with someone who would attract most of the attention. They walked together and after shaking the Secretary's hand stood behind him, shoulder to shoulder. Nick looked out over the crowd, half-listening to the Secretary's welcome when Katie nudged her shoulder into his arm.

"Pay attention," she whispered.

Nick nodded his head and smiled.

> *We are pleased to be here today to award Dr. Katie Walsh and Professor Nick Kremer from Winchester Community College our Department's highest honor – the Gold Medal Award for Exceptional Service. I am personally pleased to welcome their many friends, family and other guests that could be here with us today.*
>
> *More than six years ago we, as a nation, found ourselves attacked in a manner that few of us ever could imagine. America responded to that attack with a promise to be forever vigilant in order to prevent future attacks on American soil. That, my friends, is an incredibly difficult task because we are facing an enemy that knows no boundaries in the pursuit of hatred.*

The Secretary had the rapt attention of the room as well as the two professors standing just to his right. Nick felt Katie furtively slip her hand into his as she intertwined her fingers with his.

> *We have always known that we stand as defenders of freedom and liberty around the globe. We carry this responsibility as urgently today as ever in our country's history. Our enemies are consumed with a warped ideology, one that if left to grow will cause generations of chaos and bloodshed. Protecting the American homeland is a monumental task as we must be successful twenty-four hours a day, every day. That is why we need the help of all Americans in order to accomplish our mission. Today I am honored to present the Gold Medal Award to these two extraordinary individuals that are standing here with me.*

Nick and Katie exchanged quick smiles as she released his hand.

"This is the big moment," she whispered as the Secretary finished up his preamble to the award ceremony.

"Right. I'll try not to trip," Nick whispered in reply. He knew he was going to be the first one introduced today, and had struggled with the biographical information the administration's public relations liaison had requested him to provide. Somehow Nick didn't think that the Secretary would want to highlight his role in the Cincinnati walkway collapse or the fifteen years spent in prison for vehicular manslaughter. Nonetheless, he knew that they knew. There was no way that the Department had not thoroughly investigated him since that day Katie had helped him uncover the plot to bring down more bridges throughout the highway system. He decided to keep his information short.

First, I would like to call forward Mr. Nicholas Patrick Kremer.

Nick stepped up next to the Secretary and noticed that the temperature under the lights was significantly higher as he started to sweat.

Nick practiced as a structural engineer and recently joined the faculty at Winchester Community College. His colleagues tell me that Nick has a passion for getting things right, as well as a loyalty to his friends that is never ending. They say that he dedicates his time to finding the truth and that this dedication is consistent throughout all facets of his life. I think I speak for millions of Americans when I say that I am very thankful for this dedication which led Nick to uncover the plot that caused the collapse of the I-99 bridge in Minneapolis. A plot which our enemies wanted to repeat across our great country.

I understand that Nick lost a dear friend in that terrible collapse last August and I say from the bottom of my heart that we, as Americans, mourn in the loss of his friend and all that died that day. But I will also say that Nick showed us the true spirit of friendship in his pursuit of the truth which helped save countless more lives. It gives me great pride to award the Department of Homeland Security's Gold Medal Award for Exceptional Service to Nicholas Kremer.

The Secretary turned and placed the end of the red, white and blue ribbon around Nick's neck and clasped it. Applause filled the room as Nick looked down at the medal for several seconds before realizing that the Secretary had his hand extended towards him. Nick reached out and shook it energetically as if trying to make up for the delay. He turned and, smiling at Katie, stepped back and stood next to her.

"Your turn…don't trip," he whispered.

A subtle jab from her elbow caught him in the arm.

Next, I would like to call forward Dr. Kathrine Marie Walsh.

Katie took several steps forward and occupied the same place where Nick had stood only moments before. The chemistry professor smiled as a slight blush crept along her cheeks. She preferred not to be called by her given name. Not that she didn't like the name Kathrine, she just felt more at home as Katie. She located her parents and gave them a quick head bob, reciprocated by a thumbs-up from her dad and a little wave from her mom. They had flown in from Indianapolis on the early flight this morning and told Katie that they would meet her at the reception afterward. She was happy that they could make it as they had been there to watch over her and share in her accomplishments.

Kathrine Walsh earned a Ph.D. in Chemistry from the University of Notre Dame and was the youngest person ever to be elected a Fellow of the prestigious American Association of Chemical Researchers. Drawn by a love for teaching, Kathrine joined the faculty at Winchester Community College in 2004. Although there for a few short years, she has been recognized by her colleagues on multiple occasions for her teaching skills and her work mentoring both students and faculty alike. Her colleagues tell me that Kathrine is dedicated to her students and relentless at getting what she needs to improve their access to a high-quality education. The many accolades from her students share a common theme about Dr. Walsh — she sets high expectations and stops at nothing to help them achieve their goals. She has been called a teacher's teacher and the best colleague one could have.

Nick smiled and looked at Katie as the Secretary continued. She was, without a doubt, the type of woman that brought out the best in everyone she met.

Again I think I speak for millions of Americans when I say that I am very thankful for her determination in helping to uncover the plot behind the I-99 bridge collapse. Today we stand here as a nation safer and more secure because of her actions.

I would also like to acknowledge Kathrine's aunt and uncle that are here today, I believe.

The Secretary paused and scanned the room until he found the couple which Katie had spotted a moment earlier. The gray-haired gentleman wearing a navy blue blazer and his wife wearing a floral patterned dress smiled at the Secretary and then nodded at those around them. Nick looked at Katie, who was having a tough time holding back tears that were ready to burst forth.

Yes, there they are. I want to say how indebted we are to Kathrine's aunt and uncle for raising such a smart, accomplished and brave young woman. As a young girl, Kathrine lost her parents in another tragic collapse in Cincinnati. Afterward, her aunt and uncle raised her as one of their own. I can say I speak for all of us as I say what a fine, fine job they have done.

Nick stood stone-faced as the room filled with applause, and he did not see Katie wipe away some tears. He listened to the words that he had just heard.

Young girl… parents…collapse…Cincinnati.

He tried to process what was just said and superimpose it on his life. Katie's actual mother and father – killed in his collapse two decades ago. The reality of those words turned his stomach like someone had stuck a knife in his gut and slowly began to twist it.

> *I am deeply grateful that I live in a country that has citizens like Kathrine Walsh. Citizens that give to others without regard for their personal needs or safety. She has shown us all what it means to be a great American and it gives me great pride to award the Department of Homeland Security's Gold Medal Award for Exceptional Service to Kathrine Walsh.*

Katie stepped forward and ducked her head as the Secretary placed the red, white and blue ribbon around her neck and clasped it. Smiling out at the crowd, she made sure she gave a half wave to her adoptive parents, who were simultaneously smiling and wiping tears from their eyes. She turned back around and smiled at Nick, who was looking out at the room with a distant gaze.

"Hey, I didn't trip," she said as she reassumed her placed next to him.

Nick snapped back out of his thoughts about Katie's parents. Those with her today and those she had lost as a little girl.

"I saw that," he replied. "That medal is a good look on you."

"Thanks, you too," she said as she nudged her shoulder into his arm.

Together they waited patiently as the Secretary finished up his remarks and urged everyone to stay around and enjoy more of the reception.

"I would like to introduce you to my mom and dad – if that's okay," Katie said as she slid the gold cross along the chain that she wore. Nick watched her bracelet with the letter "K" bounce back and forth as she pulled on the cross.

"Sure," he said in a hushed and solemn tone. He turned towards his friend and looked into her brown, almond-shaped eyes.

"What is it?" she asked.

"I didn't realize that your parents that you talk about, that you spend the holidays with were your aunt and uncle. I wish I would have known that your real parents….."

His voice trailed off.

Katie recognized the pain in his words and sought to reassure him. She grabbed his hands with hers and squeezed them to make sure he understood.

"Nick, I am lucky to have had two sets of real parents. Yes, my actual parents died when I was little, but I have been blessed to have another set of parents that love me and have raised me to be who I am today. Still, that doesn't mean that I don't think about my mom and dad…" Her voice wavered a little before she continued. "That's why I still wear mom's charm bracelet every day," said Katie as she reached down and tumbled the "K" between her thumb and forefinger.

"And the "K" is for Katie?" he asked.

"Yes, it is," she replied. "She was wearing it the night she died."

Nick looked at her and saw a vulnerability that she rarely showed anyone.

"In the walkway collapse in Cincinnati?"

Katie lowered her eyes and responded faintly.

"Yes."

The memories of twenty years ago broke free from places that Nick had long since locked away. The pain the walkway collapse caused to him, and those that he knew, seemed never-ending. How was it possible that the beautiful woman standing before him had lost her parents in the walkway collapse that had ruined both his career and his life? A life that was ruined until the day he'd met her.

"Katie there is something I need to tell you. I…" said Nick, ready to reveal the one part of his past she didn't already know. The one part of his life that he was not sure she could forgive him for. He felt as if his future, their future, hinged upon the next words he would say.

"Katie! Katie! Let me give you a big hug!" called out a petite woman with silver hair that contrasted with her black Versace glasses. A moment later Katie and the woman were wrapped in a heartfelt embrace.

"Mom," replied Katie with a smile.

"Hey, can I get in on this or what?" said the gray-haired gentleman in the navy blue coat.

"Sure Dad."

Nick watched with an awkward happiness, not sure if or how he should interrupt this family moment. After another hug, introductions followed, and an easy conversation among the four started. Nick could see that communication skills ran in the family as her parents made him feel like they were lifelong friends. The crowd in the room began to thin, and the four of them decided to make plans for dinner that evening. Nick told them he would see them tonight, and said goodbye. Several steps towards the door he felt a tug on his arm. Turning around, he was met by Katie, who threw her arms around his neck.

"Thank you for everything," she said.

"For everything?" Nick's eyebrows furrowed in his confusion. "I should be the one thanking you."

She hugged him again.

"You were about ready to tell me something before my parents came over. What was it?"

Nick looked at her with eyes that longed to tell his painful association with the walkway collapse in Cincinnati. Some say that the truth will set you free, but the actual reality is that the truth is not a fixed destination, but instead a dynamic journey. One's understanding of the journey may change as time passes. This possibility of discovering a new understanding made it easier for Nick to delay his statement of the truth, especially when the truth will cause more pain.

"Oh…I can't remember," said Nick.

"Well, be sure to tell me when it comes back to you, okay?"

"Yes. I'll see you tonight," said Nick.

"Until tonight," said Katie as she pulled him close and gave him a kiss on the cheek.

If you enjoyed this novel, please consider posting a brief review on Amazon.com and Goodreads.com.

NOTES ON THE FAILURES

EQUILIBRIUM is a work of fiction that partially involves pieces of information from two tragic structural collapses that occurred in the United States in 1981 and 2007. In the book, changes may have been made to the date, location, and/or contributing cause of these failures to align with the fictional story. However, the actual failures themselves and some of the facts surrounding these failures are, unfortunately, all too real. It is not my intent, in any manner, to minimize the impact that these tragic events had on an untold number of people. As an engineer, I hope my story and the underlying historical events cause people today and generations that follow to remember these events, and help us not forget the lessons of these tragedies. I hope my story sheds some light the enormous responsibility shouldered by engineers, and the need for all to consider our sometimes-forgotten infrastructure and its impact on public safety.

The walkway collapse at the Grand Plaza Hotel in Cincinnati is partially based on the Kansas City Hyatt Regency walkway collapse that occurred on July 17, 1981. A report from the National Bureau of Standards (NBS) released in 1982 stated that this was "the most devastating structural collapse ever to take place in the United States," and some of the information found in this novel is based on the NBS report. My story's description of the orientation and composition of the walkways is generally consistent with what actually existed in Kansas City at the time of the collapse. The NBS report concluded that the "change in the hanger rod arrangement from a continuous rod to interrupted rods essentially doubled the load to be transferred by the fourth floor box beam – hanger rod connection." The NBS report further stated that if a continuous rod arrangement had still existed (instead of the "split-rod" arrangement), the connection would have "had the capacity to resist loads estimated to have been acting at the time of the collapse." One major aspect of my story that is pure fiction and should be noted is the corrosion discovered by Nick on the connection and the biological film found on it. This is purely fictional and not at all intended to, in any way, represent the actual condition of the walkway. If interested in reviewing the actual NBS report, search "Investigation of the Kansas City Hyatt Regency Walkways Collapse Report 143."

The part of the book that pertains to the "I-99N" bridge collapse that causes Joe's death is partially based on the I-35W bridge collapse that actually occurred in Minneapolis on August 1, 2007. I-99 is actually a section of the interstate system running through Pennsylvania and New York. A report from the National Transportation Safety Board (NTSB) released in 2008 found that the probable cause of the actual I-35W collapse was the "inadequate load capacity... of the gusset plates at the U10 nodes, which failed under a combination of (1) substantial increases in the weight of the bridge, which resulted from previous bridge modifications, and (2) the traffic and concentrated construction loads on the bridge on the day of the collapse." The actual I-35W bridge opened in 1967. The 40 years of service for the I-35W bridge before it collapsed was not unusual as a great number of bridges were built throughout the U.S. after passage of the Federal-Aid Highway Act of 1956. A purely fictional part of the collapse found in novel is the embrittlement of the steel due to the corrosion caused by the terror group's nanoparticle-infused paint. It is worth noting that cracking in bridges is commonly produced by a condition known as fatigue where the cracks develop due to the extraordinary number of load repetitions the structure has to endure. Interestingly, the NTSB report noted that "inspection reports from 1994–2006 did note the presence of rust, corrosion, and section loss on gusset plates" but that the conclusion reached found that this corrosion on the gusset plates was "neither causal nor contributory to the collapse of the I-35W bridge." If interested, the reader can review the actual NTSB report by searching "I-35W Bridge Collapse Report NTSB Report HAR0803."

[1] Portions of this executive summary found in the book are borrowed to some extent from the the NBS report noted above. However, the reader should be aware that the book's executive summary is purely fictional.

[2] Portions of this executive summary found in the book are borrowed to some extent from the the NTSB report noted above. However, the reader should be aware that the book's executive summary is purely fictional.

ABOUT THE AUTHOR

Thomas Burns has spent over three decades practicing and teaching in the field of structural engineering. Fascinated with technological advancements, he is particularly interested in lessons we can learn from both catastrophic failures as well as engineering triumphs. When looking at buildings and bridges, he finds great inspiration knowing that there are untold stories embedded in the vast amount of effort spent by a multitude of individuals in order to make those structures "work."

A licensed engineer, he has undergraduate and graduate degrees in civil engineering from the University of Cincinnati, and a doctorate in construction management from Indiana State University. Though new to the world of fiction, he is not new to the world of writing, having written multiple books and articles in his field during his career.

To learn more about the author and his works in progress, go to https://www.tomburnsbooks.com/ or check out his Facebook page at https://www.facebook.com/tomburnsbooks/.

73843487R00192

Made in the USA
Columbia, SC
19 July 2017